MW01230127

Tears Turn Into Laughter

By

Michele R. Leverett

Tequila,
Thank you for
supporting me. Enjoy!
Michele Leverett
7-18-03

This book is a work of fiction. Places, events, and situations in this story are purely fictional. Any resemblance to actual persons, living or dead, is coincidental.

© 2003 by Michele R. Leverett. All rights reserved.

No part of this book may be reproduced, stored in a retrieval system, or transmitted by any means, electronic, mechanical, photocopying, recording, or otherwise, without written permission from the author.

ISBN: 1-4033-7023-0 (e-book)
ISBN: 1-4033-7024-9 (Paperback)

Library of Congress Control Number: 2002094127

This book is printed on acid free paper.

Printed in the United States of America
Bloomington, IN

1stBooks - rev. 4/14/03

Dedication

This book is dedicated to my daughter, Rachel Nichole Leverett.

Acknowledgements

No goal in my life would be obtainable if it wasn't for God, who blesses each one of us with gifts and talents to use for His glory. I thank and praise Him above all else. I want to thank my wonderful husband, Kevin, who gave me loving "pushes" to finish this book.

To my Pastor and his wife, Bishop J.C. and Joyce Hash of St. Peter's World Outreach Center, under whose teaching and mentoring I have flourished and developed I can't thank you enough.

To my mother, Ann Gamble, who always believed that I could accomplish anything I set my mind to do, and my mother-in-law, Sarah Leverett, who believed in what I could do, thank you.

To my stepson, Alex, who constantly asked, "Are you finished with your book yet?" and to my stepdaughter, Jasmine, I thank you.

To my CAM family, Reverend Michael Clinton, Lakela Humphrey (my personal editor) and Cheryl Collins, who were willing to move mountains to help me obtain my goal, thanks guys.

To Karen Whitley, who for years listened to me read my book with no complaints, thank you, girl.

To Reverend Glen Johnson (www.glensgoodwork.com) who worked diligently to design my cover, and produced a fabulous work of art, thank you so much.

To Dave Hardin at D&L Computers in King, NC, who made it his personal business to help me with all my computer glitches, thanks so much.

To very special friends, Keya Kollock and Lavina Eddings, who stayed in agreement and prayer with me, encouraged and helped me through all of the challenges that came with getting my story completed, you ladies are one of a kind.

I thank you all, and I love you.

"…Weeping may endure for a night, but joy cometh in the morning."
Psalms 30:5 (KJV)

CLAUDIA

Hamel University. Office of Admissions.
Claudia took a deep breath, then ripped the envelope open. She scanned through the salutation, then breathed a big sigh of relief when she saw the rest. She'd gotten in. And it wasn't that she necessarily wanted to go to Hamel, but Marie was going. Ever since she had started at Cedar East High School since moving from the West Coast, Marie had been her best friend—her only friend. Everyone else was either rolling their eyes or talking junk. Claudia couldn't figure out why—she minded her own business, spoke to no one more than "hello" and ate lunch by herself until she met Marie.

Maybe it's because I look so strange, she often thought as she gazed bitterly in the mirror, making a face at what stared back. She was constantly finding fault with herself, and couldn't understand why Marie was always telling her how attractive she was. Her hair, a wild mixture of gold, brown and tan waves, framed what she thought was a pale, sickly looking complexion, complete with a light sprinkling of freckles. It was nothing like Marie's rich, mahogany color. In fact, Marie was just downright beautiful, with her chocolate complexion, thick eyebrows, curvy, slim build and versatile hair that knew how to stay in one style. When Claudia complained to her mother about her coloring, her mother would always rub her hair, as if trying to tame her uncontrollable waves, then she would hug her.

"Claudia, you took back after your father, honey. We can't do anything about your color."

"But what color am I?" Claudia would ask in frustration.

"Beautiful," her mother would tell her, a smile lighting up her gorgeous, mocha colored face. In reality, Claudia was just about two shades lighter than her mother, but she didn't see it that way.

Yes, Claudia did take after her father, a sandy-haired, hazel-eyed, slightly freckled man. As a little girl, Claudia thought he was the most handsome man she knew. Apparently, her mother did as well, and didn't let the fact that he was white stop her from marrying him. To top it off, the two met in the south, where some folks still didn't cotton to the idea of the two races mixing. Daniel Shipp moved his new bride to the west coast where the relationship didn't bother as many people, and they quickly produced Claudia and her younger

1

brother, named after her father's favorite vehicle, Harland. Claudia had actually been very excited about the move—she wanted to experience cold winters instead of the year round, mild weather of her home—but when school started, she would've gladly traded building a snowman for the comfort of her old home.

Claudia's biggest nemesis at Cedar East was Tallette McNeil, who made it her personal business everyday to remind Claudia how unwelcome she was. Tallette got a lot of attention from the guys at school, but that was probably because of the tight, low cut, short clothes that she wore to show off her generous curves. She had a very distinct and purposeful way of swishing when she walked, and when she knew she was drawing some male attention, that swish became more pronounced. Marie would joke that if Tallette swished any harder, she was going to throw a hip out of joint.

For all of her "femininity," Tallette was a big, territorial bully. If she felt someone was trying to squeeze in on her action, which meant all the cute, popular boys at school, she would sound the warning bell, usually in the form of a verbal and/or physical confrontation with the offender. Since Tallette had a womanly body at such a young age she was a healthy-sized girl, so most of her victims would back off. There were some who had fought back and won, and Tallette backed off, but she would still talk junk about them to redeem herself. Most of the time, she steered clear from those that weren't intimidated by her and went for the easy prey. Apparently, Claudia fell in the latter category.

Even before the incident in the locker room and her lunch room initiation, she was getting the dirty looks, the snide comments and threats from Tallette and a small band of girls who followed her around like obedient puppies. Claudia would just look the other way, or pretend not to hear them. But one day in the locker room, Tallette and her crew made sure their voices came through loud and clear.

Claudia was just putting her gym bag back in her locker after taking her shower, and barely got her hand out when her locker door slammed shut in front of her. The usually noisy room grew quiet. Claudia jumped in surprise and was about to protest when she saw Tallette's angry, heavily made-up face staring into hers.

"Listen, you zebra—you better stay away from Jimmy. If I see you trying to talk to him again, Ahma snatch you all the way around this school."

Claudia just stared back at her, terrified and confused. Tallette's numerous pieces of gold jewelry clanged and tingled from her ears and around her neck. She had on so much red lipstick her mouth looked like it had caught fire, and at the present time, she was pointing a very deadly looking, long, wild-colored fingernail in Claudia's face. Now that she was actually in Tallette's face, she could see how any man would be interested in her, but she wasn't stupid enough to let Tallette in on her opinion.

Besides, she thought. *I don't know any Jimmy*...then it hit her. Jimmy Ryan, the basketball player, who was more commonly known as "Jimmy Jam" because of the emotional way he stuffed the ball in the net, was whom Tallette was referring to as "her man." Marie had pointed out many times that Jimmy was "scoping her out," but Claudia figured it was because of her pale-freckled face and her fly-away hair. That was enough to get anyone gawking.

Not that she minded the attention. The boy was fine, and like most of the girls at Cedar East, Claudia was mesmerized by his graceful moves on the court. But, try as she would, she couldn't bring herself to believe she was someone worth looking at.

Tallette continued to address her. "Don't say you don't know who I mean, either. So just wipe that innocent look right off your face." She seemed to be getting angrier with each word. One nostril started to flare, while the one with the earring through it stayed stationary. "Jimmy is *my* man and I don't want to see you around him, you bright, yellow lollipop."

Her friends laughed so hard they almost fell off the bench they were sitting on. Some of the other girls looked at Claudia with sympathy, while the others exited quickly, smelling a nasty confrontation coming.

"Besides," Tallette sneered at her, "Jimmy likes black girls—*black*. Not no high yella half breeds."

"Look, Tallette, I don't even hang around Jimmy," Claudia had protested, near tears. "I don't even know him."

"Oh, girl—don't give me that sob story. I'm not even trying to hear it. You think you cute because you got all that long, wavy hair, that I *still* think is a weave, and you all light-skinned and think that every man wants to get with you."

"Yeah, she do," one of Tallette's idiot followers piped up from across the room.

3

"I do not think that. I don't even bother you. I don't bother anybody." Claudia was crying by now. Every time she tried to go around Tallette, who outweighed her by at least twenty pounds, and leave the locker room, Tallette would push her back. Claudia felt humiliated because everyone seemed to be laughing and no one was trying to help her.

"Aw, Tallette, just let the girl go on about her business. She gets the point," one of her friends suggested. "Come on or we'll be late for Science."

Most of the locker room had cleared out except for those waiting to see more action. Tallette slowly stepped away from Claudia and never took her eyes off of her. "You just remember what I said," she warned before she and her group flounced out of the door, laughing their heads off.

Marie was beside herself with anger. "Why didn't you push her back, Claudia?" she demanded to know after Claudia shared the incident with her. School had ended and they were headed toward the buses. "I'm telling you girl, you better learn to stand up to bullies like Tallette. She's just jealous because Jimmy doesn't give her a second look, with all of that war paint and cheap jewelry on. You should've found me—I'da put her in her place."

"She called me 'half-breed,' Marie," Claudia whimpered.

"Because she's *jealous*, girl. What have I been telling you? Jimmy ain't thinking about her. I don't know where she got the idea that he belonged to her. She's the one who's always up in his face."

"Well maybe she's right. Maybe guys like Jimmy do want their girls to look black. Why would he look at someone like me, anyway?"

Marie's face changed from compassion to confusion. "Why would you even say something like that, Claudia?"

"Something like what?"

"Why do you always act like you don't know?"

"Know *what*?"

"Know why you get so much grief from girls like Tallette and so much attention from guys like Jimmy," Marie responded impatiently. She seemed agitated for some reason. Claudia was a little confused.

"I don't understand, Marie. Why are you getting upset with me?"

Claudia was ready to bust into another round of tears. After all she had been through that day, she certainly didn't need for her best friend to be at odds with her. And she wasn't completely naïve. She knew

Marie was referring to the complexion/hair thing that seemed to be a big thing at Cedar East. It's what Tallette told her that her crime was in the locker room. It's why Marie told her she "had it going on" so many times, but for the life of her, she couldn't accept that her looks were an asset, or that people put that much time and energy into them here.

"What have I been telling you?"

Claudia hated when Marie sounded parental, but she wasn't about to let her know and risk losing the only friend she had here. "Marie, it's not always the complexion thing…"

"What else is it, then?" Marie countered.

"Maybe Jimmy just…thinks I'm nice." It sounded ridiculous coming out of Claudia's mouth, and she had no doubt Marie felt the same way.

"Girl, Jimmy doesn't even know you," Marie snapped back. "You mean to tell me that the boy can look at you and be attracted to your niceness? Don't be so naïve. And if you don't start standing up for yourself, Tallette will always feel like she can pick on you." To Claudia's surprise, Marie charged ahead of her and boarded her bus, without looking back once. Claudia stood where she was with her mouth open, wondering what in the world she had done to cause Marie's outburst.

Later on that evening, Marie called Claudia and apologized for her behavior.

"I'm sorry, Bambi," she told Claudia. "I had a rough day, and I was a little upset over what happened with Tallette."

"But you took it out on me," Claudia whined.

"I know, I know. I'm sorry. It's not your fault. It's just something I need to deal with, that's all. Don't worry about it."

Claudia, who was more than ready to have her friend back, quickly agreed. "How's your science project coming?" The conversation then turned into homework, clothes, and television shows. Claudia breathed a sigh of relief. They were back in safe territory again. She always wanted to ask Marie what that "thing" was she had to deal with each time she let her emotions fly out of control, but she never had the courage to do it. It didn't matter—all that was important was that she had her friend back.

5

Hopefully, college would be a different experience. The letter she finally found the courage to open congratulated her on her acceptance. Just what she was being accepted into remained to be seen.

EUGENE

Eugene was ready.

Eugene was ready for a change. The letter in his hand was his ticket to change. He had applied to Hamel University initially because it known for its strong English curriculum, and he had always excelled in English. His mother told him that he spoke his first intelligible word at eight months, and began speaking in complete sentences by age two. He wrote his entire name—Eugene Brian Wright—when he was three, and began reading on his own at four years old. By the time he entered the first grade, Eugene was so far ahead of his classmates that he was placed in a special accelerated program for English.

His mother couldn't have been prouder. When he brought home his first short story "The Dog That Ate New York," with a gleaming gold star and a the teachers glowing remarks, his mother had hugged and kissed him, and promptly placed the achievement on the refrigerator for the family to see.

"You are so talented and smart, Eugene," she told him with watery eyes. "I'm proud of you, baby."

His dad couldn't have cared less. When he came home from work, his jaws tight from another day of wrestling with who he called "Mr. Charlie," he barely glanced at the paper situated on the refrigerator, and grunted when his wife pointed it out to him.

"Why aren't you out playing ball with the boys, Eugene?" his dad asked after flopping down in his favorite recliner.

"I have to do my homework, dad," Eugene told him. "The teacher wants me to revise my story because she thinks it can win the school's writing contest."

"She paying you for your time?"

"Ray, what kind of question is that?" Eugene's mother cut in irritably. He just told you that she wants to enter it in the school's writing competition. That's quite an honor."

His dad grunted again, then hid behind his newspaper. Eugene stood there for a minute, waiting in vain for his father to congratulate or even comment on his accomplishment, but he stayed behind his paper—and the only comment he made was to ask when dinner would be ready.

The hints about Eugene's involvement in sports happened almost everyday. His dad even brought him a basketball for his eighth birthday and promised to set up a goal in the backyard if he would use it. Eugene thanked him, and put the ball in his closet where it sat until his older brother, Chip, claimed it for his own. The next two birthdays brought footballs, baseballs and bats, sports jerseys and sneakers. Eugene accepted all the gifts, thanked his father, and put them in his closet, where they would sit again until Chip came to use them.

"Dog Eugene. Dad brought you all this stuff and you ain't even using it." Chip would complain as he helped himself to the items. "You could at least try to play something, Eugene. You know Dad's gonna keep hounding you until you do."

So Eugene tried. His first attempt at sports was a scrimmage football game in the park near his house with his brother and some guys in their neighborhood. Eugene was ten, and Chip, at fourteen, told him that he would help him.

"Just do what I tell you to do, Eugene," Chip told him.

His dad beamed all over the place when the boys announced they were going out to play football in the park. He pounded Eugene on the back so hard Eugene nearly fell over. He had never seen his father so happy.

"See son, you don't need to stay in those books all day. Go on outside and get some fresh air—do you good."

"Chip, you watch out for your brother," his mother warned. "Eugene, you watch and don't get hurt. Wrap up real good."

"Hazel, the boy is going to play a game of football, he's not going off to war. Calm down," his father told her.

When he and Chip got to the park, the neighborhood boys were already there in the middle of a game. When they saw Chip and Eugene, they immediately stopped and starting arguing over whose team Chip was going to be on.

"You have to take me and my little brother," he told the seven boys.

"It's three against four right now," one of them protested. "We'll still be uneven."

Chip just shrugged.

"All right—we'll take him over here. You guys just line up." One huge kid said from the other side.

"Just do what I tell you," Chip reminded him, bending down beside the huge kid with the ball. Eugene bent over too, watching his brother and glancing ahead of him. Four sets of eyes and bodies looked like they were ready to run him over at any given moment.

"Hut one—hut two—hut three—hut, hut!" The big boy, who had the football, yelled. All of a sudden, everyone scrambled and Eugene looked for Chip, who was running down the grass, yelling for Eugene to follow him.

"Here, man—run!" Somehow, the ball ended up in his hand and four guys started running after him. He panicked, turned and ran in the opposite direction. He could hear Chip somewhere shouting at him—he thought he heard another kid telling him to turn around before bodies descended on him and he ended up on the ground, bumping his chin against a rock. The bodies cleared—it sounded like they were laughing.

"Boy, what's wrong with you?! You ran the wrong way!" the huge kid yelled at him. Eugene felt a sharp pain and something trickling down his neck. He put his hand up to his chin and came away with blood.

"Eugene!" Chip's face appeared over him and he reached down to lift Eugene to his feet. "Are you all right?"

"Man, yo' brotha' can't play no ball! He ran the wrong way!" The huge kid protested to Chip. The other boys started laughing. Eugene felt humiliated. He just wanted to go home.

"What's wrong with you guys, jumpin' on him like you crazy?! We ain't playin' tackle!" Chip said to the group angrily.

"Aww, your little brotha' is just a punk. He can't play ball," the huge kid told him again. And suddenly, Chip released Eugene and lunged at the big kid, who was bigger but shorter than he was. He knocked him to the ground and jumped on him, while some of the boys crowded around them and egged them on. Eugene started screaming his brother's name—he couldn't see anything but a tangle of arms and legs through the other boys. Two of the other boys that weren't cheering the fight on had the sense to step in and pull Chip off of the huge kid. Eugene had never seen his brother so angry.

"Come on, Eugene!" Chip grabbed his brother again and started pulling him out of the park. Eugene looked back—the big kid was just getting up off the ground. His T-shirt was ripped in a couple of places

9

and he had a lot of grass in his hair. He was breathing hard and looking at Chip like he couldn't believe he'd just jumped on him.

Eugene stole a look at Chip, who was frowning fiercely and breathing like a track horse. He had some smudges of dirt on his face and when he lifted his hand to wipe them off, his knuckles were covered with blood. Other than that, he looked o.k.

"I'm sorry, Chip…" Eugene told him.

"Just come on, man. Ain't nobody gonna be callin' my little brother no punk. We need to fix your chin before mom sees it. She'll have a fit."

But Eugene's mother did see his face, and she did pitch a fit—especially when she saw that Chip's hand was hurt, too. His dad laughed it off, telling her that boys got banged up all the time playing sports, but she wasn't hearing it. She refused to allow Eugene to join his brother in playing football in the park again, which was fine and dandy with Eugene. His dad complained that she was babying him, and he was going to be no good for it in the long run.

When he turned fourteen, high school brought a different set of problems. Chip was already a senior when he came on the scene, and he was sailing through the social waters of high school with ease. Eugene had problems finding his crowd. He wasn't athletic, which meant he couldn't hang out with the jocks. He wasn't Mr. Cool—that left him out of the popular crowd. And although he was in advanced classes and made honor roll every quarter, he wasn't super duper smart—that kept him away from the nerds. He was just who he was—a quiet kid who liked to read and write, and felt more comfortable in khakis and loafers than jeans and basketball sneakers. That distinction excommunicated him from a lot of the black kids in high school.

So Eugene kept mostly to himself, or he hung out with a few people like him that he managed to befriend. The problem was that they were white, and it was taboo in his high school for whites and blacks to hang out, unless it was a white person who was doing the hanging. That was acceptable. The white person was "chill." But if a black person picked a white crowd—well, that was forbidden. That person was a "wannabe," a "Tom." And it didn't help that Eugene didn't dress like the other black kids—in the more trendy styles. He stuck with his slacks and polo shirts, pressed very carefully by his mother.

"White boy."

"Uncle Tom."

"Oreo."

"Go on ahead and bleach your skin, white boy. Then you'll look like one, too."

He tried to act like it didn't bother him, but it did. He couldn't understand what he was doing wrong, but obviously he was messing up in school and at home with it, because his dad was on him about the same thing.

"Boy, do you know what color you are? Why do you hang around all those white people at school?"

"They're my friends, dad," he would defend.

"How can they be your friends? What do you have in common? Nothing. Boy, you better start acting like you black around here and stop kissing up to those white folks all the time."

That was almost everyday, then he'd go back to school and get another earful of how black he wasn't. He couldn't talk to his friends about it—what could they tell him? They were the crowd that the black students were complaining about. He couldn't talk to Chip, who had his own thing going on with dating fifty million different women, playing high school basketball, and trying to graduate by the skin of his teeth. His mother kept telling him to ignore it, but she wasn't in his shoes. Nobody understood.

He remembered the day he left school early late in the fall of his freshman year. The leaves were just beginning to fall off the trees and the air was nippy, a reminder that winter was just around the corner. Eugene had reached his breaking point that day. His homeroom teacher left the room for about five minutes to speak with another teacher, and his class of nearly all black students started whispering and giggling. Eugene didn't look up from the book he was reading, not until he felt something being forced on his head by two male students. He jerked, and felt hairs tickling his neck. The class laughed their head off.

"There's your blonde wig, white boy," one of the boys told him.

Eugene snatched the long, blonde wig off his head and looked around angrily. The white students were looking at him with confusion and sympathy; the black students were pointing and laughing, nearly falling out of their seats. Eugene threw the wig on the floor, gathered up his books and nearly ran out of the classroom. He went to the office, told the secretary he needed to call his mother

11

because he wasn't feeling well and sat there, trying to keep the tears from running down his face.

"Do you have a fever?" His mother asked when she arrived at the school and was driving him home.

"I just don't feel well, mom," he told her.

"Well, it's flu season, or it might be allergies. Your eyes are all watery."

"Might be," he said, and said no more.

She dropped him off at the house, waited until he opened the door and told him to call her at work if he starting feeling any worse. He immediately went up to his room and lay on the bed. He had never been so humiliated in his life. All he wanted to do was be himself, but that wasn't good enough for anybody—not even his father. Eugene didn't even remember getting up and going into the bathroom or opening the medicine cabinet. He looked at the bottles of headache pills, sleeping bills, Chip's shaving cream and razors…there was a brown container of pain medicine for Chip when he broke his finger playing basketball. Eugene grabbed the bottle and headed down to the kitchen.

The house was terribly quiet—he heard every footstep he made on the soft carpet, every bump and knock and swish as he filled a glass with water from the faucet. He brought the pills and glass into the forbidden living room and sat on his mother's dove gray sofa. He just sat there, staring at the bottle, thinking about that stupid blonde wig— the way the black students laughed, his father telling him he wasn't black enough. He opened the bottle and shook one of the big, banana colored capsules into his hand…

The jangle of keys in the hallway startled him. "Eugene!" his mother called. "I decided to take the day off and take care of my baby."

He fumbled the cap back on the bottle, but only managed to drop several of the capsules on the floor. He quickly tried to retrieve them and shoved the bottle under the pillow beside him just as his mother came in the living room.

"What are you doing sitting in here? And why do you have a glass sitting on my table with no coaster, young man?" She picked up the glass and paused, stooping down to retrieve one capsule that Eugene had missed. His heart beat double time.

"What is this, Eugene?"

"I don't know."

"This is one of Chip's pain pills. What are you doing with it?"

"I had a headache…"

She looked at him strangely, then pulled him off the sofa and starting grabbing and throwing the pillows. When she found the hidden bottle, she started breathing in short puffs, her eyes wide. "Eugene, what are you doing with these?! What are you doing?!"

Eugene just stood there. He started crying. "Nothing…"

She grabbed and shook him. "Yes, you were! Yes you were!! What are you doing?!" She screamed, pulling him to her and crying.

He let himself be held and they cried together.

After they stopped crying, she sat him down on the chair and he told her about the wig incident, about how tired he was of getting picked on, about his father's criticism. "Eugene, you listen to me! Listen! I told you, you are perfect just the way you are! You don't have to prove anything to anybody, do you hear me?"

He just kept crying.

"Come here." She pulled him up the stairs to the hall bathroom, and turned him to the mirror. Both of their eyes were red from crying. She grabbed his chin. "You are special—you're special to me and you're special to God! You're not supposed to be like everybody else. You're just supposed to be you—my special son." She grabbed him again and just cried all over him. He promised her he wouldn't do anything like that again.

Later on that evening when his father got home, his parents closed the door to their bedroom for over an hour. Chip asked Eugene if he knew what was going on, and he told him he didn't. He wished he had made his mother promise not to tell his father, but he was too mixed up to remember that earlier. Afterwards, his dad let up off his black kick with Eugene for a good two months, but then he started right back in with it. The taunts at school didn't stop, either—not like they knew what he did in the first place. In fact, it increased, because now the students from his homeroom were calling him "Blondie."

Somehow, he pressed through the next three years, developed a thick skin about the taunts, even took a white girl to the prom and graduated at the top of his class. He kept telling himself that college would be different—people had too many other things on the agenda to worry about who he was and wasn't. He could be who he was without any fear of rejection.

13

Michele R. Leverett

He hoped.

MARIE

"O.k., you see where it says something about the person you want to be your roommate? You do? Put my name there. S-t-e-e-l-e-t-o-n—how long have you not known how to spell my last name, Claudia?"

Marie was instructing Claudia over the phone after Claudia had called her about her admission to Hamel University. Marie had found out about her acceptance a couple of months ago, since she had submitted her application early. She had convinced Claudia to apply there as well so they could be roommates. In fact, it seems as though she was always convincing Claudia to do something—especially to have more self-esteem.

Even though Claudia was her best friend, and had a heart of gold, sometimes her whining about not measuring up to the other girls at Cedar East really grated Marie's nerves. She knew that she sometimes came off too hard on Claudia, but she wanted her to stop being so down on herself. Her self-esteem was so low, Marie felt like she had to dig a hole to give the girl a compliment. But then there was the deep-rooted reason that Marie was so hard on Claudia at times. Ever since the tenth grade when she and Claudia had become friends, Claudia had always gotten the most attention. Hardly a day went by when Marie didn't hear guys either talking about Claudia, or trying to get Marie to introduce them to her.

"Yo, Marie—when you gonna hook me up witcha' girl?"

"Look, just give her my number. Tell her to call me."

"Is she seeing anybody?"

Normally Marie would just laugh it off and keep going. But when they became juniors, then seniors and it was still happening, it started to get on her nerves. "Why don't you ask her yourself?" she started to bite back at them.

The reply was almost always the same. "Man, that girl is too stuck-up...she won't even talk to you."

But why wouldn't the guys like her friend? Marie thought she was beautiful, yet Claudia never did anything to enhance her looks. Nonetheless, the boys went gaga over her caramel complexion, long, wavy hair that she religiously wore in a ponytail, and her big hazel eyes. Marie nicknamed her "Bambi" because she reminded her of a frightened little deer. Sometimes she acted too shy and too

15

vulnerable—that's why girls like Tallette and her minded-minded followers were able to get away with as much as they did. And why Marie could, too.

It wasn't that she took advantage of Claudia's gentle nature. Marie recognized that fifty percent of the time, she could catch an attitude real quick when things weren't going her way, and her patience level could stand to rise a notch or two, so a friend like Claudia was just a natural target—except when she started to cry. When Marie saw the water well up in her big, doe eyes, her heart would immediately go out to her and she would try everything in her power to make the pain go away. Her mother always told her that she had a soft heart—too soft sometimes. The other fifty- percent of the time, she was acting like nothing bothered her when almost everything did. Both character traits were part of her survival instincts—instincts she'd had ever since childhood.

Ever since she could remember, Marie had been teased about her dark complexion, her long, toothpick legs and a thick mat of hair that her mother struggled to pull a comb through. She remembered many an agonizing night when her mom would sit on the couch and plop Marie on the floor between her legs, with a bundle of her thick hair in one fist and a comb in the other. Marie would bite her lip to keep from crying out while her mother tried to work the comb through her tangles.

"Whew, child," her mother would breathe, throwing up her hands. "I give up. I can't do anything with this head tonight and my bad wrist."

"Momma, please straighten my hair with the hot comb so it won't be nappy," Marie would beg her. "Then it'll be easier to comb." She would really have to catch her mother in the right mood in order for her to press her hair. Her mom would always complain that she was too tired or that her bad wrist was bothering her.

"No, Marie. I'm too tired to do a whole lot of fooling around with your head. Wait until tomorrow. Let me just give you two braids down the side."

Marie hated that style. It was so pickaninny. "But Momma…"

"I said no, Marie," her mom interrupted in a tone that indicated the matter was closed. It was useless to continue pleading. Her hair would just have to look fuzzy another day.

So she went to school many a day with her hair looking less than what she thought it should look—like the other girls at school. Every day she was faced with pretty pressed hair done up in curly pigtails or combed straight down with a cute flip on the sides and in the back. Her hair had the habitual two thick braids or even cornrows. The other girls would constantly snicker behind their hands and call her "African Queen" or "pickaninny." She never told her mother about the names because she would just tell Marie how silly she was being, or to just ignore the taunts. She would just come home, run up to her room that she shared with one of her older sisters and cry her eyes out. By the time her mother came home from work, her tears would be gone and her swollen eyes back down to their normal size with the help of some ice. When her mother asked her how school was, she would be ready with the usual response:

"Fine, Momma."

Her older sisters, Davette and Rolanda, didn't seem to notice, either. Davette was off in her own little teenage world of music, boys and clothes, and Rolanda was too busy being an obnoxious older sister. She was a couple of years older than Marie, and three years younger than Davette. Rolanda's looks were so unlike Marie and Davette's that people often thought they were unrelated. She had a soft brown complexion, just a few shades lighter than Marie's, and a thick head of hair that hung straight down her back. No pressing or relaxing required. Davette was old enough and skilled enough to do her own hair by the time Marie started to care how hers looked.

"I don't know where you got your hair from," Rolanda would tease her. "You look like you were raised in a jungle somewhere."

After countless battles with her mother about her hair, Marie convinced her to let her wear the latest rage in hair care in junior high school—the Curl. Her mother relented after Marie convinced her she would never have to fool with her hair again, except to take her to the hairdresser every five to six months for a retrace. She nagged her mother for nearly a month but never got anywhere. Early one Saturday morning, Mrs. Steeleton woke her daughter up and told her to get some clothes on.

"Where are we going?" Marie asked sleepily.

"To get this little hairstyle you been bugging me about," her mother said irritably. "Now come on. If you ain't ready in twenty

17

minutes, forget it. I got better things to do with my Saturdays than sit around in a hairdresser's shop."

Marie was ready in ten minutes, and beat her mother to the car. She was a little surprised when her mother pulled into the driveway of a house.

"Who lives here?" Marie asked her.

"My friend, Jerlene. We went to high school together," Mrs. Steeleton told her, getting out of the car. "Come on here."

"But I thought I was getting my hair done," Marie whined.

"Girl, come on here and stop asking me fifty million questions about what I'm doing. I know where I am." Her mother started up the driveway and around the side of the house. Marie had no choice but to follow, knowing she wouldn't get a straight answer out of her mother if she chose not to give her one.

"Yeah, I been doing a bunch of curly perms lately. I seem to do more of those than regular relaxers, these days. The young girls are all wanting them." Jerlene was talking to her mother while she prepped Marie's hair. She finally found out that Jerlene was a hairdresser whose shop was in the basement of her house. She was spreading a gooey white mixture on Marie's head as she talked to her mother. It smelled to Marie like eggs gone bad. Jerlene continued to talk as she rinsed the stuff out, and rolled big curlers all over Marie's head. Her mother sat in a chair along the wall of the shop, frowning in doubt. She didn't know if this "Curl" business was going to be worth her hard earned money.

"Are you sure this is going to look like something?" she kept asking Jerlene.

"Take a look at that magazine on the table beside you, Karla," Jerlene pointed at the table with her elbow since both hands were involved in rolling up Marie's amazingly straight hair. "You see that girl on the third page?"

"Yes."

"When I get through, Marie's hair will put hers to shame, child."

Her mother laughed. Jerlene certainly didn't appear to be shy about her work, but had to be good. Judging from her price list on the wall, she certainly charged enough to be the best.

"Well, girl, if you can do that, I'll just sit over her and keep my mouth shut." Marie's mother picked up the magazine and scrutinized the model again. "I might even let you put one in mine."

18

"You know I'll hold you to that, Karla." Jerlene put the last roller in place and pumped Marie's chair down. "Come on over to the dryer, sweetie. I'm gonna put you under for about an hour while I talk to your momma here about her curl."

"I didn't say I was definitely getting one, Jerlene. Don't get happy yet. Let's see how Marie's hair turns out first. Girl, I sure hope you appreciate all this money that's going into your one head."

"Yes, Momma," Marie told her before a big plastic dome of heat was positioned over her curlers. The heat made her drowsy and she dozed off, thinking about how she would finally be one of the "in" people at school. She could bounce around the hallways like the other girls, confident that her hair would look good.

When Jerlene finally took her from underneath the dryer and began removing her rollers, Marie thought she was going to faint with excitement. For the first time in her life, her thick bunch of hair that usually stayed stationary even when it was hot-combed, swung down on her shoulders. It *moved* when she moved her head.

"Girl, you are looking like *something!*" Jerlene raved, pulling out the last roller. She picked up a bottle and sprayed Marie's hair with something that smelled like perfumed rubber. Her whole scalp was dripping wet with it. She wanted Jerlene to turn her chair toward the mirror so she could see, but the hairdresser was too busy holding a conversation with her mother. She started to lift Marie's curls with a pick, and Marie's hands flew to her head in horror.

"Marie, put your hands down!" her mother scolded.

Jerlene chuckled. "Don't worry, baby. These curls aren't going anywhere. I'm just giving you a little body—that's all."

The hairdresser had spoken a prophetic word when she told Marie her curls weren't going anywhere. So content was she with the low hair care maintenance, the length the feel of her hair, she totally missed the year when her schoolmates started migrating back to the relaxed look. The curl was a short-lived rage, only no one bothered to tell Marie when it ended. Once again, she began to get pointed out, this time with curl jokes.

"Look at mop head over there."

"You left a big puddle of oil in front of homeroom."

Marie had enough with the jokes. Before, she would act like it didn't bother her and go somewhere and cry her pain away. Eventually, she started to fight back, facing her schoolmates who dared to say something about her hair and finding a flaw in their character to rag them about. They started to back down, figuring she wasn't a fun target anymore since she didn't shrivel up and die, but Marie went back to her mother and told her she was ready for the Curl to go.

"You done lost your mind, haven't you?" her mother asked. "You think I'm gonna jump every time you get ready for a new hairstyle?"

It had been two years since her first Curl, so Marie knew that this was another battle she was going to have to fight—on her own. She convinced her older sister, who was driving by that time, to take her to the beauty supply store where she brought herself an over-the-counter relaxer kit. All the sisters got an allowance from their father, who had been separated from their mother shortly after Marie was born.

"Who's that for?" Davette asked her when Marie came back to the car with the relaxer kit.

"Me," Marie told her.

"Momma's going to put that in for you?"

"I doubt it."

"Then who's going to do it?"

"Me," Marie repeated.

Davette was never one to question or nag or tease Marie. "All right."

Marie's first experience with her own home relaxer was a disaster. No one had told her that you couldn't put a relaxer on top of a curl without stripping the curl out first. So she wore a very short, straight style and a lot of hats while she waited for her hair to grow back in. Her second perm was better. By the time her third experience came about, Davette was asking if she could put one in hers. She began to look through beauty magazines that came to the house and recreated the latest styles on her own head. Her mother, recognizing her youngest child's natural talent, was only too happy to drag her over to Jerlene's house every week, so she could show Marie what she knew and so she could sit and talk for hours on end with her old friend. Marie suspected that her mother also felt bad for not letting youngest get her hair relaxed by a professional when she first asked her, and wanted to compensate.

Her schoolmates began to compliment her, asking her where she got her hair done. They were astounded when she told them she did it herself. She had their respect. But, by the time she learned to do her own hair, in the middle of her tenth grade career, hair wasn't the only issue anymore. It wasn't what separated her from the more popular, pretty girls at schools—the girls that always had dates, a circle of friends, a fan club of male admirers. It was complexion.

Marie began to notice that her lighter-skinned counterparts were always surround by the cutest guys in school. They would speak to Marie, be her friend, but never did they ask her out on a date, or to seat with them at lunch. They liked Marie, all right, but it was because she was on the honor roll, and she was a leader, and her hair was always hooked—but they didn't like her enough to date her, and she didn't need a highway billboard to tell her why. And when Claudia came along with her light golden brown complexion, her wavy hair and her hazel colored eyes, it was all she could do to keep from screaming. It didn't matter that they happened to be best friends; it mattered that the male attention Marie did receive was only to curry favor with Claudia.

Unfortunately, complexion was something Marie could not change, unlike her hair. She remembered how much she wanted to change it when she was younger, though. She was about eight years old, and the weather was warm—it just screamed for an active eight-year child to come out and play. Marie stayed outside by herself for an hour, enjoying the sun, sitting on the porch and making up imaginary stories. She didn't need many playmates—her imagination kept her occupied. When she came back in the house, full of the high spirits that only summer can offer a child, she immediately refreshed her sweaty face in front of their air conditioner that sat in the window. Her mother's older sister was visiting with them—she was one Marie didn't particularly care for because she was always so negative. She was sitting on the couch with her mother.

"Girl, look how dark you are from that sun!" The aunt commented. "You need to stay inside the house!"

Her high spirits left. Her mother laughed it off, thinking that her aunt was joking. Even though she was not one for holding a child to her bosom for comfort, her mother would never let anyone—family included—mess with her girls. If she thought her sister was serious, she would have went off. But Marie took the dig seriously. She vowed in her little eight-year old mind never to go out in the sun

21

again. She eventually forgot her vow and played just as hard outside as the next child, but the comment stuck with her.

So she dealt with it as best she could—by acting like the big issues didn't bother her or by going off the deep end over little ones— like Claudia's low self-esteem. The girl didn't know what she had going for her in Marie's opinion, and Marie found herself upset because she did have it going for her. She was praying that college would be different. There, the issue was bound to be intelligence and leadership ability, something Marie had no problems with, rather than hair length, hair texture, and complexion.

Hopefully.

PERCY

Percy frowned as he slid the thick manila envelope out of his mailbox and headed back into the house. *Hamel University, Office of Admissions.* He applied to at least three other schools, but this was the only one back so far—the one school he did not want to go to. This school was his mother's idea. A white school.

Percy had lived in Jackson Park all of his life. Jackson Park, with its drug dealers, prostitutes, homeless, gangs and despair, had almost shaped who he was. It took his mother to snatch him from the evil lure of the streets and set him on the straight and narrow. His sister Monica, who was five years older than him, had joined the Army right out of high school. After twelve years of studying and homework, she wanted nothing more to do with education and joined the military to travel. His mother had a small fit, but at eighteen, there was nothing she could do about her only daughter dedicating eight years of her life to Uncle Sam. So Evelyn Lyles turned her attention to her next oldest child, Percy, and starting pumping education and college into his head as soon as he got in high school. One of her children was going to college, she would make sure of that.

Percy always felt a surge of pride when he thought about his mother. In Jackson Park, she was a diamond in the rough—literally. She was a slender, cocoa-colored, woman, who loved the Lord and her family with a passion. She marched around the streets of Jackson Park like a queen in a castle, even though her kingdom was littered with beer bottles, basketball courts and pollution. Everyone on his block respected her, and more than once Percy had come home to find his mother on her knees in the living room with a female neighbor, her beautiful face frowned up and her hands lifted as she prayed the troubled person through whatever problem she was facing. There were a few catty women who wanted nothing to do with her, and dared their husbands and boyfriends to even so much as glance toward her house, not caring that she had a husband and three kids, and didn't even seem to realize how striking she really was.

Despite his mother's attempts, Percy was content as a youngster to hang with his boys in the streets, shooting hoops, breaking windows in old buildings, and every once in a while, shoplifting candy and drinks out of the gas station next door to Dell's Grocery. They never tried to lift anything from Dell's because the owner, a tall, older man with gray hair and mean eyes, always scared them and told them he'd shoot anybody with a hunting rifle that tried to steal from him. Plus, everyone in Jackson Park, hood or angel, liked and respected Mr. Dell. Still, he was no fool. He had bars on his windows and on the door that he locked every night. And he always had his nephew and oldest son with him when he locked up at night. The word on the street was that they were strapped, just like Mr. Dell was.

It wasn't until Percy was sitting in front of the television one afternoon watching a talk show, that he made his life changing decision that would rescue him from the streets of Jackson Park. He had flipped to a talk show en route to some cartoons, and saw a brilliantly dressed black man sitting on a chair, wearing a small, round cap and a matching colorful shirt that Percy would later discover was an African dashiki. The host mentioned something about the man's credentials, something about him being one of the first black millionaires in history. That got Percy's attention—he was always interested in money.

"I was born on the streets of Detroit. The only thing me and my family knew was welfare," the black man told the host and the television viewers who happened to be listening to him. He leaned forward toward the camera as if to drive his point home, and Percy leaned right back into the screen to fully absorb his words. "I made it out. I tricked the system. See, I wasn't supposed to make it out of my situation. Do you know what I used to trick the system?"

"What?" Percy asked the screen, forgetting that the man couldn't hear him.

"Education," the man answered as though he could hear. "The only way our people are going to make it is to use our heads. God blessed all of us with a mind, and it would be a sin if we waste it on drugs, alcohol, sex or some other useless activity. If we do not do something and soon, we will decrease as a race until we no longer exist."

The man went on to say more about how he had his Ph.D., but Percy had heard enough. After the show, he called his friend, Bernard, and cancelled their previous appointment on the basketball court.

"Dog—I just got some new sneaks and you fazing out on me," Bernard complained.

"Man, I gotta study," Percy told him. "If I flunk Mr. Contrell's test tomorrow, my mom will wear my behind out, then turn around and pay somebody to do it again."

Bernard laughed. He understood about parents, but would have most likely ridiculed Percy if he had told him the truth—he was putting basketball on a backburner and was going to start a little one-on-one with his books. "Check you later, man. We'll get up next time."

Eventually, his friends became a little suspicious after a few more social cancellations.

"No one can have that much homework," they would complain.

"Percy, I'm in three of your classes—how you get more homework than me?"

Percy was running out of excuses. However, he was willing to say anything to keep them at bay until he got accepted at a reputable university complete with a scholarship. He had started researching scholarships immediately, and found that funds were available for smart people, dumb people, rich people, poor people, fat people, skinny people, people with pets, people without pets... By the end of his junior year, Percy had taken his GPA to a highly respectable 3.8, was in the top ten percent of his class, and was holding down an after school job at Dell's Grocery Store about five blocks away from his house. He had spent the entire summer before his senior year applying to HBCU's—historically black colleges and universities. He wasn't sure at the time what he wanted to do, but hanging around Mr. Dell and the grocery store, he was leaning heavily toward Business Administration.

The letter congratulated him in big, bold letters after the "Dear Mr. Lyles" salutation. The enclosed material informed him about his full scholarship. He had beat out over five hundred-fifty applicants for the T. Samuel Powell Scholarship, which offered full tuition and housing coverage, complete with a monthly stipend, to one low-income minority college hopeful who was applying to a private university with a low percentage of minority students. Hamel U fit the bill nicely, with a thirty-seven percent minority roster out of over twenty-five thousand students. No telling how many of that thirty-seven percent was African-American.

"I got in," he informed his mother in a flat, emotionless voice. Her squeal of excitement almost burst his eardrums.

"I got the scholarship too," he told her in that same voice. She let out another howl of victory.

"Baby, I am so proud of you! Look at you, getting into a good school, and getting a scholarship! My prayers have been answered, thank you, Jesus!!" She sent up a quick devotional to the Man upstairs, then looked at her oldest son with tears in her eyes. Percy, you don't know how happy it makes me to see you going off to get an education. I was so afraid you'd end up like those guys you hang out with. I tell you, God answers prayers!" She closed her eyes and talked softly to herself.

"Ma, did I get any other letters?' he asked her again.

She came out her meditation. "A couple came for you last week." "Last week?" And she was just telling him today?

"Well, I wanted to see if you would hear from Hamel, Percy. This is a very good school. There aren't a lot of black people that get accepted there…"

He closed his eyes and tried to gain control of his emotions. He knew better than to mouth back to his mother, but sometimes the woman acted like he couldn't think for himself. The whole Hamel thing had been her idea in the first place. Sure, he had gotten a good offer to go along with it, but he had his heart set on going to a HBCU. His mother thought that he needed exposures to different cultures; therefore, Hamel. He didn't want to be exposed to different cultures. He wanted to be black.

Mrs. Lyles opened the drawer that held the silverware and reluctantly handed Percy two thick envelopes from two other colleges.

Mr. Dell was proud of him, too.

"Congratulations, son," he told him, pounding him heartily on the back when Percy went to work that evening. "I knew that you would make something of yourself. I knew that without a shadow of a doubt."

"Mr. Dell, I'm glad I got in and all, but Hamel is not really where I want to go." It was so easy to talk to Oscar Dell, who had been his father figure since his own daddy split—and Mr. Dell had two grown children of his own.

"Well, where did you want to go?"

Percy reached in his coat pocket and took out the two envelopes his mother had given him earlier. He had gotten accepted at both schools.

"Good schools, son? They got the program you're looking for?"

"I think so." Actually, he hadn't even looked into that. He just applied because they were two top black universities. "But they're black schools, Mr. Dell. That's what I'm concerned with. Why should I give my money to a white institution to help them out? I want to keep my money with my people."

"Percy, I hear what you're saying, but if you got this here scholarship to go to Hamel, it's not your money your spending anyway, now is it?"

He got him. "No, I guess not. But I still think it should be my decision where I want to go. My mother didn't give me these letters until today. She thinks I need to be exposed to different cultures."

Mr. Dell nodded his head in understanding. "And what do you think?"

"I think I want to be around my people—not a bunch of uptight, prejudice folk who don't want me at their school in the first place."

Percy paced around Mr. Dell's tiny office.

"So you don't think you'll face any problems at an HBCU, is that it?"

"I won't have anybody bringing me down because I'm black."

Mr. Dell widened his eyes. "Oh really? You don't think black folk bring each other down, huh?" Mr. Dell got out of his chair and walked over to the only window in his office—a tiny square that sat just low enough to see over—with bars. Mr. Dell was no fool living in Jackson Park. "Come on over to this window, Percy."

Percy followed Mr. Dell's finger outside the window. He was pointing across the street to the basketball court where Percy had spent many an afternoon and weekend playing pick-up games, one-on-ones, having slam dunk contests or just chillin' with his homies. He saw a couple of his boys over there now with puffs of smoke hanging around their heads. And Percy knew that all that smoke wasn't from cigarettes, either.

"Who do you see over there?"

"A couple of my boys, Mr. Dell—why?"

"Uh huh—and what color are they?"

27

Percy laughed, not sure where this line of questioning was leading but willing to humor the man he had a tremendous amount of respect for. "They're black, Mr. Dell. They've been that way for as long as I can remember."

"Now how did you tell me 'your boys' responded when you said you were going off to college?"

Percy got quiet for a minute. He was about to be trapped, and he knew it. "They ragged me about it—they ragged me pretty hard."

"Not one good thing to say about it, huh?"

"Not really." It had always been Percy's opinion that they were a little jealous. Very few people made it out of Jackson Park. Most of the people his age were born there, raised there, and could expect to die there. His crew all felt that way. For them, the sun rose and set in Jackson Park—Percy was determined to make it out.

"Tried to tell you it was a mistake—it wasn't going to take you anywhere because you were black?"

That's exactly what they had said, too. It just showed Percy that Mr. Dell's ears were wide open whenever he talked to him. "Yeah. They said all that."

Mr. Dell looked at Percy. "What color did you say they were again?" he asked quietly.

He knew he was going to be trapped. Mr. Dell always made him see the other side of things—especially when he had his young, inexperienced mind made up about something.

"Percy, sometimes we parents use—unique methods to get a point across. Now you know your mother has your best interest at heart, and you know she lets you make your own decisions, but just consider what she's saying for a minute. There's nothing wrong with an HBCU—we fought long and hard just to get an education in the first place. But your mother feels that you also need some social education, and I have to agree. You don't see too many races in Jackson Park, but where you're goin' son, you need to know how to deal with everyone. Whatever you decide, I'll be just as proud of you, and your mother will, too. You got in a good school, with a scholarship…just weigh your options before you make a decision."

Percy thought about it for a minute. Mr. Dell was right—the only thing he did run into in Jackson Park was his own people. Even at school, only a handful of the teachers were white. Yeah, he could get with the culture thing. He could go to Hamel and excel, proving that a black man was just as smart or smarter than a white man with his own education. "Mr. Dell, I will give it some thought," he promised him, sticking out his hand for a shake. "Thanks, sir."

Mr. Dell roped an arm around his shoulder and gave him a squeeze and a knock on the head instead. Then he told him to get back to work before he docked his pay. Percy laughed, heeded the warning, and hightailed it out of Mr. Dell's office.

When Percy came home that evening, his mother was sitting in the dim light of the kitchen, with her Bible in front of her. He came in and gave her his customary hug. "Hi, Ma. You're up late. Where's Paul?"

"Paul's in his room watching T.V. Your dinner's in the refrigerator, baby—but come over here and sit down for a minute."

Percy, already headed to the fridge, came back and had a seat at the table.

"I feel like I need to say I'm sorry for keeping your letters from you. You know I always let you kids make your own decisions about what you want to do with your life. I guess I just didn't want you to miss this opportunity, Percy. Hamel is an excellent school and…"

Percy smiled and grabbed his mother's hand to interrupt her. "Ma, it's o.k. I've decided to go to Hamel."

His mother drew in an excited breath like she was going to break into a shout, but got herself under control. "Amen! What changed your mind?"

Percy got up to stick his dinner in the microwave. "I talked to Mr. Dell this afternoon. He just made me see some things about going to Hamel that I didn't consider."

"Thank God for Oscar Dell. I am so glad you have him in your life, Percy, while your father's…not here."

Percy hated to be reminded of his absentee father. "I don't have a father, Ma. At least not a real one."

And his mother hated to hear him low-rate his father. She turned around in her chair. "You watch your mouth, boy," she warned him. "I told you about that. No matter what your father has or hasn't done, he is still your father and you will respect him in my presence, do you hear me?"

Percy sighed, feeling his mother was being extremely unfair about the way he should feel or react to a man that didn't even have the decency to be with his family, and managed to call only once a week. "Yes, ma'am."

CLAUDIA

"Claudia, speak up. I can't hear you if you whisper, girl."

"Open your mouth and talk."

"What color are your eyes, anyway? Or are those contact lenses?"

"Is that your real hair?"

"Whoever heard of a black person with freckles?"

"You think you're cute, don't you?"

"You ain't black—not all black, anyway."

"Is your mom white? Your dad?"

"High-yellow."

"Half-breed."

"Light-bright."

"Red-bone."

"Zebra."

The insults from her peers nagged at her everyday. She constantly reminded herself that college was going to be different—*she* was going to be different. All of her life, her parents reminded her that she did not have to choose one race over the other. She was who she was, and that was good enough for anybody.

"But what color *am* I?" she would ask them, confused.

"Well, I would say honey-brown," her father, the comedian, would answer.

"If you cut yourself, you'll find that you're the same color as everyone else," her mother, the diplomat, would add.

But in Claudia's world, what they said didn't hold water. She was forced to choose one color over the other in order to be accepted. Even then, her fate was not decided by her choice; it was decided by her peers.

Harland seemed nonplussed by his racial makeup. He was two years younger than her and smart as a whip, but was too lazy to do anything with his intelligence. Still, he seemed to breeze through life with a nonchalance that Claudia couldn't help but admire. And he seemed to fit in with whatever crowd was in existence. Everyone at Cedar East seemed to like him—especially the females.

"Harland, if you weren't my brother, would you try to talk to me?" Claudia asked him one day after school when he slunk in the house two hours late. He knew it was his turn to start dinner, but he always found a way to weasel out. It was three weeks before graduation and spring was in the air, so he had probably been out shooting ball with his boys. Claudia had the leftovers warming in the oven and was about to set the table when he came in, puffing and sweating and holding his basketball.

"Whoa, Claudia. That's too gross to even think about," he protested, heading to the refrigerator to drink directly out of an orange juice carton.

"I said if I wasn't your sister, big head." She grabbed the juice carton before he could get it to his mouth, and sloshed juice down the front of his shirt.

"Hey, girl—what you do that for?"

"Because you know better than to drink from the carton. Who wants your germs?" She put the juice on the counter and had a seat at the table. "Now answer my question, please."

"Man, Claudia—I don't know. It depends."

"On what?"

Harland strolled his tall, lanky frame to the table and flopped down in a chair across from his sister. He and Claudia were almost carbon copies, except for Harland's little mustache and his hair, which wasn't nearly as wavy as Claudia's. He inherited his height, hair and broad shoulders from their father, who was six feet, six inches, with straight sandy brown hair. He also had their mother's big brown eyes and cynical grin. Claudia's mother was constantly running to the hairdresser to keep her hair under control. She obviously wanted to keep the hair gene on the female side of the family. Claudia looked at her brother and could tell that he was really struggling with picturing her as anything other than his sister.

"O.k., Harly, Don't answer that," she told him, trying to let him off the hook.

"What are you trying to get at, anyway?"

"Well, I hear that a lot of guys won't approach girls that…look like me because they think we're stuck up. I just wanted to get a man's opinion on it. I mean, do you only talk to females who look a certain way?"

Harland grinned, probably liking the fact that Claudia referred to him as a man. "Well, not really. I'll try to talk to any girl as long as she looks good."

"You are so shallow."

"I love you, too. But what I'm saying is that men will try to talk to any girl that's cute. Most men, anyway. If she's stuck on herself, he'll probably shout at her when his boys are around, but he ain't gonna say nothing to her by himself. Nobody likes rejection."

"I understand all that, but what I want to know is if you associate being stuck-up with a certain *look*?"

Her brother looked confused for a moment, but then his face lit up as if a light bulb clicked on in his head. "Oh—you mean that light-skinned, long-haired thing?"

"Exactly."

"Oh," he repeated, leaning back in his chair to prop his big, dirty sneakers on the table. Claudia immediately reached over and pushed them off, feeling like a mother to a brother who was only two years her junior. And here she was, asking him for advice. *I must be desperate*, she thought.

He glared at her, but went right back to his point. "Now that's a different story. Yeah, a lot of guys I know do think that light-skinned girls are stuck on themselves. That's why they're so fun to go after." He looked up at the ceiling thoughtfully, as if remembering his last successful conquest. "It's a challenge."

"But why do guys think that only light-skinned girls are stuck-up or pretty? I mean, there are a lot of pretty girls at school and they aren't all light-skinned."

"Oh, don't get me wrong. All the pretty ladies aren't all light with long hair. Take your girl, Marie. Shoot, I'd talk to her in a heartbeat but she's almost like family. That would be a little gross."

Claudia laughed and shook her head. Harland was always trying to throw a rap on Marie, who would smile and tell him to grow up some first. She and Marie both knew that her brother loved to run his mouth, but he was otherwise harmless. "So Marie would be the kind of female that you would consider *un*-stuck up?"

"Yeah," he nodded heartily.

"Why? Because she's dark?"

"Yes—no, I mean...Claudia!" Harland looked pained that his sister would think that.

Claudia had purposely baited him. Her brother might be shallow, lazy and a smooth talker, but he wasn't hung up on skin color. "I'm sorry," she apologized. "I know that's not what you think."

33

"No, it's not what *I* think, but I'll be honest with you—a lot of my boys think that way. Some of them won't even look at a girl if she's not light and her hair ain't long enough. But it doesn't matter to me as…"

"As long as she looks good," Claudia finished for him, staring hard at her handsome, pest of a brother. With the exception of Marie, the only times that girls did talk to her was to ask if her brother was dating someone.

"There you go. So what time is dinner?" Just like that, he changed the subject. Things rolled off him like water on a duck's back. "You don't deserve anything," she told him, hurrying to the stove to take out last night's dinner before it burned. Nobody made chicken pie like her mother. The leftovers seemed to taste better than the original. "You knew it was your night for dinner and you skipped in here all late so you wouldn't have to."

"Aw, Claudia…" Harland tried to charm her with his grin, then he lumbered over to the stove and grabbed her in a bear hug.

"Get off me, boy. That's not going to work. You have dinner duty for the next two nights or I'm telling."

"I know somebody who likes you."

"Who?" she answered absentmindedly, thinking it was a ploy to get her to change her mind.

He answered immediately. "My boy, J.J."

Claudia had been reaching into the oven to take out the cornbread. She almost dropped the hot pans when she heard Jimmy's name. "You mean Jimmy?! Jimmy *Jam*?!"

Harland grabbed a fork from the drawer by the stove and grinned wide. "Yeah, he got it *real* bad for you."

She didn't want to appear too eager, not even to her brother, who was her closest friend beside Marie. Yet, she couldn't help being a little excited. This was the second time someone had told her about Jimmy's interest, but then she remembered Tallette's warning—stay away from *her* man. "No, he doesn't, Harly." Claudia told him. "Besides, he already has a girlfriend."

"Who?" Harland asked around a mouth full of chicken pie he had filched when Claudia wasn't looking.

"Tallette."

Harland almost choked on his food. "Tallette?!! Tallette, *who*? McNeil? He let out a big whoop and fell to his knees, laughing. His reaction made Claudia feel like she had said something stupid. She found herself growing angry as she watched her brother rolling around on the floor, holding his stomach like it hurt.

"Well that's what *she* said. Get up, boy. I didn't say anything that funny."

He finally calmed down and sat back against the refrigerator, wiping the tears from his eyes. "Mmmph. Claudia, where did you— no—*who* told you that?"

"I just said Tallette told me."

"Claudia." Harland got up and turned a kitchen chair around to face her. He talked in the tone of a father trying to reason with his child. "Think about how Tallette looks, and how she acts, o.k.? Now you tell me if what you just said makes sense."

"What? Tallette's not unattractive."

"How can you tell under all that makeup?"

Claudia took the plates out of the cabinet and began to set the table without answering him. Her parents would be home soon. To her surprise, Harland grabbed the silverware from her and began to help.

"Look, before you start singing your 'everybody is beautiful' song, I'm not saying that the girl is ugly. I just know she's not J.J.'s type. She's always up in his face, but he don't have no time for her."

"Well, what is his type?" Claudia wanted to know.

Harland snickered a little. "*You.*"

Now it was *her* turn to snicker. "That's funny—Tallette told me he liked black girls." She still refused to believe anything but the worst about herself—a personality trait that drove Marie absolutely bonkers.

Harland sounded like a parent again. "And just what color do you think you are?"

Claudia finished the table and sat down. "I don't know. What color are we? Mom's black, dad's white—who do we identify with? She looked him straight in the eye. "What color do you think you are?"

Harland widened his eyes and exhaled. Apparently, he hadn't given the issue much thought. "I don't know. I guess I never thought about it too much. I mean, most the people I hang around with are black, but I never really thought about what race I really am. I guess I feel like I'm black around my friends, but at home, it really doesn't matter."

But it did matter to her. It would be much easier it she were one or the other—then maybe she'd have more friends.

"Mom and dad are always telling us it doesn't matter," Harland reminded her.

"Yeah, but at least they know what color they are. They don't have anybody going around calling them 'zebra'."

"Claudia, you know how you females can be. Ya'll get all jealous of each other. You know you fly, girl."

This was Harland's version of a compliment, and Claudia couldn't resist planting a juicy kiss on the cheek of the brother who was always in her corner.

"Go on somewhere with that, girl," Harland complained, wiping his cheek off, but he couldn't hide his smile.

Given her brother's appetite for beautiful women, Claudia should have believed him, but for the life of her, she could not find anything positive when she looked in the mirror. She would have told him such, but then she heard her parents at the door, coming home from work. She let the matter drop.

MARIE

"Wake up, Marie."

Marie mumbled incoherently. She was too sleepy to try and figure out who was waking her up while she was in the deep stages of slumber.

'"Marie! Wake up!" a voice screamed at her—at least in her stage of sleep it sounded like a scream. She woke up then.

"O.k. ...I'm awake." Marie rubbed her eyes and turned to see Claudia standing over her, holding out the cordless phone. Looking at her out of her one eye that was focused, Marie wondered who in the world was calling her at nine o'clock on a Saturday morning. Unless it was...

Her roommate finished her thought. "It's Cedric."

Cedric Carter was a junior who lived in the apartments across campus. Marie had met him at a Black Student Assembly orientation when he slid in the seat beside hers, late and not wanting to cause too big of a scene.

"Did I miss much?" he asked Marie, fumbling around in his backpack for something to write with.

"Uh, not much. They're just going over the events planned for the year." Marie told him, then she looked at him. His puppy dog eyes seemed to melt into his chocolate skin. He was grinning at her—with dimples big enough to bungee jump in. She immediately turned away when she caught a whiff of some good smelling cologne, because soon her tongue was going to be hanging out of her mouth. She always told Claudia that a good-smelling man was almost worth working with even if he didn't have much going on in the looks department. Cedric conveniently had both going for him.

"So, what's your name?" he asked in a distinctively Northern accent.

"Marie."

"Marie? I'm Cedric Carter." Marie knew who he was. He was on Hamel's football team. She had noticed him on campus one day, and a fellow female student had caught her staring.

"That's Cedric Carter—he's a football player," the female informed her. "Ain't he fine, girl?"

Fine he was. His dark skin practically glowed, or so it did to her. And she caught him with his mouth open and was able to view his row of even, white teeth.

"Marie." Cedric repeated her name like he was trying to get used to it. "That is definitely not African. What were your parents thinking?"

"Well, I don't remember reading about any 'Carter' tribes in Africa," she bit back at him, her defensive fighting nature making an appearance. She wasn't particularly fond of her name, but her mother had told her more than once that when she got old enough to pay her own bills and live on her own, she was more than welcome to change whatever she wanted.

Cedric smiled at her. She felt her anger turn to butter and melt away.

"Good answer, good answer." He grabbed her hand and pumped it up and down enthusiastically. Then he let it go and continued to grin at her. She tried to maintain her cool, but found it increasingly difficult with this handsome brother cheesing at her.

"What's your classification, Marie?"

"My what?" Marie was still concentrating on the left dimple.

"What year are you?"

He probably thinks I'm an idiot. I'm a freshman. This is my first year."

"Yeah, that's usually what 'freshman' means."

Oh, goodness. "No, I meant…"

"Lighten up, Marie." Cedric rubbed her hand and winked at her. "I'm just teasing you."

Marie tried to attend to the rest of the orientation, but Cedric had thrown her focus off—especially when right before he left, he leaned over to her. "I hope to see you again, Marie. Maybe we can talk more about African names." He grinned at her.

She tried to play it cool. "Sure—I'll do my research on those Carter tribes and make sure I didn't jump the gun with you."

He laughed a little too loud. A few heads in the row ahead glanced around, frowning.

"I really like your sense of humor," he whispered to her, zipping his bag up. "It was a pleasure to meet you, Marie. I look forward to hearing about that Carter tribe." He gave her one last wink, then left.

She was literally through for the rest of the day. She did run into him later on that week, and he messed her up again when he asked for her telephone number.

Marie hung up the phone with a smile on her face. She didn't want to perform too much in front of Claudia, but this was her first official date! Guys that looked like Cedric just didn't ask her out to dinner every day of the week. Then it hit her…what in the world would she wear? The clothes she had—what little she did have—were either very formal or very casual. Nothing compared to the selection Claudia had, but hardly ever wore. Although Claudia was a few inches shorter than Marie, they were practically the same size, and Marie could wear a lot of her stuff.

"Claudia." She turned to her roommate who was standing by her desk. She appeared to be very preoccupied, but it looked to Marie like she was just moving things around on her desk.

"Yes?" Claudia responded in a soft voice.

'That was Cedric."

"I know."

"He's taking me to dinner tonight."

"Oh, that's nice. Good for you."

What's with her? Marie wasn't sure if she wanted to try and borrow an outfit, now that Claudia seemed to have an attitude about something. But she decided to push her luck anyway. "Would you mind if I borrowed an outfit from you?"

"Don't you have something you can wear?"

Well, this was a first. Usually, if Marie saw something she liked in Claudia's wardrobe, it was all she could do to keep the girl from giving it to her. And it was extremely rare for Claudia to catch an attitude with her. Extremely. She had to really be upset. Marie was nipping whatever this was in the bud. "O.k., Bambi….what's the problem? Did I say something wrong?"

"No."

"Then why are you acting like that?"

"Like what?"

"Like you're mad at me."

"Maybe I just don't like to be woke up at nine o'clock on a Saturday morning. You ever consider that?"

"Claudia, you were already up."

"So? It's still too early for anybody to be calling."

"O.k.—I 'm sorry it was so early then. I'm sorry it disturbed you."

"Sorry doesn't mean a thing if it happens again."

"All right...I'll make sure it doesn't." Marie was still trying to be congenial because she was in such a good mood, but the façade was wearing thin. She got up long enough to spread her cover up over her bed and sat back down, promising herself she would make it up later on. Right now, she wanted to sit and have some quality time with her roomie, who was apparently having a bad morning. "Would you mind sitting down so we can talk about the real issue that's bothering you? 'Cause I know it ain't about a phone call."

Claudia rolled her eyes over at Marie, then sat down on her unmade bed. Marie saw her look down and stare a hole in the floor, and knew that she was trying to hold back some tears. She immediately jumped up and sat beside her. "Claudia, what's wrong?"

Claudia shook her head and cleared her tears with a swipe of her hand. "I'm sorry, Marie. I'm not mad at you and I'm not bothered by Cedric calling her early."

"Then what's the matter?"

Claudia looked up at the ceiling and sighed. "I'm just sick of being here, already. And it's only been two months." She looked Marie in the eye. "I thought when I came here, things were going to be different. I thought I was going to feel different about myself since those silly girls like Tallette wouldn't be here. But nothing has changed for me."

Marie understood completely. She knew that Claudia, with her low self-esteem and her timid attitude would probably have a hard time at college. In many ways high school was more tolerable, since the school day was finished in a few hours. But two hundred miles away from home—that was a twenty-four seven ordeal. Marie knew she could take it. She had developed that tough exterior from years of being ridiculed. She knew how to hide her pain, where Claudia let it show. That was not going to work. Not here.

Still, her heart went out to her best friend. She looked at Claudia now, who had grabbed a tissue from her desk, wiping her face with it like it was the only one in the box—and she had to choke back tears of her own. She literally wanted to vomit when she thought back to the tenth grade, and a vindictive female named Tallette McNeil had squirted mustard on Claudia's silk shirt because "the high yella thought she was all that."

Marie was sitting at the cafeteria table with Tallette, whom she had met in junior high. Now Tallette was definitely not one of her hanging buddies, because even in junior high, she had a rep for being fast and being a bully, and had even tried to confront Marie once at lunch. But for some odd reason, Tallette had picked this day to sit down beside Marie at the crowded lunch room table and hold a conversation with her, and Marie was not one to be rude to people, even to girls like Tallette.

Tallette was giving her spiel about "light-skinned girls who thought they were cute." Tallette was just one shade lighter than Marie, and apparently thought her to be a kindred soul in the war on complexion. Ironically, Marie was about to agree with Tallette's opinion, especially when she gazed at Claudia's silky tresses and honey complexion. Her hair was in that terrible stage of needing to get her Curl redone, and she was smack dab in the middle of her showdown with her mother about getting rid of it.

Tallette nudged Marie, and pointed down at Claudia, who was sitting at the far end of the long table all by herself. "Now like her down there," she whispered. "She thinks she's too good to sit with anyone else. Look at her down there by herself, with her pretty silk shirt and her long hair—probably a weave anyway."

Marie didn't agree. "No, that looks like it's all hers to me."

"Oh, please," Tallette spit out in disgust. "That ain't even hers. And even if it is, she shouldn't be trying to swing it every which way."

Now Marie definitely didn't see Claudia swinging her hair. In fact, she had her face pointed down to her plate, eating quietly and looking at no one. Tallette apparently saw another picture. "She got one more time to roll her eyes down this way, and Ahma go down there and knock her eyeballs out."

Marie was about to protest, explain to her lunch companion that the girl was not bothering anyone, when Tallette suddenly grabbed a bottle of mustard from the table and stood up. "I'm gonna teach that redbone a lesson," she sneered hatefully, and started down the table toward Claudia. Marie wanted to stop her, but by the time the thought registered, Tallette was bumping into Claudia's chair and squirting mustard down her the front of her blouse.

The whole table got quiet. Claudia looked up at her adversary in shock. Tallette was smirking and asking Claudia what she planned to

41

do about it. Claudia looked down the table at the other students, who were staring back at her in anticipation. A few of the boys were laughing their heads off, but most of the table was quiet and had their eyes locked on Claudia, not wanting to miss a beat.

Claudia continued to scan the table pitifully with her big, doe eyes, and then her eyes locked on Marie. It caught Marie off-guard—Claudia's eyes seemed to be asking, "How could you let this happen? I wasn't bothering you." She reminded Marie of a puppy that had been kicked once too often. She had to look away.

Claudia got up from the table slowly, gathering her books. She looked at Marie one more time, then hurried out of the cafeteria with her head down. The table resumed their chatter—some laughing about the incident, others expressing their disbelief—as Tallette made her way back to her seat, triumphant, and began eating again as if decorating someone's shirt with mustard was nothing out of the ordinary. Marie looked at her in shock. She got up from the table, too.

"You through already?" Tallette asked around a mouthful of food.

Marie just stared at her. "That was so stupid what you just did," she told her. Tallette looked up at her in surprise. "That girl didn't do anything to you, Tallette."

"She deserved it, rolling her eyes at somebody." Tallette just kept eating. Normally, she would have jumped back in anyone's face who dared to oppose her, but she had much respect for Marie, who refused to be bullied by her, and let that fact be known as early as junior high school.

"Hey girl—you cut in front of me."

In the eighth grade, Marie was standing in the lunch line, in front of a much smaller but just as intimidating Tallette, who had appeared behind her in line, trying to pick a fight.

"No I didn't." Marie was content to let the incident go at that. She knew Tallette's reputation for starting trouble, and she'd managed to steer clear of her this far.

"Yes you did," Tallette insisted, getting up in Marie's face. The line stopped moving and, as students always did, looked at the altercation in the making. They even formed a crude circle, forgetting all about their appetites.

O.k.—how 'bout Tallette picked the wrong day to mess with Marie, who wasn't one to back down from anyone anyway, since she had learned survival skills from being picked on by her older sister,

Rolanda? It just happened to be the day that a so-called friend of Marie's told the guy she had a crush on that she liked him—and he laughed at her. She was not in the best of moods.

"I said, no I didn't," she told Tallette, getting right back in her face. "And you need to get out of my face."

Tallette looked momentarily shocked. Different "oohs" and "ummphs" were coming from the ringside crowd of student, who were always in favor of a good fight. "What you gonna do if I don't?" Tallette wanted to know.

"Put your hands on me and you'll find out." Marie's mother had taught all her girls not to start anything, but don't back down, either.

"And if I do?"

"Then it's on," Marie promised her. "Ain't nobody scared of you, Tallette." Now Tallette did weigh more because Marie was a string bean in the eighth grade, but win or lose, she would go down fighting.

Tallette looked confused. Normally, her victims would cower down, but not this brave little beanpole. The two stood there, staring at each other, and by that time, faculty noticed the standoff and ran over to break it up before it got ugly. Tallette gave Marie a warning look before being chaperoned to the back of the lunch line by the boys' gym coach. Marie rolled her eyes back just as hard, surprised to find that a small part of her welcomed the altercation because she wanted to try and beat Tallette down.

Marie found herself being congratulated by students all day long, even by the guy who'd found out she had a crush. He still didn't ask her out, but went out of his way to speak to her everyday after that. Tallette, at first, ignored Marie after that day, rolling her eyes every once in a while, but eventually she started speaking to her, in a quick, reluctant tone, as if Marie should be honored to even merit her greeting. After that, they were chill.

Marie had a sudden brainstorm. She stood up and grabbed Claudia by her shoulders. "Let's do a makeover on you," she suggested excitedly, already envisioning the change in her friend if she would turn her hair and makeup over to her.

"Do a what?" Claudia asked her.

"A makeover. Come on—it'll make you feel better."

"Marie, how's a makeover going to change anything?"

"Girl, come here." She stood Claudia up and steered her toward the full-length mirror that had hung on the back of the door. "Look at you. You are a beautiful girl, and you just don't know it."

Claudia tried to duck her head and turn away. Marie forced her back. "No—look!" She grabbed her hair in a ponytail and tilted her chin up. "Look at this hair and those beautiful eyes, girl. All you need is new style and a little makeup. Please?"

Claudia looked doubtful, but she at least she was looking back at herself in the mirror. "I don't know…"

"What have you got to lose?"

CLAUDIA

She tried her best to squirm out of the chair she was sitting in, but Marie kept holding her down.

"Claudia, you have to sit still, girl," she scolded. "I'm not gonna hurt you."

When Claudia agreed to let Marie give her a new look, Marie ran around the room like a madwoman, plugging up curling irons, pulling out scissors and mirrors, and turning her dresser into a pseudo hairdresser station. The entire time she was shouting with glee, promising Claudia she would look like a million bucks when she finished.

So Claudia sat down, letting Marie do her thing. Marie set up a vanity mirror on the desk so Claudia could see what she was doing, but she also warned her that if didn't stop moving around she would leave her hair in whatever state in was in at the time. The warning was heeded. She stopped squirming.

The truth of the matter was that Claudia was ready for a change. She was ready for a new look, a new attitude—a new everything. Here she was in college, feeling the same inhibitions that she felt as a silly high school girl. Marie was convinced that a complete makeover was the answer to her problems.

"Girl, let me throw a serious style on you, put on a little makeup, and get out of those big jeans and T-shirts—you'll see what a difference it will make," she told her. "It will give you confidence."

Confidence is definitely what Claudia needed. It was one of things she envied in her best friend. Marie brushed on a sweetish, sour smelling, white mixture that she joked was a "baby relaxer." And even though Marie tried to talk her out of the chemical process, Claudia refused to let her do anything to her hair if she did not first do something to straighten the waves she hated. She longed for the versatility of Marie's hair, which was worn up, down, finger-waved, rodded, french rolled, spiked, curled, wrapped, plastered to her head or just plain straight. Sometimes Marie would "add a little" as she put it, and wear funky braids, a quaint ponytail, long, curly side bangs or an elegant bun.

"Where did you learn to do hair so well?" Claudia asked while Marie carefully raked the white goo through her hair. She knew the story, but just liked to hear Marie tell it.

Marie sighed. "I just learned on my own, Bambi—mostly from watching my mother and looking in magazines. My mother got to the point where she didn't want to fool with my hair because it bothered her bad wrist, so I had to do it myself. You know my dad taught me how to cut. I shape him up all the time when I'm home."

A typical "take charge," "Marie" attitude—if you can't get anyone else to do it, do it yourself. She was so strong. Claudia never told her, but Marie was her hero.

"Come on and let's rinse you, Bambi. I don't want this stuff to stay in too long."

"What will it do?" Claudia was fearful she'd wind up with patches of missing hair.

"Girl, come on here," Marie giggled. "Don't you trust me?"

More than you'll ever know, Claudia thought. She trusted and depended on Marie—sometimes too much. Ever since the day Tallette squirted mustard on her silk blouse—a blouse that her mother suggested she wear for the school picture—Claudia had clung to Marie like a leech, drawing confidence from her presence.

She was in the girl's bathroom that day after the lunchroom incident, rubbing in vain at the mustard stains on her blouse with the school's rough, brown paper towels, and wiping tears out of her eyes. What had she done to cause a complete stranger to do this to her? All she doing was eating, minding her own business, trying not to draw attention to herself. The bathroom door opened and Marie stood there a minute before she cautiously entered.

"That'll probably spread the stain," she told Claudia after watching her futile attempts to clean her blouse. Claudia didn't respond. At that moment, everyone who was sitting at that lunch table was the enemy. Even though Marie did not laugh with the rest of the students, Claudia could not separate her from the rest. She rubbed with more vigor.

Marie put her books on the corner of a sink and disappeared into a stall. She returned with a handful of wadded toilet paper and held it out to Claudia, who swiped her eyes with it. Figuring she at least owed Marie the courtesy of speaking, she mumbled, "Thanks."

"I'm Marie."

Claudia knew who she was. On her first day at Cedar East, the first smile she received was from Marie, who told her how to get to her homeroom. She heard another girl call her name behind her, and when Claudia turned, the girl stood there and gave Claudia the once over before rolling her eyes. Now here Marie was once again, attempting to help her out. And here she was, acting like a spoiled brat.

Claudia forced a smile. "I'm Claudia. It's nice to meet you."

An awkward silence followed. Marie fumbled with her purse; Claudia resumed her rubbing.

"Claudia?"

She halted her cleaning and looked up at Marie.

"I just wanted you to know that I think what Tallette did was messed up."

"Tallette?"

"The one who squirted mustard on you. She's just jealous, that's all."

"Is she a friend of yours?"

A look of utter shock and revulsion appeared on Marie's face as she pushed out, "No!"

Claudia was so tickled by her reaction, she busted out laughing.

Marie joined her. When they had control again, Marie told her she had an extra blouse in her locker, and Claudia was more than welcome to it. "My mom bought me two blouses, and I couldn't decide which one to wear, so I just brought both of them," she explained.

After that, she and Marie became fast friends. Marie was the first person to whom Claudia revealed her hang-ups about her looks. "The girls stare at me funny, like I've done something to them," she complained almost everyday for two years.

"They're jealous, Claudia," Marie would respond in a "lets-go-through-this-one-more-time" voice.

"Of what?"

"What" is what Marie could never effectively explain to her. The excuses that it was her looks, her hair, her complexion meant nothing to Claudia. She didn't even think she was attractive, preferring Marie's deep, mahogany complexion to her own. Her hair was one big hassle, so most of time she just pulled it back in a ponytail, and ever since the mustard incident, she had taken to wearing casual shirts

47

and jeans just about everyday. "What" is what Claudia tried to figure out for her two years at Cedar East, and "what" is what she was fed up with dealing with.

Suddenly, she felt a surge of confidence ripple through her like an electric current. After they came back from rinsing her out in the bathroom, Claudia took a deep breath. "Marie? Cut it all off."

"Hmm?" Marie was caught up in combing the tangles out of Claudia's hair.

"Cut my hair short."

"Que pasa?" This time Marie heard and stopped her combing.

Claudia didn't flinch. "I want my hair cut short—shorter than yours."

Marie, whose dark tresses were just past her chin, moved around to the front of Claudia's chair and stared directly into her face. It was a tactic she used all the time when she felt like Claudia was holding something back from her. "Now Bambi, listen to me. Are you sure you want me to do this? You know once I cut, I can't put it back on—unless you want to add a little."

"Marie, I've never been more sure than I am now. Now cut it and stop trippin'. You must be afraid that you won't do a good job."

Now Claudia knew that would hit Marie where it hurt. Her best friend wasn't the bragging type, but the girl could do some hair, and she loved a challenge. The funny thing was after she did someone's hair, she was constantly checking with the person to see if she liked it.

"Oh, you don't think I can cut your hair," Marie mumbled as she readied herself behind the chair again, combing and parting Claudia straight locks into sections. "Girl, I'll throw a style on you so tough that you'll hurt yourself looking in the mirror. Afraid, my foot. Girl, after I finish with you, you'll be having guys in your dreams calling you after you wake up." Marie assumed a brother's voice. "Uh, Claudia? Yeah, my name is Tyrone. You might not remember me, but I met you in your dream the other night...girl, that head was tough."

Claudia laughed so hard she leaned forward and almost fell out of the chair. Marie caught her before she went tumbling over and laughed herself. "Come on here and let me do this head, you nut case."

"You the one," Claudia told her, feeling a rush of love for her friend come over her.

After almost two hours of cutting, combing, drying and curling, Marie was finished. She told Claudia to take a look at it the bathroom, since there was more light and she could get the full effect. Claudia practically ran down the hallway, eager to see the "new her". She was shocked when she first looked at herself and just stood in front of the mirror, angling her head in different directions. Marie had cut it down close in the back and sides, and left it longer in the top, cut in layers. That, along with the makeup Marie applied while Claudia was under the dryer, made her look like a totally different person.

"Well, what do you think?" Marie materialized behind her and was watching her anxiously. She still had her scissors and comb in hand, ready to snip, shape or comb whatever didn't please her roommate.

Claudia twisted her head some more, then grinned wide. "It looks good!"

"You mean it? Now you won't hurt my feelings if you tell me the truth."

"I mean it, Marie! You hooked me *up*, girl!"

Marie smiled in relief, then frowned as she grabbed a lock of Claudia's hair. "This piece is uneven. Let me fix it."

"Marie, stop. It's fine." Claudia laughed, feeling lighthearted and new, and headed out of the bathroom. Marie was on her heels, patting and grabbing at her hair.

"Marie, leave it alone! It looks good!"

Marie finally relaxed, putting her scissors and comb away when they got to the room. She flopped on her bed and stared at Claudia. "You know, Claudia—your hair does look good. It was a good idea to run that baby relaxer through it."

"So I was right, right?" Claudia smiled at her, still feeling giddy over her new hairdo.

"Every once in a while you come up with something." Marie glanced at the clock, then stretched lazily on the bed, letting out a big yawn. "I think I'm going to catch a nap before I get ready."

Claudia was preoccupied with her reflection in the mirror. "Ready for what?"

"For my date tonight. Don't tell me you forgot already? I sure haven't."

Claudia felt her happiness deflating like a balloon with a slow leak. For minute, Marie had helped her to forget that she had a nonexistent social life. And tonight, she would be holed up in this room in front of the television while her best friend was off being courted. She had yet to meet this Cedric, but from Marie's description, he was all that and a bag of chips. Not that Marie couldn't have exaggerated because it was her first college date. Shoot, even if homeboy was ugly, the bottom line was someone had asked Marie out, and Claudia would be left behind—again.

"Would you wake me up in a couple of hours, Claudia?" Marie asked sleepily, and she had just gotten out of bed not too long ago.

"What time is he picking you up?"

"Seven. I just need some time to get myself together—you know."

"Marie, it's only two—you need *that* much time to get ready?"

"Marie smiled and rolled over to face the wall. "Girl, I need to make sure that I'm right. I ain't going out like no sucker. This is a college man we're talking about here—a man, not some high school kid."

Oh, suddenly she was so above high school, in college all of two months. But then again, Marie had always been mature beyond her years, so maybe she wasn't being funny. At any rate, Claudia couldn't seem to swallow the little ball of jealousy that was knotting up in her throat. She looked over at Marie, who had rolled back over to face her, already asleep and breathing softly. She had a contented, peaceful look on her face. Her dark skin contrasted beautifully with the ivory pillowcase she was resting on. Claudia stared back in the mirror. Her dark tan complexion seemed pale now, and even with her makeup her freckles stood out like little dots on a map. Even with her fly cut, she was still the same little insecure Claudia Shipp—half black, half white, and never satisfied.

She spent most of that afternoon channeling surfing on the T.V.— it seemed like every channel was either showing a basketball game or a *Soul Train* rerun. When she got bored with that, she attempted to study for Biology. Someone had once told her that she should be a doctor, though they never explained why. She kind of latched on to that idea because she couldn't think of a better one. As a result, she decided to major in biology, which wasn't even her best class in high school.

Around four-thirty, Marie woke up and began getting ready for her date. Claudia pretended to be absorbed in her biology text while her roommate showered, fixed her hair and applied her makeup.

Marie had chosen a flowing, cream-colored pantsuit of Claudia's to wear. Her mother had brought that outfit on one of her business trips in some city, and Claudia didn't remember ever wearing it. When did she have an occasion to, anyway?

Her best friend looked like she'd stepped off of a runway in Paris. She had her hair slicked up and had added a long ringlet of curls to fall over her face. "How do I look?" she asked anxiously, as if she really didn't know that she looked like a million bucks.

For one nanosecond, Claudia's evil twin wanted to burst her bubble and find something wrong. "You look good, girl," she told her instead, trying to work out a genuine smile.

Marie looked relieved. "Thanks, Claudia. And thank you for letting me borrow this outfit. I promise to be extra careful with it."

"Oh, girl—don't worry about that. I don't wear it anyway. I might end up just giving it to you."

"Really?!"

Claudia shrugged. "Sure, why not?"

Marie sailed over to Claudia's bed and wrapped her in a perfume saturated hug. It smelled like *Eternity*, a scent Marie was wild about.

"You are just so special. I am so glad you're my best friend."

Claudia hugged her back, immediately regretting her unfriendly thoughts. Marie was her best friend, and she went through a lot of trouble to make Claudia feel better about herself—give her more confidence. Here she was, acting like a spoiled brat—again. "Marie..." Claudia began, about to admit how she was still feeling, when someone knocked on the door.

Marie looked at the door anxiously, then tried to stroll nonchalantly over to the peephole. She turned to Claudia. "It's Cedric," she mouthed.

"Well let him in," Claudia mouthed back, giving Marie a "duh" expression.

Marie nodded like a player who had gotten the advice she needed from her coach, took a deep breath, and opened the door. "Hi, Cedric. How are you?" Did that soprano voice belong to Marie?

"I'm fine, gorgeous. Don't you look nice?" a smooth, deep voice answered back, before the owner stepped into the room. Claudia looked up from her textbook, and found herself staring into the dreamiest eyes she had ever seen. She had figured that Cedric would look decent, but she never expected this tall, chocolate brother, whose dimples were only outdone by his pretty white teeth. He was looking back at her with curiosity, even before Marie introduced them.

"Cedric, this is my roommate and best friend from back home, Claudia. Claudia, this is Cedric Carter."

Claudia figured she may as well get off her bed. "Nice to meet you, Cedric," she said, extending her hand.

"Nice to meet you, too, Claudia. Very nice." He took her hand in his and shook it delicately, like he'd break it if he applied too much pressure. All the while, he stared at her with those puppy-dog eyes. Claudia found herself releasing her hand first—and reluctantly so.

"Well, Cedric—are you ready?" Marie asked with a funny look on her face.

"Oh, yes. We'd better go so we can get our table." Cedric looked at Claudia again. "Claudia, what are your plans for the evening? Would you like to join us for dinner? Marie, is that o.k. with you?"

Claudia saw Marie's eyes widen with surprise, then she composed herself and laughed nervously. Well—uh, that's fine. If she wants to go." Marie didn't sound like she meant a word of what she was saying. Claudia glanced at her.

"Thanks guys. That's really nice of you, but I have some studying to catch up on, anyway." She pointed to her biology book laying open on her bed.

Cedric looked unconvinced. "Studying on a Saturday night?"

"Biology is one of those subjects you have to stay on top of at all times," she explained miserably. She glanced at Marie again, whose face was even more troubled now. Something wasn't sitting right with her. "You don't want me along, Cedric—not when you have this beautiful girl to keep you company."

Cedric looked over at Marie. "Marie—I wasn't trying to be funny—I'm sorry. This is our date—I just hate to see anybody stuck in a room on a Saturday night."

"No, Cedric—it's o.k., I understand," Marie assured him, trying to smile.

"No—no it's not." He wrapped his arm around Marie and swung her toward the door. "Let's go so I can redeem myself, beautiful."

Marie turned just enough to look at Claudia. *Thank you*, she lip synched. Then out loud, "Don't study too hard."

Claudia winked at her. "I'm sure I won't."

"Claudia? Nice to meet you." Cedric turned and slowly spread his lips in a smile. She forced her mouth to stay closed.

PERCY

"Percy!"

The bellow of his name rang across the quad, grating his eardrums. Percy turned from the direction of the library and saw his roommate, Allen Downing, running and waving frantically at him. Several students glanced at him in curiosity, and Percy wanted to dive behind the nearest bush. He had just come from the Black Student Association orientation meeting, and left with a brochure and deeper passion to assert his blackness on campus.

Allen had been a thorn in his side ever since he had moved in. It wasn't the fact that he grinned all the time—too much, in Percy's opinion. Percy was immediately on guard with people who were always smiling in his face—in Jackson Park, that was usually a prostitute or someone trying to pull off some type of hustle. Allen's grin was wide enough to swallow a baby elephant. It wasn't even his impeccable neatness. Percy prided himself on his own organizational skills. He was kind of glad when his sister went off to the Army and Paul moved into her bedroom—his little brother was a first rate slob. Allen, on the other hand, made his bed every morning, used glass cleaner almost religiously to clean his mirror, the television and computer screens and the two, big windows in the room, and vacuumed the carpet just about every other day.

The reason that Allen was a thorn in Percy's side had nothing to do with his personality, his actions, or anything like that. What bothered Percy was that Allen was white, and he didn't trust white people. When Percy first moved in and found out about Allen, he tried to throw him subtle hints about where he stood with white people. Apparently, the short answers, the various, black pride, black power posters, the African art and his music didn't do the trick. Allen was just as friendly, and if he mentioned anything at all about his black collections, it was just to ask Percy where he got his "interesting items" from. Percy couldn't understand it. He thought white people where supposed to be intimidated by black people, but Allen acted like they were buddies.

"Percy," Allen breathed, finally catching up to him. "Man, you sure do walk fast."

"Yeah, well I come from a generation of people who had to walk or run—fast."

Allen looked puzzled, then laughed. "You crack me up, Percy. But listen—I locked myself out of the room when I went to the shower. Could I borrow your key to get back in?"

Now Percy noticed the damp, brown hair raked carelessly across Allen's head. For some reason, the sight of those wet tresses angered him. If Percy had jumped out of the shower with a wet head, he would have had to spend time drying it, adding moisturizer to soften it, then combing and patting it into a suitable style. All Allen had to do was wash and go. Whites had it easy in all areas.

"Where'd you get those clothes?" Percy took in the too big T-shirt, jeans and loafers. Allen looked like a little homeless waif, but the way Percy had observed students dressing so far on this campus, he fit right in.

"A guy down the hall lent me some so I could find you. His name's Eugene."

Percy knew the name. He made it his personal business to get acquainted with all the black students in his resident hall so he could distinguish the real brothers from the "Toms." He was well on his way to putting this Eugene into the "Tom" category. Why would a black man let a white man borrow clothes, when, if the tables were turned, a white man would never cut a brother some slack?

Like now. Here Allen was, grinning in his face, needing a favor out of him. Well, Percy decided that Allen was not going to get another favor out of another brother today. "I'm not sure what time I'll be headed back to the room, Allen. You may or may not be there..."

"Oh. That's o.k., Percy. I'll just head on to class. You go on. Thanks anyway." Allen smiled and started walking away, Eugene's too big jeans and shoes making his limp more pronounced than it was to begin with. Allen had shared with him that he'd injured his knee badly when he was younger, and that he would always walk with a slight limp. "There goes my track career," he joked to Percy.

Percy watched him. Why should he help him? He hadn't planned on going back to the room after class, and Allen should have thought before he locked the door going to the shower, like someone was going to steal his...

Michele R. Leverett

Percy lunged after his roommate and tapped him on the shoulder. "Here." Percy reached into his satchel and handed Allen his key.

"But I thought…"

"Just take the key, man," Percy said firmly, wanting the situation to last no longer than necessary. He could barely believe he was helping him out, anyway. "Try not to lock this one up, too."

Allen clapped him on the shoulder. "Thanks, Percy. Now I'll just leave the door unlocked and slide the key in your desk drawer…"

"Sounds good."

He smiled wide again, and trotted back across campus. Percy headed on to the library, wondering what in the world possessed him to do what he just did. His mother would probably jump straight up and down if she knew, and his boys would more likely than not disown him.

"Greeting, black brother."

Percy heard the voice to his left, and turned to face a tall, sunglassed, brother dressed in a white shirt with a tie, and dark slacks. He had a close cropped haircut, and was carrying a briefcase. Percy was immediately curious.

"What's up, man?" Percy replied automatically, sticking out his hand for the typical "brotha' grip"—one pair of hands clasped together, shoulder blades meeting, and the free hand and arm came around the back for a resounding pat. Obviously, the brother didn't know how to engage in this latest form of ethnic male greetings, or did not choose to. His arm remained stiff when Percy tried to move forward with his shoulder. Instead, he pumped Percy's hand up and down in a regular handshake.

"I'm Darryl Cross," the unsmiling young man told him.

"Percy," Percy responded, slightly taken off guard by the lack of a warm reception.

"You have a last name, Percy?"

"Yeah—Lyles. Why?" Percy felt like an idiot. Then he was angry. Why was he letting this person make him feel uncomfortable? He quickly removed his hand from Darryl's and put on his "no-nonsense" look—eyebrows knitted together and arms folded. It was a look perfected by he and his boys back home. It was their trademark, and it drove his mom crazy. She called it that "fool gangster look."

Darryl stared at him awhile, then his grim expression melted into a smile. "Please forgive my brashness, brother," he said in a

56

conciliatory tone. "But I'm used to identifying a person by both names. Both are important, you know."

Percy raised his right eyebrow, wondering where this little exchange was going.

Darryl continued to explain himself. "Percy don't get me wrong— I'm not trying to make you feel inferior. It's just that a lot of our people don't realize the significance of using both names when meeting someone for the first time. It lets a person know that you mean business." He made himself comfortable on a bench behind him and brought his shades up to look at Percy. "Please sit?"

Normally, Percy would have refused. He was not at all sure where this brother was coming from, and he definitely did not like being told what to do—especially by another male figure other than Mr. Dell. Oscar Dell and Evelyn Lyles had been all the role model he had and Percy had been the man of his family ever since his father skipped out. He remembered going into his mother's room at age eight, while she was having one of her crying spells about two weeks after his father left. He took her hand in his and told her that he would be the man of the family, not to worry. She hugged him and told him how much she loved him, and that he would be a man among men when he grew up. He never forgot that prophecy.

Despite his feelings, Percy slowly sank down on the other end of the bench, never taking his eyes off of Darryl. He was curious to hear more from him, but there was also something about Darryl that demanded respect. His tone held dignity, his dress, authority. He looked like a black man that made things happen.

Darryl templed his fingers together and leaned forward on his knees. "Percy, your probably wondering why I approached you this morning. Let me just set the record straight and tell you that I do not go around approaching strangers all the time." He chuckled, amused by the idea, and then grew serious again, turning slightly to look Percy straight in the eye. "I am part of an organization on campus called the Tri-AC—the African American Awareness Coalition. We have three basic goals—uplift of the African-American race, increasing cultural awareness on predominantly white college campuses and improving the African-American image." He spoke slowly, with purpose, as if wanting each word to sink deep in Percy's head.

Percy was momentarily stunned. How was it that he had skipped over this group—especially one that sounded like it was right up his alley? He had thoroughly researched all the groups on campus that remotely resembled a black group, but had not come across this one. In fact, he had just came from the BSA orientation when Allen halted him with his key dilemma. He still had the brochure in his hand. "Why haven't I heard of your group before?" he asked Darryl.

"We don't advertise like everyone else, Percy. We are a small but quality *organization*. The University refuses to recognize us as more than a club because of our small membership, and we refuse to be printed in their form brochures that way because we don't want just any and everybody in our *organization*."

From the way Darryl kept emphasizing the word *organization*, Percy figured he had erred in calling the Tri-AC a group. "So what does your gr—uh, organization do on campus?"

He answered without hesitation. "Our mission is to protect the rights and interests of the African-American population on campus, as I mentioned earlier."

"But if I join the Tri-AC—and I'm not saying that I will—what kind of activities would I be involved in to protect the rights and interests of blacks?" Percy wanted some straight answers.

Darryl slowly removed his sunglasses to reveal piercing brown eyes. He shook out a crisp, white handkerchief retrieved from his pocket, and began to meticulously polish each lens. Percy guessed that meant he was going to answer when he was good and ready. "You assume a lot, black brother," Darryl folded the handkerchief neatly and returned it to his pocket. The shades went back on his face. "First of all, I was not inviting you to join. I only approached you because I wanted you to be aware of our presence. The Tri-AC does not gain members like other groups on campus—we recruit candidates. You, Percy, are only a candidate. You still have to apply and pass a series of interviews to be brought on board, just like you would for a job."

"Interview?"

"Yes, interview, Percy. We take what we do seriously. We are not like other groups on campus under the auspices of African-American." He reached over and tapped Percy's BSA brochure for emphasis. It fluttered to the ground and for some odd reason, Percy felt too embarrassed to pick it up. Darryl retrieved it for him and turned it over, as if inspecting it for flaws. "You were thinking of joining them?" he asked, indicating the brochure.

"I was considering it. Is there something wrong with that?" Percy was a little peeved that Darryl had made him sound so naïve. He prided himself on always having the upper hand in most situations, but this one was not turning out that way so far.

Darryl just shrugged. "If that's what you want to do, Mr. Lyles. I would love to continue this conversation, but like most African-American men should, I must be on the move. He stood to go, then looked back down at Percy. "It's unfortunate—I was about to invite you to apply with us. A brother like you might be an asset—you seem strong-willed, determined."

Now those were adjectives Percy could deal with. Strong-willed, determined—his mother called it being bull-headed, but apparently Darryl saw the positive. He didn't know any more about the Tri-AC than what Darryl had just laid on him, and he should probably do more research, but at that moment, he was just about sold on them. Darryl had started walking toward the Student Center at a fast pace. Percy broke into a trot and caught up to him. "Uh, Darryl," he stammered. "How do I apply?"

Darryl grinned broadly. "Our office is in room 211 in the Student Center. Come by in a couple of hours and I'll have an application ready for you." Darryl held out his hand for another shake. "Thanks for wanting to make a difference for our people." He offered one last grin, then strolled off to his former business at hand.

Percy sat on the corner of his bed, reading his acceptance letter for the fifth time. His book satchel was parked at the open door to his room, because he didn't want to take the time and bring it in after checking his mail box and finding the letter marked, *Office of the African-American Awareness Coalition, Student Center, Room 211.* He had gotten his application the same day he met Darryl, and painstakingly typed in each line of information using the hunt and peck system. The call inviting him to a screening interview came a couple of days after he returned the application. The voice on the other end told him the interview process was just as intense and serious as an employment interview, so please dress accordingly— and be prompt. Percy had carefully dressed in his church suit, grabbed his leather portfolio—a graduation present from Mr. Dell—and headed across campus to the Student Center.

Darryl met him at the door of Room 211 with the same serious expression he had the day he approached Percy. Percy glanced in the generous sized office—it boasted two desks, an outdated, green, vinyl couch, a bookcase and a window with a view of the students entering and exiting the Student Center. "Mr. Lyles," Darryl greeted him, extending his hand to shake.

Percy shook, then just stood in the doorway, waiting for Darryl's invitation to sit. Darryl just went back to his desk and shuffled papers, seemingly unconcerned about Percy standing in the doorway. The portfolio in Percy's sweaty hand seemed to weigh ten pounds, so he shifted it to the other hand. He couldn't figure out why Darryl was ignoring him.

"Are you just going to stand there?"

He almost jumped when Darryl spoke without even looking up from his papers.

"Were you waiting for me to ask you to sit? I wasn't going to, you know." Darryl finally looked up at Percy, then swung his eyes to the pitiful looking couch. He moved swiftly past Darryl's desk and sat on the couch, making the patched cushions sink in with an embarrassing release of air. He hated vinyl.

Darryl snickered. "We've been trying to get rid of that couch since we moved into this office three years ago. The University is giving us a hassle about replacing it. It's probably one of the few things that we and the BSA have in common." He came around the desk and perched on the edge, facing Percy. "I'm not trying to give you a hard time this morning," he said in what seemed to be his "I'm only trying to help a brotha' out" fashion. "See, one factor that will be instrumental in your acceptance is the confidence to do what needs to be done, without somebody telling you. Now you've probably been taught that it's good manners to wait for an invitation to sit, but as an African-American male in this racist society, you have to take authority, you have to control the situation. There's not always going to be someone around to guide you, or even pat you on the back, even when you do good—especially as a black man at Hamel."

The last remark was almost hissed out—Percy sensed the hostility that Darryl had for the school. It made him wonder if he could actually tip the scales in favor of his race here, which was one of the reasons he decided to come.

"The brothers are setting up in the conference room. I'll let them know you're here. Your early arrival is a plus, Percy." Darryl grabbed a folder from the desk behind him, then stood. Percy jumped up from the couch and stuck out his hand first. He had always been a fast learner.

In the conference room, Percy found himself at the foot of a long, mahogany table, staring into the intense faces of five black upperclassmen, all dressed identically in dark suits and white shirts. *The black FBI*, Percy thought crazily. Darryl took a seat at the head, next to a brother that was already seated there. The unidentified brother had a small mustache lining his full lips, with a small part in his closely cropped fade. He looked like a corporate giant about to devour a delicious deal. At that moment, Percy felt like part of the menu.

"Good morning, Mr. Lyles," the young man greeted in a deep voice that sounded a little forced. I'm Carlos Franklin, President of the Hamel University Chapter of the Tri-AC. Of course, you've already met our Recruiting Specialist, Darryl Cross. Allow me to introduce you to the other members of the Board. Brian Samuel, Newsletter Editor, Rodney Mitchell, Special Events Coordinator, Marcus Powell, Historian, and Tamal Bailey, Treasurer. Gentleman, may I introduce you to Percy Lyles."

Each member of the board nodded as his name was called. The last one, Tamal, took his time in nodding, staring a hole right through Percy.

Carlos continued. "Your application has been carefully reviewed, and you have been granted a screening interview. If you are successful with this interview, we will grant you a second interview. If that is successful, you will become a trial member of the Tri-AC for thirty days—weekends are included. Now if we feel that you don't require a trial period, you can become a full-fledged member after your second interview. That just depends on you. Brothers, are you prepared with your questions?"

The board nodded, almost in sync.

"Mr. Lyles, do you understand everything I've said?"

Percy answered yes.

"Very good...first question..."

Starting with Carlos, the board asked him about his background, his affiliations with other black organizations, and his future plans. He answered openly and honestly, instead of just telling them what he thought they wanted to hear. Most of the things he had already answered on his application, so there were really no questions that caught him off guard. What did catch him off guard was that no one appeared to be taking any notes on what he said.

"Percy, why did you choose Hamel as opposed to a historically black college or university?" Rodney, the Special Events Coordinator, asked.

Percy cleared his throat, excused himself, then relayed his story about how he initially planned to go to a black school, but decided on Hamel because it presented a challenge.

"What challenge was that?"

"That I could excel in the white educational system as well as my own," he told Rodney, noticing some brief nods of approval from the other board members. He added that Hamel was also paying his way. This time, some raised, impressed eyebrows accompanied the nods.

"So you're on a scholarship?" Carlos asked, sounding pleased. Darryl grinned briefly, knowing Percy was his find. "Which scholarship would that be?"

"T. Samuel Powell."

Everyone nodded again, except Tamal, who looked stunned, then angry as he narrowed his eyes at Percy, slowly pushing away from the table.

"Excuse me." Tamal got up and slammed out of the conference room, to the surprise of everyone. The board members looked at each other in confusion. Darryl leaned over and whispered something to Carlos, who nodded, looking relieved.

"Percy? The board thanks you for your time. We will contact you on our next step. Brothers, we need to have a brief meeting as soon as Mr. Lyle exits."

Percy stood, grabbed his portfolio, and purposely made his way around the table, shaking each hand. Carlos looked like he was trying to hold in some strong volcano of emotion that would erupt as soon as Percy left. He didn't know what the deal was with that brother, Tamal, but he was sure that their "brief meeting" involved him.

Darryl ushered him to the door. "Good job, Percy," he whispered before shutting him out.

A week later, Percy was reading his acceptance letter. He hadn't even had a second interview, and he was already in!

The phone rang. "Congratulations, Percy," Darryl said on the other end. "You're in, brotha'. I'm sure you've gotten your letter by now."

"Thanks, man. Yeah, I just got it. But what happened to the second…"

"Percy, the Board was very impressed with you—I told you that early arrival would be a plus. It's one of the first things they mentioned. You were confident, honest—we just got a very good feeling about you. That's why we had that quick meeting at the end. As soon as you left, Carlos told us, 'I know we need to vote, but in my opinion, that brotha' is in.' We could've ended the voting right there."

Percy was pleased and a little proud. "Thanks man. I was just being real."

"Hey, that's all we ask. We don't want any phonies in the organization. We have enough of those in other groups on campus." Percy knew he was probably referring to the BSA, for starters, and wondered what in the world the beef was between the two, who both seemed concerned about the black student population.

He didn't realize how close he was to finding out.

EUGENE

Eugene wanted to let the phone ring. He knew who it was. It was his father, calling to see how he was doing at Hamel like he did almost everyday for the first two weeks Eugene had arrived. The conversation was always tense although his dad tried to appear pleasant, but Eugene had learned to read in between the lines. The conversation was almost always the same:

"Hello?"

"Eugene, This is your dad." *The one that is basically funding your education. Show me some respect.*

"Oh, hi dad."

"How are you?" *Are you ready to leave that lily-white school and go to a predominantly black school where you belong?*

"Just fine. School is keeping me pretty busy."

"Well, good." A pause. "So, have you made any friends yet?" *Have you ran into any Blacks that aren't Uncle Toms?*

"A few."

"Are they nice?" *Are they black?*

"Yes dad, they are nice people."

"O.k. Well, here's your mother."

Eugene would breathe a sigh of relief when his mother took over the phone. She would ask about the usual motherly things— schoolwork, his health, if he were eating right, did he need anything. His conversations with her were the typical "no, mom, yes, mom" call and response.

"O.k., baby. Take care. Your father would like to speak with you again."

His dad again. "Let me know if you need anything." *Call immediately when you come to your senses and want to transfer to a black school.*

"Right, dad. Bye."

Eugene decided to let the answering machine pick it up this time. The fourth ring was short, then the machine clicked, and his roommate's voice came on, informing the mystery caller that there was no one there to take the call. He then added the caller had forty-five seconds to leave a message; afterwards, the phone would self-destruct.

Beep! "Eugene, this is Irene. I was calling to see if you wanted to come to a study session, but since you're not in…"

Eugene lunged across the room and grabbed the phone, banging his knee on the bedpost in the process. He barked in pain just as he picked up the receiver.

"Hello? Hello?! Is anyone there?!" He heard the faint female voice as he waited for his injured knee to flare painfully, then subside to a dull throb. He exhaled the breath he had been holding and sat up. "Hi Irene. It's Eugene."

"Are you o.k.? Sounds like someone was trying to kill you."

He laughed—more in nervousness than amusement. Irene Poe was a sophomore volleyball player in his Cultural Differences in Literature Class. He was one of the few freshman because Composition 101 and 102 were prerequisites and he had tested out of those classes. Hamel University was one of the few colleges that would allow students to submit writing samples to test out of a freshman English class. Eugene was one of the fortunate few that did.

Cultural Differences in Literature was an interesting class, to say the least. The professor, a balding, spectacled white-haired gentleman in his fifties led the class with a religious enthusiasm that sometimes caught Eugene off-guard. He would hover over his class like a vulture, inviting them to join in a lively discussion that he usually pulled out of the clear blue. He and Irene shared the perception that Dr. Grayvine's elevator might not go up to the top floor.

When Eugene first entered the class, he noticed two things right off. First, he was one of the few males in there, second, he was definitely the only black. He quickly took a seat near the door, ready to run if someone should so much as glance at him. Irene came in a few minutes after he did with her light brown ponytail swinging, looked around, and then chose the empty seat behind him.

"Hi."

Eugene almost jumped out of his seat. His new five-subject notebook plopped to the floor and before he could retrieve it, a female hand reached down and held it out to him.

"Thanks," he managed to smile.

"I'm Irene."

"Eugene," he responded, taking the notebook and shaking the hand that was still outstretched. Her deep green eyes twinkled at him, and he looked down quickly so she wouldn't notice him staring. Irene sank back in her chair, still smiling at him. He could feel himself smiling back, like an idiot. He wanted to slap himself. Man, she was cute.

"Is this your first class with Grapevine?" she asked.

"With *who*?"

Irene leaned forward again. "Grapevine. You must be a freshman. Us English folk gave him that nickname because we spread so many horror stories around about him."

"Oh, really?" The last thing Eugene needed was to be stuck in a class with a nutty professor.

"Don't worry—he's harmless. He's just a little…different."

"Different?"

Irene laughed. "Don't let it worry you—you'll do fine. Have you ever known a professor that wasn't weird in some way?" She looked at him expectantly, then snapped her fingers. "Oh, that's right. You're just a freshman."

"What are you?"

She gave him an arrogant look. "I am your superior—a mighty sophomore. I would usually require you to bow at my feet, but I'll give you a break this time."

Eugene laughed, feeling a little more comfortable. Irene gave him a light tap on the arm and told him she was just kidding around with him, don't mind her. He was about to respond when Dr. Grapevine marched in, smiling possessively over the room. *You're mine now*, his grin seemed to say.

"Good morning!" he boomed, wide-eyed. "I am Dr. Julian Grayvine, and this is Cultural Differences in Literature. If you have stumbled into the wrong class, now is your chance to leave. Otherwise, you're here for the duration." He let that sink in, while a few worried students quickly fumbled out their class schedules. "Just kidding," he assured them, as they laughed nervously.

"In this class, we will be discussing the differences in literary writings based on culture, as the name of the class indicates. I will tell you right now that if you harbor any prejudice against any race, creed or national origin, do not have an open mind, or are easily offended, then this is not the class for you. I will assume that most of you have either completed the prerequisites for the class and are at least sophomores, or you were fortunate enough to test out by passing the English Proficiency Exam if you are a freshman…"

"That's you," Irene whispered to Eugene, poking him.

"....do we have anyone that represents that fortunate minority?"

Eugene looked around, just like everyone else did. He swallowed, then slowly raised his hand, feeling twenty-three sets of eyes on him, including the four from Grapevine. He could have easily done without all the attention.

"Welcome aboard, young man," Grayvine greeted with his peculiar smile. "I'm sure you'll find this class unlike anything you've been used to."

You're telling me, Eugene thought.

"I must express my disappointment at the small number of minority students in here," Grapevine continued, having a seat behind a small table in front of the room. "I thought that a class such as this would attract more minorities. Nevertheless, we trod forward. Perhaps it will help my Anglo-Saxon majority to be a little more open-minded, huh?" Grapevine shuffled his papers, explained the other goals of the course, and immediately assigned them work.

"Your semester long assignment will be done with a partner. You are to look at any major work from a list I will provide, and approach it as a team, analyzing the work from two different cultural standpoints. I want you to record everything from day one of your research—your agreements, disagreements, headaches, victories—the whole nine yards. It is to be fifteen typed, double-spaced pages to hand into me, and a twenty to thirty minute oral presentation for the class. The oral presentations will start mid-October—if I were you, I'd schedule early and get this project out of the way, since it is forty percent of your overall grade.

Now since our minority pool is so limited, this project will really challenge some of you to look at literature from a different standpoint. I would suggest as many male/female pairings as possible, which also appears to be a challenge. Please don't bombard our minority students—I'll need your teams by the next class meeting. Good day."

Just as quickly as he entered, he left the class, who sat there like they didn't believe they could leave so early.

"He gets straight to the point, doesn't he?" Irene commented.

"Yeah, he sure does." Eugene could feel eyes on him again, like everyone wanted to rush over to him and ask to be his partner.

"Want to team up for this one?" Irene asked. "Thought I might as well get my bid in before anyone else."

"Uh, sure. That's fine."

"Well, let's exchange numbers and work out a schedule. I'd like to get this thing over with as soon as possible." Irene ripped out a sheet of paper and wrote her number down. Eugene followed suit.

"No fair, Irene," a male student sitting across from Irene said. "No one else got a chance to ask him."

"Back off, Richard," Irene told him, grabbing Eugene's arm. "He's mine, now."

Eugene didn't know how that comment would go over. Irene certainly appeared to be very liberal in her attitude towards him. He didn't know if he liked feeling like the last pack of beef on sale at the grocery store, but it felt different to be appreciated because of his color, no matter what the circumstances.

MARIE

No, she wasn't dreaming.

Just to make sure, Marie blinked. Yep, Cedric was still there, still walking beside her. She wanted to turn a few cartwheels. He was saying something to her, but she couldn't hear him—she was too busy concentrating on the way his dimple made that lovely indention in his smooth complexion whenever he moved his mouth. He chose that exact moment to look down at her, parting his lips to show that million-dollar smile. "Am I boring you with all this talk about football?"

"No, go right ahead." *Talk about anything—football, the weather, the price of tea in China, for all I care. Just talk.*

"Why do I feel like I'm rambling?"

"Football is your thing, Cedric. Everybody likes to talk about what they enjoy."

Cedric stopped walking and brushed his fingers lightly across her cheek. She vowed right then in her mind not to wash that side of her face for as long as she could stand it.

"I'll call you later, o.k.? I might stop by if I have time." With these parting words and a wink, he streaked into the English building, already late for class.

Marie walked away slowly, smiling down at the ground. She could still feel the pressure on her cheek where Cedric's hand had grazed it. And to think—she had been concerned when he came to pick her up the other night and met Claudia for the first time. It was probably her imagination that his eyes had widened with interest when Marie introduced them and he shook her hand a second too long. He might have been busy admiring her new do and forgot to let go. And so what he had invited Claudia to dinner with them? Didn't he apologize for being too polite? It was like saying, "have some" to somebody when you were eating, even if you only had enough for yourself. And no, she was wasn't going to get all bent out of shape because he had asked her a couple of questions about Claudia when they were at dinner, like how long she and Marie had been friends, and did she usually study on a Saturday night.

"Why isn't she going out somewhere with her boyfriend? Or is her boyfriend back home?" he asked.

"She doesn't have a boyfriend, Cedric," Marie replied honestly.

"Mmm hmmm," he mumbled thoughtfully, then changed the subject.

She had felt a twinge of something then, just like she felt when they were up in her room. But now, she let all that slide. It was Marie he took to the movies, ate lunch with, and walked to and from class sometimes. This was not high school, this was college, and Cedric was a mature man who knew what he wanted. Still, she refused to read anymore into his actions then friendship—until he stated otherwise. How she hoped for otherwise. Marie was in such deep thought that she almost walked past her roommate, talking with a nice-looking brother wearing a Greek letter shirt.

"Marie! There you are!" Claudia called cheerfully when she noticed her. She made a beeline for her. "I'll call you later, o.k.?" She called over her shoulder to the brother. "I promise."

"I'll be waiting, Claudia," he responded.

Claudia grabbed Marie's elbow and nearly walked her into a sprint. Marie glanced behind her—the brother was staring at them then turned on his heel, going about his business.

"Girl, I am so glad you came when you did," Claudia said in relief, slowing down to a normal pace.

Who was that?" Marie wanted to know.

"Some guy named Darius," Claudia said offhandedly. "I met him in the bookstore last week."

"He's a cutie."

Claudia just shrugged. "Yeah, he's cute, but I think he knows it. That's a turnoff."

Listen at her. Marie looked at her best friend, the former Ms. Shy, talking with gumption about what turned her off. That hairstyle and makeup must have hit a couple of nerves with her. Even her outfit was spunky. She had on a brown suede miniskirt with a thick brown and tan striped sweater and brown tights. Cute. Chic. Very un-Claudialike. At least, the Claudia she knew before her transformation. And look! She even had the nerve to be wearing some sassy little shades. Marie looked down at her collegiate outfit—sneakers, jeans, a huge Hamel U sweatshirt that had cost her more than she cared to remember in the bookstore, and a baseball cap, because she didn't feel like fooling with her hair today. She didn't even bother with her contact lenses on Thursdays, slapping on her glasses instead. She only had one class on Thursday at 9:30, and she was usually headed back to her room to finish sleeping by this time. She had run into Cedric purely by accident and was totally devastated by the way she was dressed. He didn't seem to notice.

"Let's go get some breakfast," Claudia suggested.

"I'm not real hungry, but I'll go with you. I want to hear more about this Darius." Marie also wanted to get back to the residence hall as soon as possible. Cedric had mentioned stopping by if he had the time. That might mean later on this afternoon or this evening. She wanted to make sure she was halfway decent either way.

Claudia was in the mood to eat a full-course breakfast, so they headed to The Appetizer, the newest eating place on campus. The meal card didn't go far there, but they had the best food on campus. And they served a mean breakfast. Marie got a banana nut muffin and orange juice, while Claudia showed no shame and ordered a "sho-nuff" breakfast—biscuit, eggs bacon and grits. She offered to treat Marie to breakfast but Marie declined, though the smell from Claudia's plate was driving her crazy.

As they made their way to a table, a couple of brothers sitting down stopped their conversation and gawked. "Dang, she fine," one said.

"Which one you looking at?" the other asked.

"That little redbone. She's a honey, man."

"I hear you." The two high-fived each other.

Marie walked on by, pretending not to hear or see the exchange. However, she felt her heart drop. She was never able to command the attention Claudia did. She had witnessed guys drop whatever they had in their hands to stare at her friend, even during Claudia's jeans and ponytail stage. They found a table and Claudia did manage to bow her head before diving into her plate. She may have been shy in a lot of areas, but eating was never one of them.

"Have some?" Claudia offered politely, not really slowing down to see Marie's response.

Marie shook her head, nibbling on her nut muffin slowly.

"Marie, I don't see why you're trying to diet, anyway. You're slim enough as it is."

"I'm not dieting—I'm just watching my fat intake. What's wrong, you feeling guilty eating all that food now?"

71

Claudia put a forkful of egg in her mouth. "Do you see me stopping?"

Marie had to laugh. Even Claudia's sense of humor had improved. She could be so serious at times. "So tell me about Darius."

"There's really nothing to tell. I met him last week while I was in the bookstore. He asked me for my number."

"Did you give it to him?" She didn't remember any guys calling the room for Claudia.

"Of course not."

"Why not?"

Claudia looked at Marie like she should have known better. "Because. I'm not going to be giving my number out to some strange guy, girl."

Well, he might not be so strange if you got to know him." Marie couldn't take it anymore. She helped herself to a slice of Claudia's bacon. Claudia slapped at her hand, but missed. "Don't be so uptight." She wasn't going to tell her, but it would make her feel more comfortable about Cedric if Claudia had a guy to occupy her time.

"Listen at you. Did you give Cedric your number the first time you met him?"

"No, but that's different."

"Oh, really? How?"

"He didn't ask me for it."

"So you're saying you would have if he had asked for it?"

Would she, or would she have played hard to get? While she was thinking of a suitable answer, Cedric and another brother who looked like a football player approached their table, carrying trays of food. Marie immediately put down her bacon and wished for an inconspicuous way to way to check her lipstick level. She could feel the grease and crumbs on her mouth, but didn't want to remove any trace of lipstick there by wiping it off. She did a quick swipe with her tongue anyway and smiled as the guys approached.

"Hello, ladies," Cedric greeted with charm.

"Hi, Cedric. I thought you had a class?" Marie tried to keep the extra pitch out of her voice.

"I did—but my buddy here forced me to skip it and have breakfast with him." Cedric nudged his companion with an elbow, then turned his attention to Claudia. "A little hungry this morning, Claudia?"

"Very," Claudia replied calmly. Her lipstick was still intact, despite the almost inhumane attack on her food. She wiped her mouth delicately, and smiled up at Cedric. "Was I oinking?"

Cedric and his companion busted out laughing. Marie chuckled a little, but then felt that uneasiness creeping in again. Why did Claudia have to show off her new personality *now*? Why couldn't she revert back to that timid little creature Marie saw in the cafeteria in high school?

"Ladies, this is a buddy and teammate of mine, Junte'. Junte', this is Marie and Claudia."

"Very pleased to make your acquaintance," Junte' greeted in a heavily accented voice. Marie guessed African, especially with a name like Junte'.

"May we join you?" Cedric asked.

"Please do," Claudia answered before Marie could get her mouth open. Marie was pleasantly surprised when Cedric chose the seat next to hers; Junte' sat across from him, next to Claudia.

"Junte'—that's an interesting name," Claudia continued, the perfect hostess. "Where are you from?"

Junte' smiled. "West Africa. Senegal."

"Really? You came here just to go to school?"

"Well, I came to attend school on a football scholarship."

"And go pro," Cedric added after swallowing a mouthful of food. "Don't let his humbleness fool you. This boy is being heavily scouted. Heavily."

Marie and Claudia both looked at Junte' with interest. "That's great, Junte'," Marie chimed in, beating Claudia to the punch. "Do you play offense or defense?"

Junte' looked surprised at her question. "Offense. Lead block. You know the game?"

"Know it? I watch it every Sunday and Monday night during football season. I've been a Cowboys fan ever since the fourth grade."

Junte' nodded appreciatively.

"Marie knows her stuff." This was Cedric, finally acknowledging her presence. "We just got to work on her taste in teams." He winked at her, a diehard Redskins fan, and she felt some of her uneasiness leave.

"So you are knowledgeable in sports as well as being a beautiful black woman," Junte' told her, while she tried not to smile like an idiot. "You have such pretty skin, Marie—like an African Queen."

Marie was overwhelmed by the compliment. The last time she had been called "African Queen," it was not positive. "Thank you, Junte'. I appreciate that." She glanced over at Cedric to see his reaction, but if he heard Junte's compliment, he didn't acknowledge it. He had his head in his plate eating like he had to put out a fire. She swung her eyes across to Claudia, who had stopped eating and even looked a little miffed. She reached down and pulled up her book bag.

"I've got to get to class." Claudia stood up and grabbed her tray. There was a trace of attitude in her voice. "It was nice to meet you, Junte'." She dumped her tray at the trashcan and sashayed out the door, forgetting to even tell Marie or Cedric goodbye.

Cedric watched her leave, and glanced down at his watch. "I've got to run myself. Junte', man, I'll see you later. Marie—talk to you later?"

"Sure, Cedric," she said with more cheer than she felt. She turned and watched Cedric head out the door catching up to Claudia, who hadn't gotten that far. Claudia smiled up at him, and they sauntered off at a casual pace. Marie told herself that she didn't have anything to worry about. What was the big deal? So they were walking together—they were probably just headed in the same direction.

Yeah, but did you see the way he blew you off when Claudia left? "Talk to you later, Marie." That's all he said.

Claudia's my best friend. Even if Cedric was playing games with me—and I doubt that he is—Claudia wouldn't diss me like that. One, she's too good of a person. Two, she's too timid.

Timid?!! Take a closer look, Marie. That girl's shyness is obsolete. Face it—you created a monster with you "be more outgoing" advice and your makeovers.

Marie shook off that pessimistic voice that was talking to her. Junte' was looking at her with interest.

"You seem deep in thought, Marie."

"No… I just, no. Don't mind me." She took a sip of her orange juice and ventured a question. "I guess Cedric has a busy class schedule today, huh?"

Junte' laughed in amusement. "When he makes it to class. We have practice in fifteen minutes, so I imagine his errand does not require much time."

"Fifteen minutes?"

"Yes, and we need to hurry. Coach Bell makes us run a lap for every minute that we are late."

"But I thought Cedric just said you guys just skipped class?"

"I'm not in the habit of missing class, Marie. There is too much at stake. Cedric was only joking. He has no class right now, but it would not make much difference if he had one, anyway." Junte' rose and stretched out his hand. "It was an honor to meet you, Marie. I am going to head over to the field so I won't be Cedric's running partner." He laughed at his own joke. "To tell you the truth, I think Cedric's on a quest."

"A quest? What kind of quest?"

"I think he is questing after your friend." Junte' talked like he had no idea exactly whose "friend" Cedric was supposed to be. Then again, when Cedric introduced Junte' to her and Claudia, he didn't add any special tag to her name to make that distinction.

"No, we all just know each other. Everyone's just friendly." Marie was stretching the truth slightly to spare her feelings.

Junte' shrugged. "I could be wrong. It was only a theory, but I guess you know best. Well, it was an honor to meet such a beautiful woman. I hope to see you around." Junte' smiled in parting and strolled out of the cafeteria.

Marie sat where she was a minute, trying to keep nonsense tears from her eyes. She was just being silly, and she needed to cut it out. Guys didn't like girls that had no trust in them. Jealous, possessive females. Maybe Cedric had to run back to his apartment and get something real quick. It wasn't that far away. Comforted by this thought, she picked up her tray and headed to the trashcan, totally missing Cedric as he streaked by the cafeteria from the opposite direction to catch up to Junte'.

PERCY

"What we need is more representation in the Student Government."

The meeting room in the Benson Student Center was packed with BSA members, Tri-AC members, and what appeared to be a good majority of the black student population at Hamel. The meeting was an attempt by the BSA to unite with the Tri-AC. Percy found out later that his membership with the Tri-AC "negated" any membership with the BSA, though he didn't understand why. It wasn't explained to him, either.

A letter was sent from Terrell Connor, President of the Black Student Association, to Carlos:

As President of the Black Student Association, it has come to my attention that the two major black organizations on campus are not a united front. There have been rumors of discord and strife that are not conducive to a healthy environment for our black student population. As President of the BSA, and as a member of that student population, I am requesting a meeting between these two strong units on Tuesday, October 7 in Room 5 of the Student Center. The meeting should be a very informal discussion, addressing areas we need to tackle in order to promote unity.

There is power and strength in unity. Let us, the black leaders and representatives of Hamel University, work together to gain that power and achieve that strength.

In brotherly love,
Terrell Connor
President, Black Student Association

At their weekly Tri-AC meeting, the eight board members flanked Carlos as he read the letter to the twelve regular members, most of which were still in their trial period. He told the members that they would attend the "so-called unity meeting," and see what the BSA what talking about.

Right now, Percy was sitting on the second row in room 5 with seven other new members. The board members were seated on the first row, and the remaining new members were behind Percy. All of the Tri-AC, including Carlos, were dressed in conservative, dark suits, white shirts, and ties. A campus dress code was not enforced for the members, but it was "expected" that each member maintain a positive image, and avoid articles of clothing that were labeled as "stereotypical"—oversized jeans and shirts, baseball caps turned backwards, fancy basketball sneakers, etc. Percy had studied his wardrobe after finding out that tidbit of information. His dress clothes were limited since the only time he really dressed up at home was for church, weddings and funerals. With his savings from working at Dell's, he had bought what he thought would be appropriate for a campus environment—casual shirts, sweaters and pants, underwear, socks, sneakers, a pair of boots, a pair of casual shoes, and a heavy weight coat for the cold weather. His brother's eyes had popped out of his head when he lugged his bags in the apartment after his mother had taken him shopping.

"Yo, man—let me sport some of this," Paul said, pawing through his clothes the minute he put them down.

"Nah, Paul—these are for school." Percy told him. Paul stayed in his closet. Percy would go to get a shirt or a pair of pants, and they would be missing. Nine times out of ten, he would find it in his brother's room or on his brother's back. That was because Percy always had a good eye for fashion. He just knew how to put clothes and colors together and make them look good. He couldn't count the number of times that Monica had bribed him with candy, money, or switching chores if he would come shopping with her and help her pick out something. Now when he was younger, Percy thought it was very uncool to be with his sister in a clothing store—it was almost comical when they went. He would be in the mall, standing on the outside while Monica went in the store. She would have to come to the entrance, clear her throat to get his attention, and show Percy whatever outfit she wanted his input on. He would look away, scratch his head for "yes" or rub his nose for "no."

The scratch and rub went on for about four years, and that was only because Monica left to go to the Army. His mother took him shopping with her once after she recognized her son's gift, but she refused to do the "scratch and rub" method and loudly bragged about her son's keen sense of fashion all over the store, instead. After that, he flat out refused to go shopping with her again, so she would go on her own, bring outfits home, and return them to the store if Percy gave the outfits a thumbs down.

So Percy had no major beef with the Tri-AC's dress code—the big jeans and caps were never his flavor, anyway. But at the same time, he didn't know if he were completely comfortable with dressing like nineteen other brothers. But it wasn't a big thing, since they didn't have to wear the same thing all the time—just when they were together in public as an organization. He turned his attention to the head table up front, where Terrell and his Vice President, Veronica Little sat opposite Carlos and Darryl. Each leader had a microphone in front of him or her. A podium separated the two pairs and behind it stood Dr. Donald Forrestor, a professor of African-American Studies, and the faculty advisor for the black organizations on campus. He was mediating this historical meeting between the two groups that spent most of their time at each other's throats.

Dr. Forrestor asked for the room's attention, and welcomed each person to the unity meeting. He suggested that instead of this meeting being a gripe session, that each group be open about its issues, and work on coming to a resolution, not pointing fingers. He also pointed out something that Percy thought all along—the BSA and the Tri-AC were both supposed to be advancing the interests of the African-American student population, so they should be working together, not against one another. Percy looked at the leaders' reactions: Terrell was nodding and mumbling what looked like "Amen"; Veronica was punctuating each of Dr. Forrestor's points with an emphatic but low-volumed "yes"; Darryl frowned like he was in deep concentration and Carlos just looked bored.

"And now I'd like to turn the meeting over to Terrell Connor, President of the Black Student Association," Dr. Forrestor said. "Terrell?"

The audience clapped as Dr. Forrestor sat in a chair behind the podium and Terrell smiled like a politician and leaned into his mike. "The Black Student Association was established on Hamel's campus in December of 1971, by five of the thirty students who made up the school's black population..." Percy was surprised to learn that the BSA had existed now for nineteen years. Terrell was explaining the purpose of the BSA, and the many accomplishments of it over the last twenty years. He boasted about the groups that had developed from the BSA's fight for racial equality—the fraternities and sororities, the

Black Athletic Council, etc., and their crowning achievement—the purchase of the half acre of land between the academic buildings and the athletic fields, known as "The Plot."

Hamel was the first predominantly white university to have what was more common on HBCU's. Percy had learned in a Tri-AC meeting that the University fought the Plot tooth and nail, but after the black organizations raised the money and the black Hamel alumni supported it, there was nothing they could do. So there it was, a half-acre of land that paid tribute to all of the African-American organizations on Hamel's campus. Artistically carved, hand painted stone structures were placed all over the plush green land. It was the pride and joy of Hamel's black population. Each organization had a hand in building a piece of history. Next to Yardley Tower, it was the second most popular hangout spot for the black students. The organizations alternated in cleaning and other upkeep of the Plot to keep it looking as pristine as the day it was completed. So far, it was the only symbol of complete black unity on the campus. Unless the unity meeting currently in session proved to be a success.

So far, Terrell wasn't delving into any issue concerning the BSA and Tri-AC. He was talking more about the battle the BSA had been in for many years, and the low number of black representation in the Student Government. He noted that black students just didn't have the interest in the working of political matters like they did during the beginning years of the BSA—they were getting too comfortable. "Now, I am sure my brothers over here representing the Tri-AC would have to agree." He motioned in the direction of Carlos and Darryl, who said nothing, but appeared to be giving Terrell their full attention. "No, we have not been pen pals over the years, which is probably more of a tragedy than the low black representation in the Student Government. Carlos, perhaps it would help if we all understood the purpose of the Tri-AC..." Terrell didn't sound like he was being sarcastic, but judging from the fidgeting and whispering from the board members in front of Percy, that's the way it came across.

Carlos, however, didn't show any offense taken—he smiled a little, whispered something to Darryl, and then surrounded his mike with his fist, bringing it to him. "The purpose of the African-American Awareness Coalition, *brother* Terrell, is to uplift the African-American race, increase cultural awareness on predominantly white college campuses, improve the African-American image and most important, protect the rights and interests of the black students here at Hamel."

Terrell was nodding. "It sounds like we have the same goals, brother."

Carlos was shaking his head. "It *sounds* like we do, but while the BSA focuses in on the Student Government, dealing with things on the student level, the Tri-AC puts its focus on administration, faculty and staff—the people that run the school, the decision makers and breakers."

The board members looked redeemed. They were nodding along with Carlos. Percy had heard the stories of the Tri-AC meeting with the Dean of Students, demanding action over an injustice, sending letter after letter to the Financial Aid Office, insisting that more funds and scholarships be made available to black students, and making professor turn red in class when they would question comment after comment made if it appeared to be "racial"—even in classes like math and science. Every year since they came on board five years ago, the University has threatened to boot them off campus, but they fought back just as hard—and remained.

Up front, Carlos had switched gears in his speech. "Now I do want to address an issue that my esteemed brother pointed out—the low number of African-Americans in the Student Government, which is definitely a concern to the Tri-AC. Out of the seventy-two committees and departments we have in the student government, there are only ten African-American leaders—ten. And that number already includes the BSA, the Tri-AC and the fraternity and sorority leaders. Brothers and sisters, that is beyond sad—it is a tragedy. We need a student government that will have the proper amount of representation to satisfy our needs."

Terrell was nodding in agreement, which was a shock. The two organizations spent most of their time at each other's throats. Even the audience seemed to be relaxing more. The two leaders seemed to be on common ground so far.

"Brother Carlos, I agree one-hundred percent," Terrell told him. "That's why we need to start a campaign to get more blacks on the ballot. Our students need to be educated on workings of political matters so they can find their niche."

Carlos shook his head again. "I don't think you understand what I'm saying. Yes, there does need to be more minorities interested in the running of things. That is why the Tri-AC suggest starting an all-black student government here at Hamel."

The audience gasped, along with Terrell. Even Percy's Tri-AC brothers sucked in their breath. Carlos had not discussed this one with his members, but then again, Percy was finding out he didn't discuss a lot of decisions with the members. Darryl was quick to point out that this was the mark of a good leader when Percy brought the matter to his attention.

Terrell leaned around the podium to stare in disbelief at Carlos. "A separate government?! Are you serious? What will that accomplish?"

Carlos seemed prepared for the question. "Simple. We run *our* government so that it meets the needs of *our* Student Body."

"But that's separatism, Carlos." Terrell had now dropped the "brother" title. "How in the world are we going to promote racial harmony if we form our own government?"

"Who's talking about harmony?" Carlos replied. "We are talking about equality. Harmony is just a potential by-product of equality. If it happens, wonderful, if not—so be it."

Terrell looked ready to respond, but hands were flying up all over the room. Everyone seemed to be talking at once. The body was itching to get in on the action, but Percy and his brothers sat still. Darryl had instructed them to sit and listen in on this meeting—let the BSA members do the talking. They needed to look controlled at all times. Carlos' announcement was not supposed to be a shock to them, even though it was.

Dr. Forrestor stood up from his perch behind the podium and held up his hands. "All right—we need to establish some order here. Remember—I am not here to interfere or offer any opinion. I'm here to mediate. Why don't we take questions from the audience?"

Several hands stayed up. One young lady stood up to the dismay of those obediently raising their hands. "I would like to know how you would propose starting a black government and running it beside the one that is already established?" she asked Carlos.

Carlos smiled at her, all charm. "Sister, all we would have to do is combine our forces, meaning all the African-American organizations coming together to form a strong union. The present government is not working for us like it should, do you agree?" He addressed that question to the whole audience. Heads were reluctantly nodding around the room. The body had to admit that their representation wasn't where it needed to be. They had been complaining for years, and the problem kept getting swept under a rug. Action needed to be taken—they just didn't know what.

Carlos seized the moment. "And do you know why the current student government is not working for us?" He had their full attention now. Percy was reminded of how he felt when his TV mentor had talked to him a few years ago. They even leaned forward in their seats as he had leaned into the TV that afternoon.

"It's not working because they don't understand us," Carlos informed them. "It is impossible for the white man to understand the plight of the black. They don't go through what we go through, because they've never been where we came from. They think they know how to appease us, but they really could care less. See, they think we are stupid—unintelligent, when, in fact, we are far superior to them in every aspect—physically, mentally, spiritually..."

"Carlos, man—do you know how you sound?" Terrell's face was swollen like a balloon, he was so upset. His demeanor had done a one-eighty since the beginning of the meeting. He was pure "brotha'" now.

"No, Terrell—how *do* I sound?"

You sound like—you sound like a racist. I mean, what is the difference in your attitude right now and the attitudes that you speak against?"

"The difference is in the color of my skin, your skin and the skin of all these people in here, *brotha'*." Carlos spit out that last word. Darryl flinched a little, afraid that his leader's composure was slipping. The Tri-AC couldn't risk showing any signs of not being in total control. That was their trademark.

Carlos wasn't quite finished with Terrell. "See the thing with the BSA is that you think the problem can be solved through step shows, parties and loud speeches. That's not doing a thing but perpetuating the stereotype that we are nothing but a race of shuffling, 'yassah boss,' Uncle Tom idiots." His tone was quite nasty now. "The white people on this campus don't take you guys seriously. They just tolerate you because they think it gives black folk something to do with their idle time and they don't have to be bothered with you."

Terrell was doing the balloon impression with his face again. "Typical, man. You are so typical of the way white people stereotype the blacks already. What do you want to do, roll on over to administration and beat somebody up? You think the problem can be solved with your gangbanger attitude and tactics?"

"Whoa—gentleman…" This was Dr. Forrestor, sensing trouble. The audience was getting riled up, too.

Carlos allowed a smile to spread slowly across half his face. "The response I would expect from a house nigger."

Terrell jumped straight up in his chair, as did the thirty or so odd members of the BSA in the room. There was a mad jumble of chairs, legs and words all around. Through the chaos, Percy caught glimpses of Dr. Forrestor waving his hands for order and Darryl desperately trying to hold back Carlos, who had gotten in Terrell's face. Some students were rushing to the front, while several were headed out of the door, already socialized in what to do in cases such as these. Percy sat wide-eyed, not knowing what to do. He saw the other new members looking around in bewilderment, too. Some of the board members were up front trying to help Darryl control Carlos, while others were surrounding and holding off Tamal, who seemed to randomly select a BSA member's face to jump into, and was trying to make it a physical confrontation.

Up front, Dr. Forrestor had restored some order by managing to sit the two leaders back in their seats. His eyes looked angry and his mouth moved rapidly back and forth between Terrell and Carlos. Percy couldn't really hear his words or see much else, because people were still milling around the room like a pack of wolves, waiting to see if there were going to be any more flare-ups.

Dr. Forrestor had the mike again. "I believe this meeting is adjourned," he announced firmly, breathing like he'd run ten miles. "But before anyone else leaves, I have something to say." Several students sat back in their seats. Others just froze where they were. "I am deeply disappointed in what just took place. I *do* not, and I *will* not, condone this type of behavior in further meetings!" He turned to look at Carlos and Terrell, who were either looking down at the table or rolling their eyes at each other. "I am sorely disappointed in you two so-called 'leaders.' You came together for the purpose of uniting—*uniting*, and you're acting no better than someone out on the street. You and your *educated* selves!" Dr. Forrestor opened his

83

mouth to say more, but then clamped it shut. He threw a disgusted look to both leaders again, shook his head, and headed toward the door. All eyes followed him. He suddenly turned and addressed the head table again.

"Don't even think about asking me to mediate one of these meetings again until you get your acts together." He turned to the audience, and Percy could've sworn he looked straight at him. "I want to caution everyone of you to always think before you act. Don't let *anyone* talk you into doing *anything* that doesn't feel right to you."

After he left, the room settled into an uncomfortable silence. Someone coughed. Terrell cleared his throat and gathered his notes together. His board members took the cue and prepared to leave as well. The other students started a rippling whisper conversation as they made their way out of the assembly room. After a while, the only people sitting in the room were the Tri-AC.

Carlos took time to carefully adjust his papers that had flown every which way when the altercation broke out. He looked calmly out at his members, as if chaos were all in a day's work. "Brothers, you have just witnessed why the BSA and the Tri-AC cannot be united. It's a shame—our people need to come together under the same political ideology, but the BSA wants to keep us in bondage under the existing structure. It's just the way it was in the days of slavery—you had some slaves that were willing to die for freedom, and the others were content with their plantation life or just too afraid. The BSA resembles the latter group of slaves. So I say if they aren't with us on the idea of a separate student government, we march forward without them. He became silent, looking expectantly at the members. Darryl nodded his head in agreement, staring at Carlos like he was a wise old sage.

"Yeah, I'm with that, Carlos," Tamal boomed out. He had finally sat back down after his run-in with a BSA member. "Tired of these white folk telling me what to do."

Carlos looked at him with a slight disapproving frown on his face. "Thank you, brother. How about you other members?"

The board quickly nodded and mumbled their agreement. Percy and the other new members just sat in silence. What were they supposed to say? If their leader thought they needed a separate government, then they needed a separate government—bottom line.

But Percy was sure having problems with the almost blind agreement they were expected to give their leader.

Michele R. Leverett

EUGENE

Eugene could get accustomed to being one hundred fifty miles away from home. He could get used to sharing a small, closet like dorm room with a complete stranger, and a bathroom with eleven other strangers. He could work his way through the less than tasty cuisine in Hamel's cafeteria, and on the days he just didn't feel like making the trek there, he could live with the packs of cheap noodles with imitation seasoning, two bags of microwave popcorn and the sodas from the vending machine in his residence hall's lobby. He could deal with the stuffy and bare study rooms when his roommate wanted to watch TV, or talk on the phone or play his radio, and he could probably make it off of three hours sleep when he had to cram for a test. He could successfully ignore his father's frequent calls and pokes about Hamel—he could even pretend that his lack of athletic skill didn't bother him.

Eugene could get used to all of the quirks and adjustments that he would experience in a college environment, but he still struggled with the looks he got when he and Irene walked together on campus. Both blacks and whites alike would steal a quick glance or deliberately stare when the twosome headed to Grapevine's class, or made their way to the library to meet with their study group. Not that he didn't get the same looks in high school, but he thought it would be different in college.

Irene didn't seemed phased by the stares. She would jabber on about their project, or ask about his family and hometown. When she laughed or made a strong point, it was not uncommon for her to lay her hand on his arm, or squeeze his hand for emphasis. "Let's do lunch," she suggested one day when Grayvine's class had ended. She didn't appear to be concerned that there was a crowd of students around when she spoke—she just looked at Eugene expectantly when he didn't answer right away.

"Sure," he answered quickly, looking around to see who had heard their exchange. If anyone did, they didn't acknowledge it. They bustled busily through the hallways, going about the business of being educated.

"The Food Court or Dining Hall?" Irene asked.

He contemplated. Both were busy this time of day, but the food at the Dining Hall left a lot to be desired. His meal card didn't go far at the Food Court, which was downstairs in the Student Center, but the food was better there.

"Let's do Food Court."

The Food Court was jammed with students grabbing a bite between classes. Long lines were forming at the hot bar, grill and deli sections, while two harried looking cashiers tried to swipe meal cards and handle money as fast as they could. Eugene had a taste for a cheeseburger, but he chose the shorter deli line instead. In minutes, he had his food and was headed toward a table. Irene opted to wait in the long pizza line and quench her craving for pepperoni. While eating his overpriced ham and cheese sub with chips, Eugene read through Grapevine's research project once again. Sometimes the man acted as if his were the only class on campus—never mind that Eugene had four other subjects to deal with.

A tray clattered down on the table. "Man, this project is not to be believed," he complained to the tray clatterer, assuming it was Irene. "Can you believe he wants us to turn in a ten-page paper in addition to our group paper?"

"That sounds like a lot."

Eugene looked up sharply at the unfamiliar voice. Across the table from him stood a short, mocha-colored female with cat-shaped brown eyes. She laughed lightly at his reaction.

"Oh, hi," he started, amused himself. "I'm sorry—I thought you were someone else."

"Obviously," the young woman answered, still grinning at him. "What's *her* name?"

The emphasis on gender was lost on Eugene. He was too busy staring at the beautiful eyes that were twinkling at him. He had a thing for eyes. *Man, she's pretty*, he thought to himself.

"Oh, no. I don't want to sit down. I like standing up when I eat," the female told him, moving aside as a couple of Food Court patrons made their way to their tables.

Again, Eugene's ears failed him. "I'm Eugene."

"Renee'—and I'm still standing!"

"Oh—sorry. Please have a seat," he invited, standing in respect and also to look over her head for Irene, who was lost in the mass between the food sections and the cash registers. Renee' followed his stare.

"Are you looking for someone?"

"Well, my classmate," he explained. "She's probably back there in line."

"She?"

"Irene," Eugene told her, as if mentioning Irene's name would help Renee' identify who she was. Renee' just looked at him with that slight grin on her face. He felt the need to explain who Irene was, though he didn't understand why. "Irene's my partner on this project for English class. We're doing some research and…" he stopped, realizing that he was rambling and probably making no sense. Besides, Renee' looked like she didn't give a fat baby who Irene was. She calmly began to peel the wrapping off of her deli sub, and Irene coming on the scene was no big deal.

"So where are you from, Eugene?"

"Harrisburg, Pennsylvania."

"Oh, way up there, huh? What brings you down here?"

What did bring him to Hamel? He was trying to get as far away from his father as possible, but he couldn't share that with her. "Hamel's got a pretty decent English program."

"So you're an English major?"

"Well, I haven't declared it yet, but yeah, you might as well say that. What about you?"

"Social Work. I'm just starting to take classes in my major, so we're kinda in the same boat." She started to take a bite of her sandwich, but looked up at him first. "You're in my Sociology class at ten."

"Dr. Caldwell?"

"Yes. You sit all the way in the back—like you're scared."

He sat in the back of the big lecture hall because it was near one of the exits. He wanted to be the first one out when class adjourned.

"I like what you had to say about social violence. You sound like you really know your stuff."

"Thanks, but I just said what I felt. I really don't know all those technical terms yet."

"Mmm." Renee' chewed her sandwich, boring those feline eyes right into his. It was funny—in high school, black females would barely give him the time of day because they had him labeled as a sell-out. Now here he was, having his first real conversation with a gorgeous one who apparently didn't think he was. Maybe college would be different, after all. He was about to expound on his point that he made in class when Irene walked up with her tray. She stopped short when she saw Renee', then gave her a big smile.

"Hi! I'm Irene." She sat her tray down beside Renee' and held out her hand. Renee' gave Irene a strange look, glanced at Eugene, then finally extended her hand to her.

"Nice to meet you," Renee' said in a quiet voice. She continued to stare at Irene who sat down and tapped her straw on the table to loosen the paper. Eugene once again felt like he had to explain himself.

"Irene, this is Renee'. She's in my Sociology class."

Irene took a sip of her Pepsi. "Oh, really? So you guys met in class?"

"No, we just met," Renee' answered, sounding like she had a slight edge to her voice. And she had stopped eating.

"Well actually, that's how we found out we were in class together," Eugene explained, feeling like an idiot.

Renee' stood up suddenly and grabbed her tray. "I have to run. Eugene, I'll see you in class." She started to walk away and then turned back to them. "Oh, nice to meet you, Irene."

"Yeah, same here. Hey, why don't we all do lunch together when you can stay a little longer?"

Renee' gave her that funny look again and shook her head. "Yeah, let's." She turned and disappeared into the crowd.

Eugene couldn't explain what just took place. All he knew was that Renee' was acting cool until Irene showed up. It was like a Jekyll and Hyde experience.

"She's pretty," Irene commented. "A little on the shy side, don't you think?"

Eugene didn't know what to think. Irene lapsed into a conversation about their project, and he just sat there, half listening, feeling like he had done something wrong.

Edward D. Wesley Library—home of the English major.

Eugene was more familiar with the library than he wanted to be. It seemed like research was all he did, and most of it was for Grapevine's class. On top of the project he had, Dr. Grapevine had now assigned a one thousand word essay on any of the authors they were studying that year, and the catch was that students had to pick an author that was from a different cultural background than they. Well, that was a piece of cake for the majority of the Anglo-Saxon students, but Eugene had to settle in on an Eastern European author to avoid anyone with African heritage. Hating the impersonal atmosphere of the huge, airy building, Eugene chose the first book he found on his author and sat at a small desk to jot down some notes. Just then, he heard a familiar voice around the corner of the book rack.

"Trina, please just check out the books you need and let's go. I'm not trying to be in this library all evening while you read."

"Renee', I'm just making sure I have the right information. I don't want to come back here, either. This library has too many floors for me. And why are you in such a hurry, anyway? You expecting a call from your boy?"

Eugene felt a little disappointed. Here he thought Renee' might have had an interest in him, but it sounded like she had her eyes on some other guy. Oh, well. He went back to his book, but immediately looked up from it again when he heard the conversation continue.

"What's his name?" Trina asked.

A pause. "Eugene, for the fiftieth time. You don't know him, so don't rack your brain."

"That's because you never told me anything about him, except you had your eye on someone. Is that the guy you were sitting with in the cafeteria?"

Renee' must have nodded.

"Girl, he's pretty cute. Where'd you meet him?"

"He's in one of my classes. He's *just* a freshman."

"So? You're *just* a sophomore. You better go for it, chick. Ya'll been out yet?"

"No, I haven't even given him my number."

Trina sounded outraged. "What's your holdup? You waiting for him to ask *you*? Girl, this is the nineties, get with the program. Just give him your number and tell him to call you some time."

Eugene couldn't help but smile. He had wanted to ask for her number, but was too afraid to do it. He could barely believe a beautiful young lady like Renee' was really interested in him. And she was black. Wait until Chip heard this. *Come on Trina, keep talking to her.*

Renee again: "He's not interested in me, Trina."

Yes, I am!

"How do you know?"

"Because. Every time I see him, he's with that white girl. That might be his thing, you know?"

Eugene couldn't see from where he was sitting, but he felt for sure that Trina was nodding in understanding. He felt a tight fist balled up in his chest. Maybe that's why Renee' had acted so strange that day in the cafeteria.

Renee' continued. "They might be just friends, but I don't know. So many brothas are going that route these days. You never know."

Trina: "Mm hmm. It's like a sister's not good enough for them. I mean, I could see if it was the real thing—like they just met a female they liked and she just happened to be white. But going after one just because she's white and it makes you feel like you have something? Uhn uh."

Renee': "That's what I'm talking about. I'd date a white guy if I happened to run into one that I really *really* liked. I ain't gonna advertise for one, though. It's hard enough to find a black one that ain't in jail or has kids or something."

Trina: "So you really don't think he's interested?"

"I honestly don't know, Trina. He's a really nice guy, but I'm not trying to get my feelings hurt."

"I know that's right. Well, just see how he acts with you. I'd give him my number, anyway. Nothing's wrong with having a friend, is there?"

"Yeah, you got a point. I might, I don't know. You ready?"

"Yup. Let's go."

Eugene got up quickly, knowing they would have to pass his table to get to the elevators. He disappeared into the men's room until he heard the elevator arrive and the girls get on—he hoped. He opened the door slowly. They were no where in sight. So now he knew. Renee' was interested, but she thought he liked white women exclusively. It was high school all over again. He wondered how many black girls had been interested in him then, but had given him the same label.

PERCY

The ringing phone snatched Percy out of a deep sleep. He reached down and fumbled for the phone on the floor while across the room, Allen rolled over and mumbled something in his sleep.

"Hello," he hissed out, ready to go off on whomever was disturbing him at such a late hour.

"Percy—this is Darryl." Darryl sounded wide awake. Percy opened one eye and glanced at the clock on his desk: 2:17 AM. What in the world did the Tri-AC want with him at this hour? "Look, man. I know it's a strange time to be calling, but we got a problem. A big problem."

"Darryl, what could happen at 2:00 in the morning that couldn't be handled tomorrow?"

He heard Darryl exhale hard on the other end. "They—man, get dressed and meet me at the Plot as soon as you can. I can't explain over the phone." Darryl's voice was trembling—he had never heard him when he didn't have his emotions under control.

As foolish as he felt, he told him, "O.k., man," hung up the phone and tiptoed over to his closet for some clothes.

Allen rolled over again and mumbled at him. "Percy, wha' you doin'? Where you goin'?"

"A friend of mine has some trouble. I'm going to see if I can help," he explained, sliding on some jeans he had worn the day before.

Allen turned on the lamp clipped to his bed and squinted at Percy. "Uh, can I help? You need me to come along?"

"No man, I'll handle it. Thanks."

"You sure?"

"Yeah." Percy slid into his heavy coat and pulled on a baseball cap. He sat down at his desk to put his sneakers on, and was about to grab his door key from his dresser when he saw keys dangling in his face.

"Here, Percy. Take my car."

"No, Allen. That's…"

"Go ahead. "It's not exactly wise to go hoofing across campus at 2:00 in the morning."

Percy had to chuckle. "Yeah, if I was a girl, Allen."

"O.k., then it's freezing cold outside. How 'bout that?"

Percy slowly took the keys, and surprised himself because he actually felt grateful to his roommate for his hospitality. He thanked him again, then slid out of the room quietly. He could hear someone's television playing down the hall, reassuring him that he wasn't the only idiot up late on a weekday.

Percy was glad he took Allen up on his offer to drive once he got outside. Even though his roommate's 1976 Grand Prix had very little heat, it beat walking across campus in thirty-three degree weather. To tell the truth, Percy was a little surprised by Allen's old car. He was under the impression that a little upper class kid like Allen, whose parents had footed the bill for his education, would be driving a later model car—at least one with a radio and heat. Allen admitted to Percy that when he wanted music, he would lug his box radio to the car and hide it under a blanket. Percy had laughed, but his roomie was proud of his car that he warmly referred to as "Old Diane." He told Percy he would drive it until it fell apart.

The thing sounded like it *was* falling apart as Percy bumped across campus in it. It knocked, creaked and popped as he turned up the street by the Admissions Building and hung a quick right around the parking deck. Even a half mile down the road, he could see a huge crowd standing around the perimeter of the Plot. From his angle, he saw what appeared to be small, white banners waving in the air. What type of celebration was going on so early in the morning?! Percy crept closer and parked behind several cars along the sidewalk. Several heads turned to glance at him as he got out and banged Allen's metal door shut. He could see campus police cars, sirens flashing, parked further up the road and blocking the street, and heard loud, angry voices rising and falling. He edged closer. The white banners he saw flying through the air were actually toilet paper strewn through the tree limbs. But that wasn't even the worst part.

Darryl's head popped out of the large crowd of people, black and white, and he met Percy on the sidewalk.

"What's going on here, Darryl?" Percy asked, confused.

"It's a mess, Percy. I've never seen anything like it since I've been here!" Darryl's voice was still trembling with anger. "The entire Plot is ruined!"

"Ruined?!"

"Destroyed, Percy. Vandalized. You get it?!"

93

Surely Darryl was exaggerating, but as the two made their way through the crowd, he saw that he was wrong. The stone structures were either pulled straight out of the ground or broken in large pieces. Benches were turned over. The beautiful oak trees had large gashes in them. Trash and toilet paper littered the entire yard. Several of the students stood over their respective organization's pieces of land, shaking their heads in disbelief. A few of the women were crying. Some were trying to lean their stones upright, only to watch them tip back over in the ground up earth. About ten campus officers were on the scene, trying to control the angry crowd that wanted answers and weren't moving until they got some. Other officers were scribbling in little notebooks as they surveyed the damage. Percy spotted Carlos gesturing angrily to an officer over by what used to be the Tri-AC's shield. The stone, cut in the shape of Africa, was painted in the continent's red, green, black and gold colors with an African warrior holding a spear straight up in the air. The stone was lying in two huge pieces on the ground. About ten feet away, Terrell and three of his board members were slowly marching around the BSA's structure. It was still whole, but completely coated with thick, black paint or tar or something that was still dripping. Destruction was everywhere, and Percy's stomach did flip-flops.

Darryl was back in his ear. "It took three years to get this land from the University. We paid for it with *our* money—*black money*! Do you know how many fundraisers we threw? Do you know the sweat we put into all of this?! Now look...." Darryl kicked viciously at a piece of broken stone and sent it flying across the Plot. Percy sunk deeper into his coat to get away from the cold night air, and the unbelievable nightmare he saw before him. "You know, I can even feel sorry for the BSA and the Greeks," Darryl continued. "Despite what we feel about each other, this land was about the celebration of a culture."

Percy just nodded. He wasn't ready to speak just yet—he was still in shock.

"Percy, we built this with *our* bare hands!" Darryl held his hands out to show Percy which body parts he was talking about. "This was ours! We didn't go to the University for the money—*we* raised the money!" Darryl bent and perched on a bench that happened to be upright. It belonged to the ADK's but no one seemed to be concerned about who was sitting where. What appeared to be the entire ADK sorority was huddled around two campus officers, shivering, but demanding answers.

Carlos finally spotted his two comrades and marched over. Even in the dark, Percy could see the intensity on his face. "Percy," Carlos nodded at him and stuck his hands in his pockets. "Looks bad, huh?"

That was the understatement of the year. He assumed Carlos was being sarcastic to hide his real feelings. If it mirrored what Percy was feeling at the moment, Carlos wanted to go out and hurt a few people. "Carlos, what's up? I mean…what's up with this?" Percy held his hands out. "Does anyone know who did this…?"

Carlos didn't answer right away. He watched the campus officers trot from one group to another, warning people not to touch anything, and insisting that everyone leave the area. No one was obeying either command. He finally walked toward an oak tree that didn't have people hanging around it, turned and motioned for Percy to follow him. Percy threw a glance back at Darryl sitting on the bench, who had now dropped his head in his hands. Carlos stopped at the tree, looked toward Darryl, then behind him. "The cops know who did it." He told Percy in a low voice.

"Who?!" Percy practically yelled. Carlos quickly shushed him. "Percy, please keep your voice down. The cops don't want any information leaking out before sun up, so they only told me, Terrell and the Greek presidents. We promised not to say anything so there wouldn't be a riot—and that's about the only order from them I'm complying with." Carlos hesitated and studied the ground. He looked like he was trying to put his anger in check before he spoke. "Twelve white pledges from Lambda Sigma destroyed what used to be the pride and joy of the African-American campus community. The police brought them in for questioning about thirty minutes ago. They should still be talking to them right now."

Percy could feel his blood boiling. "How do they know who it was?"

Carlos chuffed out a short laugh. It made a small cloud of smoke in the crisp, night air. "They found one passed out drunk in front of the Lambda Sig house down the road. They thought he was dead so they went to investigate. He still had a can of black paint in his hand which was responsible for the fine artwork on the BSA shield." He pointed to the fallen stone, where Terrell and his board were stationed.

95

Carlos continued. "When the cops questioned him, he got scared and sang like a drunk canary. It didn't help that the entire house was still up drinking and partying. Probably celebrating what they did."

"You mean to tell me this was some kind of fraternity initiation stunt? That's why they did all this damage?" Percy kept his voice low, but his anger was still evident.

"Percy, the white Greeks have been against this Plot from jump street. They don't think it belongs on their conservative white campus. They tried to run some game and argue that it promoted separatism between the races. That's why we had to build this ourselves—the University bought that lie."

"So Lambda Sig did this for all the white Greeks, or what?"

"Lambda Sig—them boys were the most vocal over not wanting this. See, they're a bunch of rebel-flag-waving-good ole' boys. They were founded on some school in Mississippi, right before they starting integrating colleges. Biggest racists you ever hoped to meet."

Percy couldn't help but be a tad bit impressed. "Sounds like you've done your homework on them."

Carlos gave Percy a sideways glance that made him feel like he'd made a dumb comment. "You must know your enemy just as well as you know your friend, Percy, because sometimes they can be one in the same—don't ever forget that."

"So what's going to happen to Lambda Sig? They're gonna be suspended by the University, right? Kicked off campus?"

"Don't fool yourself, Percy," Carlos told him. "These are white boys with money. The school's not going to give them any more than a slap on the wrist. But don't worry…justice will be served."

"By who…?"

"Mr. Franklin?" A tall black campus officer with a deep voice approached them and addressed Carlos.

"Yes?"

"We need to clear this area. We need for you and the other group leaders to help move this crowd along so we can tape off this area. We'll be in contact with you later on. Go home and get some sleep."

Carlos nodded. "I'll see what I can do." The cop shook Carlos' hand and moved on. "Percy, why don't you do the same—I'll be talking to you tomorrow."

"All right." He turned and noticed Darryl again, who had found Marcus, Rodney, and Brian somewhere in the crowd, and was deep in conversation. "Where's the rest of the members?"

"We didn't tell all the members, Percy. Just the ones that we felt were the most responsible." Carlos followed his eyes to where his board members were congregated. "We usually meet as a board before we bring information to the other members, but we made an exception in your case, Percy. Darryl insisted that we call you—he sees something about you, and I trust his judgment." Carlos looked at him like he had just bestowed an honor upon him.

"Oh…thanks, man."

"You notice all the board members aren't present either, right?"

"Yeah—Tamal…"

"Is a hot head that doesn't think before he acts," Carlos finished, to Percy's surprise. Tamal was a board member, and the leader was selling him out to a new member. Still, Percy agreed. He didn't care too much for Tamal Bailey. He had a smart mouth and a street attitude. Percy couldn't understand why Carlos would trust him with the organization's money.

"He'll find out tomorrow like everyone else. Go on and get some sleep, Percy. Keep up those good grades." Carlos stuck out his hand, then walked toward a crowd of people and waved his hands forward, telling them to go back to their rooms, they would know something by tomorrow, he promised. Terrell was doing the same thing a few feet away, but making no promises.

Percy made his way back through the crowd that was actually listening to Carlos and Terrell and were headed out of the area. He climbed back into Allen's loud hoopty and watched the crowd leave while the police began to tie bright, yellow tape around the perimeter of the Plot.

Later on that morning, he felt Allen shaking him like he thought he was unconscious. And he very well might have been. "Wake up, Percy. You're going to be late for class."

How much sleep had he gotten? A one-eyed glance at his clock told him it was 9:15—he didn't remember what time it was when he got back to the room. Allen was fully dressed and shoving books into his backpack.

"How's your friend doing?" Allen asked him.

"Huh?" Percy was still asleep, legally.

"Your friend. The one that was in trouble that kept you out until four o'clock this morning."

So he'd been gone for about two hours. "Oh yeah...I guess he'll be all right." Percy sat on the side of his bed and grunted, squinting at the light streaming in through the blinds. "What're you doin' up so early?" he asked Allen, whose first class that day wasn't until eleven.

Allen grinned and rubbed his stomach. "Man, I'm starved. I always get hungry after a good night's sleep. I'm gonna run by the Center for some breakfast before class."

There was a soft knock on the door. Allen opened it and there stood Eugene from down the hall, also fully dressed and looking wide awake. Percy was beginning to feel like a lazy bum, and he was surprised. Eugene never stopped by. He would wave if their door was open and he was passing by, but he never actually stopped.

"Hi, Eugene." Eugene nodded in response to Allen, who let him in.

"What's up, Percy. Sorry—I didn't know you were still in bed."

"Nah, I'm woke," Percy told him. "What's up?"

Eugene gave Allen a funny look. Allen was perched against his dresser, waiting to hear what Eugene was going to say. Percy was too curious himself to tell Allen to step.

"I just wanted to know if you heard about what happened to the Plot last night."

"Yeah—I *saw* it." He was surprised Eugene knew about it. Percy had already filed him under "Wanna-Be."

"What happened?" Apparently, Allen wasn't as hungry as he made himself out to be, because he sure wasn't making any strides to go to breakfast now.

"Somebody tore up our Plot last night, Allen. It was a mess," Percy told him.

"What plot?"

Percy forgot who he was talking to. "The place behind the Student Center where all those stones were..."

"The ones that the black students built," Eugene cut in. Percy looked at him in surprise, again. Eugene sounded a little short with a fellow who had worn his clothes just a few weeks ago.

If Allen noticed anything in Eugene's voice, it didn't register on his face. "Yeah...I think I know what you're talking about... Oh, man—who would do something like that?"

Eugene and Percy exchanged a glance. Percy knew for sure, and he assumed Eugene was at least in the race ballpark.

"Man..." Allen acted like he was taking the whole thing personally. "Hey, is that where you went this morning?"

"I was there, and so were about one hundred other people. Did you see it, Eugene?"

"Yeah, I saw it this morning on the way back from class. Blew my mind. There was a bunch of people standing around then, too. Someone said it happened last night?"

"About eleven," Percy confirmed from what he heard floating around the Plot earlier that morning. Some students were headed back from that free movie in the Student Center and went and woke folk up. My Tri-AC brother called me about two o'clock this morning, upset."

"Can't say I blame him. It took three years to get it built."

Now Percy was completely shocked. That was surprise number three. He shook his head to clear the last remaining cobwebs of sleep and began to think that maybe Eugene was o.k., after all. Maybe he couldn't judge a book by its cover—or the other books it hung out with.

"Well, I just hope they find who did it—soon," Eugene said.

Percy just nodded, realizing that he needed to get dressed and see if he could catch up with Darryl or Carlos and find out what was going on. Carlos had sounded very ominous when he mentioned that justice would be served. Percy wanted to know what he meant and, more importantly, how he factored into that equation.

Allen suddenly remembered his appetite. "I gotta run, guys. Hey, keep me posted, o.k.?"

"Yeah, sure Allen," Percy told him. Allen smiled and headed out the door. Eugene excused himself too, and headed back down the hall.

Percy showered, dressed and hightailed it to class in record time. His psychology professor droned on about the id, ego and superego and some other stuff that wasn't going to land him a job when he graduated. Class finally ended, and Percy headed straight to the Tri-AC office where Carlos and Darryl where already sitting. Tamal was also in the office sitting on the couch. Percy was immediately on his guard.

"What's up, brothers?" Percy greeted everyone collectively.

99

"Hey, Percy…come on in the house." Carlos waved him in from his desk by the window and motioned to where Tamal was sitting on the couch. Percy felt like he had walked into the middle of a private conversation, but both Darryl and Carlos were smiling at him reassuringly.

"Hey Carlos…do you think we can get Percy in on time?" Darryl was asking.

"I don't have a problem with that."

"Whoa, fellas. Let's think this through," Tamal said, holding up his hands in a time-out gesture. "He's not on the board, and he's just a freshman."

Darryl counter-argued. "He's not on the board *yet*, Tamal. Remember? We talked about this already."

"Yeah, and I *still* think it's a bad idea to put a new member on the board!"

Percy's mind was reeling from confusion and lack of sleep. "Excuse me…what exactly is everyone talking about?"

"Sorry, brotha'. Here we are, discussing you like you weren't even here." Carlos grinned in amusement. His mood was noticeably lighter than it was earlier—so was Darryl's, for that matter. "Actually, I'm glad you stopped by. See, we have a vacant spot on our board, and Darryl felt like you were the man for the job—if you want it."

Percy was immediately flattered. Just when he was beginning to have his doubts about the Tri-AC, they pull this out on him. He didn't know what to say.

"Well—uh, thanks. I—what position are we talking about, here?"

"Mine," Darryl answered casually.

"Yours?! Where are you going?"

"Percy, let me explain." Carlos shot Darryl a "let-me-handle-this" look, and leaned forward on his desk. "See, we need to march forward with what we discussed in the meeting the other day—organizing a black student government and infiltrating the political system here. We've got to become more visible, because the BSA's just not getting the job done. Naturally, that means more work for me, but I need someone to lead the organization when I'm tied up. Therefore, I'm appointing Darryl here…" he nodded in Darryl's direction. "…as Vice President of the Tri-AC, so he can carry on duties in my absence. Obviously, we still need someone to recruit…"

100

"I told him you were the man for the job, Percy," Darryl couldn't help but chime in. "I've been very impressed with you since you became a member. An intelligent man like you should have a little more responsibility."

Again, Percy was speechless. He really didn't think he had done anything that spectacular. He noticed Tamal sitting quietly, with his mouth set in tight line. Percy wondered what he had against the idea besides what he said earlier. After all—he was already on the board.

"I think we should bring the whole idea before the board. How do you think the other new members will feel with Percy being appointed without their vote?"

"They'll know after we tell them, Tamal." Carlos was very short. "And to tell you the truth, *you* were supposed to find out with everyone else. The reason that you're here is to anty up on the treasury and talk fund raising for my campaign. You're not here to vote on any decisions."

Tamal wasn't finished with his opinion, though. "I'm just trying to be fair to everybody."

"Brotha', you can save your griping and complaining." Darryl had an edge to his voice. "Now the decision has been made whether you like it or not. We'll take the heat from the board if there's any to take. I seriously doubt there will be."

Good. That saved Percy the trouble of opening his mouth, because he could feel his old Jackson Park attitude coming on strong. In his neighborhood, Tamal would be walking around with a busted lip—if he was still walking. And Percy knew he didn't give two hoots about what the new members thought, because he spent half his time coming down on them. No—that brotha' had a personal beef with Percy, for whatever reason.

Tamal stood up slowly, eyeing both Darryl and Carlos like they'd talked about his momma. He snatched his kenti print book bag from the couch and left, slamming the door behind him. Percy flinched a little, but Carlos and Darryl didn't bat an eyelash...and Carlos even had the nerve to chuckle.

"Tamal's going to have to learn some anger management," Carlos remarked to Darryl, who nodded in agreement.

"Has he always been like that?" Percy wanted to know.

"Not always—he used to have a real nasty attitude," Darryl answered with a straight face, then burst out laughing with Carlos at

Percy's confused expression. "Percy—lighten up. Don't let that brotha' bother you. He has some personal issues that he needs to deal with, one of which is his temper. That's why he always acts like he has a chip on his shoulder."

Carlos agreed. "Mmm hmm—and he also wanted Darryl's position. He raised quite a fuss before you showed up."

Percy finally sat down on the empty couch. "Not that I mind, but why me instead of him? He's been in longer."

Darryl leaned back and twirled a pen he was holding. "You've been around Tamal enough. He doesn't have the right character to recruit anyone. He wants to run the recruitment like a fraternity—put brothas on line, get in their face and yell. We don't deal like that."

"No *sir*," Carlos agreed. "Tamal would look for guys he could intimidate. We don't need any wimps in the Tri-AC." He winked at Percy, and once again, Percy felt like there was something under his words.

"Wait a minute—did I hear you say something to Tamal about a campaign, Carlos? Are you running for something?" Percy suddenly remembered.

Carlos smirked. "Can you keep a secret?"

"Yeah…"

"I got my eye on being the first black Student Body President at Hamel. Watch and see."

Percy was impressed—and shocked. He didn't think Carlos was interested in running what he termed as a "slave block of higher learning."

Carlos caught his look. "Oh, I'm going to have my black government—one way or the other. And what happened with the Plot is just what I need to boost my campaign."

"So what do I do? When do I start?" Percy wanted to know.

"Don't worry about that right now, brotha'. We've got bigger fish to fry." Carlos stood and grabbed his briefcase. "I've got to run to class. They're trying the Lambda Sig members on January 8—one o'clock. I'd get there early if I were you so you can see the case." Carlos patted Percy's shoulder on his way out.

"Come on, Percy. I'm treating you to lunch to celebrate your new position." Darryl got up and Percy followed him out of the door. "Anywhere you want to go."

"Anywhere, Darryl?"

"Be reasonable, man. Don't try to break a brotha'."

Percy laughed. "I wouldn't do that to you, man. But seriously, I don't know this town, so why don't you pick?"

"All right—how about this place called Cow Pattie's? They can work a steak dinner."

"The name's kinda strange, but steak sounds good to me."

CLAUDIA

It was a relief to get out of class.

On Tuesdays, Claudia had a Biology lab that lasted for three hours. Her lab partners always seemed to know what they were doing, mixing the right solutions, identifying the correct cells and drawing the logical conclusions. She couldn't tell an amoeba from an amino acid half the time. It was five o'clock by the time her dreaded lab ended, and she couldn't wait to grab a bite at the Student Center, go back to her room, kick off her shoes and take a breather before starting her studying for the evening. She was trying to discipline herself to allot a certain amount of time each day for studying, like her disciplined little roommate, Marie. Most of the time, Claudia gave up and flicked on the television, promising herself that she would finish before the evening was over—or at least the week. She never knew college would be this intense.

Actually, Claudia thought as she walked slowly away from the science building, college wasn't that bad. She kind of felt like an adult, working with a schedule, being responsible for her own meals, doing laundry, cleaning. Not that she didn't do those things at home, but she had her mother breathing down her back there, and now it was she who determined when she did what. And ever since Marie had taught her the virtue of makeup and hair care, she found herself being a lot more sociable. In fact, she and Marie were planning to check out the ADK interest meeting in a couple of weeks.

"Claudia!" The loud voice came from behind her, and she turned to see Cedric streaking toward her, waving and grinning.

He sure is cute, she thought, then immediately put herself in check. Cedric was trying to hook up with her roommate. She had no right to even think of him as being cute.

He caught up to her, exhaling but still smiling. Claudia put herself in check again. "How are you, gorgeous?" he asked. Wasn't that the pet name he used on Marie?

"I'm good, Cedric. Glad to be out of Biology lab. I don't know why they feel the need to have a boring lab to go along with a boring class."

"Is that what you're doing on campus this late in the day?"

"Yeah. The dumb thing doesn't let out until five o'clock. It's three hours long."

"Yeah, ya'll underclassmen got to pay the price—what can I say?"

"You could show a little sympathy," she joked.

He frowned, and shrugged. "I left my violin at home, Claudia."

She rolled her eyes at him, and he laughed, telling her he would leave her alone before she hurt him. Claudia really enjoyed his playful nature. He was always in such a good mood. *Boy, Marie lucked up on this one*, she thought as she sized him up again, and once again, put her thoughts in check. She had no right even standing here having a conversation with ole' boy, let alone think about how cute he was. What had gotten into her?

"So, where are you headed?" he asked, staying right beside her as she started a forward walk.

"I was going to grab a bite to eat at the Student Center, then head on back to Belten."

"Would you mind joining me for dinner?"

Lord, no. No, no, no... . "Well, o.k. I can stay on campus and eat." Maybe he was just being friendly. Maybe he wanted to talk about Marie. That was probably it. Cedric wanted to take their friendship to another level but didn't know what to do. He had to seek out her best friend for advice.

Cedric stopped walking and looked down at her shyly. "I was thinking more of an off-campus thing. The food here gets on your nerves after three years—same old thing everyday."

Claudia swallowed. Here was the man her best friend was crazy about, asking her out to eat. What would Marie say if she knew? Then again, Marie kept insisting that they were "just friends", but her voice had a strange, high-pitched keen to it every time she made the argument. She couldn't do it; she wouldn't do it. No matter what Cedric's motive was, it just wasn't right. It...."What about Marie?" she made herself blurt out.

"What *about* Marie?" he responded casually.

What did he mean, what about Marie? "Don't you think she might want to join us?"

Cedric looked around, then shrugged. "Marie's not here, Claudia. I just wanted to grab a bite to eat. I ran into you and thought you might want to come along. If you don't, that's chill..."

105

Well, o.k…that sounded a little—safer. "Sure, that sounds good, Cedric."

He grinned. Claudia had to avert her eyes to keep from staring at those pretty teeth. "Great. I'm parked underneath the deck today, so we don't have to walk far. I got all the way to the apartment and remembered my car was over here. That's where I was headed when I ran into you."

"Got a little lazy this morning, right?"

"No, I was running late and decided to drive, Miss Thang."

They strolled to his car in silence. Cedric kept glancing down at her and grinning, and Claudia could not keep her mind off of Marie. She kept expecting her to appear, catching she and Cedric walking together to his car. Her conscience kept telling her that what she was doing was all wrong, but her excited mind kept fighting that feeling.

When they reached his car, Cedric took her book bag and placed it in his back seat, which Claudia noted was very neat, like the rest of his car. He opened her door for her, and a pleasant aroma like men's cologne drifted from the interior. *Even his car smells good*, she thought, then mentally slapped herself. *Stop thinking about his assets and go have a nice, friendly dinner.*

"Now I hope my driving doesn't bother you," he said as he climbed in the driver's seat and strapped on his seat belt. He stuck the key in the ignition and the car dinged in approval.

"What do you mean?"

"Well…" he began, popping the clutch into reverse and easing out of his space. "I have a tendency—to drive a little—fast!" He suddenly pushed the clutch into first and sped out of the parking lot. Claudia was unprepared and flew back against her seat in surprise. Cedric laughed at her shocked expression. "I warned you," he told her as he shifted higher. His car vroomed loudly in response.

"Have you lost your mind? Aren't you afraid of tearing up your transmission, or better yet hurting somebody out here?" She shook her head, and pulled down his visor looking for a mirror. She just knew that sudden jolt had messed up her hair.

"I'm sorry, Claudia. I didn't mean to scare you. You're right."

"I guess I forgive you." Claudia found a mirror and was patting her hair back into shape.

"Don't worry…you're still as beautiful as ever. You know you fly, don't you?"

She could feel a blush coming on, and with her complexion, it would be noticeable. She looked for something to start a conversation about, and noticed a huge class ring on his hand holding the gear. It had a football engraved in it. "What position did you say you played again?"

"Tight end. You should come to a game sometime. There's one next Saturday, as a matter of fact."

"Oh, I don't know too much about football. I wouldn't know when to cheer and when to keep my mouth shut."

He smirked at her. "I'm not surprised—most women don't know a lot about sports. But I'll bet you could tell me the latest movie Denzel is in, can't you?"

"Oh, all you men think that all women are hung up on Denzel. Now why is that?"

"So you're telling me you're not?"

"I mean, he's a good actor—he's a great actor as a matter of fact—but I'm not 'hung up' on him. I just like good acting, no matter who it is. Like ya boy Morgan Freeman and Danny Glover—now they're some decent actors, too."

"For real? I like them, too. Hey, I'll tell you a secret, but you can't tell anyone."

"O.k."

Cedric stopped at a red light and pulled down his right turn signal. Claudia could see a gigantic bull in the parking lot of a restaurant. That had to be their destination.

"Nah," Cedric decided. "I better not say anything."

Claudia shrugged. "All right."

"See? Why can't more females be like that?"

"Like what?" she asked with genuine confusion.

Cedric was pulling into the parking lot with the huge bull. Claudia had guessed correctly. "Most girls would keep pressing a brotha' to talk. You just let it go."

"I mean, if you want to tell me, fine. If you don't, that's fine, too."

"That's what I'm talking about, Claudia. That's a good thing. I like that about you."

O.k.—why was he telling her what he liked about her? Why wasn't he telling her what he liked about Marie? As Cedric stopped the car and ran around to open her door, she decided she was going to address the thing with Marie head on. She would let him know that what they were doing was wrong, even if it was just a friendly dinner. Yes, she had to explain "The Laws of Friendship" to him. If two girls were best friends and one had just an inkling of an interest in a guy, the other friend did not show an interest in that same guy. And never, never was she seen with him except in the company of the friend who had an interest—even if they were not an official couple. In fact, even if the first friend lost interest in the guy, he was still off limits to the other friend. He just did not exist in their world anymore.

Men were different—they didn't understand the unwritten rules of friendship between women. She had to make him understand without appearing ridiculous. They entered the loud, crowded restaurant and waited to be seated. Everyone in the place looked like a football player. There were several people in the lobby that were waiting to sit down, but Cedric excused himself from Claudia and approached the hostess, who broke out in a big grin when she saw him coming. He whispered something to her, and the next thing Claudia knew she and Cedric were following her to a table.

"How did we get around all those people?" Claudia wanted to know after they were seated.

Cedric winked at her. "I'm pretty good at getting what I want, Claudia. Rarely do I take 'no' for an answer."

Claudia acted like she didn't hear that loaded answer. "What did you say to her?"

"I just asked her if she could work something out with a table, because I didn't like to keep a beautiful young lady waiting for anything." He flashed that grin at her, and Claudia felt her face heat up. Fortunately, a waitress came up with menus. She used hers to hide her blush.

"Are you ready for my big secret?"

"Uh, yeah." Claudia put down her menu, relieved that the conversation was going in another direction.

Cedric said, "You mentioned that you liked Danny Glover?"

"Yes."

He took a deep breath. "O.k., here it is—you know his movie, *The Color Purple*?

Claudia nodded, intrigued by what he was about to tell her.

"I—still cry when I watch it." He looked at her, waiting to see her reaction.

"What did you say?" she asked, not sure that she heard right.

"I said, I cried during *The Color Purple*."

Claudia tried to hold the laugh in, but she was getting an image of big, macho Cedric blubbering in front of his television or in a movie theatre, clutching a tissue. She couldn't help it—she busted out laughing.

"Wait a minute…what are you laughing at?"

She couldn't stop. It was so rare for her to laugh that when it finally came out, it was nearly uncontrollable. She had once scared Marie so bad when she laughed non-stop for five minutes, that Marie was going to call 911.

Unfortunately, Cedric wasn't laughing with her. "Claudia, I didn't tell you that so you could laugh at me."

"I'm s-sorry Cedric," she coughed out.

"See? I knew I shouldn't have said anything," Cedric complained. "I just thought I could let you know that I have a sensitive side. You women think we're always so hard core. I don't tell a lot of people about that side of me. Sometimes, they take that for weakness."

"Cedric, I'm sorry. I didn't mean to laugh at you." She touched his hand that was resting on the table. How unlike her to offer comfort to a male besides her brother. "I wasn't making fun of you—I just thought you were going to tell me something like you were adopted or you'd been in prison or something. It's o.k. for a man to cry. I think it makes him stronger—not weaker."

To her surprise, Cedric removed his hand and placed it on top of hers. Oh no. She quietly slipped it from his grip. "I'm sorry, Claudia. I guess I got a little carried away."

"It's o.k." No, it wasn't o.k. and she knew it. She was enjoying the attention. She was flirting with him. She was breaking one of the laws.

"Cedric, I need to ask you a question."

"Sure."

"Do you—do you have an interest in Marie?"

He didn't answer right away. He looked down at his menu as if he were thinking of a suitable answer, then the waitress appeared again with their drinks and took their orders. Cedric ordered a well-done steak with fries, and Claudia had the same, since she had not taken the time to study her menu.

"Marie and I are friends," he finally told her. "Why do you ask?"

109

Why did she ask? Did she want to make sure that there was nothing but friendship between them? Claudia hated to admit to herself, but she was definitely attracted to this man sitting across from her. He had a charming, funny personality, and knew what to say to make her feel good. Not to mention that he was handsome—his smile and eyes could get a date all by themselves. Before Claudia could answer him, two husky guys approached their table and greeted Cedric with a hardy pound on the back. Cedric had been in the process of sipping his ice tea and coughed in surprise.

"What's up, Romeo?" one of them asked. He was tall and white, with sandy brown hair and grey eyes. He spoke with a southern accent. His counterpart was black, and had closely shaven sideburns ending in a goatee at his chin. Both grinned first at Cedric, then at Claudia.

"Yo, fellas. Can't ya'll find a normal greeting for a brotha'? I coulda choked." Cedric wiped his mouth with a napkin and glared up at the two, who were still grinning innocently. "Claudia, these two fools are Vince and Travis, my roommates and teammates. Ya'll, this is Claudia."

"Hi, Claudia. I'm Vince." The black guy grabbed Claudia's hand and pumped it up and down. She figured by process of elimination that the white guy was Travis, who greeted her with a kiss on her hand.

Vince pounded him in the arm. "You trippin', bru. You ain't in Georgia. A brotha' will kill you for coming on to his woman up here." He gave him another pound to drive his point home. Travis pounded him back and gave him explicit instructions on what to do with his comments.

"Look, ya'll are in the presence of a lady. Don't use that language around her," Cedric scolded. "Claudia, please forgive these two. I swear—sometimes they act like they were raised by wolves."

Travis grabbed Claudia's hand again and sat down beside her. "Please forgive me, Claudia. I'm so used to being around these idiots that I forget how to talk sometimes. You know you only have to have a third grade education to communicate with Cedric, right?"

"Man, forget you," Cedric laughed, throwing a wadded up napkin at him.

"It's o.k.," Claudia smiled at him, enjoying the good-natured ribbing the roommates were giving one another.

"Yo Ced, you coming to practice on time tomorrow?" Vince asked, sitting down at the booth beside Cedric. Both he and Travis settled in like they were going to stay awhile.

"Yeah, man—three thirty tomorrow. I'll be there. Now if you'll excuse me, we are trying to have a private conversation."

Vince and Travis exchanged a knowing look across the table.

"My bad, man."

"We out. Don't stay out too late. Nice to meet you, Claudia.."

They gave Cedric one more hearty back pound and migrated back to their table, which was filled with other football looking types. Claudia saw Vince whisper something to the table, and several of the players turned to look at them, holding their glasses up as if to propose a toast.

Cedric rolled his eyes.

"More roommates?" Claudia wanted to know.

"No—teammates. It seems like I picked a fine time to eat here, huh?" He put his attention on the steaming plate that had just arrived in front of him. Claudia wanted to remind him of her question about Marie, but didn't know how to bring it up without sounding completely stupid. He saved her the trouble. "You were asking me about Marie." He stared straight at her with his dreamy eyes. No wonder Marie was so gaga over him. "Marie and I are friends, like I said. I don't know if she told you any different, but…"

"No! Marie hasn't said anything to me about this. Don't get me wrong." Whew, that was close. She had almost sold her best friend out. "I just assumed you were trying to get to know her better, that's all. You two—hang out a lot, right?"

"I do spend time with her, yes. But I thought we both knew it was just a friendship," Cedric explained. "Where I come from, it's not a big deal to take a young lady out to dinner or to a movie—we're enjoying a dinner with no strings attached, right?"

"Right…"

His face took on a worried look. "I hope I haven't given her the wrong impression, have I? I mean, I have a lot of female friends. I just think women deserve special treatment, even if they are just friends."

Boy, was she confused. Claudia didn't know what to say, now. Marie seemed to have an interest in Cedric, who apparently didn't return the favor.

"Marie reminds me a lot of my little sister, Robin."

111

Wouldn't Marie appreciate that—a little sister that went to lunch, dinner and to the movies with her big brother. She knew what she had to do then. She had to talk to Marie about taking her interest off of Cedric before she got her feelings hurt. Apparently there was a big misunderstanding about where their relationship was headed. And now, here was Cedric, reaching out to grab Claudia's hand again. Only this time, she didn't pull away.

"Claudia, I don't want to run you off when I say this, but I guess I'll take my chances. I would like to get to know *you* better."

She couldn't concentrate. What did he just say to her? Was she even sitting across from him in a restaurant? What day was it?

"Did you hear me?"

She blinked and looked at him. "I heard you."

He put his other hand over hers. "How do you feel about that?"

Why me, and not my roommate? she wanted to scream. Marie was the outgoing, strong one with all the talent and the beautiful complexion. She was the one who could hold an intelligent conversation and had confidence. And she always knew which block to check under "race."

Claudia pushed back her insecurity. She was so tired of worrying about her looks, her personality—how black she was. Why couldn't she be just as appealing to guys as Marie? Why couldn't she be labeled as down-to-earth, funny and intelligent? Was it a crime for her to enjoy the fact that her hair was a little softer and her complexion was a little lighter? She probably lost out on having a boyfriend in high school because she let someone bully her out of it. Now here was another absolutely, gorgeous man who had approached *her*—and he obviously did not think that she was stuck on herself. He was free, she was free—where was the crime?

"I know I put you in an awkward position, Claudia. But it was going to come out sooner or later. And I didn't want to tell you because...well..." he stopped talking and played with a french fry.

"Why? I promise I won't laugh this time."

"Well, for one, I figured someone as pretty and sweet as you already had a man. But even if you didn't I didn't think you would give *me* the time of day."

"Cedric, why would you think that? You have a lot going for you! You're funny, nice and....well you're a nice-looking young man." That was the understatement of the year.

He looked back at her in surprise. "You really think so?"

"Really," Claudia told him. She never realized he was so shy about himself. Like her.

That comment seemed to give him renewed confidence. He grabbed her hand again. "So I can I see you again, Claudia? I mean, as more than just a friend?"

She had no idea how she was going to explain any of this to Marie, and deep down, she knew she needed to nip the whole thing in the bud right then and there. But for the life of her, she just didn't want to. And it was time for her to come out of her shell and stop missing out. "O.k.," Claudia said. Cedric grinned widely at her and leaned back in his chair contently. Claudia tried a smile back at him. It worked.

MARIE

It was her third head this week.

Her mother had always told her that bad news traveled fast, but in Marie's case, it was good news that was traveling at the speed of light. Claudia's hair cut was such a hit that Marie actually had girls leaving their names and numbers all over her message board, wanting appointments. They couldn't believe that Claudia didn't step out of a salon with her style. Claudia had done some great PR. She told Marie that when girls stopped to compliment her on her style, they would ask how much Marie charged. Claudia told them it depended on what they wanted, but Marie wouldn't break them.

Right now, Marie was across the lobby on her floor, working on a sophomore named Vanessa Gibson. Vanessa's dark brown tresses were long, but the ends were split and she was badly in the need of a relaxer. Vanessa had the misconception that she had wash-and-go hair, and didn't like to use a lot of "heavy moisturizers," as she put it. The result was a rather dry, wild look and a comb full of damaged hair. Marie had a time convincing her that ethnic hair had a tendency to be dry, and needed to be moisturized.

"Not my hair, girl," Vanessa argued. "My whole family is blessed with nice hair. I've got to wash it at least three times a week to get rid of the dirt and build up."

Lord, have mercy.

"The reason it's not straight the way it usually is, is because I switched shampoos. I need to go back to my Mane Attraction."

That horse shampoo. She calmly explained to Vanessa that shampoos like that were designed for animal hair, not human hair. She warned her that if she didn't change the way she was maintaining her hair, she would need a wig real soon.

That hit the right note. "O.k., o.k.—do what you have to do. I don't need to lose any hair," Vanessa quickly told her.

Coupled with being ignorant about hair, Vanessa was also very nosy. And a gossip. Before they had been at school a good month, Marie and Claudia knew all there was to know about a lot of the females on their floor, in their residence hall and across campus. Their resident advisor, Chelsea, was the first person to visit them and welcome them to the floor. Vanessa was the second.

Now, Marie was in her room, listening to her chatter away, pausing only to make sure her hair was being done right. Marie wanted to take the towel she had draped around Vanessa's shoulders and shove it in her mouth. She wondered how the girl's roommate put up with it.

"My roommate tells me to shut up sometimes," Vanessa told Marie, like she'd read her mind. "Can you believe that? She says I talk too much."

Your roommate speaks with a wise tongue, Marie thought, as she cut away at Vanessa's damaged hair. She was going to lose about an inch and a half, but Marie had a style in mind that would really become her.

"Marie, what's up with you and Cedric Carter?" Vanessa asked out of the clear blue.

"What?" The question caught her off guard.

"I see you two together quite a bit on campus. Are ya'll dating?"

Marie could feel her inner blush heating up. So—they were being coupled together already. Not that she minded, but she didn't want to talk anything until things were more concrete. She knew that she was more than interested in him, and liked to believe that he felt the same way. Still, she didn't want to jump to any conclusions. They were building a good friendship, despite that troubling scene at breakfast a few days ago. She had finally managed to convince herself that she was being ridiculous to be jealous of her best friend. Just because Claudia looked like a miniature Halle Berry was no reason for Marie to be jealous.

"Isn't that your roommate getting out of Cedric's car?" Vanessa had pulled away from Marie and was looking out of her window. Her room was on the west side of the residence hall where the parking lot was, and she had a clear view of who was coming and who was going. How convenient for her.

Marie's face heated up. Her throat felt dry. The ole' green-eyed monster began to surface and she forced herself to push it back down as she joined Vanessa at her window. There was her prim and prissy roommate, Halle Berry, Jr., standing just outside the open passenger door of Cedric's black 626. Cedric was propped against the door that he obviously ran around and opened for Claudia, being the gentleman that he was. Her glamorous best friend was laughing at something he had just said, then she started walking toward the residence hall,

115

stopping to turn and wave sweetly at him. Even from the eighth floor, Marie could see the hint of a smile on Claudia's lips. She felt her chest tighten.

"Come on, Vanessa. Let's finish up." Marie was anxious to get away from Ms. Motormouth and go see her roommate. She wanted to find out exactly what Claudia was doing getting out of Cedric's car. For the moment, she calmed herself with the idea that he had just seen her walking back from her evening lab and gave her a lift—being the gentleman that he was.

"The three of you must hang pretty tight," Vanessa commented.

Marie was trying to keep her concentration on wrapping Vanessa's hair. "Huh?"

"I said the three of you must be pretty close."

"What makes you say that?"

"Well, I wouldn't be so trusting with my man and another female. Even if it was my best friend."

Marie stopping her brushing. Her fingers were slick with the setting lotion she had sprayed on. "Vanessa, what is the big deal? So he gave her a lift back to her room. Anyway, Cedric and me are just friends. Now I really do need for you to hold still so I can finish wrapping your hair."

Vanessa shrugged and held her head very still, but not her mouth. "So I guess it wouldn't bother you if they started seeing each other?"

"Vanessa, why are you harping on this?" Marie could feel herself getting angry. She had to stifle the urge to pop Vanessa in the back of her wet head with her brush. *Shut up!* She wanted to scream. *I'm having a hard enough time dealing with it myself without you running your mouth about it!*

"Oh, I'm sorry, Marie. I didn't mean to upset you."

Marie finished wrapping and tied a scarf around the perimeter of Vanessa's head, pulling the knot extra tight. Vanessa flinched and reached up to loosen it while Marie packed up her hair care supplies in her duffel bag. She told Vanessa to sit underneath her dryer for about twenty minutes and she would be back to comb her out. *I'm being silly*, she told herself as she lugged the heavy bag across the lobby. *He probably just gave her a lift from class like I told Vanessa.*

"Hi, Marie." Chelsea Richards, her Resident Advisor, was coming out of her room armed with a book bag when Marie got in the hallway. That was the beauty of living next door to your RA—you pretty much always ran into her. Chelsea was a bright, bubbly, blonde senior who never seemed to have a bad day, or meet a person she didn't like.

"Hi, Chelsea."

"How's everything going for you?"

"Fine. Just keeping busy with school work."

"Boy, don't I know." Chelsea shook her head and hoisted her book satchel up further on her shoulder. "I'm headed off to study with my boyfriend right now. I'm on duty tomorrow, so this is my only chance to sneak away."

RA duty—that glorious time when the RA in charge was confined to his or her room, leaving only to roam each floor on the prowl for violators of the housing policy. Marie often saw one walking around, clutching a black three-ring binder that Chelsea explained was for recording the events of the evening. Marie felt fortunate not to have to deal with that life. Hers was convoluted enough.

"Hey, be sure to come to the mixer Thursday. It'll give everyone a chance to get acquainted."

"I'll see what I can do."

Chelsea smiled and started to walk off, but then remembered an item she neglected to mention. She sidled up to Marie like she was about to share a juicy secret. "I forgot to mention that tomorrow is the last day for room changes. So if you want to room with someone else or want to pay for a single, tomorrow is it."

Marie almost laughed at her. "Thanks anyway, Chelsea. I think me and Claudia are o.k. We're best friends from back home."

"That's right—you did mention that. I'm sorry."

"No problem."

"Well, Kenny's probably waiting for me downstairs. Isaac Dryer from eleven is on duty tonight. If you have any problems, just let him know. See ya!" She swished off, her ponytail keeping rhythm with her steps. Chelsea was a nice person, but she had a tendency to hover over her residents like a mother hen. Or maybe Marie was just being too judgmental. After all—the mother hen *did* leave her chicks for a study rendezvous with her rooster—and she didn't mind telling Marie where she was going. Maybe one day she would be able to "sneak off" and go study with Cedric.

117

The door to her room was halfway open. Claudia was standing by the small refrigerator, one of Marie's contributions to the nest. She turned with a wide-eyed look when Marie walked in.

"Oh hi, girl. You scared me, sneaking in like that."

Was that surprise or guilt Marie heard in her voice? I didn't think I was sneaking. I guess I just walk soft."

Claudia nodded and headed to the closet to hang up her jacket. Why was she acting so nervous?

Claudia told Marie, "I'm glad I don't have to see that lab until next week. Three hours is too long for any one class to last. I don't care if it is a lab."

"Yeah…I spent about that much time on Vanessa's head this evening."

"Oh, you had to deal with Super Mouth, huh?" Claudia grinned and appeared to relax a little. "I know she must've talked your ear off."

"She bent it real good." Marie slid her duffel bag of supplies under her bed and sat down at her desk. She was trying her best to read Claudia's face for some sign, but couldn't. She wondered how many clues she would have to drop before Claudia would mention coming home in Cedric's car. Her failure to mention it, like she wanted to keep it a secret, was making Marie uneasy. She watched her best friend hang her book bag on the back of her chair, and head back to the fridge. Marie cleared her throat and threw out the bait. "We saw you coming back to the residence hall."

Bingo. Claudia fumbled and knocked over a cup by the refrigerator. She bent quickly to pick it up. Marie sat and waited calmly for her explanation.

"You did?"

"Yes, we did. Actually, Vanessa saw you first. She said, 'isn't that your roommate getting out of Cedric's car?' It was funny, because she had just said something about me and Cedric not two minutes earlier. I told her that he probably saw you walking on campus and gave you a lift."

"Yeah…he gave me—he gave me a ride over here. He had left his car parked on campus. He was on his way to get it when I ran into him."

So, it was just like Marie had originally thought. She let herself relax. He saw Claudia on campus and gave her a lift. She felt the knot in her chest loosen and was about to comment on what a busybody Vanessa was when her eyes rested on the container that Claudia had been trying to stuff in the refrigerator since she came in—*Cow Pattie's—Thanks for Dining With Us!* The name sounded vaguely familiar, then *very* familiar. Cedric had told her about a restaurant where the football players got a special discount because they ate there all the time—Cow Pattie's. Marie had laughed at the name, and Cedric promised to take her there one day when he had a free afternoon. Obviously, Claudia had caught him on one of those rare afternoons.

"Did you go anywhere else, Claudia?" Marie lowered her voice to keep it under control.

Claudia caught Marie staring at her food container. "Oh…we ran and got a bite to eat."

"I thought you said he just gave you a ride back to Belten?"

"I didn't say 'just,' Marie. I said he gave me a ride back to the room, and he did." Claudia shrugged and headed back to her desk where she began pulling books out of her bag, like she really intended to study. Marie knew that she waited until the last possible minute to do any school work. She wasn't disciplined in that area. Besides, she couldn't believe that Claudia was trying to make dinner a small matter.

"Claudia, I think you know what I mean. You never mentioned that he took you out to eat. You just said you ran into him on campus, and he gave you a ride back to the room. You ain't say a thing about dinner."

Claudia sat at her desk, something else she never did. If she had any homework, she would flop on her bed with the remote in her hand and do it. "Marie, I'm sorry I didn't mention going out to eat. I didn't think it was that big of a deal. And he didn't 'take' me out to dinner. We decided to get some food off-campus."

We decided? *We?* "Who paid?"

"Excuse me?"

"Who paid for dinner?"

"Does it matter?"

"Apparently, it does. I asked, didn't I?" Marie was making no attempts to hide her anger now. She did not like what she was hearing.

And Claudia had the nerve to look shocked. "Am I on trial, here?"

"Why can't you just answer the question?"

"*He* did, o.k.? I mean, what is the big deal? I'll pay him back if that'll make you feel better."

"Claudia, cut the drama, o.k.? You paying him back does not change the fact that you went with him in the first place, does it?"

"Marie, he asked *me*, all right? I didn't run him down and force him to take me to dinner. I was on my way to the Student Center…"

"Girl, please—save that," Marie cut in rudely. She stood and walked to the window. "I ain't ask you all that. What I want to know is this—how would you feel if I did that to you?"

Claudia's mouth was tight. There was no mistaking the guilt in her eyes now. "Did what?"

O.k.…so she was all set to play stupid this evening. "How would you feel if I went out with a guy that I *knew* you liked?"

"Marie…"

"How would you feel if you were me, watching you get out of his car, acting like you had something to hide then lying about where you've been with him?" Marie was raising her voice now.

"Marie, why are you yelling at me?" Claudia looked near tears, but she could have cried a river for all Marie cared now.

"Because you could have least been mature about it. You could have come to me and told me that you liked him. We're supposed to be best friends, Claudia. Friends don't do each other like that." Marie felt tears coming. "How many other times have you two been out?"

How she hoped she was blowing things out of proportion. She wanted Claudia to jump up and deny everything and tell Marie she was making a mountain out of a molehill. That, in fact, she and Cedric had spent the whole evening talking about Marie and his feelings for her. He didn't know how to approach Marie about it, so he decided to seek advice from her closest friend. Or that yes, Marie blew it. They were planning a surprise birthday party for her. Or Cedric wanted to buy her a present and needed to know what she liked. *Something.*

Instead, Claudia just sat there, looking down at her pants, picking invisible lint off of them. Being silent. Looking guilty. "I didn't know," she finally said in a low voice.

"What?! Speak up!"

"I said, I didn't know." Claudia looked up. I didn't know I liked him."

Marie stared at her a minute, trying to accept what she was hearing. "Please explain something to me—how can you *not* know you like somebody? I can see you not knowing what time it is or what the weather is going to be, but how can you *not* know you like someone?! You sound like those stupid soap operas you watch, girl. Give me a break!"

"Marie, just listen…"

"Listen to *what*, Claudia?! Listen to you try to explain how you dissed your best friend over a guy? Are you that desperate? As far as I'm concerned, you don't have a thing to say to me—not one thing. You threw yourself at Cedric because you felt like he would go for you with your light skin and good hair." She had never spoken so rudely to Claudia before, but she deserved it, dissing her the way she did. She still felt like crying, but was not about to break down in front of her.

"I can't believe you said something as tripped out as that, Marie! You sound just like them girls in high school with that nonsense!" Claudia had the audacity to jump up and stand defiantly in the middle of the floor. Her hands were perched on her tiny excuse for hips, and she looked…was that anger? Yes, Marie definitely read anger on her face.

Oh, give her a new hairstyle, tell her she looks good and she wants to catch an attitude after all these years of being timid. Well, well. "Well, maybe those girls were reading you right the entire time, Claudia," she said calmly, wanting to do everything in her power to hurt her feelings. "You came off all innocent and timid, but you was just perpetrating a fraud, that's all."

Oh yeah, Claudia was hurt. Marie saw her bite back some tears, which was a shock in itself. "I can't believe you said that…"

"And I can't believe you went behind my back with Cedric!"

"You were the one who said ya'll were 'just friends,' anyway!"

"You knew that I liked him!"

Claudia was crying now, but still standing toe to toe with Marie."I knew what you told me."

"You knew what I told you?!" Marie repeated, wondering if Claudia was trying to be funny or if she was seriously brain damaged.

"You had no idea I was interested in him?"

"Like I said before, Marie—I knew what you told me."

"Girl, you need to shut 'cho lying mouth! You..." Marie realized that they were yelling at each other. And she was mad enough to snatch Claudia. But no—she had to maintain control. No matter what. It was a wonder that no one was knocking on their door, telling them to chill out. Anyway, the conversation was going nowhere. It was obvious that Claudia thought her actions were justified, or she just wasn't budging on this Cedric thing. Marie felt defeated, humiliated and used. She had to get in one last dig to break Claudia down.

"I'm not even going to discuss this petty mess anymore," Marie told her. "It's obvious that Cedric was just being nice to you because you sit around feeling sorry for yourself all the time, so don't get your hopes up."

That seemed to have the opposite effect of what Marie was hoping for. To her surprise, Claudia wiped her tears and smiled. "Well, I'm sorry to disappoint *you* and I was going to try to sit down and tell you like an adult, but Cedric told me at dinner that he wants to get to know me better, and that you're just a friend to him."

"Why you wanna lie, Claudia?" However, something on the inside told Marie that Claudia wasn't lying. Especially when Claudia picked up the phone and handed it to her.

"Here, call him and ask him. Go ahead."

Marie looked down at the phone. Somehow, she was going to exit this situation with dignity. If Cedric wanted Claudia, he could have her. And vice versa. They deserved each other. She had never cried over a man, and wasn't about to start now, no matter how much she hurt inside. "I'll have my things out by tomorrow," she told Claudia.

And Claudia had the nerve to look shocked, like she didn't understand why. "Fine, if that's what you want to do, Marie," she told her in an irritating, calm voice. She just had it all together now—a fly cut, a better personality, and a new man. Marie wanted to vomit. She had to get out of the room.

"You don't have to leave now," Claudia said. "I can go so you can get your things together."

"No, don't do me any favors. I'll leave. I need to, before I go slam off on you." Marie still wanted a physical confrontation. The only thing that stopped her was the thought of fighting over a man, something she had vowed never to do.

"Oh, what is that, a threat?" Claudia was trying her best to put up a brave front, but Marie knew that she was probably scared stiff that she'd haul off and hit her. She needed it. And just for good measure, Marie walked right up in her face. Claudia readied herself for action, but took a few steps back.

"Claudia, believe me…if I wanted to hit you, I wouldn't waste my time by telling you about it. Cedric ain't worth fighting over, and you ain't either." Marie turned and left the room. It was almost time to comb Vanessa out, anyway.

The next day, she contacted Chelsea and had a new room assignment. Chelsea wanted to know if everything was all right and Marie told her it was—and didn't elaborate. Claudia had the decency to be gone while Marie moved her stuff. She had also got ghost when Marie returned from combing Vanessa out. She didn't know where she was—maybe she was over Cedric's—but she came sliding back in around midnight when Marie was in bed. When she woke up the next morning, she was already gone, and her class wasn't until later that afternoon.

Marie finally finished moving everything she owned except the refrigerator—it was too heavy for her to move and too old for her to care about it and her new roommate had a huge one. She took a final look around the room and noticed a bottle of Sizzling Red nail polish on her dresser and a card still taped to her desk. A picture of jewels and coins spilling out of a treasure chest was on the front of it, with the caption—*A Friend Like You is a Priceless Treasure*, scripted across the top. Marie grimaced. Claudia had given her that card shortly after she came to Cedar East, and discovered that Marie did consider her a friend. Marie had the card tucked in her mirror at home, but gave it a special place of honor on her desk when they moved in. She grabbed the nail polish and untaped the card from the desk, reading the contents: *Marie, thanks for always being there. You are a true friend. I love you!! Claudia.*

She was tempted—tempted, to tear the card up and throw the pieces on Claudia's bed, then open the bottle of red nail polish and empty the contents over all the stuff she'd returned to her. Instead, she snatched a pad of sticky notes and a pen from Claudia's desk and scrawled out a quick message: *Since this obviously does not pertain to us anymore, I am returning this card, along with the other items left on your bed. Marie.* If there was an ounce of the old Claudia in the person she had encountered yesterday, she would be severely wounded by those few, simple words. She placed the card on the bed right on top of that fly white pantsuit Claudia practically gave her for her date with Cedric, looked around again, and then left, slamming the door behind her.

CLAUDIA

Claudia drummed her fingers on the arm of the couch while she crossed and uncrossed her legs. It was no use—she was nervous. It wasn't like she hadn't been in Cedric's apartment before, but that was only once and it was for no more than five minutes. He had invited her up because he'd forgotten his wallet on their way to a movie. Now, she was invited over to spend a "quiet evening" with him, which meant pizza, videos—and no roommates.

The apartment was pretty decent, she noted. Cedric and his roomies had stored away the university's furniture and brought their own—a plush, deep green couch and two matching easy chairs occupied the living room. She hadn't had the chance to check out the bathroom, but unlike the doors to the three bedrooms, it was open. That let her know it was at least clean.

"How's the movie?" Cedric called to her from the kitchen where he was getting them something to drink.

"Oh, it's fine, I guess. I really haven't gotten into it yet."

"How 'bout rewinding it for me? I'll be there in a minute."

Claudia picked up the remote and rewound the movie, but to tell the truth, her mind wasn't even on it. She was too busy thinking about Marie. She hadn't meant to hurt her feelings—that was never her intention. But Cedric said that he and Marie were just friends. Could she help it that Marie felt more for him than he did for her? Claudia told Cedric that she and Marie had a difference of opinion and Marie moved out. He asked if it involved him and she just told him it was a personal matter and left it at that. Despite what she felt towards Marie, she still wasn't going to sell her out.

But didn't Marie have some nerve, running up in her face, talking to her like she was two years old? Claudia never had the nerve to tell her how much her bossiness bothered her—until two weeks ago. Marie had gotten so bent out of shape over that dinner. They could have discussed the matter like two adults. Claudia might have even told Cedric that she couldn't see him again if Marie would have been nicer, but no, that would be asking too much. Marie had to get ghetto, but that was because she was so selfish—always wanting her way, always wanting to be the center of attention. Claudia had felt like an ugly duckling at breakfast when Cedric's partner, Junte', had went on and on about Marie's beautiful African skin and her wealth of knowledge about sports. And Claudia was sure she heard him stress the word *African*. The African princess and her zebra friend, Claudia—what a pair. Well, Claudia had enough. She hadn't meant to flounce out of breakfast like that, but she would have started to scream if she stayed any longer. Marie this, Marie that....Marie's friend, Claudia. Marie's roommate, Claudia. It was showtime for Claudia now.

"Here you are, gorgeous." Cedric came into the living room carrying two big, frosty mugs of soda. Claudia thanked him, and sat her drink down on the table in front of her. It sure was a lot of soda—maybe she'd get the chance to check out that bathroom after all.

"That's not too much for you, is it?" Cedric asked, taking a sip of his drink.

"No, it's fine. I'll probably need it after the pizza, anyway."

"If that ever gets here." He frowned down at his watch. "I know I'm getting some kind of discount. It's been almost forty minutes."

"Do they offer that deal? If the pizza's late, you get a discount?"

Cedric winked at her. "You watch me. I told you I'm good at getting what I want." He leaned back and casually tossed his arm across the couch, smiling and putting his dimples on display. For some odd reason, Claudia envisioned a tiger in a jungle right before it pounced on some poor, unsuspecting deer, just like the film she saw in Biology yesterday. She edged a little closer to her end of the couch. "Am I making you nervous, Claudia?" He winked at her and removed his arm.

She shrugged. She didn't want to appear prudish, but she also wanted his respect—the same respect he had shown Marie. "No, I'm fine," she lied.

"Everything's 'fine' with you, girl. The movie's 'fine,' you're 'fine'...." He reached over and tugged a lock of her hair. "And you're right. You are one *fine* sistah."

She wanted to kick herself for blushing. "Thank you."

"No—thank *you*." Cedric continued to stare at her and play with her hair.

Claudia felt her stomach board a roller coaster and take off. "Relax, Claudia—I don't bite." Cedric showed her both rows of pearly whites and Claudia tried not to look. She picked up her mug and attempted to drink, but all she managed to do was swallow too much too fast and cough in a choking fit. Cedric patted her back. She had heard somewhere that you weren't supposed to pat a person's back when that person was choking. As long as the person was coughing, air was getting through. Patting only made things worse. "You all right?" he asked when her coughing had eased some.

"Yeah," she choked out in a husky voice. She pushed out one last cough and that seemed to do the trick. Her throat cleared up. "I'm fine now," she reminded him, because he still had his hand on her back. Only now, his patting had turned into a caress up on her shoulder. She inched away from his hand. "I said I was fine, Cedric."

A kid with his hand caught in a cookie jar could not have looked more shocked. "I'm sorry, Claudia. I guess I got carried away again. It's your fault, you know."

"*My* fault?!" Had the boy lost his mind, or did she in some unconscious way lead him to believe that he could get cozy with her? Her next move would be out the door.

Cedric lowered his head and focused one puppy dog eye on her. "Yeah. You're so beautiful and sweet—I can't help myself sometimes. I've never met anyone like you."

Her heart thumped double-time. Could he be serious? Marie would know. She would know right off if he was feeding her a line. And there she went again, comparing herself to Marie. When was she going to trust her own instincts?

"Claudia, I have a very special favor to ask you."

Favors sounded safe. She felt a little relief. "What is it?"

"You have to promise to say 'yes'," Cedric told her.

"I don't know what it is yet, Cedric."

"Will you at least say you'll consider it?"

"O.k. Cedric. I'll consider it. Now what is it?"

Cedric let a grin slowly spread across his handsome face, then he leaned closer to Claudia. She could smell the cologne that used to send Marie into another dimension. She felt herself blacking out right now.

"I wondered," he started, bringing up a finger to stroke her cheek, "If you would give me the privilege and the honor of kissing this lovely face?"

Oh no—not that. *You see, Cedric—it's not that I don't want you to, but things are moving a little too fast for me. I've never kissed a guy before, did you know that? I can't tell you that, because then*

127

you'll think I'm weird. So please, hold my hand, look into my eyes— *but don't ask me for a kiss. Not just yet.* "Uh…" Claudia managed, but it might have been too late. Cedric was leaning in closer, and she didn't know if she had the power to stop him.

There was a knock at the door. Cedric huffed in frustration and moved back. Claudia exhaled and relaxed. "It's probably the pizza," she told him.

"Yeah…" Cedric reached in his back pocket for his wallet. "Their timing is perfect." He went to the door and opened it on a young delivery boy. "Yo, man—ya'll said forty minutes or less—it's been almost an hour."

The pizza boy apologized—they had been very busy that evening, and if he would call the restaurant and talk to the manager, he was sure he would give him his next pizza free of charge. Cedric said he'd do that, paid the worker and sent him on his way without a tip.

Pizza was one of Claudia's all time favorite foods, but her appetite was history. Cedric sat the greasy, savory smelling box on the table and took his seat beside Claudia. He smiled and grabbed her hand. "Now, where were we?"

"Aren't we going to eat?" she asked, willing to do anything just to keep the conversation off of intimacy.

"We'll eat in a minute," he told her. "But I want to know if you gonna do me this favor, girl." He was serious, too. He had a funny look in his eyes, and he was rubbing her hand with his thumb.

Fear gripped her. "No, Cedric—I can't."

"Why not?" he asked, sounding rather frustrated.

"I'm not—ready for that yet." Goodness, she sounded like she should be sitting on a front porch swing in a hoop skirt, on the set of one hose black and white fifties' shows. Why couldn't she just tell him that two weeks just didn't seem long enough to be comfortable with a kiss? He had taken Marie out for over a month, and hadn't as much as held her hand—why was he trying to bumrush her? Oh yeah, they were "just friends"—a different set of rules applied for friendship. When you were trying to hook up with a girl, the rule book was thrown out of the window.

Cedric released her hand and pulled back to his side of the couch. He grabbed the remote and put his attention on the movie.

"Cedric, what's wrong?"

Silence.

"Cedric."

Still nothing.

Claudia exhaled slowly, confused. Now he wasn't talking to her. How could she have made such a mess of things? How did Marie do it? She had kept him calling her, taking her out, and she didn't remember them having any tiffs like they seemed to be having now. But no, here she comes along, and she can't keep peace with a man for one evening. She unconsciously reached over and touched his hand. At least that made him look at her. "Why aren't you talking to me?"

"Because I don't see how you can play a brotha' like that. I thought you were different than those women I used to date."

"*Play* you? What are you talking about?"

"I'm talking about you, acting all funny when you know how I feel about you. I can't be played like that. And ya'll wonder why the brothas won't tell you their feelings half the time. Nobody likes rejection, Claudia. You wouldn't."

Where had she heard those words before? Didn't she have a conversation with her brother about the same thing? Didn't he tell her that guys wouldn't go after girls that they thought would reject them? "Cedric, I'm not rejecting you. I'm just not ready to kiss you." She didn't know what else to say. It was how she felt. Why couldn't she get him to understand that?

He shook his head. "Let me ask you something. How do you feel about me?"

That sounded like a trick question. "I…like you, Cedric. I think you're a nice guy."

"How much do you like me? Maybe we're on different channels on how we feel about one another. 'Cause see—I like you a lot, Claudia. A whole lot."

The roller coaster hit a loop. "I like you a lot, too, Cedric."

"No—I don't think you understand." He looked her straight in the eye. "I've never felt this way about a woman before. You had my heart when I first met you in the room that evening. "I want you to be my lady, Claudia. Now I wasn't going to tell you that yet because I didn't want to scare you off. But I can't keep denying how I feel about you."

Oh my. No one had ever swept Claudia off her feet like Cedric was doing now. This gorgeous man wanted to date her—exclusively.

Was she reading too much into this kissing business? She had absolutely no experience, but she thought a kiss was supposed to be a mutual thing. Maybe she should just count to three, get it over with.

"I just want to express how I feel about you," he was telling her in a soft voice. "Is that so wrong?"

"No," she said without thinking.

His dimples were back. "Good." He leaned closer to her again.

O.k. here goes nothing. One, two... "I can't Cedric. Not yet. I'm sorry."

Cedric had been holding her hand, but now pulled his back abruptly. "And I can't do *this*."

"Do what?"

"This, Claudia. Play these games. The way I feel about you... I'm not trying to get my feelings hurt. It might be best for both of us if we just ended everything right here and now."

Ten minutes ago, he was serving her a drink and waiting on a pizza. Now, he was ending a relationship that hadn't gotten out of the starting gate good. All over a kiss. Now on top of her best friend, she was about to lose this fine specimen of a man who just wanted a kiss. It seemed so simple, but she was all torn up inside. She didn't know what to do or say. All she knew was that she managed to mess up two meaningful relationships that came into her life. So she did what she was used to doing in crisis situations. She starting crying.

Cedric immediately reached over and embraced her. That made her cry harder.

"Claudia, Claudia. It's o.k.," he soothed. "I didn't mean to make you cry."

Now she really felt like an idiot. Once she started crying, there was no immediate cut off. "I've made such a mess of everything."

She rested her head on his shoulder and tried to control her tears. She was so tired of fighting people, situations, things. She just needed some peace.

Cedric took a finger and lifted her chin. She took a quick glance at his shirt and saw her foundation smeared on it.

"Don't worry about that, Claudia," he told her. "I need to apologize. I shouldn't have pushed you like that. It's just whenever I look at you—my stomach gets all knotted up and my tongue gets all tied...ah, I didn't mean to tell you all that." He pulled away from her, looking embarrassed.

Claudia's tears were evaporating. How could someone who seemed to be so confident be so shy? And around her?

"Look at you," he was saying. "You all fly—you could have any man you want. I guess I just wanted some assurance that you weren't trying to play me."

"Cedric, I wouldn't play you. To tell you the truth, I'm just scared."

"Of me?!"

"Well, not you, necessarily—I just don't have a lot of experience with men." Shoot, she might as well be honest. He was. "I really don't have…any experience with men."

What was up with the twinkle in his eye? "You mean you're a…you ain't had a boyfriend before?"

No! Don't answer that! Please! a voice screamed insider her head. And the more she thought about it, the more that voice was beginning to sound like Marie, who had no business here. This was *her* situation—*her* man. Yeah, she liked the sound of that—*her* man. "Not even a first date until I met you."

"Really?! What about the prom? Did you go?"

"Yeah, I went—with Marie." She remembered that evening that was just a few months ago. She felt humiliated because not one guy approached her about the prom, and she wasn't about to take Marie's advice and ask one of them, although Marie told her that several guys had approached her about Claudia. A couple had even asked if she would ask Claudia to the prom for one of them, but Marie refused. Marie was going with a good guy friend of hers from another school, but when the week of the prom came and Claudia still didn't have a date, she suddenly decided she wanted to do something "contemporary" and go stag.

"Come on, it'll be fun," she told Claudia. And it was. It was one of the most special nights of her life. It wasn't because, believe it or not, she danced with guys for the first time, laughed with them without feeling uncomfortable, and even shared a slow dance with Jimmy Ryan despite Tallette's murderous glares. It was because Marie had sacrificed her happiness just to make sure that little, shy, insecure Claudia wouldn't be embarrassed. O.k., she had to kick that memory to the curb. It didn't help in her present situation with Cedric.

Cedric smiled at her again. And she would have been completely happy about that, except his grin looked like a wolf's. "Ah, girl. And here I am thinking you were rejecting me. You're just inexperienced, that's all. No wonder I scared you." He pulled her back into an embrace, and this time she didn't seem to mind being close to him. "Now, I'll tell you something, but you can't share it."

"I know—you cried over *The Color Purple*."

"No, it's something else." He took a deep breath. "I don't have a whole lot of experience with women myself."

"Really, Cedric?"

"Really. You sound shocked."

"Very."

"So I guess we just have to help each other out, huh?"

Claudia nodded, letting herself be held. Someone finally understood her. She had let herself be bullied out of Jimmy Ryan, but she wasn't about to let another one get away. No matter what.

EUGENE

Renee' didn't have the edge he had experienced that day when he met her in the Food Court. Not until the day they met for lunch on the patio of the Student Center, on an unusually warm day in October. Renee' was right in the middle of a story about their sociology professor, when Irene flounced around the corner.

"Hi," she greeted, smiling her sunny smile. She was dressed in a white T-shirt and black Umbro shorts, and was carrying a gym bag, which let Eugene know that she had probably just left volleyball practice.

"Hi, Irene," Eugene grinned back. "How was practice?"

"Grueling, as usual," Irene looked over at Renee', who was eyeing her warily. "Hi, Renee'."

"Hi," Renee' pushed out. Eugene caught her expression out of the corner of his eye. She was not smiling back. In fact, she dropped the french fry she was holding back in her plate, never taking her eyes off Irene.

Irene turned her attention back to Eugene. "So how's the paper coming?"

"Slow. I don't know where Grapevine found that author. There's one book on him in the library and a couple of journal articles. I had to do an interlibrary loan."

"Yeah? Well my author was married five times, lived in Russia under an assumed name for three years, and never learned how to write—he dictated all of his stuff. And I'm supposed to discover a theme to his works? Come on, give me a break."

"I'll switch with you," Eugene offered.

"Hey, no way. He may be complicated, but I'm almost done."

Renee' cleared her throat—not loud, but enough to make herself heard. Eugene glanced at her and she cut her cat eyes at him quickly, then looked away.

Irene caught the look, too. "Oh, I didn't mean to interrupt your lunch with boring English talk. I'd better run. I'll see you in class, Eugene. Renee', it was good seeing you again."

"Mmm hmm—bye," Renee' mumbled.

Irene frowned up a moment, then walked away back toward the center of campus. Eugene couldn't understand Renee's abruptness.

133

He remembered the conversation in the library, but he thought Renee' now knew that he and Irene were just friends, especially now that they had done lunch together. But looking at her now, he could tell that she was still bothered by something. She was picking slowly with her food, not looking at him.

"Renee'?"

"Mmm hmm?"

"Is something wrong?"

"No." She bit into her cheeseburger and chewed thoughtfully, still not looking at him.

Well, maybe nothing was wrong. He shrugged. "You never finished your story about Dr. Caldwell."

"I was pretty much through."

"Oh, o.k. Well, you ready for the test on Friday?"

She nodded, swirling a french fry around in a small pool of ketchup.

Eugene tried again. "Renee', are you all right?"

She cut those cat eyes at him. "I'm fine."

He wanted to throw his hands up in defeat. Was he supposed to guess? Why couldn't she just come out and say what the problem was? It may have been that she was a tad bit jealous, a thought that didn't bother Eugene. In fact, it was kind of flattering. "O.k., well— let's talk about the test Friday…"

"Eugene!" Renee' interrupted, frustrated.

"What?!"

"I don't want to talk about Sociology."

"What do you want to talk about?"

Renee' looked him straight in the eye. "Do you like that girl?"

"Who? Irene?"

"Whatever her name is."

"Her name is Irene, and we're just friends."

"Then why is she always up in your face if you are 'just friends'? Does she like you?"

He didn't know whether to laugh or holler. "Irene and I have a research paper we're working on in English, Renee'—that's one reason why we're together so much. We're friends—that's it. Is that what you're so bent out of shape about?"

Uh oh—wrong choice of words. Renee's eyes grew big, and her hands went straight to her hips. "I am not *bent out of shape*, Eugene

Wright. I just wanted to know why that white girl was always up in your face. Can't she find a white guy to buddy with?"

Whoa—this was much more than he bargained for. Renee' was turning into his father right before his eyes. She stood up and grabbed her books off the table, mumbling about the nerve of some black men, who couldn't see the forest for the trees. He hadn't meant to upset her.

"Renee'—wait." He grabbed her wrist gently before she flew off. She pulled away and sat back down, frowning at him. "I'm sorry. I didn't mean to offend you. I was just trying to understand why you were so upset with me."

Renee' stared hard at him, then dropped her eyes. "I guess I owe you an apology, too. I shouldn't have blown up at you like that. I just get so tired of these white women trying to steal our black men."

"What?!" Eugene heard every word, but didn't want to believe that he was hearing it again, like in high school. Not when things were starting to look up for him.

"And what really gets me are these black men breaking their necks to run after a white woman, like sistahs aren't good enough for them. We have to stick together as a race in *all* areas."

Good Lord. Every time he turned around, someone was telling him how black he needed to be—his father, his classmates in high school and now Renee'. And not only her. There were the other looks from students on campus when he walked somewhere with Irene, like that guy that lived down the hall from him. Irene had been by the room a couple of times and the guy had seen them coming down the hall together. Ever since then, he acted like Eugene's skin color was changing right before his eyes, the way he looked at him sideways. He thought the guy's name was Perry or something like that. He had lent his roommate some clothes one day when he locked himself out of his room.

"...So maybe I did get a little bent out of shape," Renee' was still talking. "To be honest, I don't see where you two have anything to talk about outside of class. A black man and a white woman—what can you possibly have in common?"

Eugene, I don't see why you hang around all those white folks. What do ya'll talk about?

"I have to run." Eugene glanced down at his watch and got up from the table.

"Are you all right?"

"I'm fine," he lied. "I'm just late for a meeting. I'll call you later." He grabbed his books and streaked away from the table, without waiting for her to respond.

"Eugene, can I ask you something?"

"Sure, go ahead."

"Are you embarrassed to be seen with me?"

Late Friday afternoons on campus were about as lively as a graveyard. Most students were loading their cars or waiting on rides to whisk them away for the weekend. The unfortunate few who were still trudging from one building to the next had crazy classes like architecture and geology. Very rarely did Eugene go home or anywhere else for the weekend. He had been invited out a few times by Renee' but ever since that altercation on the patio about three weeks ago, he had been doing a lot of keeping his distance. He and Irene were sitting on a bench near Yardley Tower. Her question caught him off guard.

"Why would you ask me that?"

She paused, reflecting on a suitable answer. "O.k., it seems like lately whenever we're together on campus, you're always looking over your shoulder. You get kind of fidgety. And when we pass someone black, you hold your head down or walk ahead of me. What gives?"

That was the thing about Irene—she was very direct. She didn't look angry or upset. She just wanted an answer. With her tone of voice, she could have just as easily asked him about the weather.

"Irene, how can you say that?! When do I do that?!" He knew what she was saying was true, only he didn't know how to explain the "Black Man's List of Do's and Don'ts." One was that if you didn't want your "brotha'" card revoked, you did not talk to, walk with associate or be seen in anyway with a person of the white race— especially if that person was also of the opposite sex. Violation of the Do's and Don'ts could result in disapproving looks, unfriendly comments, labels like Wannabe, Uncle Tom, Oreo or, at a worst case scenario, being completely ostracized from the African-American race. Eugene had to deal with the Black List in high school, but tried to do away with it at Hamel. But he was finding it hard to survive outside of it. Still, Irene was a good friend, probably the only one so far who understood him. But he was getting tired of fighting against the Black List. Real tired.

"Look, Irene," he started, unsure of what was going to come out of his mouth. "I just...I just think we should keep our association on an...academic level."

She looked confused and rightly so.

"What I mean is that...that we've already finished our project..." She continued to frown. "What are you trying to say, Eugene?"

He could feel himself starting to sweat, and it was about fifty-five degrees outside. He felt lightheaded, and really wanted her to stop staring at him with those huge, green eyes. He tried a firmer tone. "What I mean is that maybe we shouldn't, you know..."

"Know *what?!*"

"...hang out so much." There. He'd said it.

Irene shook her head and studied the ground, trying to grasp what he was saying. "What is this about, Eugene?" she asked in a strange, low voice. "Did I do something to you or something?" She finally looked up at him and delivered the bombshell. "Or is it because you're ashamed to be seen with a *white* girl?!"

He started to open his mouth and deny everything, but she didn't give him the chance. "You don't have to say a word. I'm not stupid—I've seen the looks we get on campus and I've noticed how rude Renee' acts toward me. And then the thing with the Plot—a lot of black people are angry, and might not like you buddying with a white person. I just don't choose to let it bother me." Her voice held the hint of a tremble.

"Well, if you've noticed, then you can understand where I'm coming from." That way he wouldn't have to go into the Do's and Don'ts.

She shook her head furiously. In fact, she looked furious, anyway. "No, Eugene, I *don't* understand. Why try to understand someone else's ignorance? What is the big deal about us being friends, because we're different colors? That was the mentality that kept the races at each others' throats for decades."

"No, Irene—that *is* the mentality," he corrected her. "That mentality didn't disappear because we have a few laws on the books to protect against racism, or because we had people who died fighting against it. That mentality is in each of us, black and white. We can't get around it. It's been there from day one."

"But where did it come from, Eugene?" She was standing now, too wired to remain seated. "It isn't some kind of gene that manifests into a physical trait, like eye or hair color. Prejudice and racism—it's all learned behavior. *Learned.* What…law of nature says that blacks and whites can't be friends?!"

She was making it extremely difficult for him, and though her points made sense, he somehow resented her saying what she said. There she stood, waiting for him to answer incorrectly so she could cut him off with her theories that painted a rosy picture of the world. Maybe her world of acceptance was all peaches and cream, but his wasn't.

"Irene, look. All I'm saying is that we are making it harder on ourselves by hanging out together. Maybe the mentality is unfair, but it's there. We can't change that by not liking it. School is hard enough without being a public spectacle."

"I'm really surprised at you, Eugene. I thought you were above all that petty mess." Her words stung like little sharp arrows. He could feel himself wincing with each one.

"Well, maybe I'm not," he told her, still not looking at her in the face. "Why is it so important for you to be friends with me, anyway? Are you on some racial guilt trip you're trying to get over by hanging out with me?"

"How dare you try to turn this around on me!"

"It's the truth, isn't it?!" he shot back at her. "You're trying to prove how unprejudiced you are by hanging out with a black man?!"

Irene looked shocked, then hurt. "No, Eugene. I thought I was hanging out with a nice, intelligent person. I thought I had a friendship with someone I had something in common with. I can see how wrong I was."

Eugene was past feelings now. It didn't matter anymore. He had taken care of the hard part—the rest was just a matter of words. He looked her squarely in the eye, knowing that his next words would cut deeply. "How can we possibly have anything in common?" he asked quietly.

Irene straightened up quickly, as if a hot poker had been pushed between her shoulder blades. "I guess we don't," she told him, snatching her book bag from the bench and flinging it over her shoulder. Eugene saw her hand swipe at her eyes as she marched away from him. She never looked back.

He inhaled deeply, and then exhaled with a force. He dropped his head into his hands and sat there, listening to the four o'clock bell. He was tired. He was just so doggone tired.

MARIE

Quite honestly, Marie was happy to be back at school after the holidays. It seemed like her family kept harping on why she and Claudia weren't roommates anymore. It was easy to distract them when they bugged her over the phone at school. She could always make up some convenient excuse that she had to study, her roommate had to use the phone, she didn't want to run the phone bill up, but when she got home in December after mid-terms, her family was right back at it.

"Well, what happened, Marie?" her mother would ask. "Why did you move out?"

Marie would have loved to talk to her mother about the whole thing, but they didn't have that type of mother-daughter relationship. "We just had a difference of opinion, Momma," Marie told her.

"Oh, please...and it took you to moving out?" her mother responded, just like Marie thought she would. "Ya'll young girls can be so silly at times."

At least Mrs. Steeleton let it go at that. Rolanda, on the other hand, had to take things to another level.

"Did ya'll have a fight or something?" she wanted to know. "Why did you move out?"

"Because I wanted to that's why. Mind your own business," Marie snapped at her.

But Rolanda loved to get Marie riled up. "You must've said something you had no business saying. You know you got too much mouth, anyway."

"I know you ain't talking about somebody running their mouth, Rolanda." Normally, Marie would ignore her pesky older sister, but she was still seething over the Claudia thing so it didn't take much to get her going. They went back and forth until her mother entered the scene, and both knew to shut up, no matter who had started what.

At least she got some reprieve from Davette, who was supportive of her little sister.

"Is it a better situation for you?" Davette asked her. Davette had done community college and was working on getting her own place. She was working at a bank downtown. Marie was happy for her, but secretly did not want her only support system in the household to go,

140

even though she was twenty-four and it was time for her to leave the nest.

"I think so," Marie told her.

"What happened?"

Marie shrugged. Even with Davette, she didn't want to go into detail about the whole, painful event. "It was over some guy," she told her.

"Marie, you don't have to tell me about it unless you want to, but let me tell you something from personal experience—don't ever let a man come between you and a true friend."

The brightest spot in Marie's time off was being able to spend time with her dad, whom she adored. She'd always secretly hoped that her mom and dad would get back together, even though she had no idea what split them up in the first place, and barely remembered when they were together, she was so young. Davette was the only one old enough to clearly remember when her parents did live in the same house, but all she would tell Rolanda and Marie was that they just argued a lot, and one day dad moved out. Her mother kept the married name, Steeleton, which gave Marie hope that perhaps she didn't want to completely dissolve the marriage—they weren't even legally divorced after fifteen years apart.

Marie loved her father's sense of humor. He was always ready with a corny joke, or an oddball story—especially about his girls. He wouldn't talk about the break up, just like Marie's mother, but whenever his youngest would ask him about coming back to live with them, he would give her a hug and tell her, "It's not that simple, baby girl."

She definitely took after her father in the looks department, something her mother reminded her of often. "If you ain't the spittin' image of your daddy, I ain't standing here," her mother was fond of saying. Her father was tall and chocolate brown, with the prettiest white teeth Marie had ever seen on a man. It's probably why she was so hung up on Cedric's million-dollar smile.

She also loved her father's affirmation of her. She could always count on him to say something positive about her looks—especially since she looked so much like him. "Here comes my black beauty queen," he would declare every time he saw her, or "How's my chocolate princess?" Marie always suspected that if it wasn't for his positive strokes, her self-esteem would probably be as low as

Claudia's—at least, the way Claudia's used to be. Her father didn't harp too much on why she and Claudia weren't roommates—he just told her he hoped everything worked out for them.

Marie's new roomie was Corrie Fletcher. She was quiet, at first, but very polite. Corrie's first roommate decided to go home after only two months at Hamel, and left a space open for Marie, who really didn't want to move to another floor. She later found out that Claudia opted to keep their old room to herself, and shell out the extra fee for a single. She could afford it—her parents weren't hurting for money.

Corrie was from Florida. Her father owned a large car dealership, but had insisted that all four of his children work if they wanted spending money. Marie gathered that much from the snippets of conversation they had the first couple of weeks she was there. Corrie didn't volunteer much, but at least she didn't act like Marie was going to rob her, which had been her biggest concern with having a white roommate.

Marie could tell that Corrie wasn't used to black people. She would catch her staring occasionally, especially when Marie was doing her hair or putting on makeup. And after Christmas break, she finally worked up enough nerve to talk to her. Marie was putting her hairdresser's bag back in place and Corrie was coming in from the shower, dressed in a big fluffy robe, rubbing her wet head with a towel. Marie had just finished another head on the tenth floor and was preparing to study for her first test of the semester, and Corrie was getting ready for a sorority rush party.

Marie smiled at Corrie when she walked in. "Hi, Corrie. Getting ready for your party?"

"Yeah, and I've got plenty of time. I just need to give myself some time to relax. I'm pretty nervous." Corrie returned her shower basket to her closet.

"That's a pretty outfit you're wearing." Marie pointed to Corrie's bed, where she had her clothes laid out and ready. A roomie after Marie's own heart.

Corrie smiled brightly. "Thanks! You can borrow it anytime." She looked surprised to hear the words coming out of her mouth. Marie was just as surprised to hear it.

"Well, uh—thanks. I appreciate that."

That seemed to open up a reservoir for Corrie. "I'm serious. Anytime you want to borrow or use anything of mine, feel free. I don't mind."

"That's really nice of you, Corrie. The same goes for me." Marie didn't have as much materially as her new roomie, but felt she should return the favor. Even though her mother advised her never to borrow other people's clothes, something she constantly did with Claudia, Marie thought she just might take Corrie up on her offer. That outfit was pretty fly.

Corrie sat on her bed and looked at Marie. "Marie, can I ask you something personal?"

Well, it was about time. "Sure." Marie put her Biology book down with glee.

Corrie appeared to be searching for just the right words. "Why...why don't you wash your hair everyday?"

Marie was shocked, then she wanted to laugh. Is that what Corrie had been wondering for the past month or so? Corrie immediately turned a light shade of red, so Marie stifled her laugh into a smile.

"I'm sorry, Marie..."

"No, no—it's o.k." At least Corrie was bold enough to ask. Quite honestly, there were some things Marie wanted to ask her about. "A lot of black women don't have to wash their hair but once a week, or even every two weeks—it just depends on the person, Marie told her as Corrie's complexion returned to a normal peaches and cream.. "See, our hair has a tendency to be dry, and washing it everyday would strip all of the moisture out of it."

"Oh," Corrie nodded, like she'd just discovered the answer to an ancient riddle. "I've always wanted to know that. I wish I could go that long without washing this stuff." She pulled up a section of her long, brown hair that hung straight down her back, even when it was dry. Marie had never attempted Caucasian hair, but she longed to throw a style on Corrie that would enhance her face better. Her practically self-trained eye told her that if Corrie lost some of her length, she could get some body out of her hair.

"Well, Corrie, let me turn the question back on you—why do you wash yours everyday?"

Corrie opened her mouth to answer, but then hesitated. "I don't know. I really never thought about it—I've just always done it. I thought everyone did. I guess if I didn't, it would get real stringy and greasy. And the smell's not that great, either." Corrie laughed at herself, and Marie joined in. It was very refreshing to have this type of exchange without anyone taking an offense.

Corrie was ready for a real tell-all session then. She sat back further on her bed and folded her legs under her. "How in the world do you get your hair into so many different styles? You hardly ever look the same."

Marie sat back herself. "I learned to do different thing to it when I was in high school. I guess it just holds styles well."

"Well, it looks great all the time, really." Corrie sighed. "I wish I could do something different to mine."

That was Marie's in. "You ever thought about cutting it?"

"With hedge clippers," Corrie declared, sounding disgusted. Marie was beginning to think she had some personality after all. "It's such a headache, washing and drying it everyday. It takes me forever."

"Why don't you get it cut? I think it would look cute, cut to your shoulders in a bob."

"You think?"

"Yeah. You've got big, pretty eyes—you need to show them off."

Her new roomie brightened visibly. Apparently, no one had ever clued her in to her eyes, and how the right hairstyle would set them off. Corrie was a little like Claudia in her personal maintenance. She wore very little to no makeup, and wore her hair in two basic styles— up in a ponytail or straight down. She was an attractive girl, Marie thought. She always thought the combination of dark hair and blue or green eyes was so pretty. Then, Corrie totally blew her out of the water.

"Can you cut it for me?"

"Huh?!"

"My hair—can you cut it for me?"

Marie looked at Corrie like she didn't understand English. "Well—yes, I guess. I can cut it for you."

"Great! Where do you want me to sit?"

"You want me to cut it *now?!*"

"Unless you're busy. I'm sorry—you were trying to study, weren't you?"

"No, no...that's o.k. I'll cut it now. Just uh, have a seat over here at my desk." Marie felt a surge of excitement. Sometimes, she felt like she wanted to just do hair for a living and forget about her lifetime ambition as a lawyer. Corrie settled in Marie's chair, while Marie drug her bag out again and assembled her equipment on the desk. A lot of things had come from Jerlene, who took a great amount of pride in being Marie's first teacher in hair care. She carefully raked through Corrie's wet strands, took a deep breath, and cut her long hair up to her shoulders.

Unlike Claudia, Corrie didn't flinch. She sat contently, jabbering away about the pledge party and how much she wanted to get into Delta Rho Sorority. "I really hope they pick me," she gushed.

"You mean you have to be picked? That's all there is to it?" Marie asked in disbelief.

"Well, yes. Isn't that the way it works with bla…"

Marie patted Corrie's shoulder in reassurance. "It's o.k., Corrie. How else are you going to describe it? But no, I don't think black sororities work that way, from what I understand. I haven't been through the process yet."

"Oh, are you thinking about rushing?"

"Rushing with what?" Marie thought she meant her hair. Then it hit her. "Oh, you mean pledging?"

"Yeah."

"I thought about it. There's an interest meeting next week. I may go." Marie clipped contently, working on evening up Corrie's edges. Corrie's hair was thicker than she thought, which was wonderful. That bob style was sure to be a winner with her thickness.

"Do you have any setting lotion and rollers, Corrie?" Marie asked, not sure if Corrie wanted to use her stuff, even though she washed her rollers thoroughly every time she used them.

Corrie got her setting lotion, but told Marie she didn't use rollers. "You don't have enough of your own?" she asked, indicating the various sizes of rollers on Marie's desk.

"Well, no…I've got plenty. I just thought—never mind. I've got enough."

"Oh." Corrie settled backed and picked up where she left off in her conversation. Marie rolled her hair on her biggest rods, and held a vanity mirror for Corrie so she could apply her makeup while she was under the dryer. Marie advised her to add just a "tad" more makeup than she was used to wearing for this occasion, and Corrie, again, did not question her advice. Marie felt that was part of what made her a

145

good leader—she had an uncanny ability to generate people's trust in her and her decisions. By the time Marie took Corrie's hair down and worked her loose curls through with her fingers, Corrie looked like a different person. She didn't want to look at herself in the mirror until she got dressed and could experience the full effect. Marie couldn't help but be awed by her handiwork. Corrie looked terrific, in her opinion.

Just as her roommate was getting dressed and ready to look, her friends who were rushing with her, Amanda and Chrissy, were knocking on the door and peeking their heads in. They took one look at Corrie and both mouths dropped open. They stared at their friend like they'd never seen her before. Marie's heart shot to her throat. Had she messed up Corrie's hair? Maybe she should have just let it be—told Corrie to let a professional do it. It was her fault, trying to be a jack of all trades, thinking she had no limitations on what she could do…

"Corrie, you look terrific!" Chrissy or Amanda squealed. They both approached Corrie and took a slow tour around her head. Amanda or Chrissy reached out to touch it.

"You look so *good*!! I *love* this on you!!"

Corrie beamed, and then squealed along with them when she went to the mirror to see it for herself. They went into a couple of rounds of cooing over her hair, and one of them asked, "Who did it?!"

"My roommate," Corrie announced proudly, as if Marie were a great secret she alone had uncovered. "She did just a little while ago."

Amanda and Chrissy stared wide-eyed at Marie. They looked at Corrie, who nodded in confirmation, then turned their big eyes on Marie again. She could almost read their thoughts. They didn't know a black person could do white hair and make it look so good.

They marched around Corrie's hair once more and came over to where Marie was sitting on her bed. "You did a great job. Fantastic."

"Thank you."

"She doesn't even look the same. Does she Chrissy?" Chrissy, who had straight strawberry blond hair and looked like a bubbly little cheerleader, nodded. Amanda was obviously the other one. She was slightly pudgy, and had rather plain brown hair that hung to her shoulders. Tonight, she had it sprayed or moussed into a style that was probably meant to add volume. It looked kind of wild, instead. Marie itched to get into it.

146

"Come on guys. Let's go or we'll be late." Corrie picked up her purse and headed out the door with her friends. She came back in almost immediately.

"Marie, thank you sooo much," she said, leaning to give her a warm hug. "It looks great!" She opened her purse. "How much do I owe you?"

Marie waved her off. "It's on the house for roommates."

Corrie was shaking her head. "No—I want to give you something." She reached into her purse and pulled out a twenty—twice as much as Marie normally charged.

"Corrie, that's too much..."

"I don't care. You deserve it." She forced the bill into Marie's hand and looked toward the open door. "They'll probably try to get me to ask you about doing their hair—just wait and see," she whispered. She gave her a big smile, shook her bouncy new hair, and left.

Marie sat back, looking at her hands like they didn't belong to her. Twenty dollars! Wait until she told Claud...oh—there was no best friend to share her successes with anymore. No Claudia to tell secrets, laugh or go to lunch with. That part of her life was over with, she thought sadly. Then she toughened up. Claudia had made her choice. She had chosen Cedric over the friendship, and there was nothing Marie could do about it, except go on with life as it was.

The next day, she got a call from Amanda, who rather cautiously asked if Marie would do her hair. Marie said yes without thinking. Then, Chrissy asked if there was anything Marie could do with her hair to make it more perky. Marie did. She told her she needed it cut short above her ears to make her small features more prominent. Chrissy went to a professional, but she was so thankful to Marie anyone would have thought Marie did it herself. The next thing Marie knew, her weekends were filled with studying and hair care for both black and white, which filled both her pockets and her social calendar, but not the empty feeling on the inside. She was hurting from both her dissolved friendship and the reason it dissolved—the void the situations left was almost unbearable at times.

Michele R. Leverett

PERCY

Percy lugged his suitcases up the sidewalk as the bus pulled off. It had been a long, three hour ride home, but he was anxious to leave campus with its different issues and he also wanted to surprise his mother, who was all set to pick him up from the bus station later that evening. The station was only about a mile from his neighborhood, so it wouldn't be that bad of a walk, even if it was seriously cold outside. He passed the post office and Dell's Grocery as he neared his home. He sat his luggage down for a minute and looked around. No—nothing much had changed in four and half months. Same old ragged neighborhood, with the same old houses. As he walked toward his rented home, he wondered if the heat was out again, or if his mother was running the kerosene heater while she waited for the maintenance man to come in on his camel caravan from Timbuktu to fix it.

Percy neared his house, wrapping his scarf tighter around his neck to keep the wind from biting his face. During the summer, he would most likely hear the continuous pounding of a rap tune shooting out of several windows and cars, and the sidewalk and porches of the neighborhood would be littered with all types of colorful people. But in the winter, it was quiet, for the most part. An occasional drunk would go stumbling down the street, cursing at an invisible companion, but the only person out in the cold weather today was Ms. Cleo from two houses down, sitting in a chair on her porch like she did everyday.

"Hi, Ms. Cleo," Percy greeted as he climbed her stairs.

"Percy, how you doin', baby?" she replied, with a smile full of motherly warmth and love. She was a little younger than his mother, who would only tell Percy that she was "a fabulous forty-something and lovin' it" when he asked her age, but Ms. Cleo appeared to be so much older. She held her arms up so Percy could hug her. "You home from college?"

"Yes ma'am. I'm home for Christmas break."

She nodded. "That's precious, baby. I know Evelyn's proud of you."

"Yes ma'am."

Ms. Cleo smiled at him again, then her eyes became troubled as she looked anxiously down the street toward Dell's Grocery. "Percy, did you happen to see Jarrod anywhere?"

Percy shuffled his feet, uncomfortable. "No ma'am, I didn't."

"I sent him to the store a little while ago for some brown sugar and a jar of molasses so I could make him a pecan pie. He should be back by now."

Percy cleared his throat and studied his shoes.

"Well, I guess he'll be back shortly. You know how you young boys like to hang out somewhere, talking to some girls or shooting some ball."

"Yes ma'am."

"Go on in and see your momma, boy. Come by when you can. Jarrod thinks so much of you."

"Uh, Ms. Cleo? Wouldn't you be a lot warmer inside?" Ms. Cleo didn't have on much in the way of a coat—just a thick sweater that she had pulled tightly around her, and a scarf on her head.

She waved him off. "I'm fine, Percy. This cold don't bother me. I just want to make sure Jarrod gets here all right. There's been a lot of bad things happening around here lately. You go on—don't worry about me."

Percy gave her another hug, then retrieved his luggage from the bottom of the stairs and walked toward his house. He stole one last look over his shoulder at Ms. Cleo, who was perched on the edge of her chair, looking down the street toward Dell's again.

The door to his house was partially open, and Percy could hear the soft tones of a gospel song playing somewhere in the back and his mother singing along with it. He tiptoed in the house, slid out of his coat and looked around. The Christmas tree was up and decorated, standing in its usual spot right in front of the window where everyone could see it. Mrs. Lyles found a brass baker's rack at a yard sale and put it in the living room to display family pictures, plants and a stereo system—she had her three, hand-knitted stockings for each of her children fastened to it. Percy loved Christmas at his house, even after his father left, it was a time that his whole family got together, Monica came home, and they all enjoyed each other.

His mother was in the kitchen, judging from where the tangy, delicious smells teasing his nostrils were wafting out. As quick and as quiet as a cat, he made his way past the living room into the kitchen

149

and grabbed his mother around her waist, swinging her up in the air. She screamed in surprise and the pack of flour she had in her hand went flying. Percy laughed at her terrified expression when he finally put her down.

"Boy...what in the world...have you lost your mind...I'm gonna..."

"Hi Ma." He greeted, as if he had done nothing wrong. His mother looked like she wanted to go upside his head. Her hair was flying every which way. She narrowed her eyes up at him a minute, then reluctantly smiled.

"Don't you ever sneak up on me like that again, boy!" She scolded him as she grabbed him in a hearty hug. "What are you doing home so early? I wasn't expecting you until later on. How'd you get home from the bus station?"

"I caught an early bus, and I walked," Percy explained, looking in the cabinets for something to snack on. "My roommate dropped me off at the station on his way home." Percy found some of his favorite breakfast cereal and fixed himself a bowl, sitting down at the table.

"Percy, you mean you walked from the bus station with your bags? It's a wonder you weren't mugged on the way. What have I told you about being safe?"

"Ma, what have I told *you* about leaving the door open so anyone could walk in when me and Paul are gone?" he retaliated in a respectful but firm voice.

His mother looked playfully shocked as she put her hands on her hips. "And how do you know that Paul is not here, smarty?"

Percy just looked at her and twisted his lips.

She nodded. "O.k., son. You're right. I'll work on mine, and you work on yours."

"Sounds fair." He shoved a spoonful of cereal in his mouth. "I saw Ms. Cleo outside," he told his mother, his mouth full.

Evelyn sighed heavily, shaking her head and lifting her arms toward the ceiling. "Lord, please heal that poor woman's heart. Help her, Father. She ain't been the same since Jarrod got killed."

"No, I guess not." Percy was always saddened when he thought about Ms. Cleo and her family. She had lived down the street with her husband and her only child, Jarrod, who was two years younger than Percy, on the quiet side and an excellent student. He had wanted to befriend Percy back before he died, but Percy had his crowd of homies who were the exact opposite of Jarrod.

Four years ago, Ms. Cleo had sent Jarrod to Dell's for a jar of molasses and some brown sugar to make him a pecan pie. Two hours later, police were outside of Ms. Cleo's door with Jarrod's baseball cap. Jarrod was on his way home with the groceries when two boys burst out of the gas station next door, failing in their attempt to rob it because the cashier had pulled a gun on them. Eye witnesses said that one gunman bumped into Jarrod on the way out, and then just shot him when they were scrambling to get off of the ground and kept running. Jarrod died in the hospital the next day. Ms. Cleo had a nervous breakdown, then went into a state of denial after the funeral. Unable to deal with his wife's detachment from reality and his only child's death, Mr. Cleo left, but, from what Percy's mother had told him, continued to pay for his wife's living expenses. In Percy's estimation, Mr. Cleo was not better than his father and a lot of other black men in his neighborhood—when the going got tough, they got going. His mother frequently checked on her, making sure she had food, sometimes shopping for her, and persuading her to go in from the cold on her many lookouts. Other neighbors shied away, chalking Ms. Cleo up as just another sad oddity in Jackson Park.

Shortly after Ms. Cleo started her porch watches, Percy's mother sat down with Percy and Paul and told them they would show the utmost respect for Ms. Cleo, despite her ill state. They would not, she told them, make fun of her or refuse to help her if she needed it. "The Lord loves Ms. Cleo just as much as He does anyone else," she told them sternly. "And no matter what, you *will* treat her with respect, or you'll have me to deal with."

"Did you take her inside?" his mother was asking, getting the broom and dustpan out of the closet to sweep up the mess of flour that had landed in a white heap beside the stove.

"I asked her if she wanted to go in—she said she was all right. I'll get that, Ma."

His mother looked at him impatiently. "Percy, you know she's not all right. It's cold outside. You have to take her in when you see her out like that—she'll catch cold. I guess I'll have to do it myself. The poor child probably hasn't eaten today, either. I'll go down and see if I can fix her something."

"Hey Ma...didn't you say she had family somewhere down South?" Percy asked, sweeping up the mess he had caused his mother to make.

"I believe her people live in North Carolina."

"Why don't they come get her or something? Don't they know she's sick?"

His mother snorted. "They know. And they got the money to keep her, too. All they have to do is come get the woman and..." She stopped mid-sentence, looking like she had just committed a crime. She dropped her head. "Lord, please forgive me for putting my mouth against Marilyn's family. I'm so sorry."

"What? It's the truth, isn't it?" Percy asked. Sometimes his mother's rigid beliefs exasperated him. She'd always get an inconvenient conviction right in the middle of a conversation.

"Percy, you know what the Word says about that. I can't teach you children to follow the Bible if I'm not doing it myself."

Percy decided to change the subject before his mother got going on that. "When's Monica coming home?"

"She called and said her flight would be in on Saturday." Evelyn washed her hands in the sink and dried them on her way out of the kitchen. "Let me go get this girl in from the cold."

Percy followed her, grabbing his coat from in front of the front door where he'd parked it. His mother grabbed hers from the hall closet, muttering in her strange prayer language. Percy made sure he shut and locked the front door after them. When they got to Ms. Cleo's, she was standing on her porch in front of her chair. She smiled and sat back down when she saw Percy and his mother.

"Wooo, Marilyn...it's getting a little cold out here, isn't it?" Evelyn commented, climbing up the steps to give her a hug. "Don't you think you'd better go on in the house?"

"Well, I wanted to wait for Jarrod to come home," Ms. Cleo explained. "I thought I just saw him down the street."

Percy and his mother threw each other a concerned glance. She had never talked about actually seeing her dead son before. She must be getting worse. "Marilyn, why don't you come on in?" Mrs. Lyles coaxed patiently. "Have you eaten? Let me get you something to eat."

"Evelyn—you don't have to..."

"No, I insist. Percy…" Mrs. Lyles reached into her coat pocket and pulled out some folded up bills. "Run down to Dell's and get Ms. Cleo a hot plate. You want pork or chicken, Marilyn?"

"Pork is fine."

"Make sure you get some cornbread, too. Go on."

Percy took the money and headed down the steps.

"Aren't you proud of him, Evelyn?" Ms. Cleo asked, reverting back to her sane mode that Percy always found so eerie.

"Yes, my baby is making me proud. He got a scholarship and everything."

"Oh, is that right? Well, you are smart, aren't you Percy?" Ms. Cleo and his mother smiled down at him, pride showing all over their faces. Percy felt a little bashful and checked the steps under his feet for cracks.

"Percy, make sure you get her some ice tea with lemon," Mrs. Lyles told him.

"Yes ma'am."

"And Percy?" This was Ms. Cleo's voice stopping him.

"Yes ma'am?"

"If you see Jarrod, tell him to hurry up and come home."

When Percy opened the front door to Dell's grocery, he was immediately enveloped in vise grip. He looked down, and Mr. Dell's wife, Rose, was squeezing him with as much strength as her petite, short stature could muster.

"Hi, Sugarplum!" she greeted him, lowering his face to plant a juicy kiss on his cheek. "I didn't know you were coming home today!"

"Hello, Mrs. Dell," he smiled down at her. Mrs. Dell, with her bouncy, motherly self, meant just as much to Percy as her husband did. She treated all of the workers like her children, down to a serious threat of "slapping the fool" out of them if they got out of line. Because the last of her five grown children were finally out of the house, Mrs. Dell came in three days a week to supervise the hot bar.

"What's up, Percy?" One of the bag boys, Stanley, stepped away from his counter and grabbed Percy's hand in a grip. "What's goin' on, man?"

"Ah, man. Nothin' much, nothin' much. Just tryin' to do what I gotta do, yo."

"I hear that. Good to see you, man. Keep up the good work."

Several of the other cashiers and bag boys stopped their work for a moment to greet him. He had practically spent most of his teenage years with them, and they were like a second family. As far as he knew, he was the only one who had made a decision to leave for college, and everyone was extremely proud of him.

Mrs. Dell playfully ordered everyone to get back to work. "You act like the boy's been away for years!" She scolded, before turning back to him. "You're looking good, Percy! How's school? Boy, I am so proud of you!!"

"Thank you. School's fine. Just a lot of work."

"You can do it, honey. Just stay on top of things and don't go out partying or hanging out with a bunch of hoodlum friends who ain't serious. Keep your grades up, Percy. I'll slap the fool out you if you don't."

Percy chuckled. "Yes ma'am."

"You here to see Oscar? He's in the back."

"Yes, ma'am. But I also need to get a plate for Ms. Cleo."

Mrs. Dell, looped her arm in his and led him toward the hot bar in the back of the store. "How's she doing?"

"About the same. "Ma's with her right now."

"Good, good. I need to make my way over to see her this week myself. How's Evelyn doing?"

"She's doing good."

The Dell's hot bar was in the back corner of the store, right next to the meat counter and Mr. Dell's office. Anita, the Dells' oldest granddaughter, was behind the partition, ringing up a customer's order. She smiled widely when she saw her grandmother and Percy approach.

"Hi, Percy," she grinned, flashing a row of gleaming silver braces at him.

"Hi, Anita. You heard anything from Johns Hopkins yet?"

"Yeah, I got in!"

"Congratulations!" Anita was a year younger than Percy, but her parents enrolled her in a private school about thirty minutes away from Jackson Park. She had applied to a few medical schools, but had a strong desire to attend Johns Hopkins in Baltimore. The girl was a walking brain cell, in Percy's opinion. She also had a tremendous crush on him, but Percy just let it slide. It wasn't that she was unattractive or anything because she was cute, but he'd just always thought of her as a younger female relative. Nothing more.

"Nita, Percy needs a plate for Ms. Cleo. What's she want, baby? Barbecued ribs or baked chicken?"

"Ribs, please."

"You want anything?"

"No, ma'am. I need some ice tea with lemon, though."

"Nita, fix Ms. Cleo a rib plate with some green beans and macaroni and cheese, and fix Percy a chicken plate."

"No, Mrs. Dell. I'm fine…."

"Just hush, Percy. The chicken's real good today." Mrs. Dell waited while her granddaughter fixed the plates and set them at the register, then she waved Percy's hand away when he pulled out his mother's money. "Come on in and say hello to Oscar right quick so the food doesn't get cold."

"Bye, Percy," Nita grinned at him. "I'll leave my address with my grandparents when I find out where I'm staying."

"Girl, quit flirting with this boy and work!" her grandmother told her.

Mr. Dell was on the phone when Percy walked in his office with his wife. He smiled broadly, and told whoever it was he'd call them back. "One of my sons just walked in, home from college," he told the caller, and Percy couldn't help but grin. *Good ole' Mr. Dell.*

"Boy, how ya' doin?!" Mr. Dell came over and gave him a hearty hug pound on the back. Man, was he heavy-handed. "What cha know good?"

"I'm good, Mr. Dell. How are you?"

"Slick as ever, son. You know me. Have a seat, have a seat. Tell me about school."

"Oscar, he's got to get Ms. Cleo her dinner. You know how you can be," his wife told him.

"Baby, we've got this, now," he waved playfully at her. When she left, he rolled his eyes. "Son, let me tell you something—before you put a ring on a woman's finger, you better be prepared to have two mothers running around."

Percy chuckled, knowing full well that even though Mr. Dell complained constantly about his wife being a mother hen or "bossy" as he put it, he adored her.

"How's school goin'?"

"Oh, it's all right. I don't get into my major classes until next semester—I'm just taking my goal courses right now."

"So no business courses yet?"

"Not yet."

"That's all right—you'll be ready when they come." Mr. Dell had shown Percy quite a bit about running the store—he was the reason Percy decided to major in business in the first place. "So how is it goin' to a white school? Is it as bad as you thought?"

"Well—yes and no. The classes are all right and my roommate's cool, but we did have some race trouble already on campus."

"Get out! What happened?"

So Percy told Mr. Dell about the Plot, about the Tri-AC, about the upcoming trial.

Mr. Dell was shaking his head. "Sometimes I can't believe that we have that kind of ignorance in this day and time. Back in my day racism was right out in the open like that... Well—don't let what happened break you, Percy. You keep on keepin' on. And you be careful with this group you're in, too."

"They're cool, Mr. Dell. They're positive."

"Still, when it comes down to race relations, even 'positive' groups can make the wrong decisions—I saw it in my day many, many times. You just be careful—look out for number one."

"Yes sir."

"How's your family."

"They're good. Monica should be home Saturday."

"Oh yeah? Good, good. Your brother just turned sixteen, right?"

"In October. October 7."

"I thought so. I told him to come see me when he turned sixteen so I could put him on here at the store. He said he was coming. Everytime I see him he tells me he's coming. Boy hadn't been in here yet."

"I'll talk to him." And Percy was going to make good on that, too. His mother was big on her children keeping their word—if you're tell someone you're going to do something, you had better do it. Percy was a little surprised at Paul—he was usual very dependable.

"Well don't jump down his throat son," Mr. Dell said. "I offered him a job because I'm a little concerned about him. I've seen him around with some of those boys that ain't up to no good. I just don't

156

want to see him get in any trouble. He's always seem so level-headed."

"He usually is."

"I'm telling you, being around the wrong people can change you. You'll find yourself doing things that you normally wouldn't do. Keep an eye out for him, Percy. I know your momma's working a lot and can't be home all the time, but call and check up on him. I'll keep at him about working for me. Let me handle that part."

"Yes sir," Percy said, thinking that if Mr. Dell told him to quit school and come work for him full-time, he'd probably do it. That's how much respect he had for the man. But he would try to keep in contact with his brother. He didn't want him becoming another statistic in Jackson Park.

"You better get Ms. Cleo her food before Rose comes back in here. Wait a minute, Percy." Percy, who had been standing to leave sat back down. Mr. Dell opened a drawer in his desk and handed Percy a white envelope. "I forgot to give that to you before you left for school. That's a graduation present."

"Thank you, sir," Percy said taking the envelope.

"Go ahead and look—I know you want to."

Percy laughed. The man knew him up and down. He peaked inside and his eyes grew big. There were two, four, no...eight, Good Lord, ten...was he dreaming?!...twenty, crisp, one hundred dollar bills inside. "Mr. Dell...I...wha...." He couldn't speak. His mouth felt dry. His heart was pounding.

Suddenly, Mr. Dell was over his shoulder. "Now that present comes with some stipulations. First, you give the Lord his..."

Yes sir..."

"Then on Monday, you come on down to the store around one o'clock, and you and me are going to the bank so you can open a checking and a savings account. You're old enough to start tracking how you spend your money and saving some for a rainy day. You take out the Lord's portion, put about fifteen-hundred in savings and the rest is for you, however you want to spend it."

"Yes sir. Thank you sir." Percy stood up and grabbed Mr. Dell's hand, pumping it up and down in a hearty handshake.

"Now Percy, I wouldn't do that for everybody, but I see something in you. I saw it since you were a young rascal getting ready to throw a rock in my window..."

157

Percy remembered that day, ten years ago—his first encounter with Oscar Dell. His father had been gone for about a month and Percy was walking past Dell's with three of his homies—Dennis, Domino and Kevin. Percy remembered feeling very frustrated, very angry, very broke. When his father was home, he'd always managed to give his children a small allowance, now his mother said she needed every penny to take care of them and couldn't spare anything.

"I dare you to throw a rock at Dell's," Kevin challenged him. Kevin was a known troublemaker, but he had guts, and Percy couldn't help but admire him.

Then again, he wasn't stupid. "Man, you crazy. I ain't gettin' in no trouble. I ain't throwin' no rock," he told Kevin.

"Aww, you just chicken," Kevin laughed at him, Domino and Dennis joining in.

"Nah, I just ain't stupid. You do it."

"I would, 'cause I ain't no chicken."

"Well, do it then, Kevin."

Kevin looked around his feet and spotted a chunk of broken sidewalk. He picked it up and hefted it in his hand. He cocked his arm back like he was about to aim it, then reconsidered. "I give you two dollars if you do it."

Percy doubted it. Kevin's situation was just as bad as his, if not worse. His grandmother was raising him and his four brothers and sisters. "Man, you ain't even got no two dollars."

With the hand that wasn't holding the concrete, Kevin reached into his jeans pocket and pulled out two tattered and worn one-dollar bills. Dennis and Domino were practically slobbering over it.

"Dang, Kevin—where you get two dollars from?" they asked.

"None o' yo' bitness." He turned back to Percy. "What cho' goin' do, Percy?"

Percy looked down at the money, and up at the row of small, square windows right above the entrance to Dell's. Mr. Dell had closed the store about an hour ago—at seven o'clock—no one else was around. He couldn't remember the last time he'd had a quarter to spend on himself, let alone two dollars. Before he knew it, he was taking the concrete chunk out of Kevin's hand and backing up to get a good angle. The next thing he knew, he heard rubber flapping on the sidewalk as his three homies took off like a shot. He barely turned his head around to see what had spooked them when he was snatched up

158

in the air, and looking down into two very angry eyes. The concrete slipped from his hand and made a "plunk" sound as it hit the ground, breaking in two pieces.

"Boy, were you goin' to throw a rock in my window?" A very irate Mr. Dell asked, shaking Percy's bony frame.

Percy was beyond scared. He could only breath in short huffs.

Mr. Dell shook him again. "I asked you a question! Were you getting ready to throw a rock at my store?"

"N-no, s-sir," Percy said, tears springing to his eyes.

Mr. Dell shook him again, bringing Percy's face right into his. "You lying to me, boy?"

"It was—it was a piece of s-sidewalk," Percy told him, feeling the tears running down his face.

"You smartin' off to me?!"

Percy, now into full-fledged sobbing, shook his head and pointed down at his feet. Mr. Dell followed with his eyes and saw the broken concrete. To Percy's terror-stricken surprise, Mr. Dell's started to laugh, and placed his little juvenile delinquent back on the ground.

"Well, I guess you told the truth after all—that sure ain't no rock."

Percy just stood there, too scared to move and too emotional to answer.

"Dry up, son, and follow me."

The next thing Percy knew, he was inside the store with Mr. Dell who shoved a broom in his hand. "Sweep up the front here while I get these registers ready for tomorrow. Good thing I decided to come back and take care of this tonight, huh? Otherwise, I might've been paying for some new windows tomorrow." Mr. Dell laughed, but Percy, diligently sweeping, could not find anything to crack a smile about. He swept harder. "All right, that's good enough. Give me back my broom and get out of my store."

Without looking at him, Percy handed back the broom and took off for the door. A heavy hand on his shoulder halted that.

"Aren't you Evelyn Lyle's oldest boy?"

Ah...man! Please don't let his mother find out. Anything but that! "I'm sorry about the window, Mr. Dell..."

"Calm down, son—what's your name?"

"Percy."

"Percy, you mind telling me why you were about to destroy my property?"

Well, the truth had saved him last time. "My friend bet me two dollars."

Mr. Dell frowned down at him, then reached into his pocket, pulling out a roll of bills. He licked his thumb and counted off four dollars. "That's for sweeping my floor," he told Percy, who took the money like it would turn into a snake and bite him. "Don't be scared to take it, Percy. Don't ever be scared to take what you earn by working, not stealing or a stupid bet. Now you go home where you belong and come back here tomorrow. I'll find you something to do around here. Go on, now."

Percy shoved the money deep in his pocket. "Thank you sir. Thank you." He came back the next day and the day after that, until he was sixteen and could work legally as a bag boy.

"It was a piece of sidewalk, Mr. Dell," Percy said softly, laughing as Mr. Dell howled in amusement.

"You are right about that, son! I almost forgot about that!"

"Mr. Dell—I don't know…how to thank you for this…I mean…man, I don't even know what to say…"

Mr. Dell draped an arm around him. "Boy, let me tell you something. You're like a son to me. I feel like I raised you myself. I would do the same for any of my children who were trying to do the right thing. You got a good head on your shoulders and you know how to make good decisions. Don't let me down."

"No sir. Thank you Mr. Dell. I…thank you." Percy zipped the envelope up in his coat pocket and shook Mr. Dell's hand again.

The office door opened. "Oscar, you still have this child in here?" Mrs. Dell scolded. "Please let him get that woman her dinner!"

"We're done, we're done. Percy, I'll see you on Monday."

"I'll be here, Mr. Dell." Percy followed Mrs. Dell to the front of the store, barely hearing her motherly chatter about him wrapping his scarf tight around his neck so the cold wouldn't get to him. Sure, his father had jetted without explanation, but it was like God had blessed him with Mr. Dell to take his place—at least that's the way his mother would explain it. He gave Mrs. Dell another squeeze and headed back to his house, ready to leave the troubles at Hamel behind and feel good around his family. Sometimes Jackson Park wasn't so bad, after all.

EUGENE

Snow was just beginning to fall when Eugene drove up in his driveway. Christmas was just two weeks away, and then he had three weeks of vacation from school to look forward to, or three weeks of dealing with his dear old dad to dread. He parked behind his mother's maroon Buick, noting that his dad's Bronco was gone. Maybe he could get settled in and rested up before he came home. It was almost seven o'clock—his dad was usually home from work by this time, unless he had one of his lodge meetings, which he usually didn't have on Fridays. Chip's car was gone, too—unless he had parked it in the garage.

The house was quiet except for the continual ticking of the grandfather clock in the living room. His mother had found the clock at an antique store before he was born. She had his dad restore the finish on it, and it was her pride and joy. The clock had been ticking for almost twenty-five years without fail. He shook his head, thinking that the clock and his dad's attitude were the two consistent things in the house, if nothing else.

Eugene stopped and looked around. His mother had been hard at work, decorating the house for Christmas. The tall, white tree with blue Christmas balls, lights and garland stood in front of the bay window in the living room. Two huge, blue stockings and two little ones hung from the fireplace mantle in between Christmas cards from previous years. His mom had even found some animated Santa and Mrs. Clauses, who held candles and moved fluidly, grinning like they were on top of the world. The figures were black, of course—his dad had probably seen to that.

"Hey, little bro." Chip's voice caught him off guard from the top of the stairs in the hallway. His brother came down the stairs smiling at him, but his eyes looked tired.

"What's up, Chip? I didn't know you were here. I didn't see your car." He met Chip at the bottom of the steps and gave him the grip. He was learning fast.

"It's in the garage. They're calling for snow this weekend. I'm surprised that you came home to get stranded."

"Ah—I needed a break."

161

"Woo—I was sleeping good, too," Chip said, rubbing his eyes and yawning. He followed Eugene into the living room and flopped down on the couch, stretching out and looking up at his little brother. "So how are you, Genie? Mr. College Student—look at ya."

"All right, I guess." Eugene put his luggage bag down and eased into his dad's La-Z-Boy, pulling up the leg support. His mom desperately wanted him to move the chair downstairs in the den because it was seriously out of place with her plush, dove gray furniture that Chip knew she would kill him over if she found him lounging on it. But his father liked to have his quiet time up in the living room where there was no television.. "Just tired from all that driving. What's been going on here?"

"Nothing much—just work as usual. Except for mom…" Chip interrupted himself, looking like he'd let something slip that he shouldn't have.

"What, mom quit her job?"

"She made some killer meatloaf, Genie. There's some left in the fridge. You don't want to have to fight me for it."

Oh yeah. Eugene immediately got up and headed toward the kitchen. Chip didn't play when it came to his mother's meatloaf. Come to think of it, Chip didn't play when it came to food, period. Eugene was surprised he told him about it, instead of gobbling up what was left for himself. Eugene put a generous portion of it on a plate and stuck it in the microwave, forcing himself not to eat it cold. He set the timer and headed back to the den, where his brother was now sitting up, staring at the floor.

"Chip, did you say mom quit her job?" Eugene asked, licking cold meat loaf sauce from his fingers. Chip continued to stare at the floor, looking more fatigued than when he first came down the stairs.

"So how is Hamlet College?" He asked Eugene, subtly changing the subject.

"It's *Hamel*—Hamel University. It's going o.k., I guess."

"You change your mind about going to a black school?"

"No, and don't you start anything with that, Chip. I'm staying at Hamel. What'd dad do, tell you to lean on me a little?"

Chip laughed. "I know dad's been giving you a hard time. I was just messin' wit ya."

"Yeah, he gave me a hard time in the beginning. He hadn't really been saying too much about it here lately.."

"Probably because he's had other things on his mind," Chip responded, almost to himself.

"What other things?"

Chip just shrugged, and changed the subject again. "So, you got a girl at Hamel?"

Ah—sooner or later, he knew that question would be asked. He thought it would be his dad who would ask first, then immediately try to find out what color she was. Of course, Chip could be just as curious. He was engaged as of two months ago and was walking around on cloud nine. Eugene didn't know how to answer the question. Renee' was interested, but she really wasn't his girlfriend, and probably wouldn't want to be either, not after the way he'd been ducking and dodging her lately. "Maybe I do, maybe I don't."

"Is it *Irene*?"

How'd he know about Irene?! "How'd you know about Irene?!"

"You know mom. She said you had a little friend at school."

"Irene is—well, *was* just a friend."

Chip reclined on the couch again, ready to hear a juicy story. *"Was*? What happened—she wanted to take it a step further?"

"No, nothing like that. We just stopped being friendly. We didn't see eye to eye on some things." He hoped that was a good enough explanation for his nosy brother, because he didn't dare tell him the real reason they weren't friends anymore. Chip might have let that slip to his father, who would have walked around the house singing, "I told you so." He decided to change the subject himself.

"How's Deidra?" Deidra was Chip's fiancée. They had been dating for three years—and now Chip had proposed to her. Eugene felt that at twenty-one, his brother was too young to be engaged, but Chip was as stubborn as an old mule. His parents had finally convinced them to wait a year or two so they could get financially established and finish school. Deidra was getting her RN in nursing at the local community college and Chip was working at a car dealership during the day, and taking classes at the community college at night.

"Oh, she's great, man. I haven't seen her as much lately because she's doing her clinical third shift at the hospital. I'm proud of her, though. She's sticking with it. She said somebody in our family needed to know what to do in case of an emergency."

"You never told me what dad said when you told him you'd gotten engaged."

Chip snickered. "He asked if she was pregnant."

Eugene bit his lip. For the first time, he and his dad were thinking alike. Growing up with Chip, he knew that his brother had been a bit on the irresponsible side when it came to females. He had always been a handsome rascal, and usually had at least three females a week calling the house. That was until his mother put a stop to it, threatening to tell the girls' mothers if they didn't slow their little hot tails down and stop calling her house so much. Then she brought home pamphlets on sexually transmitted diseases and teenage parenthood and told Chip he better not go near the phone until he read every last one and reported accurately to her what each of them said. The phone calls decreased significantly.

Chip must have recognized Eugene's look, because he immediately sat up and frowned. "Don't tell me you were thinking the same thing?!"

"I didn't say anything."

"You don't have to. What, you and dad never heard of being in love?"

"Yeah—you can be in love, Chip. Go ahead—be in love. I just grew up with you, so I know what you used to be like."

"That's not me anymore. I am strictly a one-woman man. Deidra's different than those other girls I used to date. She's a church girl—keeps me in check. She said she absolutely does not engage in premarital activity. Get that, man. She calls it 'premarital activity.' I mean, she won't even say the word. I just do get to hold her hand." Chip leaned back and gazed thoughtfully at the ceiling, and although Eugene heard the story of Deidra at least a thousand times since Chip had been dating her, he leaned back to and let his brother tell it for the thousand and one time. "I tell you, Eugene—Deidra made me respect her. I practically had to lay on a bed of nails to get her to go out with me in the first place."

"That's because of that weak line you gave her. 'Excuse me, but my doctor wrote your name on my prescription for a heartache'—you didn't even know the girl's name yet." Eugene laughed at him.

"Oh, you remember that line?" Chip laughed hard at the memory. "That line got me about five dates in one month—one month. Oh, but your girl immediately told me where I could get off…"

"Did you ever get on that slow boat to China?"

Chip laughed again. "Ah man—I got blessed with this one—that's what mom keeps telling me. I keep telling her that two years isn't too long to wait, especially with Mom being sick..."

Beep! Beep! The microwave screamed from the kitchen, but Eugene wasn't budging. The pieces were starting to fall into place now. His brother looking bothered and tired, the sudden changes of conversation when his mom's name came up...

"All right, Charles—what's really going on?" Eugene demanded, not knowing if his brother heard him over his loud, pounding heart.

"You'd better get your food, Eugene." Chip got up quickly and headed towards the stairs. Eugene jumped up and blocked his way. "Come on, little bro—move." Chip sounded tired again.

"What did you say about mom being sick, Chip?! Is she just not feeling well, or is it something more serious?"

Chip tried to push past him, but Eugene pushed him back. His brother outweighed him by twenty pounds of muscle, but he fell back like a ninety-eight pound weakling.

"Talk to me, man! Is it the flu? A bad cold? What?!" He had raised his voice, but he was already fearing the worst. His mom was the stabilizer in the family, the one who had coached him through the rough times in high school, by telling him he was perfect just the way he was. For something to be wrong with her was not what he wanted to hear.

"I promised Mom I wouldn't say anything." Chip gave up his attempt to move past Eugene and went back to the couch, plopping down hard. "She wants to tell you herself."

Eugene couldn't believe what he was hearing, which was nothing so far. "Tell me *what?!!*"

"Look, calm down and quit yelling—don't you think it's hard on me, too?"

One more vague statement and Eugene was going to put his fist through the wall. As much as Chip liked to run his mouth, this was fine time for him to change his ways. "Chip..." Eugene sat down beside his brother and tried to keep himself calm. He could tell that Chip was very distraught, and he wasn't going to get a thing out of him if he lost control of himself. Chip had dropped his head into his hands. And was that sniffling Eugene heard? "Chip—please tell me what's wrong with Mom. I won't tell her that you told me—please."

Michele R. Leverett

Chip lifted his hands and he did have tears in his eyes. He barely spoke above a whisper. "She's...she's got cancer, Eugene. Ovarian cancer."

Eugene felt something like a sledge hammer smack him in the back of the head. He tried to formulate a question, but nothing came out of his mouth. Chip didn't look like he was kidding this time. He blinked, and tried to ask his brother another question, but just then he heard keys rattling in the kitchen door.

Chip threw him an anxious look. "Don't tell Mom I told you," he warned and Eugene nodded, still in shock. He wondered how he was going to pull off this charade.

"Eugene?" his mom called from the kitchen. She sounded normal, for the most part. Still, he hadn't seen her yet. He envisioned a walking skeleton, but his mom came into the living room, looking as healthy as ever. She smiled and held her arms out to him. "Hello, baby. When did you get in?" She patted his back like she did when he was a child, he held onto her for dear life, feeling like he was going to start bawling at any minute.

His mother gently pulled him back and looked him in the eye. "You know, don't you?"

"Know what, Mom...?"

"Don't lie to me, boy. "I can read my children like a book. And I knew that Chip couldn't keep it to himself." She rolled her eyes over at Chip, who had jumped off the couch and was standing by the stairs, trying to look innocent.

"Mom, he *made* me. I didn't want to..."

"Hush, Charles," she scolded him playfully. You would have never known that she had been diagnosed with a potentially terminal disease.

"Where's dad?" Eugene realized that his father had not made an entrance.

"He's outside, pulling my car in the garage and putting the cover over the Bronco. You know how he is about that truck."

"I keep telling him that cover is going to freeze on the Bronco in this weather," Chip said.

"He's hard headed, just like my boys. Go move your car, Chip, so he can pull the Bronco in the garage." Chip got up and headed to the steps again. "And tell him to come in and see his son, Chip."

166

His mother pulled Eugene into the kitchen and sat him at the small breakfast nook, while she went to the refrigerator and pulled out a carton of milk. That could only mean one thing—she had some fresh baked cookies stashed somewhere. He smiled, reliving childhood memories of sitting in the kitchen with his mother while she pulled out a secret cache of cookies just for him. Sometimes, he would read her one his stories that he had gotten a gold star on, and at other times he would just be there with her, while his brother was out with his father on some manly activity.

His mother went to the pantry and brought out a box of wheat and grain cereal. She reached in the box and pulled out an aluminum foil bundle, which she opened to reveal about a dozen chocolate chip and walnut cookies. Eugene had to smile. Anything to keep the human garbage disposal named Chip from finding them. His mother knew he would never touch anything healthy like wheat and grain cereal on his own.

"I made these about two hours ago," she told him, taking a glass from the cupboard and filling it with milk. She brought it to the table and sat down across from him.

He looked at her in surprise. "You want me to eat all of these?"

"Either that or share them with Chip," she told him, laughing. He really wasn't in the mood to eat, but he couldn't get his thoughts and words together at that moment, anyway. Eugene grabbed a cookie and gobbled, washing it down with milk and keeping his eyes on his mother the entire time.

"Eugene, I was just kidding. Don't you eat all those cookies," she told him, tweaking his nose. She waited until a few more cookies were devoured then she rubbed his hand. "I know you must be feeling confused right now, so why don't you ask me everything that's running through your head."

The cookies that had tasted so good a minute ago now sat like a lump in his stomach. He wasn't sure he wanted to know anything—except that what Chip told him wasn't true.

"Come on, honey," she rubbed his hand briskly. "Ask me what you need to know."

"When did you get cancer, Mom?" He sounded like she had caught it like a cold.

"I went to the doctor last month because I hadn't been feeling well. They ran some tests, and told me I had ovarian cancer," she answered. Plain and simple. No beating around the bush. Heck—she didn't even seem upset about it. He, on the other hand, was terrified. Cancer was something that other people had—not someone in his family. Especially not his mother.

He had to ask; he had to know. "Mom...will you..."

"Live? I plan to." She grabbed a cookie and nibbled thoughtfully. "They're going to remove my ovaries after the holidays. At my age, I don't need them for much, anyway." She laughed, then stopped when Eugene didn't join in. She got up and enveloped him in a hug that smelled like her perfumed dusting powder and fresh baked cookies— a comforting smell he remembered from childhood.

"Now promise me something," she said.

He could feel tears welling up in his eyes. It was only her strength about the whole thing that kept him in check. "What?"

"Promise me you're not going to do something crazy, like drop out of school or even take time off for this. And don't even think about transferring to a school that's closer to home. You stay at Hamel."

He was flabbergasted. "Mom, how can you expect me not to want to be closer?! How can you expect me to concentrate at school while you're sick?!" He pulled angrily out of her embrace and sat there, pouting. "And why did you wait so long to tell me, anyway?"

"Because I knew how you would react."

"Can you blame me?! You just told me you have *cancer*—not the flu. How can you expect me not to be concerned?!" It was like she couldn't see things from his point of view. Everyone knew what was best for him except *him*. His parents, his brother, his peers—he couldn't win.

He got up from the table and stormed down the hall toward the front door, grabbing his coat off the couch where he'd left it. It was freezing outside and the snow was falling steadily, but he needed to clear his head. His father said something to him from the garage, but he didn't even acknowledge that he'd heard him.

When he returned, cold and hungry, his dad and brother were seated in the dining room, while his mother hustled from the kitchen, bringing in steaming plates of food. Eugene stripped off his wet coat and scarf, aiming them at the coat rack but missing the mark badly. He'd get it later—right now, he needed to apologize to his mother for storming out like a child. He couldn't remember the last time he'd gotten upset with her, but the thought of her being ill and not telling him was a hard pill to swallow. He bypassed the dining room and headed straight for the kitchen, where his mother was turning off burners on the stove. He swallowed.

"Mom..."

"Well, you did come back, after all. Go wash your hands and get ready for dinner." She didn't even look up when she spoke to him.

He tried again. "Mom, I wanted to say I'm sorry for..."

"We'll talk about it later, Eugene."

"But..."

"Eugene." His mother finally looked up to face him. "I said we'll talk about it later."

He nodded, and headed to the hallway bathroom to wash his hands. He knew he had hurt her feelings when he walked out. He and his mother had always been able to talk about anything. Still, it was out of character for her to hold a grudge, especially when he was trying to apologize. And the only thing he really needed to apologize for was for walking out—not what he said, because he meant it.

When he came into the dining area, his mother had taken her seat and joined hands with Chip and his father. "Sit down, Eugene," she said. "Chip's getting ready to bless the table."

Chip mumbled out a quick request about blessing the food for nourishment, and then ended it with a barely discernable, "Amen".

"Amen," Eugene and his mother echoed. His dad grunted out something that sounded like "Amen" and begin helping himself to the food. His mom had laid out a spread: roast beef, mashed potatoes, greens, homemade rolls and sweet potato casserole. It seemed like his mother had always spent a lot of time cooking. Once, his dad wanted to hire someone to do the cooking and cleaning, but his mom refused. She told him she wasn't about to let some strange woman come in her house and take over. It had always been Eugene's assumption that his dad wanted to show off to the neighbors. In fact, he would not have been surprised if his dad had a white woman in mind for the job.

The foursome ate in silence for the first few minutes, except for Chip's loud chomping, slurping and other caveman table mannerisms. Eugene's mother frowned at her oldest son, and Eugene poked his brother with his finger.

"What?" Chip asked around a mouthful of mashed potatoes. He sounded annoyed at being interrupted.

"Can you please cut out the sound effects and eat like a normal person?"

"Man, mind your own business. I'm trying to enjoy my dinner."

"Yeah, but you sound like you should be underneath a table somewhere, eating out a bowl with your name on it."

That even got a snicker out of his dad. Chip reached over and thumped Eugene in the back of his head. Eugene stomped on his foot underneath the table.

"All right, you two, all right," his mother said. "Cut that nonsense out. You ought to be ashamed of yourselves, two grown boys at the dinner table, acting like children."

"He started it," Chip complained, sounding like the child his mother had just accused him of being. "I was sitting here minding my business…"

"Chomping like a pig," Eugene finished.

"Why don't you quit worrying about how I eat, Genie? You need to dig in yourself—put some meat on them scrawny bones."

"Look at all that meat on yours. Are you any smarter with it? Muscle head."

Mr. Wright was laughing out loud now. His mother picked up the hand that wasn't holding her fork and slammed it on the table. "I said cut it out!" she practically screamed, to the surprise of everyone. Hazel Wright barely raised her voice—ever. "You two are brothers and you *will* get along. Is that understood?"

"But Mom…" Chip started.

"Don't 'but Mom' me, Charles. You need to learn to eat like a civilized human being."

"Hazel, Hazel—the boys are just having some fun with each other. Lighten up." Raymond Wright winked at Eugene, to Eugene's surprise. Was his dad actually supporting him in something? "They're just being boys."

"Ray, I can't believe you're defending their behavior. You're laughing at this nonsense instead of correcting…"

"Hazel, I think you need to calm down," his dad told her in a low but firm voice. Eugene and Chip glanced at each other, then back down at their plates. Usually, when their parents had a disagreement, they would go to another room and shut the door. This was new. But for once, Eugene agreed with his dad. He and Chip went at it quite often, and rarely were they ever serious, even when they were young.

There were only a couple of times when things got bad, and his parents had to step in to keep them from coming to blows. Besides those isolated incidents, Eugene and Chip had no problems with each other. Maybe it was his mother's condition that was making her so testy.

The family resumed their eating. Dishes were passed and Chip did cut down significantly on the sound effects. Eugene was still marveling over his dad's defense of him. Maybe he was finally accepting Eugene for who he was. Maybe they could finally get along.

And as if to confirm Eugene's thoughts, Mr. Wright asked, "How's school, Eugene?"

"Uh, fine. School is fine." Eugene almost dropped his fork in surprise. Even his mother stopped sulking and turned wide eyes on her husband.

Mr. Wright grinned. "Good. You making good grades, and all that?"

"Well, some classes are tough, but I think I'm doing all right."

"Oh, I'm sure you're doing better than you think, Eugene. You have what it takes."

"Thanks, Dad." Was he actually having this pleasant conversation with his dad? And in front of witnesses?

His mother had completely forgotten her anger by now and grinning widely. Chip nudged Eugene with his elbow as if to say, *See? I told you it would work out.*

"Eugene, did you tell your dad about testing out of your general English classes?" his mother asked proudly, seemingly encouraged by her husband's new attitude. She didn't give her son a chance to answer. "He had to write an essay to test out. Now, he's taking junior and senior level English courses, isn't that right, baby?"

"Mom, I wasn't the only one…"

"You're the only one I care about." She reached across the table to squeeze his hand. If she was upset with him earlier, she wasn't showing it now.

"That's just great, son." His dad told him.

Son?! Eugene blinked, and expected Bill Cosby to be sitting in the chair where his dad had been. No, his dad was still there—Raymond Eldridge Wright. Eugene felt like taking a few gymnastic leaps off the kitchen table, he was so happy. After all these years of never

171

measuring up in his father's eyes, his dad had seemingly settled in his mind that his son was who he was. Maybe his mother's health had something to do with it, he didn't know. Maybe it shocked his father into realizing just how important family was. Well, Eugene made up his mind right then and there that if his father was making an effort to smooth out the rough spots in their relationship, he was going to do the same. Maybe he'd take in ball game or two with his dad, just to show...

"You know, Crowler University has an outstanding English program," his dad said before shoving a forkful of roast beef in his mouth.

Eugene stopped his own fork midway to his mouth, the wheels and cogs in his head doing overtime. Out of the corner of his eye, he could see his brother going into overdrive on his dinner, putting it away like he had to hop on somebody's fire truck.

"I hear they have some pretty good faculty over there," his dad continued. Eugene knew about Crowler. It had a good reputation and it was only about forty-five minutes away in a neighboring city. And like his dad, he had heard about the faculty being extremely skilled. But Crowler was also predominantly black.

"I know the program's supposed to be pretty decent," he responded cautiously, still not wanting to jump to any conclusions.

"Maybe we should check into it, Eugene. I talked to a buddy of mine in Admissions and I think he can get you in with no problems. You probably won't even lose any credit hours on a transfer." His dad leaned back confidently, liked he'd just presented his youngest with the opportunity of a lifetime. "He might be able to arrange a full scholarship for you—save me a few bucks."

"I appreciate the offer dad, but I like the program that Hamel has." The happiness he had felt earlier was rapidly ebbing away. He felt the calm before the storm in the room now.

"Now, listen son—don't be so quick to shoot the idea down. Just think about it some." Mr. Wright leaned forward, about to negotiate. "Crowler is an excellent school. It's private, like Hamel, only not as big. You'll get that individual attention that a larger school can't offer. It's got professors from all over the nation—you can get a variety of new ideas. It's cheaper and it's closer to home. You won't have to be on the highway so much, putting all those miles on your car..."

"That's fine, Dad. But I really don't want..."

"Eugene, keep an open mind about it..."

"My mind is open. I don't want to go to Crowler. I want to stay at Hamel."

His dad's expression was starting to harden. Eugene smelled his old nature coming back. Well, it was nice while it lasted.

"I don't understand you, boy. Here you have the opportunity to go to an excellent school that turns down hundreds each year, has a top notch English department and you're shooting it down to stay at that lily-white institution you're at now." His dad's tone was nasty again—the one Eugene was used to hearing. "What's wrong? You ashamed to be around your own people?"

"Ray, Maybe Eugene just doesn't want to switch schools," his mother cut in hurriedly, trying to defray a confrontation. "Now, can't we have a nice dinner without an argument? Anyone ready for dessert?"

"No thanks, Mom. And you're right—I don't want to switch to a predominantly black school," Eugene said boldly, eyeing his father. "And no, Dad—I am not ashamed to be around black people, but this world is made up of more than just blacks—I don't need to go to a black school to be black—I *am* black."

"Then you need to act like it then," his dad snapped back nastily. "I should think you would want to be a little closer to home, with your mother being ill."

"Ray, that is not fair!" his mother declared, shocked.

"No, don't defend the boy, Hazel. He'd rather stay holed up at that school, under all those snobby white folk, then to be close to his family and his people." His dad emphasized the phrase, *his people*. "This boy has been housed, fed, clothed and educated with black money all his life, but he'd rather spend his time around people that don't care a lick about him. I bet you don't know the first thing about your history, do you boy?! I bet you don't know how many blacks died at the hands of those people you love so much just so you can enjoy the freedom you have now, do you?! Who was the first black man to die in a war, huh?! You know that?!"

"What does it matter, dad?!" Eugene slammed his hand on the table and yelled. "Why do I always have to prove myself to you?! Why do I always have to prove how black I am?!"

"Boy, don't you raise your voice to me!!" His dad stood up and looked down at him. You aren't too old to get knocked on your butt! You will respect me!"

"Then I think I deserve a little respect myself, dad!" Eugene stood up, too. He didn't know where he was getting the guts—or the stupidity—to talk to his father like he was, but he was rolling with it before he lost his nerve. Whatever happened just happened. "For years, all I have heard about what I wasn't doing right—how I needed more black friends, play more sports, get my head out of the books. You've never been satisfied with me the way I am, dad. Never!"

"Maybe that's because you don't really know who you are!" his dad countered.

"Ray, come on..." His mother sounded weary.

"No, I'm not biting my lip about it, Hazel! The boy doesn't know who he is! He's been socialized in the white man's world, and now he thinks that's the way he's supposed to act—*white!*"

"Dad, what in the world is acting white and acting black?! Can you explain that to me?! Why can't I just be acting like who I am?!"

"I'll tell you why." His dad got right up in his face, lowering his voice. "Because you are my son. You were raised by me and your mother—you've never seen one of us kissing up to or buddying with anybody white. We are proud to be who we are—proud. And I'll tell you something else that may come as a shock to you. I don't care how many white schools, white people or white ideas you associate yourself with, you're a black man, they despise you and they aren't going to let you go any further then they want you to go. You're better off sticking with your own people who you can trust."

Eugene was breathing hard. His dad's look challenged him, dared him to say something back. His mom was looking up at them with fear in her eyes, and even Chip had stopped eating and was watching with a cautious interest.

"You know what? I think I'll stick with who I am, Dad. You may not like it, you may not accept it, but you'll have to live with it because like you said—*I am your son*!" Eugene stepped back from his dad and headed out of the dining room, stopping and turning back. "And the first black man to die in a war, which was not technically a war, but a brawl that catapulted into the war, was Crispus Attucks." He had the satisfaction of seeing a look of shock on his dad's face before he turned and headed up to his room.

174

PERCY

Carlos and Darryl stormed out of the Assembly Room, breathing fire. Percy walked slowly behind them, feeling numb. Tamal followed, walking in circles in the hallway and slamming his fist into his palm. The whole court case had been a farce.

The three stony-faced, white student justices sat behind a large mahogany table, placed on the stage in front of the room, microphones and legal pads placed before each. As many black students as humanly possible squeezed themselves into the elevated benches that surrounded the perimeter of the room, looking ready to do battle. Percy had taken Carlos' advice and he and Darryl arrived at least an hour before the trial, and already, a small line was forming outside of Room 7, where the majority of the Student Court cases were heard. Three Lambda Sig members were sitting at a table placed to the right of the justice table, wearing business suits and carrying briefcases. They were the President, Vice President and Dean of Pledges. The other members—the fun guys that were merely obeying the orders of the leaders, were seated in the rows behind the other three, also dressed in suits. They all looked more like Wall Street wizards than vandals.

The President of the fraternity, Randy Something-or-the-Other, spoke on behalf of his brothers. He admitted, solemnly, that what they did was wrong, but in no way was it racially motivated, oh no. The brotherhood of Lambda Sigma did not condone racism. Because of the sinful influence of alcohol that their pledges were under, their mental faculties were "skewed."

And they were not under any order from the Dean of Pledges to perform this act? one justice wanted to know, pen lifted to record his response.

Randy What's-His-Name looked pained at the thought. They were under order to roll the trees and paint some graffiti, but not to target one specific group's property. This comment caused a loud, collective groan from the black students, and a subsequent warning from the justices to keep down the noise.

What about the other damage—the broken structures, the turned over benches, the trash all over the plot? another justice asked after looking up from his notes.

175

Randy dropped his head for a minute, as if he were embarrassed by the whole chain of events. There seemed to be some miscommunication, he explained, and because they had all been drinking so heavily that night, there might have been a careless, yet innocent request for the other, serious damage, and the pledges carried it out. Alcohol, he reminded them, impairs good judgment, and what they and the pledges did was not representative of good judgment. Randy Whatchamacallit continued, nobly stating that there was no excuse for what they did, and that Lambda Sigma was willing to clean up the mess, pay for any damage and offer a formal apology to each and every organization affected by the vandalism, as well as the black student population.

The justice scribbled furiously on their legal pads. Was there anything else they wanted to add? They asked Randy. Randy looked near tears when he concluded that the brothers of Lambda Sigma were willing to do whatever was necessary to restore the racial harmony at Hamel University.

The justices convened for no more than fifteen minutes, and returned to the Assembly Room as solemn faced as ever. On the charge of a racially motivated act of violence, they found the defendants—not guilty. On the charge of vandalism, they found the defendants guilty, with the sanction of three weeks' probation, a formal letter of apology to each organization, and the hope that Lambda Sigma would be true to their word and carry out their offer of personal restitution and cleaning up the Plot.

Case closed.

Half the audience jumped straight up in the air. The campus security officer on hand in the room tensed up, anticipating trouble. The justices and faculty advisors screamed for order. One of the presidents of one of the fraternities went boldly down to the front of the stage, and was immediately shadowed by two campus officers. How could they let Lambda Sigma off so easily when their property was utterly destroyed? he asked in a loud angry voice that managed to quiet the crowd. Structures would have to be rebuilt, trees would have to be replanted—all of those things required money. And there was no guarantee that Lambda Sigma would carry out the restitution without a legal order.

The justices understood that, but it was not in their legal power to order a fraternity to make any type of financial compensation. That was the Interfraternity Council's jurisdiction.

But how could the justices ignore the fact that the Plot was the only property destroyed? The surrounding area was untouched. This question came from a BSA board member who joined the president at the stage. There was a collective, loud affirmation from the audience. The Lambda Sigma members looked for a side exit.

The justice believed that the pledges did not purposely target the Plot. It was the closest property to the Lambda Sigma house, and was far enough away from the population that it would not cause a disturbance.

That wasn't satisfactory to the audience. What about indefinite probation? Suspension? Cultural awareness seminars? Something?

The justices grimaced. One leaned forward into her mike. They had rendered justice as they saw fit, and they were not going to retry the case, she stated firmly. The advisors in the room winced and dropped shaking heads, feeling that was a wrong move for the justices. But, like all faculty advisors should, they were there to oversee, not take over.

Case closed. Again. The justices rose from their seats and started to leave. The audience, who had never really sat back down, stormed out after them, angry and confused. Those who happened to still be sitting looked in disbelief around the room, then slammed out. Lambda Sigma stayed where they were until the room was clear, then hightailed it out of there followed by campus police. Carlos, who was usually so cool, calm and collected, was furiously pacing up and down the small hallway. Darryl tried to talk to him, but he waved him off. Darryl then walked over to Percy, who was trying hard not to snatch the first white justice or Lambda Sig member he saw and drill a hole through them with his fist.

Darryl was livid. He was about to express his opinion when Carlos flew by and tapped him on the shoulder, indicating for the two of them to follow him. They went down the hall through the angry crowd of students, rounded the corner and into their office. Carlos slammed the door and continued his pacing. Outside, the crowd was getting louder. Percy could hear the advisor and the campus police asking everyone to vacate the area. A female voice shouted back that they had just as much right in the Student Center as anyone else, and they weren't going anywhere.

"This is exactly what I expected," Darryl stated furiously. "Three *white* justices, and a slap on the wrist..."

Carlos held up his hand for silence, and Darryl reluctantly clammed up. "It's time for us to take some action, brotha's. See, I'm not at all surprised by this. I'm not surprised at all. Angry, yes. Surprised—no."

Percy was getting a little impatient. He was getting weary of all the "One Day We'll Get to the North" speeches by the black organizations. He had been exposed to racism early in life, and here it was again. Somebody had to pay.

"Well, I know one thing that's definitely going to happen. They're gonna boycott. That's what going on outside right now, as disorganized as it sounds. But I was thinking on a more intimate level..."

"Hey, what's going on in here?" Tamal suddenly burst into the office, bringing all the noise from the outside in with him. "Why didn't somebody let me know we were meeting?" He gave Percy a hard, sideways glance, as if he were behind it all.

"Tamal, this isn't a meeting. We just needed a quiet place to think." Darryl was exasperated.

"Yeah, well...Terrell's trying to plan a sit-in out there. He was looking for you, Carlos. He wants to get all of the leaders together."

"Where is Terrell?" Carlos threw Percy and Darryl an "I-told-you-so" look.

"He said something about meeting in Room 5. I guess that where everyone is headed now."

Carlos chuckled bitterly. "I bet he wishes he had been with me on that black student government idea now, doesn't he? Let's go, men. Let's see what Terrell and his group are planning. Then, we'll talk about what *I* have in mind."

MARIE

She couldn't believe what she had just heard. The pledges, who had just about demolished the Plot, had gotten off with a kick in the pants. Marie was sitting in the Assembly Room of the Student Center, where Terrell was trying to calmly explain the events of the hearing, even though his round face looked ready to burst. For once, the members present at the weekly BSA meeting were silent, too angry or too stunned to offer an opinion. Terrell talked about meeting with the various leaders of the black organizations, and the consensus to stage a daily sit-in in the Student Affairs building, until the Dean of Students agreed to retry the case fairly.

The black Greek organizations agreed to boycott the Interfraternity/Intersorority Council meetings, no matter how much they were penalized. Kendrae Adams, President of the Black Athletic Council, told everyone that the black athletes could not boycott the games since many were on scholarships, and required to play. They would, however, be willing do whatever else they could for the cause.

"How about if we only cheer when a black player scores?" someone suggested.

"Yeah, let other schools know Hamel had a racial problem," someone else added.

Kendrae shrugged. "That's fine with me. Just understand that I still have to respect my teammates."

Everyone understood. Kendrae was on Hamel's basketball team, and they were doing very well so far.

"So we agree—we cheer only for the black players at any sporting event until justice is served?" Terrell asked the body.

Marie slowly raised her hand when the "ayes" voted, wondering what she was really getting herself into. On the other hand, all the blacks were uniting—it could turn out to be a milestone event, and all in her freshman year.

"Is anyone sitting here?" she looked up to see none other than Cedric looking down at her, late for yet another BSA meeting. She couldn't believe that he had the gall to sit next to her, after what he and Claudia had done. Then she looked around the room—there didn't seem to be another empty seat left except the one next to her.

"No," she said, and turned her attention back to the front, where someone was proposing that the black students go as far as to boo when a while athlete scored. Kendrae asked if he could think about that—it might be pushing things too far.

Cedric settled in beside her and Marie caught a whiff of his cologne. Despite what she felt, his cologne still made her heart do acrobatic leaps. "What'd I miss?" he asked, fumbling for a notebook and a pen in his bag. Marie felt like she had replayed this scene somewhere in the past.

"They're taking minutes and sending them to all the black students, so you'll have a record of what you missed," she answered blankly.

"They still talking about the Plot?"

"That's what this meeting is about, Cedric." Where had the boy been, anyway? He acted like he had just gotten off a pickup truck bound for Alabama. The biggest news ever to impact the black student population, and he wanted to know if they were still talking about it. Maybe he was spending too much time with her ex-best friend to know what was going on. That thought alone made her more aloof.

"Have you seen the Plot?"

Dumb question number two. "Yes I have, Cedric. It's a mess."

"I haven't gotten a chance to go by there, I've been so busy."

She just bet he had been busy. And why was he trying to act like everything was all right between them? He hadn't contacted her since she and Claudia fell out, and the few times that she did see him on campus, he acted like he had been caught doing something illegal— especially when he was with Claudia.

"So what are we planning to do about it?"

Marie was fed up. "Cedric, I told you we were going to get the minutes. I'm really trying to pay attention to what is going on here, o.k.?" She didn't mean to catch an attitude—yes, she did. How dare he waltz in there, with his fine, good-smelling self, and sit beside her, talking as if he didn't use her to get to her best friend? And what exactly did he want with her now?

He caught her attitude, and even had the nerve to look surprised by it. They were silent for a long moment, then he leaned over to whisper to her. "Are you upset with me?"

Up front, Terrell was asking for volunteers to make posters, banners, and signs for the BSA boycott, and to help organize the events for the Forum. Marie raised her hand, and so did Tony Sadler from the other side of the room. Tony glanced over at her and winked. He was a saxophone player on the band, and an excellent artist—Marie had been telling him to put his talent to use. She met him after the BSA meeting when Terrell and Carlos locked horns. She gave him a quick smile in return.

"O.k…Tony. I have you and Marie down for those things. Now we need…"

Marie put her hand down and Cedric was at it again. She was surprised to find that he was getting on her nerves. "Why would I be upset with you?" she whispered harshly.

"I don't know—but I'm sensing this negative vibe from you." He was trying to joke, but she was not in a joking mood.

"It was just a dinner," he muttered, but it was not like he was trying to keep it to himself.

"What?"

"I said it was just dinner. I just went to dinner with Claudia, that's all."

What was that supposed to mean? A couple of heads swiveled around to look at Cedric, and he stared right back at them. Then he shook his head and put his notebook and pen back in his bag. "Can I call you?"

"Why, Cedric?" she desperately wanted him to be quiet and stop drawing attention to both of them.

"We need to talk, Marie." He was getting louder. "Can I call you?"

"Yes, yes…" she said hurriedly, wanting to end the conversation. He sounded like he would keep at it until she agreed, anyway.

"What's your new number?"

She hissed that out to him.

"Thanks. I'll call you tonight." He slunk out as smoothly as he had slunk in, leaving Marie feeling like she had fallen into some kind of booby trap.

"Marie!" Tony called out to her as they were leaving the Student Center. "So what do you think?" he asked, catching up to her.

"I guess we have our work cut out for us," she told him. "I like the name of the boycott."

"Oh, 'Operation Blackout'? Yeah, that is kind of sweet. I've never been involved in an all-out boycott before. I feel like we're back in the 60's, in Montgomery, Alabama or something."

She laughed. Tony had a very pleasant personality and a good sense of humor. And getting a good look at him now, he was pretty cute. She felt like she had ignored him in the past when he tried to hold conversations with her. Then again, she was so wrapped up in Cedric her first semester, she didn't have time for anyone else.

"Have you eaten?" he asked.

"No...what time is it?" She glanced down at her watch. The BSA meeting had started at noon and it was now 2:15. They had been in there for over two hours, and she hadn't had a bite to eat since breakfast. "You want to grab a bite back inside?"

Tony grinned at her. He was always grinning. "I've got a better place in mind. The food is excellent. My treat."

"O.k.," Marie agreed, pleasantly surprised. "Lead the way."

"You like spicy food?"

Marie was sitting in Tony's on-campus apartment which, like most of the on-campus apartment arrangements, he shared with three other people. He was talking to her from his kitchen, where he was demonstrating his much bragged about culinary skills. Marie was at the table in the living room, thinking up slogans for "Operation Blackout" posters and waiting to be fed. At the moment, he was reheating what he called "Tony's Chicken Delight" and he refused to share the recipe. He did warn her that after one bite of his dish, her taste buds would take on human form, climb out of her mouth, and hold her for ransom until they could get some more of his chicken. With a warning like that, Marie was more than eager to dive in.

"Yes," she told him. "Spicy is fine."

"Good, 'cause it's spicy." Tony hummed as he took other pots to the stove to reheat. A savory, tangy smell soon wafted out of the kitchen and traveled up Marie's nose. Yum. If the smell was any indication of the taste, then she was in for a treat.

"Can I help?" she offered.

"Sure. You can relax out there and look beautiful. Can you handle that?"

Marie giggled, feeling giddy. "I'll try my best," she promised him, going back to her work. She felt bad for always dissing Tony. She found herself enjoying his company.

His humming had now turned into full-blown singing. He was singing a gospel song that Marie recognized from her church's choir—and he was good. Real good. It wasn't just that he had a beautiful voice; there was something in his singing that made Marie want to cry, or shout or do something. It gave her goose bumps. She jumped out of her chair and applauded him when he finished. Tony look surprised that she was listening, and would have turned red if his Hershey's chocolate complexion would have allowed for it.

"Girl, what are you doing?" he asked, smiling down at the floor. "You have got a *voice*, Tony. I mean, a *sho-nuff* voice!"

"Aww…"

"You do," she insisted. "Where'd you learn to sing like that?"

Tony pulled the hot chicken casserole out of the oven. "I've been in the choir since I was five, but my mom used to sing professionally. She gave it up to raise me and my brother and two sisters."

"Oh, your mom was a professional singer? What's her name?" Tony told her. Marie told him she hadn't heard of her before.

"She sang gospel music. You listen to gospel?"

Marie didn't, except when her mom played the radio on Sunday morning before church. For some reason, she felt embarrassed to tell him that she didn't. "Not really…"

"It's o.k. A lot of people our age don't except when our parents turn the radio on Sunday morning," he smiled at her, and Marie was amazed—he was like he read her mind.

She changed the subject. "So there are four of you?"

Tony stopped moving around in the kitchen to stare at her. "Now, Marie—think. Do you think I can be duplicated. They broke the mold with me."

Marie gave him the front of her hand. "O.k…you took me there. But you knew what I meant, smarty."

He laughed. "I'm just playin'. Yes, there are four of us. I'm the youngest."

"Really? Me too."

"See? We have so much in common. Let's just go ahead and get married tomorrow."

"I can't. I've got class until 3:30."

"Uh, oh…she came back strong. I can't mess with you, girl."

Marie laughed—something she hadn't really done since the Cedric/Claudia Adventure. All she did until now was try to keep from crying. Then here Cedric came today, wanting to talk about the situation. "Forget him," she mumbled.

"What?" Tony was bringing the steaming casserole to the table.

"Oh, nothing. Let me move this poster board."

Tony finished brings all the dishes in and returned for plates and silverware. Marie's mouth watered at the chicken, baked macaroni and cheese, cornbread and green beans he had laid out. This was Sunday dinner at her house. He must have cooked all day yesterday. He returned and sat down diagonally from her. He bowed his head and reached out for her hand. Marie stared at him a moment, then slowly placed her hand in his.

"Father, God, we thank you for this food we are about to receive. We thank you for another day, another opportunity to be in Your glorious presence. I thank You for allowing this time of fellowship with my beautiful sister, and for allowing me to be Your child. In Jesus' name, I pray, Amen."

"Amen," Marie echoed, touched by his prayer. Tony sounded like he meant every word. She had never heard any man pray like that outside of a church. Even when she sat down to eat with her father and he bowed his head, she could repeat his grace word for word. It was always the same.

"All right, time to eat." Tony grabbed her plate and began heaping food on it. Marie waited impatiently for him to fix his own plate, and then took a bite. She had to stifle the urge to throw her face in the plate, gobbling her food up like a pig in a trough. The brother could cook.

"Well?" He asked.

"Tony," she began after swallowing. "This food will make you wanna slap yo' momma!"

"Well—I wouldn't say all that…but thanks for the compliment." He grinned and pushed his chair back. "I almost forgot the drinks. Be right back." He disappeared into the kitchen and came back carrying a pitcher full of red liquid.

"Is that Kool-Aid?" Marie asked, happening to be a Kool-Aid fanatic since she was knee high to a grasshopper.

"You know it."

"My brotha', you are truly ethnic. Chicken, green beans, cornbread...and red Kool-Aid. You go, boy!" She held up her hand and high-fived him.

He settled back at the table and started to eat. "Hey, did your mom ever make you those fried baloney sandwiches with the splits in them?"

Marie nodded and chewed enthusiastically. "How about those frozen fish sticks? Did you get them?"

"Mmm hmmm." Tony had his mouth full of macaroni. "And fried Spam sandwiches."

"You too?"

"Every Thursday. We ate grilled cheese sandwiches, fried egg sandwiches, beanie weenies..."

Marie was about to add her input about biscuits in a can, when someone burst through the front door. A rather angry looking black man looked over at Marie and Tony. He had a kenti bag slung over one shoulder. She looked back at him, not knowing what to expect, but Tony just glanced up and kept on eating.

"Hi, Tamal," Tony greeted the person at the door.

"What's up, little man?" Tamal nodded at him. He looked at Marie like he was waiting for her to introduce herself.

"Tamal, this is Marie. Marie, this is one of my roommates, Tamal."

"Hi," Marie said.

Tamal came forward and held out his hand. "Nice to meet you, Marie." He gave Tony a sideways glance that Marie recognized. Why some guys immediately jumped to conclusions when they saw the opposite sex together was beyond her realm of comprehension. She was automatically on her guard against him.

Tamal looked at the loaded table with interest. "Been cooking again, man?"

"I whipped up a little something yesterday. Marie and I are having a little lunch and working on the boycott signs." Again, Tony seemed to read Marie's concerns, and explained why they were alone in the apartment.

"Yeah, I'm looking forward to that. They lucky they didn't get more than a boycott." Tamal said, balling up a fist and smacking it into the other hand. "When you coming on in, Tony? You know we need a brotha' like you."

"No thanks, Tamal. You know my slant on that. Besides, I'm too busy with the band and the BSA to join anything else."

Tamal snorted. "Man, you need to drop that sissy band. It ain't 'bout nothin'. You know you just a token anyway."

Marie was immediately angry and wanted to go off on the brother herself. She braced herself for Tony's reaction, but he just continued to eat. He even helped himself to some more cornbread. "Well, if I'm a token, then maybe I can pave the way for more blacks to come on board. And as sissy as is it, it's paying my way through school."

"Yeah, but if you were a *real* brotha', you'd give that money back and try to get a black scholarship somewhere."

Tony just shook his head. "That wouldn't be wisdom, Tamal," he told him calmly.

Tamal stared at him a minute, then shook his head. "I guess you'll see the light one day. I've got to run to a meeting. Save me some food." With that, Tamal disappeared briefly down the hallway and then headed out the front door he had just burst in. Marie felt the tension in the apartment leave with him.

Tony noticed that she wasn't eating. "You finished already?"

"What? Oh no…I just—can I ask you something?"

"Absolutely."

"You're o.k. with him talking to you like that?"

Tony looked confused. "Like what?"

"Like he was talking. Putting you down. You know, calling you 'little man' and talking about the 'sissy band'." Marie couldn't understand why he wasn't angry or offended or foaming at the mouth—something. Tamal reminded her of Tallette.

Tony just shrugged, enjoying his meal. "Oh, he talks like that all the time."

"To *you*?"

"Pretty much."

Marie wanted to scream. "Why don't you say something back to him, Tony? Maybe he would straighten up."

"What good would that do?"

She was not dealing effectively with his passive answers. She would have felt better if he told her that he was just scared of his roommate. That she could have understood.

186

"Marie, what Tamal says about me doesn't make or break me. He doesn't define who I am—God does. Now if I get upset, that means that he's telling the truth, right?"

Well, color her put in her place nicely. "Well, if you look at it that way…"

"That's the only way to look at it. "Tamal's a very troubled young man. And that group he's in doesn't help matters."

"What group?"

"The Tri-AC."

So that's what Tamal meant by Tony "coming on in." Marie remembered the confrontation at the Unity Meeting vividly now, and recalled where she first saw him.

"I've got mixed feelings about that group," Tony said, gulping down his Kool-Aid like it was an oasis in a desert. "They've got the right idea, but the wrong approach."

"I don't know much about them. I do remember that mess at the Unity Meeting."

"I'm not surprised you haven't heard from them. According to Tamal, they don't advertise—they recruit. He's been after me to apply since last semester."

"Apply? Why can't you just join? It isn't a fraternity, is it?"

Tony shook his head. "I don't know, really. I just know you apply, you interview, and you are chosen—in that order."

"So what makes them so terrible?"

"Well for one, they're real militant. And not that being militant is all bad, but they border on being a hate group. Tamal detests anything white. He barely speaks to our two white roommates—and his brothers seem to act the same way. I can't get with all that. That ain't God."

"He's probably just upset about the Plot," Marie rationalized. "A lot of blacks are acting that way right now. It'll wear off soon."

"I'm telling you—Tamal has been that way since he became a member of that group. I've tried talking to him, but you see how he feels. That's enough negative talk, Marie. I didn't invite you over for that. Tell me something about you—I know that's a pleasant topic."

The rest of the lunch conversation focused on Marie—it was refreshing. When she was hanging with Cedric, all he talked about was himself or football. Granted, she had listened and told him it was o.k. but that was her infatuation talking. Now, conversing with a gentleman like Tony, who was genuinely interested in who she was, she could see the difference. He was so comfortable to be with, easy to talk to. And she was still puzzled as to how he could remain so calm with Tamal, but where she would have normally looked at his non-confrontational style as weak, Tony actually appeared to be standing ten feet tall, and Tamal just looked goofy. It was weird, but she found herself wanting to unlock the key to this mystery.

MARIE

Claudia was the last person she expected to see on the other side of her door.

Marie was trying to type a paper on Corrie's word processor that was due tomorrow, when she heard a knock at her door. Claudia looked a little taken aback when Marie opened the door, like she really didn't expect for her to be there. She was holding a department store bag.

She spoke first. "Hi, Marie."

"Hello, Claudia."

Claudia shifted the bag to her other hand. "You got a minute?"

"Yeah..." Marie moved back to let her in. Claudia glanced around the room, and then stationed herself by the door. Her hair had grown out of its style, but at least it wasn't snatched back in a ponytail. And she had on a cute little casual jumper. Marie hated to admit it, but Claudia didn't appear to be suffering from their dissolved friendship. She looked good.

"I came to give you this." Claudia held the department bag out to Marie.

"What is it?" Marie asked, wondering if it was something she had left behind. She had packed in such a hurry, it was possible.

"My mom got it for you. She brought it with her when they came down for Family and Friends Weekend. She thought we were still...roommates, I guess."

It wasn't unusual for Mrs. Shipp to buy Marie something. Ever since she and Claudia became close, her mother would bring Marie something back from a shopping spree or from one of her business trips out of town. Marie's mother had taken offense—at first.

"Does that woman think I can't provide for my own children?" she would complain.

"No, Momma. She just does it because I'm Claudia's best friend. I'm actually her only friend here. She's not trying to show you up or anything," Marie would explain.

After a while, Marie's mother accepted the generosity and would fawn all over Claudia's mother when she saw her out, and thank her sooo much for being sooo nice to her daughter. Marie would bite her lip to keep from laughing out loud, thinking her mother deserved an award for her performance.

She looked inside the bag, and gasped when she pulled out the hunter green blazer that was inside. Mrs. Shipp always complimented Marie on her complexion, and thought that rich, deep colors enhanced it even more. Marie didn't know what to say. The jacket was gorgeous, and would go well with a skirt she had. "Claudia, this is beautiful! I love it!" She held it up to her, forgetting she was supposed to be at odds with Claudia.

"Try it on," Claudia advised.

Marie slipped in on over her T-shirt—it was perfect. Her long arms were sometimes hard to fit, but this blazer looked like it was tailor-made for her.

"It looks good on you. It really brings out your complexion." Claudia looked like she wanted to stay and chat awhile, like they used to. Marie did miss her company, but she couldn't quite shake the incidents of last semester. But that wasn't supposed to be bothering her, so she could at least make an effort.

"How's your family doing?" she asked Claudia.

"Oh, they're fine. Harland keeps bugging me for Vanessa's number."

"Vanessa *who*?! Not Super Mouth?!"

Claudia nodded. "He thinks she is all that and a bag of chips. He's talking about coming here next year when he graduates just to get with her."

That brother of Claudia's was something else. He talked a big game, but like his big sister, he wouldn't hurt a fly…well, like his big sister *used* to be.

"He told me that Tallette was pregnant."

"What?!" But when Marie thought about it, she wasn't all that shocked. Tallette had trouble etched in her forehead. She had quite a rep back in high school, but still Marie never thought she would actually get pregnant. "How far is she?"

Claudia leaned against the door, a little more relaxed. "Girl, Harland told me she was due any day now. Guess who the daddy is?"

A name automatically popped in her mind, but nah…he couldn't be that stupid. But Claudia was nodding, like she'd read the name that popped up.

"Not…"

"Yes, girl—Jimmy. I couldn't believe it myself."

"Lord, have mercy. Was he *that* desperate?!"

"Harland said she kept throwing herself at him. You know how she was. Jimmy's saying the baby isn't his."

"Then how does your brother know that Jimmy is the daddy?"

"He said they hooked up at some party around the time she said she got pregnant. Now you know Jimmy is Harland's boy, so he has the scoop on something. Jimmy is at State on a basketball scholarship, so you know he's not thinking about being a daddy and child support and all that."

Marie shook her head. Jimmy seemed to be so decent in high school. He wasn't stuck on himself even though he was drop-dead fine, and had a million and one women after him. Not that she was in any way condoning Tallette's actions, but Jimmy could at least have the decency to admit his wrongdoing. "Well," she said to Claudia, caught up in the conversation and not the company. "Aren't you glad you didn't get mixed up with him? Tallette turned out to be a blessing in disguise."

"Yeah, that's what Harland said. Jimmy's his boy, but even he thinks what he's doing is foul. He said Tallette was talking about marriage and all that, but Jimmy ain't going for it. He said Tallette doesn't look good at all."

"At least she's keeping the baby."

"That's the good part. I don't know what kind of mother she'll make, though."

Marie didn't either. She envisioned a little baby with long braids and big gold earrings, crying *all* the time. "Well, what can I say? Tallette made her bed for a long time. Now she has to lay in it."

"So you think Tallette deserves what she got, huh?" Claudia asked in a strange voice.

"I think she was asking for trouble by throwing herself at Jimmy. You saw how she was in high school, wearing those tight jeans and short skirts. Blouses halfway open to her belly button—and heels. Who wears heels in high school? How many times was she sent home to change her clothes?" Marie recalled many a time when Tallette would sashay out of the building in some too tight, too short outfit, headed for home to change.

Claudia's demeanor changed noticeably. She looked sad, hurt. "So she was asking for trouble?"

191

"I'm not saying that Jimmy is innocent in all of this," Marie clarified. She didn't want to give the impression that she thought teenage pregnancy was all the girl's fault, but she had a thing against fast girls like Tallette. To her, it put a label on all females. "It definitely takes two. But I will say this—if girls start telling these boys where to go, and stop throwing themselves at guys like they lost their mind, guys would start respecting them."

If Mrs. Steeleton had taught them anything, it was to wait for marriage, or "treat their stuff like it was expensive jewelry—keep it locked up until somebody who could afford it came along to buy it"— as she put it. She told Marie and her two older sisters that if they gave it away anyway, not to bring a grandchild or a venereal disease home to her. The two older ones had boyfriends and dates, but if the guy started tripping about getting intimate, they were sent on their way— see ya later, don't call me, don't write me, don't send me smoke signals. Guys respected the Steeleton girls. Marie's mother made sure of that.

Marie was about to continue, because if she felt strongly about an issue, it was hard for her to release it. But she saw Claudia's bottom lip start to quiver, and round drops of water fall out of her eyes and land on her jumper. "Claudia—what's wrong?"

Claudia looked down, trying to control her tears. She breathed in heavily, then lifted her head. "I guess I'm no better than Tallette," she said in a shaky voice.

No better than Tallette?! What in the world…? "Claudia look," Marie started, not sure how to start this forgiveness thing but willing to try, since she was supposed to. "I'm …over the thing with you and Cedric, so you don't have to go through all that. I mean…" What did she mean? "What's done is done, o.k.? You don't have to compare yourself to…"

"Marie," Claudia interrupted. "That's not what I mean."

"Then what do you…you slept with him?"

Claudia tightened her lips, but nodded.

"Are you pregnant?"

"I don't know," Claudia sobbed uncontrollably. Automatically, Marie's heart went out to her and she zoomed over to the door and led Claudia to her bed. This must have been the beginning stage of the forgiveness process, because she completely forgot that she was supposed to throw Claudia out instead of put comforting arms around her.

"I'm sorry, Marie," Claudia choked out, when she was able to speak. "I got some nerve, don't I—crying on your shoulder."

"That's all right," Marie said before she realized she meant it. "You wanna talk about it?"

Claudia shook her head and wiped at her eyes. "No, I better go." She got up and headed toward the door, then stopped. "I feel so cheap," she turned and confessed. "I mean, he told me all these lies about how he cared so much for me… I was so dumb."

"Well, I guess you thought he meant it," Marie answered stupidly.

"That's just it—I should have known better. I should have known it was just a line." She started pacing the room like she had an important business decision to make. "Something kept telling me, 'Claudia, it's a trap—he don't mean it, he don't mean it. I mean, there he was, saying all the right things…he even had the nerve to tell me that he didn't have a lot of experience with women. And I believed him."

Well, Maybe Claudia had been *her* blessing in disguise like Tallette was with Jimmy. "When did it happen?" Marie found herself asking.

"A little over a month ago." Claudia had taken a seat at Marie's desk, looking exhausted from all her raving.

"When's the last time you heard from him?"

Claudia huffed. "I haven't. He's been avoiding me like the plague. He won't return my phone calls and he barely speaks to me on campus."

"You mean he just dissed you?"

"Basically."

"Umph." Marie still didn't know what to say. Claudia was hurting, that much she could tell, and there was nothing she knew to say to make her feel better. But Marie was starting to see the value in what her mother had taught her. She had been ragged a little in high school for being a virgin, and felt bad about it from time to time, but she was starting to see the flip side. *Thank you, Lord.* "Are you late?"

"About two weeks," Claudia said, sounding like she wanted to break down again.

"The Health Center gives free, first-time pregnancy tests," she offered.

Claudia looked a little hopeful. "They do?"

"According to that little pamphlet they gave us in our welcome box." Marie went to her closet shelf and took a pink box down with the words, *Welcome, Ladies of Hamel U* emblazoned on the top. The University Made sure that every female resident received a goodie box complete with small samples of deodorant, lotion, shampoo/conditioner, perfume, cold medicine, headache medicine, a pen, a Hamel U bumper sticker and various pamphlets outlining the different services provided on campus, including the one for the Health Center that Marie was looking for. The pamphlet had a scenic picture of the Lorraine P. Dobson Health Center with the words, *What Every Woman Should Know* across the picture. Unfortunately, advice on how to get over a guy that had played you like a cheap fiddle was not part of *What Every Woman Should Know*.

"It says so right here." She showed the pamphlet to Claudia, who was busy staring at her. "What?"

"You still have this?" Claudia asked, a small smile on her face.

"Yeah...you don't have yours?"

"I guess. I don't know where the heck it is, though. I think I threw it away."

"Oh." But that was just like Claudia. She had nice things, but she just tossed them around and ended up losing half of them. Marie couldn't count the number of times she had found nice jewelry or an expensive shirt laying in a corner of Claudia's bedroom back home. Sometimes, the clothes would still have a store tag attached to them. Claudia just didn't bother to hang it up in the closet when she got it. "I was getting around to it," she would tell Marie when Marie pointed it out to her. "A cluttered room means a cluttered mind," Marie would respond, quoting one of her mother's many pearls of wisdom.

Claudia took the pamphlet. "I guess I know what my next step is."

"At least it's free."

"Yeah, my parents won't find out." Claudia let out a bitter laugh. "My father would have a fit if he found out. He would expect something like this from Harland, but his little girl? It would break him."

"But you're not telling him, right?" Marie didn't see the need— not yet, anyway.

"If I turn out pregnant, I don't have a choice. Abortion is out of the question. I...I just have to wait," Claudia realized sadly, walking to the door again.

Marie found herself doing something that she felt she deserved a Purple Heart for. She went over to Claudia, and grabbed her hand. "Do you want me to go with you?"

Claudia looked stunned. "You would do that...?"

Marie held up her free hand. "Claudia, we won't even talk about that, o.k.? If you need me, I'm here."

Claudia grabbed her in quick hug, then added, "Thanks, Marie. But I think this is something I need to do by myself. I got into this mess by myself."

Marie nodded in understanding. "Just let me know."

"I will." Claudia gave her another smile and a disbelieving look before she left.

Marie closed the door, feeling like she had just stepped out of someone else's life. Surely, that had to be one of those tests that Tony said she'd face after she'd put God in control of her life. And she had a funny feeling that she'd passed with flying colors.

CLAUDIA

She had never been so terrified in her life.

She made an appointment at the Health Center two weeks after she talked to Marie. Eight o'clock in the morning—the time she would be least likely to run into someone she knew. Claudia spent the evening before her appointment worrying and crying. When her eyes were so swollen she could barely keep them open and her head hurt so bad from crying that she had to lay down, she finally went to bed.

That night, she had a terrible dream. She was in a doctor's office and the doctor was leaning across his desk with a grim expression on his face.

"Congratulations," he told her. "You're having twins."

"Twins?!!! No!!" she exclaimed.

The doctor smiled crookedly and pointed at her stomach. She looked down. Her stomach was inflated like a helium balloon.

All of a sudden, Cedric appeared behind the doctor's desk. "It ain't mine," he told both of them.

Claudia was about to protest when she felt a hand on her arm. "Girl, I know how you feel." Tallette was sitting in the chair next to her. Her braids looked like they needed an update and she was holding a wailing baby on her shoulder. "Jimmy did the same thing to me. Get a blood test. Sue him for child support."

"But it was just one time," Claudia cried to everyone in the room, which now included her parents and Harland.

"That's all it takes," her mother said sadly. "How could you do this, Claudia? Why couldn't you wait until you were married?"

"It ain't mine," Cedric reminded everyone. "And I ain't marrying nobody."

"You are such a dog," Marie told him from behind Claudia's chair. He leered at her in return.

"That'll be two-hundred fifty dollars." The doctor stuck his hand out to Claudia.

"For what?!!" she cried.

"Your pregnancy test," the doctor answered patiently.

Claudia turned to Marie in desperation. "You told me it was free!"

Marie stepped back with a sheepish grin. "Oops."

Tallette's baby started to scream. The noise was deafening.

"What are you going to do, Claudia?" someone asked, then everyone was asking her that question over and over again. Claudia slammed her hands over her ears, and her screams blended in with the baby's.

She woke up shaking and sweating. Her clock told her that she had only forty-five minutes to get ready and get over to the Health Center.

She walked swiftly through the woods, wishing she had worn her sneakers instead of the uncomfortable flats she chose. She felt each rock in the ground. The Lorraine P. Dobson Health Center was just a short walk through the woods across from her residence hall, and to her relief, the small waiting area was empty when she arrived. The only noise was the blare of the morning news on the floor model television. The receptionist's station sat across from the waiting area, and a young, blond-haired girl who looked like a student was sitting behind the glass partition.

"Hi. May I help you?" the girl asked when Claudia approached her.

"I have an eight o'clock appointment. My name is Shipp— Claudia Shipp."

The girl typed in some information on a computer that beeped in response. Claudia waited for the girl's expression to change from bubbly to disgust when she saw the reason that Claudia was there, but her face held its professionalism.

"O.k., Ms. Shipp." The receptionist slid a clipboard to her. "Just fill out the top half of this sheet and someone will be with you shortly."

Claudia settled herself into one of the plush chairs in the waiting area and began to write in the information as fast as she could. The sooner this thing was over with, the better.

"Claudia! What a surprise!"

Claudia looked up at the voice, and felt for sure that God was punishing her. Vanessa was smiling down at her. "Girl, we keep running into each other, don't we?"

"Yes, I guess we do." *That's it, I'm transferring schools. I hear the University of Moscow has an excellent Biology Department.*

"So," began Vanessa, nestling down beside her. "What are you here for?"

Was that a question that people normally asked? Did you actually make small talk in a doctor's office by asking people what they were seeing the doctor about?

Vanessa didn't give her time to answer. "I think I have some sort of bug. I've been throwing up for the past couple of days. I sure don't need to miss any class over being sick."

You sure don't, thought Claudia. *How could you ever keep up with everyone's business lying up sick in your room?*

"It's either a bug or I'm pregnant. And I can't be pregnant," Vanessa laughed. Claudia gripped her pen a little tighter. "How about you?"

If Claudia were like Marie, she would tell Vanessa where to go and how to get there. "I'm here to make sure everything is all right, too," she told her instead.

"You know you haven't been looking a hundred percent lately," Vanessa told her.

"I haven't?"

"No. Now you know I have to keep an eye out for my girl, Claudia. But you've been looking rather pale lately. Are you all right?"

"Must be that bug that's going around." And his name was Cedric.

"That's what I thought. Don't let that thing get a jump on you, girl. But I guess that's why you're here."

"Exactly," Claudia said, and put her concentration back on her sheet. When Vanessa saw that she would get no more conversation out of Claudia, she picked up a magazine and flipped through it.

Claudia scribbled answers and checked boxes and fast as she could on the sheet. After she turned it back into the smiling receptionist, she sat down and watched the television screen intently, though she had no interest in what was on. It was just something to do to keep Supermouth from starting another conversation to get in her business.

"Claudia Shipp?" A nurse came to the doorway of the waiting area. "You can come back now."

"I hope it turns out negative."

Claudia's heart slammed into her throat. "What?!"

"I said I hope you feel better," Vanessa repeated, looking at her strangely.

"Oh. Thanks." Claudia followed the nurse to the back, where she was handed a cup and shown a restroom. She prayed the whole time she was in there, not even sure if God heard her. All she knew was that she did not want to be pregnant—not now, and especially not with Cedric's baby.

Fifteen minutes later, she was in a room, listening to the nurse tell her the results. She thanked the nurse, then walked out of the Health Center in a daze, passing buildings and people on her way to class. "Claudia!" Marie was suddenly rushing up to her. "What's up, girl? You look kind of out of it."

"I had my test today," Claudia whispered dully.

Marie's eyes grew wide. She grabbed Claudia's elbow and led her to a deserted spot behind the Architecture building. "How was it?"

"Negative."

Marie exhaled loudly, visibly relieved. It made Claudia feel like an even bigger heel with Marie showing such relief over her news, especially since she had practically slapped her in the face with Cedric. "Claudia, that is such a relief! Aren't you happy? You look disturbed. Don't tell me you wanted to be…"

"No, please—don't even go there." Claudia almost felt nauseated at the thought. "I'm happy about that. I just feel so…empty. Marie, I gave away something that I can't get back. And to a man that used me. I wanted my first time to be with the man I marry."

Marie nodded, empathizing. "Well, I'm sure a lot of girls wanted the same thing, but things happen, girl. It's forward from here."

Claudia smiled at her. "Thank you, Oprah."

"What? Oh, girl, please," Marie laughed. "My mother just taught me to learn from your mistakes and move on."

"I know I know. But I feel so different now. I don't feel like the same Claudia who came here in August. I feel…violated."

Marie's look was one of concern. "So what are you going to do now?"

Claudia shrugged. "I don't know. I guess go on with business as usual. I can't take it back now, can I?"

"No, you can't. I wish you could, though."

"Marie, I'm going to have a rep!" Claudia cried, the thought suddenly jumping into her mind. "He'll tell all his male buddies, the football team—and they'll think I'm easy."

Michele R. Leverett

Marie shushed her and shook her head, looking around. "Don't even think that way."

"But it's the truth," Claudia insisted. "I'll be marked. I might as well walk around campus with a big sign around my neck—"I slept with Cedric Carter!"

Marie shushed Claudia again, whose voice had risen in anguish. "Don't you have a ten o'clock?"

"I'm skipping. I'll go to the two o'clock."

"Come on. Let's go get something to eat and talk in private." They started walking toward the Student Center, when Marie stopped and snapped her fingers. "Shoot, I forgot. I'm supposed to meet Tony in ten minutes."

"Who is Tony?"

"A friend of mine. We're working on the events for the Forum."

"Oh."

"You're coming, aren't you?"

"I kinda forgot about it." She was too wrapped up in Cedric to even care. "Are you doing that with the BSA?"

"Yeah. They nominated Tony and me for the Events Planning Board. We're the only underclassmen on it," Marie said with a hint of pride.

"That's great, Marie. It sounds like you've been busy."

"Well, yeah. Kind of. They want me to run for Sophomore Class President. I don't know. I'm still thinking about it."

"That's wonderful," Claudia told her, feeling like dirt. Marie had ambitions, goals, places to go and people to see, while she just wandered around aimlessly from one day to the next, not sure what her future plans were. But not busy little beaver Marie—oh, no. Her future was all mapped out.

"Here he comes now," Marie said, looking towards the center of campus. A slim, attractive, neatly dressed brother waved at Marie as he approached them.

"Hi, Tony," Marie greeted him, grinning.

"Hello, lovely lady," Tony smiled back, then he held out his hand to Claudia. "I'm Tony."

"Hi," Claudia said. He continued to smile at her, but it was just a friendly smile. She had just met this brother, but she could already tell that there was something different about him.

200

"Claudia, this is Tony. Tony, this is Claudia," Marie introduced. "This is my best friend from back home."

"Really? It's nice to meet you, Claudia." Tony turned back to Marie. "You ready to get to work?"

"Sure. I've got a couple of ideas I want to bounce off of you." "Bounce away, girl." Tony turned back to Claudia. "Did Marie tell you she's running for Sophomore Class President?"

"Tony!" Marie cried, laughing. "I haven't made up my mind yet."

Tony ignored her. "I'm going to be her campaign manager." He threw an arm around Marie's shoulder and studied the sky. "I can see it now—'vote for Marie; she'll set you free'."

Marie rolled her eyes and pushed at him playfully. "O.k., that is too corny, boy. You are officially crazy." Tony laughed, and Claudia felt left out.

"Well, I'm not going to hold you guys up. I'll see you later, Marie. Nice to meet you, Tony."

Marie grabbed her hand. "We'll talk tonight, o.k.?"

"Sure, that's fine. I'm going to go on to class, I think."

Marie smiled and punched her lightly in the arm. "Good idea, girl. I'll talk to you later, o.k?"

She and Tony moved on, already in deep conversation about whatever. Even from their brief encounter, Claudia could tell that Tony though a lot of Marie. And vice versa. He seemed to be so genuine, for some reason. She headed back towards the English building reluctantly, looking down at her feet so she wouldn't have to look anyone in the face. When she did glance up, she thought she saw people clumped into little groups, watching her. Were they talking about her? Eyes seemed to look at her knowingly. How many friends did Cedric have, anyway? Who had he told already?

Guys she passed leered at her; girls rolled their eyes and turned their heads. Claudia walked faster, but she was headed away from her class towards the residence halls. She felt sick—she needed to lay down. And she needed to get away from all the whispering, pointing and staring.

PERCY

Operation Blackout was in full swing immediately after the holidays. Every day from eight o'clock in the morning until five o'clock in the evening, the lobby of the Dean of Students building was filled with black students. The Dean, Thomas Atrell, was stunned on the first day of the boycott. When he entered the building, he was faced with a crowd of close to three hundred black students, standing around the perimeter of the building, which immediately began yelling at him about the injustice of the Lambda Sigma decision, but still parted cordially to let him enter the building. Then, he was hit with a lobby full of more black students—along with a handful of radical white ones—that stopped their low volume conversations to stare at him in silence. They lined the walls of the lobby, sat on the floor and in every available chair. Dean Atrell paused in the middle of the lobby, tried to smile but failed, then hurried up the stairs to his office.

About an hour later, he sent a secretary down to the lobby to clear the students out, but they refused to leave. Two more hours passed, and the Assistant Dean of Students, Lilly Kelly, came down and used a firmer voice to clear out the lobby. Still, the protestors refused to budge in unsettling silence. They just looked at her and held up their various signs about injustice and racism. Twenty minutes later, five campus police officers came in through the back door, threatening to detain all of the protestors if they did not clear the lobby immediately. One student walked confidently up to the officer that spoke, pointing to a white brochure she was holding.

"It states right here in the *Hamel University Student Rules and Regulations*," she stated in a cool, unruffled voice, "That 'students will have the right to peacefully assemble in any area of campus excluding residence halls, cafeterias—before or after normal operating hours, and academic buildings. If the assembly is considered to be harmful to the well-being of the campus population (to be defined as possession of firearms or other weapons, unusually loud, profane language or other types of behavior commonly defined as 'violent'), then campus security will be alerted and the assembly will be dispersed.'

"Here," she handed the brochure to the officer, who automatically took it. "Each one of us has a copy."

The officer scanned the language carefully, his facing turning red with frustration. He rudely thrust the brochure back into the young woman's hand. "You call this *peaceful*?"

"There's no violent behavior, no profane language, and we're being extremely quiet in this lobby," she replied in that same calm voice. "And all of us are willing to undergo a search for weapons. Even the ones outside."

All five officers looked at the mass of students in the lobby, and then the crowd outside, most of whom had stopped marching and were watching the proceedings in the lobby through the large front and side windows. A weapons search would take forever, and would definitely require more than five officers. They seemed to reconsider.

The red-faced officer glared around at the students in the lobby. "Just make sure this doesn't get out of hand," he warned snappishly. "The first time it does, we'll come back and break it up, no questions asked." He motioned for the other officers to leave, and then started up the stairway, most likely to report the outcome to the Dean.

One of the BSA members stopped him. "Would you do us a huge favor?" he asked in a pleasant yet sarcastic voice.

"What?' the officer huffed back.

"Would you tell Dean Atrell that he can talk to us, or Chancellor Donaldson can—it Makes no difference to us. We know where his office is, too." The young man smiled, then quietly moved back to his post against the wall.

The officer narrowed his eyes, opened his mouth to respond, but then shut it immediately. He strode up the steps two at a time. The other officers were still in the process of leaving, but the tall, black officer who had been at the Plot the night it was destroyed stayed behind a minute, holding up both fists in a gesture of unity and agreement. The students clapped and cheered for him as he made his way back to the campus station with the other officers. The word from upstairs was that the Dean refused to talk until the boycotters disbanded. The protestors refused to disband until the Dean heard them out; as a result, the whole issue was at a standstill, and was still at that point a couple of days later, when Percy and Marcus were assigned to sit in the lobby for the Tri-AC.

Percy was holding his sign that read "Hamel U—The University of Jim Crow" when he saw Darryl walk in, looking around. He finally spotted the two on the floor and headed over to them.

"I bring you greetings of peace and unity, my strong, African brothers." Darryl greeted them with the Tri-AC public greeting.

"We receive your blessings, warrior, and pray that you receive all the richness and happiness our race has to offer," Marcus answered back, speaking for both he and Percy.

Darryl looked at Percy. "Mr. Lyles, if I may have a minute of your time, please."

"It would be an honor," Percy recited, feeling the same way he felt in the beginning about the "Tri-AC Code of Public Speaking"—it was cheesy, but he would be obedient. "Mr. Powell, would you be so kind as to hold my sign while I converse with Mr. Cross?"

"It would be an honor," Marcus told him, taking the sign. A couple of students sitting next to them shook their heads and hid laughs behind their hands, and Marcus threw them dirty looks.

Percy rose and followed Darryl out of the door, where the crowd immediately parted to let them through. They weren't so swift for whites, who had started trying to avoid the Dean of Students Building altogether—if they could help it. They walked up the hill from the Dean's Building and found a bench near the Student Center.

"How are things going with the phones?" Percy asked. Carlos, Darryl, Terrell and his Vice President, Veronica Little, had set up a command station between the two offices. They were calling Dean Atrell at least ten times a day, but were unable to get through to him. Since the boycott began a couple of days ago, they must have left at least thirty some odd messages.

"Man, he still won't talk to us. Carlos is in the office now, probably leaving another message."

"He's going to have to talk to us eventually," Percy predicted. "He'll get tired of seeing us around."

Darryl kicked at a stone in front of them. "Percy, this boycott is a pretty good idea, and will probably produce some results—one day. But those Lambda Sig boys are still walking around, free as birds. With a slap on the wrist, as far as we're concerned."

"Yeah, what's this probation mean for them, anyway? It doesn't sound like much of anything."

"It's not. It just means they can't participate in any functions under the name of Lambda Sig for three weeks. And they can't attend any Interfraternity meetings, which means they have to pay a fine for being absent for three weeks. Oh—and no wild keg parties, either. That's about the worst part of it for them." Darryl looked Percy straight in the eye. "But we're about to change all that."

"Who's *we?*"

"The Tri-AC, Percy. We can't wait around for Administration or this boycott. And even if the boycott does succeed, what will we get out of it? They'll hear what we have to say, but that doesn't guarantee us another trial or a stiffer sanction against those redneck hillbillies."

"What about the Black Alumni Forum?" Terrell had thought of another tactic to put Hamel's administration on the spot—they were going to contact the black Hamel alumni—those who had donated money to purchase the land for the black students—and see if they would be willing to sue Lambda Sig in civil court for destruction of property. So far, Terrell had contacted about five of the property owners, who actually wanted to come on campus and meet with the Dean, face to face. Terrell decided that it would be a great idea to turn the whole thing into an open forum, so that everyone could be privy to the meeting. He had left a message about the idea for the Dean, but had not heard anything about that, either.

"Another excellent idea," Darryl told him. "But it still ain't enough. Percy, do you understand what happened the other night? Do you really understand?"

"Yeah, those white boys tore up our Plot…"

Darryl was shaking his head. "No—the white man sent a message to the black man that we still have no right to enjoy the freedom we fought long and hard to attain. They don't want us in their school, they're threatened by our ability to think, learn and apply knowledge, and they resent the fact that we were emancipated over one hundred years ago, that's what happened the other night."

Percy's mind was reeling. "O.k. …"

"The mindset doesn't change, brotha'. The times may change, the people may change, but the white mindset toward the black man is constant. You're seeing proof of that right now. Look at how the Dean is ignoring us—how dare we protest when our civil rights have been violated? Why aren't we out in the field, singing and showing our teeth and picking cotton like we don't have a care in the world?"

205

Wow. And here Percy thought he topped the charts with having the biggest vendetta against white people. He knew the Tri-AC was extremely pro-black, but Darryl was reading deep-seeded, southern, antebellum mansion, plantation racism into everything.

"No...those boys have to know that they can't mess with us and get away with it—no sir."

"So what do ya'll have in mind, Darryl?"

"Percy, I'll be honest with you. Carlos wanted me to get a feel on where you'd be on what I'm about to tell you."

Percy didn't waste time with more questions. He knew that whatever they had in mind, it was violent and risky. "Man, you know I think those boys deserve it. I just don't want anything coming back on us." In reality, he didn't want anything coming back on him. He had escaped the violent lifestyle by the skin of his teeth growing up, and he wasn't willing to revert back to his old way of doing things. And then there was the exchange program that his Business Administration professor, Dr. Adams, told him about—he had a good chance of spending his sophomore year as an exchange student in England, studying business at one of the top British universities. Dr. Adams was extremely impressed with his business proposal assignment last semester—Percy had Mr. Dell's tutelage to thank for that—and told Percy she was putting in a personal recommendation for him as a contender for the program. If he was involved in some trouble, he could pretty much kiss that opportunity goodbye.

"We've considered that Percy. We're taking precautions to ensure that doesn't happen. Come on—let's take a walk."

The two walked in the direction of the Plot. The crowd that had surrounded the area before Christmas break was gone now. Most of them were marching around or sitting in the Dean of Student's Building. The curious white students would pass but kept stepping, like a built-in radar was warning them that they dare not stop to gawk. The only thing surrounding the area now was the bright yellow police tape. Other than that, it looked desolate. The black students had literally forbidden Lambda Sig to step foot back on the land, let alone repair the damage.

Darryl stopped when they reached the area. His face was set in what looked like a mixture of pain and anger. He inhaled, then let the air out slowly and stayed silent, just staring out at the mess.

Daring to break the silence, Percy asked him, "So, uh…what are we planning to do?"

"We're planning a little tit for tat, Percy. They destroyed our property…"

"So we destroy theirs," Percy finished, thinking that it might not be so bad, after all. A few spray painted logos on cars, a little graffiti on the sides of the house…

"Percy, I want you to understand something—we're not just talking about a few smashed car windows or some graffiti—though that is definitely a nice start. We're talking about teaching these boys a lesson. If everything goes according to plan, that precious house of theirs will look like a tornado hit it—and some of their members, too, if they don't cooperate."

Percy wasn't sure he heard correctly. "So we're talking about what? Breaking in the house, doing some damage? Are we going to make sure they're gone first?"

Darryl looked at Percy for a minute. "Make sure they're gone?! No, man—we *want* them to be there. See, we're a tad bit more cordial than they are. They did their dirt in secret—we're going to make them watch ours."

"Darryl, man… we can't do that!"

"Why not?" Darryl asked calmly.

"Because—because it's…illegal, that's why!" Luckily that area was deserted. Percy had raised his voice in anguish.

"So what they did to us is legal and moral, right?" Darryl pointed out at the Plot. "Percy we can't patty-cake with these boys. They set the rules to this game—not us. We're going to cover ourselves, sure, but legality and morality—that's out the window, bru."

"O.k., so what if we don't cover ourselves well? What if we get caught? Man, they'd throw us under the jail cell! Have you forgotten we're black men?!"

"No, Percy—have *you* forgotten?!" Darryl retorted in anger. "You just gonna let these redneck white boys walk all over you and you sit back and don't do a thing about it?! They already killed your ancestors, made slaves out of them—called them everything but a man…" Darryl crossed his arms and studied Percy a minute. "Tell you what…why don't you just go to those Lambda Sig boys, give them a whip, take your shirt off, lay on the ground and tell them to give a whipping you'll never forget, huh? Or better yet, tell em' to call your mother and call her a nigger…"

"Darryl, man—you need to chill on that." Percy could feel heat rising in his face. Like most African-American men, he didn't play when it came to his mother. Tri-AC brother or no, Percy didn't have any loyalty when it came down his mother, the woman who had practically given her right arm to make sure her children had what they needed.

Darryl's face still showed anger, but he nodded in understanding. "Percy, I meant no disrespect toward your mother—I was just giving you a real picture of how the world is—how the white man really thinks about us. You think the problem is going to go away by itself? You leaving it up to the white man to get over his hang-ups? Nah, brotha'. This is a war we're in—we fight, or we die. Simple as that."

What Darryl said sounded justifiable to him—but what about what the man on television said—that education was the way to beat the system? How about his mother and Mr. Dell, who told him he'd be somebody without fighting? Who was right? He didn't know—he needed to think; sort things out. "Darryl, I don't know. I need to think about it."

"You go ahead, Percy. You think about it. Meanwhile, we're going to do what we have to—see we don't have the luxury to stop and think—that gives the enemy the opportunity to act."

"Darryl, my point is…"

Oh, I understand your hesitation, brotha', don't get me wrong. Who knows? You may be a better man than me, because you can still feel moral and legal about this racist society we're in. But like I said, we gotta do what we gotta do, whether you're with us or not. Peace, man." With that, Darryl turned and started swiftly toward the center of campus, leaving Percy alone with the Plot.

He turned to look at it one last time—the trash jumping across the land in the soft wind, the broken stone structures, the graffiti—he could almost hear the loud, drunken hooping and hollering as the pledges trampled through the Plot, hacking and littering and breaking and rolling…

"Darryl!" Percy called out, running to catch up with Darryl, who had gained a good distance between them. Darryl stopped and turned to look at Percy. "When's it going down?" Percy asked, puffing to catch his breath.

EUGENE

Eugene sat before the microfiche reader in the library, unable to concentrate. The words in the article whizzed by his eyes like little ants, giving him a headache. He probably passed the page he was supposed to be looking at half a dozen times, but he didn't really have his mind on what he was doing. His mother was having surgery today, and she had practically threatened him to make him stay at school. She even went as far as to say she would refuse the surgery if he did come home. She was serious. Even his father had argued his case, but she put her foot down—she would not have her son missing time away from his studies when she was going to be perfectly fine.

Christmas vacation had been a grim affair. His mother had tried to liven it by suggesting they all decorate the tree with Christmas music, hot apple cider, Christmas cookies and popcorn. Eugene almost fell over when his father agreed, and everything was going fine until his mother told him to put on some Christmas music. "What is that?!" his father asked when he came back upstairs from the den where the stereo was.

"It's Christmas music," he told his dad, grabbing the other end of the lights that Chip was struggling to untangle.

"It's *white* Christmas music," his dad spat out, giving him a hard look and heading down the stairs to the den. Bing Crosby's crooning about Christmas was halted, and after a few minutes, the Temptations famous falsetto singer was humming a seasonal, soulful tune.

"Let it go," Chip whispered to Eugene, while working furiously with the lights and nibbling on a cookie.

His dad came back upstairs. "Now why in the world would you want to listen to a white man sing about Christmas? What does he know about Christmas in a black family?"

"Ray, please..." his mother began.

"No, Hazel—you told the boy to put on some music, and he can't do any better than Bing Crosby?! I want to know why!"

Eugene decided not to help his dad make a scene. "I just picked some music, Dad. I didn't think it mattered."

"Yes, it matters!" his dad argued. "What do you think that man meant when he sang about a white Christmas—snow?! No, he was talking about a Christmas with no black folk..."

"Ray!" his mother pleaded. "Let's just finish the tree. You changed the music, so it's over with."

"Hazel, the boy needs to know these things so he won't keep smiling in white folks face like they're going to be in his corner..."

Chip nudged Eugene. "Let it go," he mouthed to him.

His dad laughed bitterly. "You know he's not learning anything about black folk at that lily-white school he's at..."

That was it. Eugene jumped up, nearly tripping over the lights he was trying to untangle. "Why can't you just lay off me for one minute?! Just one minute?!" he fired at his dad.

"Boy don't you raise your voice to me in the house I'm paying the mortgage on! I told you before, you better learn some respect! And you better learn how to handle the truth....!"

"Whose truth, dad?! Yours?!"

"Stop it! Just stop it!" They both stopped to look at his mother, who was shrieking and jerking her arms in frustration. "I get so sick of hearing you two argue over nonsense! You can't even try to get along! I can't take it anymore!" She ran down the hallway and up the stairs, crying, leaving the three men standing around in the living room, mouths hanging wide open.

His dad looked at his two sons, dropped his eyes, and headed down the hall to go after their mother.

"Come on, Eugene—let's just finish the tree," Chip told him, resuming his work with the lights. Eugene sat back down beside his brother, feeling numb, and really not in the Christmas spirit anymore.

The rest of the holiday was pretty much the same. He and his dad barely spoke to each other, his mother was moody because the atmosphere in the house was so tense, and Chip ended up spending most of Christmas Day with Diedra and her family because he couldn't take it, either. Eugene couldn't wait to get back to school.

He threw his pen down and hit the rewind button on the machine. He wasn't getting anything accomplished. He gathered up his stuff, put the microfiche in the return basket and headed out of the library, promising himself he would come back tomorrow and knock out at least two hours of research. Right now, he wanted to get back to his room and call the Polyclinic Hospital—check on his mother.

Outside, he saw a big crowd gathered around the Dean of Students office. Some people were standing and yelling, their words coming out in puffs of smoke courtesy of the chilly fall weather, while others

210

were marching a circle around the building, holding signs. Eugene zipped up his coat and pondered—then it hit him. "Operation Blackout" began today. He had gotten a letter about it in the mail—all students were invited to join in a protest against the Plot, but blacks in particular were "encouraged" to join. The three-page letter talked about the actual incident, the atrocious Student Court ruling, and what the leaders of the black organizations planned to do until the punishment fit the crime. In addition, the leaders were contacting the black alumni and community leaders to hold a Forum to discuss the issue. They planned to turn this into a big media circus. When Eugene first read the letter, he inwardly cringed. Once his dad caught wind of what was happening, the "I-told-you-so's" would be inevitable. That's all he needed.

"Hi, Eugene." Renee' waltzed up to him holding a sign that read, "Montgomery Alabama 1965—Hamel University, 1991." She was all bundled up and looked like a political Eskimo. He couldn't decide whether or not he was happy to see her, because it reminded him of his falling out with Irene. "Are you joining in the boycott?" She nodded back to where the protestors were congregated.

"I almost forgot about it," Eugene admitted. I've been so busy trying to get this paper done."

"How could you forget about something like this?" Renee' asked.

"I just did, Renee'."

She looked at him a minute, then shrugged. "They've got plenty of signs left. You're supposed to register at the BSU office so they can keep a record of how many students actually participated, but everybody's not doing that. You can just jump right in with the rest of the crowd down there."

Wasn't she being presumptuous? "Who said I was going to participate?"

She looked at him like he had spoken a foreign language. "Not participate?! You mean to tell me you're not going to join in this fight against racial injustice?!"

"I'm telling you I'm not sure yet. I've got a busy schedule."

"Well so do I, Eugene. But we've also got a responsibility to our people..."

A responsibility to our people—a responsibility to our people. A responsi...

"You could at least march for a little while. Maybe thirty minutes at least."

"Eugene, you need to hang around your own people and stop kissing up to those white folks at school. All they're doing is making fun of you behind your back. You're just a token."

"I've been out here since my eight o'clock class let out. A lot of us have and our schedules are just as busy…"

"There goes Eugene WHITE. What's up, white boy? Oreo? Black on the outside, white on the inside."

"That's the problem with our people. They're always crying about racism, but they never want to do anything about it."

"Girl, don't even look at Eugene. He ain't gonna talk to you because you don't have blond hair and blue eyes. That's all he dates."

A responsibility to our people. She just told him he had a responsibility to his people. His people—the first ones to criticize, ostracize and judge him.

Renee' was looking at him like he was wearing a white sheet and holding a burning cross. Her self-righteous attitude was too much to bear. "Renee'," he began quietly. "I'm going to say this one time, so listen carefully. Do not ever run up in my face again about my responsibility to my people, o.k.? I don't owe them, you or anybody else anything."

Renee' appeared stunned. "I didn't mean…"

"I don't care what you meant, Renee'! I heard what you said! I get so fed up with this list of criteria for being black. You have to do this, you can't do that—if you do, you ain't black anymore."

"Eugene, I think you're making too much out of what I said…"

He held up his hand. "Renee', save it, all right?" He pointed at the marching crowd. "If it makes you feel a little blacker to carry around that sign and march and be in with all 'your people,' go right ahead. I don't need a march, a school or a group of friends to prove how black I am."

Renee's face went through a series of transformations. She looked shocked, confused, angry and hurt all in about five seconds. She opened her mouth to speak, but Eugene didn't give her a chance before he stormed off, leaving her standing there with her mouth open. He kept going, plowing through the crowd of protestors.

"Hey brotha'—you joining in?"

"You need a sign?"

"They need an extra body in the lobby…"

Where are you going, man? The boycott is right here…"

"Kenny, give this brotha' a sign…"

Eugene set his face and kept going, ignoring all of them.

"See, you got over there at that lily-white school and now you're afraid to stand up for what's right."

Eugene turned sharply at the voice he thought he heard and saw about one hundred faces that looked like his father's, smirking at him. They were wearing sweatshirts that read, "Crowler University English Department" and all their signs read, "Down with Lily-White Institutions". He shook his head and kept walking.

"What's wrong Eugene? Your white friends won't let you sit at their table today?"

He turned again and this time saw a young black girl with an asymmetrical haircut and braces frowning at him. She looked just like his biggest nemesis in high school, Katrina Denton—the one who had started the rumor that he didn't date black girls. It was leaked to him that Katrina had a crush on him but he didn't return the favor. She was attractive, but she was also loud and extremely ghetto, in his opinion. He believed that's how the rumor got started. The sad thing was that most of the black girls believed her, which is why he ended up taking Wendy Johnson, a white girl and a very good friend of his who felt sorry for him, to the prom. Needless to say, his dad hit the ceiling. His mother couldn't even display his prom picture, so he kept it hidden up in his closet.

Eugene kept walking, almost running now. It seemed like he could hear other voices taunting him, asking him why he couldn't play football, basketball… why he wore such "white boy" clothes like loafers and khakis, and why in the world did he talk so proper? Did he just want to *be* white? He did start running then, trying to escape the voices. He heard a car horn and stopped, nearly running into a car in the middle of the street. He started running again, and heard someone calling his name from the car. He didn't stop until he heard tires screeching a female voice yelled his name.

"Eugene!" Irene was parked on the side of the curb and leaning out of her driver's side window. "Are you all right?!"

He just looked at her, huffing from all his running. He tried to nod, tried to tell her that he was all right, but all he could do was shake his head. "No..." he managed to huff out.

She pulled herself back in the car and leaned over to unlock the passenger door. She waved her hand at him to get in. He opened the door without hesitating and climbed in.

"Why were you running so hard?! I almost hit you!" Irene told him, looking at him with a concerned frown.

Eugene looked the other way, fighting back his emotion. "My mother had surgery today—she has cancer."

He heard Irene gasp, then he felt the car move as she pulled onto the street and headed toward the campus entrance. He didn't say a word as she drove off campus and onto the highway. He leaned back and closed his eyes, feeling Irene grab his hand and squeeze it. He wanted to ask where they were going, but found that he really didn't care.

MARIE

She trudged in her room, worn out. She had been at the Dean of Students building ever since her ten o'clock class adjourned, causing her to eat a late lunch around two o'clock. All she wanted right now was a hot shower and her bed.

Corrie was sitting at her computer typing away when Marie came in. "Hi, Marie."

"Hi, Corrie." Marie threw her book bag down and slid out of her heavy coat and gloves. She snatched a tissue off of her desk to blow her runny nose. Cold wasn't the word for what it felt like outside.

"You catching a cold?" Corrie asked.

"No...it's just so cold outside, everything is running. Nose, eyes..."

"Were you at the boycott again?"

"Yeah." Marie flopped down on her bed to catch her breath and enjoy the warmth of her room.

"I see you guys out there every time I go to class. I didn't realize there were so many bla..." Corrie widened her eyes.

"It's all right, Corrie—remember? 'Black' is not a dirty word." Corrie relaxed her eyes. "I know—I'm sorry. I know you guys are kind of upset about what happened. I didn't want to offend."

"Well, yes—I'm upset. But you didn't have anything to do with it, did you?"

Corrie laughed. "Yeah, really. I masterminded the whole thing."

"I thought I saw a sledgehammer in your closet." Marie was surprised that she could joke about it. When she'd first heard about the Plot, and then actually saw the damage, she was almost in tears. It was like someone had vandalized her personal property.

Corrie grew serious. "Lately when I walk to class, I feel like I had a big part in it."

"What do you mean?"

Corrie turned completely from her computer, glad to finally share. "I get dirty looks from the black students. Me and my friends. It's like I was out there, destroying that property. I just started taking the back way to class just so I don't have to pass the Dean's building."

Marie nodded slowly, not really knowing what to say. The black student population was a little perturbed right now, and they were not going to be sharing warm fuzzies with the white students.

Corrie leaned forward. "Do you know what that girl that lives at the end of the hall said to me the other day? I think her name is Sandra?"

Marie didn't really know her, but she spoke whenever she happened to see her. All of the black students in Belten and around campus for that matter, spoke to each other whether or not they knew each other. It was like some kind of unwritten code of black conduct.

Corrie didn't wait for her to respond. "She and a friend of hers were getting on the elevator when I was getting off. I guess they had been talking about the Plot. Well anyway, when the door opened, they stopped talking and just stared at me. Then Sandra said, 'I'll bet you're happy about it, aren't you?' and she's been snubbing me ever since. I don't know what to say to her, so I just don't say anything. You think I should say something to her, like ask her if I did something to upset her?"

"I think you should just leave her alone," Marie answered harshly. Corrie looked stunned, then Marie realized she might have take her comment to mean that Sandra's actions were justified. "What I mean that if she wants to act silly, then let her. I think she's being ridiculous."

"Marie, I'll be honest with you. I don't know that much about black people. That's why I didn't say too much when you first moved in. But then you were so friendly, I felt comfortable asking you all the questions that I did."

Well, thanks Corrie. That's nice of you to say."

"I think what happened to the Plot was awful, and I think Lambda Sig should pay to have it fixed. Then they should be bounced off campus. And that's what I would tell those students who keep acting like I'm to blame."

Marie didn't know Corrie felt so strongly about the whole thing. She guessed she had been buying into the attitude of the black student majority about white people. She remembered justifying the attitudes of the black students to Tony just last week. Now, hearing the experience through the eyes of her roommate, she realized a few things about herself.

"Corrie, you can't waste your breath convincing others how innocent you are of another person's crime. You can't apologize for something you didn't do. It's just as wrong for Sandra to second guess you because of your race than it is for whites to stereotype blacks. Lambda Sig was wrong—not you. Please don't feel responsible for the mistakes of others, no matter what you have in common."

Corrie nodded thoughtfully. She sat quietly for a minute, looking like she wanted to say something else. "I got into Delta Rho."

"Really?! Congratulations!" Marie smiled at her, then realized that her roommate didn't look too thrilled.

"I'm not accepting."

"What?! Why not? You've been wanting this for a long time, Corrie."

"I know—but they said some things at the Rush party that I didn't agree with."

"What, they want you to go through some strange rituals?" Marie joked.

Corrie smiled briefly. "I wish it was that simple. No, they said they didn't understand what all the fuss was about the Plot, since Lambda Sig offered to clean up their mess. The President of Delta Rho said that the sisters should support Lambda Sig through this 'challenging time.'" Corrie rolled her eyes. "I found out later that she had been lavaliered by the President of Lamba Sig."

"Lava-who?"

"Lavaliered. It's a ceremonial thing a girl goes through when she and a fraternity member get real serious about their relationship. It means they're 'pre-engaged.'"

"Interesting." Marie had never heard that concept before, but then again, she and Corrie were finding out new things from one another almost every day.

"After that little speech, I thought about it for a while and decided I didn't want anything to do with an organization that condoned what Lambda Sig did. Amanda and Chrissy thought I was deranged."

"Are you sure that's what you want to do? You were real excited about the invitation."

"I'm positive. They're a bunch of snobs, anyway."

Marie laughed. What she wanted to do was run over and throw her arms around her roommate, who had taken a stand for justice when she didn't have to. So she did. "Corrie, you're a great person," Marie told her, giving her a squeeze.

Corrie grinned and squeezed her back. "Oh, by the way…some guy called you a few minutes before you came in."

"That was probably Tony." Marie grabbed her bucket of toiletries from her closet floor.

"No, he said his name was Cedric. I wrote his number down and left it on your desk."

Marie fumbled her bucket of supplies. So he did call. Not when he said he would, of course, which would have been last week.

"What's the matter—you have so many men you can't keep up with them?" Corrie laughed.

"That'll be the day."

She started not to call him back. She didn't want to give him the pleasure, but she was curious about what he had to say. Marie compromised by waiting a couple of hours before she called, so it would appear she had called him back at her leisure. So she took her shower, lay down for a while, and then dialed his number.

"This is Travis," his roommate answered. She didn't understand why the three of them announced themselves when they answered the phone, instead of saying "hello" like normal people.

"Hi, is Cedric there?"

"Yes, hold on. Yo Ced! Phone!" The greeting wasn't the only part of their phone etiquette that needed work. Her ear was ringing.

"Sorry, sweetheart. I didn't mean to yell in your ear," Travis apologized.

"No problem."

"Is this Marie?"

Great. She had wanted to keep her identity a secret. "Yes, how are you, Travis?"

"Hey, girl! Long time, no hear from! Where've you been?"

"Oh, I've been around. I'm actually returning Cedric's call." She wanted Travis to understand that she was not chasing after his roommate.

"Oh all right…"

"Give me the phone, man," Cedric demanded in the background. Travis said something she couldn't make out, and then he and Cedric laughed.

"This is Cedric," Cedric announced when he took the phone.

What kind of tone should she use? Professional? Detached? Jolly?

"This is Cedric," he repeated, insistent.

"Cedric, this is Marie."

"Hi, beautiful. It's a pleasure to hear from you."

"I'm returning your call." Did he think this was a social call? And calling her beautiful—did he think she was going to melt over that? "My roommate told me that you called."

"I did. I told you I was."

Yeah, last week.

"I know I should have called sooner, but I've been so busy lately."

"Oh, well...I forgot about that anyway." And she did, so it wasn't like she was lying. She had been consumed with the Forum and Operation Blackout.

"So you forgot about me, huh?"

She let out a plastic laugh.

"Why haven't I heard from you?"

Marie took the phone away from her ear and looked at it cross-eyed. Was she hearing right? "What did you just ask me?"

"I asked why I haven't heard from you in a while."

"Cedric, you mean to tell me that you have no idea why I haven't called you?"

"I figured you were just busy."

"You figured?" She just couldn't keep the sarcasm out of her voice.

"Either that, or you were upset with me about cha' girl."

"Why would I be upset about you and Claudia? I think it was messed up that you two felt the need to sneak behind my back, but I'm over that now."

"Marie, we just went to get something to eat. Just like I told you before. That's it."

She got an image of a lightning bolt headed straight for Cedric's apartment. "It really doesn't matter, Cedric. We don't even have to go there..."

"Will you just hear me out?"

She sighed. "All right."

"Thank you. I mean, one minute, we're really getting to know one another good, and the next minute, you're not speaking to me anymore. You move out of your room with Claudia, and then you guys aren't speaking."

"Sounds like an accurate summary to me," she told him.

He chose to ignore her sarcasm. "I don't know what Claudia told you, but all I did was take her out to eat a friendly little dinner and give her a ride back to her room. Now what did 'we' sneak behind your back with?"

Marie's mind was spinning with questions. What about this conversation when he told Claudia he was interested in her? How about telling Claudia that "Marie was just a friend?"

"Did Claudia tell you something different?"

Did she spill her guts about what Claudia told her, now that she was starting to wonder how much of it was true? Or did she cover for her, because Cedric's credibility was as reliable as an elephant in a china shop?

Cedric obviously took her silence as consent. "Ah, Marie. I think I made a big mistake. That's what I get for trying to be a Mr. Nice Guy."

"What do you mean?"

"I hope I didn't lead her on." He sounded really bothered. "To tell you the truth, I felt kind of sorry for her. She seemed so…alone all the time. If she wasn't with you, I didn't see her hanging with anyone else…and she was studying—on a Saturday night. And when she mentioned just grabbing a bite to eat that day and heading back to her room…well, without thinking, I suggested going off campus to eat. Maybe she misunderstood my motives. What was I supposed to say, 'Claudia, I feel sorry for you, so I'm taking you out to eat?'"

Now that part could be true. Claudia had clung to Marie like Velcro all through high school because Marie had shown her some kindness. Claudia became attached real quick.

"Cedric, why didn't you tell me this earlier?"

"Because I didn't think it was that big of a deal," he protested, echoing Claudia's words. If I had known it was gonna to lead to all this, I would've told you a lot sooner. You moved out the next day, and I didn't have your new number or anything."

Please. "It's not that hard to locate someone if you really want to."

He was silent for a while. Marie thought he had hung up for a second. "I guess I was too embarrassed," he finally said. "By the time you found out everything, I figured you thought I was a dog and anything I said would've sounded like a lie. That's why when you saw me walking with her on campus, I would barely speak. I was still just trying to be nice to the girl—give her somebody to walk with. Now tell the truth—how many guys would take a female that looks like Claudia out to eat because they felt sorry for her? Or walk with her on campus?"

She had to give him that. "Not many," she admitted.

"O.k. then, so what would you have believed?"

Now she was really confused. Cedric, Claudia, Corrie, Tony, the Plot...it was too much to think about at one time. She needed to get off the phone, clear her head. "Hold on Cedric...there's a call coming in." She pressed the mute button and took a deep breath. It was an old high school trick she'd learned. "Cedric, I have to go."

"So can I call you again?"

"I really have to go, Cedric. I'll talk to you later." She hung up without giving him another opportunity to plead his case.

CLAUDIA

She didn't know what made her snap at Marie. All she knew was she was tired of hearing Tony this, Tony that. Tony, Tony, Tony. Claudia was sitting on the wall outside of the dining hall, waiting for Marie. The wall surrounded the area that stretched between the dining hall and the ladies' residence hall, and was unofficially known as "The Block." Marie had made dinner plans with Claudia earlier, and asked her to meet on the Block at 5:45. She was hitting close to being fifteen minutes late, Claudia noticed, looking down at her watch. Marie was usually so punctual.

Cedric had called her today. She wasn't in, so he left a message on her machine, apologizing for not calling in a while, but he'd been soooo busy. He even invited her to call him back. She listened to that message about five times to see if she could detect anything in his voice that wasn't sincere. She couldn't wait to tell Marie, who would be overjoyed that she didn't return his call, even though she had considered it for a split second.

Claudia didn't say too much when Marie talked about Tony, but muttered the appropriate "mm hmms" and "that's nice" when necessary. Marie would constantly ask her, "You don't mind me talking about him, do you?" Claudia would respond, "No, girl. Please. Talk about the boy if you want," even though it did bother her to hear how the young man who was just "her friend" treated her like a queen.

Lately, it seemed like whenever Claudia wanted to do something with Marie, she couldn't because Marie had to meet Tony about the Forum. Or when Claudia called, Marie couldn't talk right away because Tony was on the other line. It was a total shock when Marie approached her about dinner.

"I feel like I've been dissing my best friend," she told her when she came by the room earlier that day. "I've been so busy with the Forum—you want to meet for dinner?"

Claudia agreed to meet her, happy to spend some quality time with her former roomie. Marie told her she had a 4:30 meeting that she expected to last no longer than an hour. She suggested 5:45, just to be on the safe side. It was now 5:58. Claudia sighed, then looked up just in time to see Marie headed towards her—with Tony. He was

222

talking with animated gestures, and Marie was laughing gracefully. If Marie's hair had been long and flowing, Claudia was sure she'd be tossing it back right now.

Marie spotted Claudia and started waving. Tony looked over and waved, too. Claudia produced a slight grin and waved back, wanting to jump up and head right back to her room. Here she had been waiting almost fifteen minutes, and Marie was strolling down the sidewalk with her new "friend" like she'd lost sense of time. She was probably thinking, "Oh Claudia won't mind—she ain't got nothing else to do."

Claudia stayed seated and glared at the two behind her sunglasses, even when Marie and Tony got to her, all smiles.

"Hi, sweetie," Marie greeted, bending down to give Claudia a quick hug. "Sorry I'm late. That meeting ran over."

"No, Claudia—it's my fault," Tony confessed solemnly. "The meeting did run over, but I spent about five minutes trying to convince this lovely lady to have dinner with me. I made a roast last night."

"You cook?" Claudia was surprised, in spite of herself. That was one tidbit of information Marie had neglected to tell her.

"Cook?! The boy throws down," Marie answered emphatically. "Claudia, he Made a baked chicken dish that Made you want to hurt somebody."

"Come on now, girl…" Tony protested.

"It did," Marie insisted to him, then turned back to Claudia. "Girl, the cornbread was so light and fluffy, it melted in your hand before you could get it to your mouth."

"That good, huh?" Claudia said with fake enthusiasm.

"Marie's exaggerating," Tony said shyly. He looked like he wanted to shove his hands in his pockets, hang his head and say something like "Golly gee whiz."

"You know, Claudia—the invitation is open to you, too. I made enough for an army."

"That's so sweet of you, Tony," Marie chimed, now sounding like a southern belle.

"Well…" Claudia began. She really wanted to talk to Marie by herself, but the invitation *was* tempting. She looked up at Marie, hoping she would lapse into an explanation about how this was their little get together time. But Marie just stood there, looking

223

expectantly and wistfully at Claudia, then something must have clicked. Her pleasant smile faded slowly.

"I think we need to do some girl talk, Tony," Marie told him. "Maybe some other time."

"No problem. I can't say that I'm not disappointed, missing the opportunity to dine with two lovely sisters, but the food won't go to waste. I guarantee that roast will be history by tomorrow once my roommates get a hold of it. I probably need to go home and practice anyway while my roommates aren't there."

What a charmer, thought Claudia. *And such a cutie*. She could figure out why he didn't have a girlfriend already. But then again, he wasn't bopping around, throwing loud lines on women, either. Or driving around in a fancy car trying to impress somebody. For some reason, most girls flocked to guys with that "bad boy" image, and didn't give the time of day to the ones like Tony. It was usually the quiet, nice guys like Tony that really knew how to treat a girl. And he and Marie seemed to get along so well, like good friends—the same way she wanted to start out with Cedric.

"You ladies enjoy your dinner," Tony said, starting to back up. "Marie, can I call you later?"

"I guess I can permit that," she joked. Wasn't she cute? Tony cracked up like she'd brought the house down at the Apollo.

"Well, thank you for your permission. I'll see you, Claudia."

"Bye."

Marie watched him disappear down the sidewalk. "That boy is something else," she remarked almost tenderly. She turned back to Claudia. "You ready to go in?"

"Yeah." Claudia snatched off her shades and they made their way into the dining hall, which was surprisingly crowded, considering the quality of food they served. Students that didn't feel up to the hike to reach the Student Center settled for the dining hall's imitation meat, undercooked vegetables and watered down drinks. They did a decent job on the desert, but it was hard to mess up on store-brought ice cream and cookies. The cake pieces that looked less that appetizing were usually left standing in place, only to appear the next day underneath a new layer of icing.

Claudia and Marie got behind a line of chattering students at the hot bar and looked over the selection—beef stroganoff, chicken pan pie, green beans, corn, mashed potatoes and what resembled cornbread. The unsmiling woman behind the counter moved the students along like an assembly line. The two guys ahead of Claudia questioned the server about each item of food like they were from another planet.

"What's that?" one asked, jabbing his finger on the plastic shield that separated the food from the students.

"It's beef stroganoff," the frustrated server answered, pointing to the sign in front of it labeled, "Beef Stroganoff."

"Dude, who killed Mr. Ed?" his companion asked, and the surrounding students broke out in a fit of laughter. Even Claudia and Marie found themselves giggling over that.

The red-faced server asked if they were going to get anything—if not, she needed to move on. They chose the pan pie and moved on. Claudia ordered the same, not sure if she could separate the beef dish from that lovable television character. Marie got a vegetable plate.

They chose a table near the window and Claudia immediately bowed her head. She was surprised to see Marie's hands reaching across the table. "What?" Claudia asked.

"Let's join hands and pray," Marie explained, taking Claudia's hands. "I learned this from Tony."

Tony already. Marie lapsed into a prayer that would have made Jesse Jackson holler. Claudia kept glancing up to see who was watching, then she'd look at Marie who had her head bowed, praying away.

"Amen."

"Amen," Claudia echoed, not sure what she was amening. She would usually mutter a quick, "God is great, God is good" prayer she learned as a child and commence to eat, but Marie sounded like she was standing behind a pulpit. And the scary part was, she sounded like she meant every word. For some strange reason, it made Claudia feel a little uneasy.

"Did you learn how to pray like that from Tony, too?" she asked Marie, trying to keep her voice normal.

Marie smiled. "No—I just prayed what was in my heart. Tony just taught me that joining hands is a sign of coming into agreement."

"Tony's a special kind of guy, isn't he?" Claudia said to herself, jabbing her fork into her chicken pie. The crust was surprisingly flaky. Maybe it wouldn't taste so bad after all.

"What?" Marie asked her.

"Nothing."

"Oh." Marie played around with her green beans. "So, how have you been, girl?"

"Fine, I guess." Claudia was hoping Marie would pick up on the heaviness in her voice. "Same old, same old."

"No excitement—no drama?" Marie asked before forking vegetables into her mouth. She grimaced, then added salt to her plate. "These vegetables need a little work. Tony needs to show these cooks a thing or two."

Claudia wanted to scream, but shoved a forkful of chicken pie into her mouth, instead. That was a big mistake, because the pie had so much pepper in it, her mouth caught fire. She fumbled for her drink and let the watery lemonade soothe her burning tongue.

"You all right?"

"Chicken pie is too spicy," Claudia gasped, inhaling to get her wind.

"We should've taken Tony up on his offer, huh? At least we would have had a decent meal."

"Marie, if you want to go eat with Tony, go ahead. Don't let me stop you."

"No, girl! We haven't chatted in a while. I'm sorry. That did sound kind of bad, huh?"

"Don't worry about it." Claudia played around in her plate, wondering how she could tell Marie about Cedric. Marie seemed different somehow. It wasn't just the thing with Tony—it was her whole attitude lately. She appeared so—nonchalant all the time. Calm. It made Claudia feel guilty for some odd reason. Still, she needed to bounce off her what had happened today. Shoot, she needed to bounce it off of *somebody*. "Cedric called me today."

Clank! Marie's fork hit her plate. Well, at least Claudia had her attention now.

"And just what did he want?"

"I don't know—he left a message on my machine. He said something about being busy lately and wanted me to call him back." She paused for dramatic effect. "I haven't called back."

She expected a triumphant smile, a pleased look, a pat on the head for obedience—something. Instead, Marie gave her one of those sharp, parental stares. "You weren't going to, were you?"

"I just said I didn't call him back."

"Yes, I heard that part, Claudia. It just didn't sound very conclusive. It just sounded like you haven't called him back *yet*."

"I never said I was planning to call him back. Those words never came out of my mouth."

"Claudia, honey—I know what you said. It's what you didn't say that concerns me. I just wanted to clarify that you weren't going to call him back, that's all."

What was up with her attitude? Anger heated up Claudia's face. Who did Marie think she was over there, acting like Claudia didn't know how to handle herself? She had a thousand and one things she wanted to tell her then, but she decided to keep her cool. "Let's just drop it, all right?"

Again, Marie's face registered surprise. "Drop what, Claudia? All I said was...all right. We'll drop it." Marie shrugged and resumed playing with her food. She shook her head, like she couldn't figure out where Claudia's attitude was coming from. They were supposed to be having a friendly little dinner.

But Claudia wasn't satisfied with her response. "I did want to talk to you about it," she pushed.

Marie stopped her playing again. "We can talk about it, Claudia. I thought you said you wanted to drop it. So that's what I did."

"Well, I just said that because you were..."

"I was what?"

"Never mind."

Marie folded her hands and looked at her. "Claudia, if I said or did anything to offend you, please forgive me." She sounded like she was reciting from a Hallmark card. "If you want to talk about Cedric, I'm listening."

Marie was making her feel smaller and smaller by the minute. The person sitting across from her was not the same friend she knew in high school. Then again, Claudia *had* dissed her with Cedric, but Marie claimed to be over that. Everything was supposed to be love-love now...or was it? Marie might still be bitter, but as was her nature, she wouldn't admit it.

But what about Tony? Marie certainly talked him up enough, but that didn't mean that she still wasn't upset about Cedric. Yeah, Claudia could see it now. Marie had a new thing, wanted to get back at Claudia for stealing her old thing, so she talked her out of seeing Cedric so she would wind up with nothing.

227

"Why shouldn't I call him back?" She was looking for something in Marie's face—in her tone—to prove that she was right.

But Marie kept a perfect poker face. "You do what you feel is best," she answered safely.

"Oh, I will," Claudia assured her. "But you don't think I should, do you?"

"I think you should do whatever you want to do."

"But you don't think I *should*?"

"Does it matter what I think?"

Claudia egged her on. "You already said you thought I shouldn't."

Marie was keeping her cool pretty good. Claudia was sure she would have exploded by now. "All I remember asking you is if you were going to call him back, Claudia. Now I'm not going to lie—the idea didn't set well with me and I don't think you should call him back after what he did to you. But if you have a driving desire to talk to him, call him. That's on you. I don't have anything to do with it."

If there was one phrase that Claudia hated to hear, it was someone telling her they didn't have anything to do with whatever she had shared with them. That statement, and "I don't know what to say" irritated her to no end, especially if she had shared something extremely difficult. It was like the person was washing their hands of the whole ordeal, or didn't want to be bothered with her problems. And she was sure she had mentioned that pet peeve to Marie more than once since she and her brother were really the only people she shared her problems with.

Claudia couldn't stop herself from thinking the worst. *Look at her over there, with her organized little life. She has a new "friend," a good GPA and activities to occupy her time. And now she's on some spiritual high, trying to make me feel like the devil's child. "I don't have anything to do with it"...who asked her that in the first place? And why shouldn't I call Cedric back? He may want to apologize. Shoot, for all I know, Marie made up that story about Cedric calling her, trying to get his rap back on. She's not dumb. What happened with me and Cedric gave her the perfect opportunity to twist a lie against him. After all, a female is liable to do anything when she's jealous. I did.*

"I think I will call him back," Claudia decided out loud.

"Like I said before, Claudia, I..."

"Yeah, yeah, I know. You don't have anything to do with it," Claudia cut in rudely. "You've made that clear already."

"I didn't mean it like you're making it sound. If I offended you…"

"You're sorry, I know," Claudia interrupted again. "You've said that phrase already, too. It sure would be nice to hear something new."

The look of shock on Marie's face said it all. Little, timid, gullible Claudia was trying to break bad on somebody—again. And on her, of all people—the one who had reached out a helping hand when she was going through, even though Claudia had put a man before their friendship. Good. It served her right for trying to be Ms. Perfection, Claudia thought. She wanted to see some anger like she'd seen the day Marie found out about her and Cedric. This new calmness of hers was a little unsettling.

"I get the feeling that this isn't just about Cedric. Is there something else going on? Are you mad at me for some reason?"

Claudia wasn't quite ready to put Marie back on her Christmas list. "Why should I be mad at you? You got it going on, don't you?"

"Girl, what are you talking about?" Uh oh. *Now* the sister was coming out. Her little choir girl façade was gone. Marie looked like she wanted to roll her neck a little. "We're supposed to be having a nice dinner, but you've had a chip on your shoulder ever since we've sat down. Now I've apologized for being late—is that what you have your lip poked out about?"

"The problem is that I have been trying to talk to you about Cedric calling me, but you're too busy trying to find out if I'm going to make another mistake with him."

"Claudia, I wasn't even trying to go there…"

"You didn't have to, Marie. Your whole attitude says it all."

Marie looked like a frustrated parent dealing with an unruly child. "So *talk*, Claudia. *Talk.* I've been sitting here waiting for you to finish. Talk—*please.*"

Claudia glanced around. A few diners near them were looking their way, but turned back to their tables when with a nervous smile when she made eye contact with them. She didn't realize their conversation was that audible. She looked back at Marie, who seemed oblivious to the attention they were drawing. She was sitting back in her chair with her arms folded. *Hurry up and let's get this over with so I can go back to my room and call Tony, and tell him how I had to face a very challenging situation with my ex-roomie, who is wrapped up in this guy that is no good for her. He's not like you, Tony. But she won't listen to me. I guess we'll just have to pray for her. Come on—let's pretend we're holding hands so we can come into agreement,* the look said.

Oh, Claudia was going to talk, alright. She was going to tell her everything she wanted to say, but didn't have the guts to say it—until she got angry.

"You got a lot of nerve, sitting over there like you're all that, Marie. Trying to make me feel small. But that's the way you've always been. Always trying to boss somebody around, like you never made a mistake. But you got crunched when Cedric picked me instead of you, didn't you? That was a mistake, wasn't it? You thought he liked Miss Black African Queen but he liked little shy zebra Claudia instead, right? Acting like you forgave somebody about it. Quit lying to yourself, girl. Quit trying to act like nothing bothers you. You know you're still upset about what happened with Cedric, and you probably still like him, don't you?"

Marie took one deep breath. Claudia braced herself for the explosion, but Marie was looking at her like she had spoken a foreign language. "That is the most ridiculous thing I have ever heard," she answered in an infuriatingly calm voice.

"Yeah, it is ridiculous, ain't it? Considering how you told me you were over him, and what a dog he was." Claudia lowered her voice and leaned forward. "And I bet you were disappointed when I told you I wasn't pregnant, weren't you?"

"O.k., Claudia. That's it. I'm not going to listen to this nonsense anymore." Marie reached down for her purse, scooted her chair back and stood. "You're upset, I know. But I will not sit here and be a target for your anger. When you are ready to talk to me like an adult, you know where to find me."

"Oh, don't worry about that, Marie. I've said all that I had to say to you."

Marie looked down at her. "Whatever, Claudia. You probably need some time to yourself, anyway. Like I said, you know where to find me if you want to have a civilized conversation." Marie turned on her heel and walked away, just like that. She didn't even give Claudia the chance to have the last word. She could feel the anger seething inside of her.

Fine, then. She didn't need Marie's advice or her friendship. Marie left because she couldn't take the truth about herself. She needed to come down off her high horse, anyway. Claudia didn't know whether or not she should cry, so she just picked up her lemonade, surprised to find that her hands were shaking.

PERCY

"Good news, ya'll," Carlos said as he slapped down a card. "The Dean has agreed to attend the Forum discussion."

Percy, Carlos, Darryl and Andre', Darryl's cousin and roommate, were sitting at the small kitchen table in Darryl's apartment, playing a vicious round of spades. Seven pizza boxes, some empty, some getting there, were sitting on the kitchen counter. The retaliation on Lambda Sig was three weeks away, coinciding with the Forum, so that there would be very little witnesses on campus. Carlos felt like the Board needed a little breather from all the fuss of Operation Blackout, and time to mentally prepare for what lay ahead. Two of the other board members, Marcus and Brian, were sitting in the living room, alternating between eating and coming over to the kitchen table to see who was winning. So far, Andre' and Darryl were ahead. Another board member, Rodney, was sitting in front of the entertainment center, rifling through Andre' and Darryl's video and music collection.

"I didn't think he'd agree to it," Darryl remarked, studying his hand.

"I told you he would," Carlos replied as he slapped a spade over Darryl's ace of diamonds. Percy breathed a sigh of relief because his hand was bleeding bad—nothing but diamonds and hearts, for the most part. "The man's a racist—not a fool."

"I just better not see any diamonds showing up later on, Carlos," Andre' told him, throwing out his deuce.

"I told you in the beginning—me and Percy do not have to cheat to win this game, like ya'll have been doing. Ain't that right, partner?"

Percy reached across the table and high-fived Carlos. "True dat, true dat."

"Don't confuse cheating with skill," Darryl told him.

Percy was pleasantly surprised that the usually serious board members could relax and enjoy themselves—it was almost like hanging out with his boys back home again. Darryl was wild when he played. He started talking junk as soon as they hit his door, promising that he and Andre' were going to pull out the paddle on Percy and Carlos.

"Man, when is Tamal coming?" Marcus asked around a mouthful of pizza. "We could've had another game going."

"Tamal said he'd be running late, but he'll be here. Be patient— two of you can play the winners of this game. Me and Percy, in other words."

"Nah, man...I was trying to be nice, but you blew it. Andre', we taking these suckers out on the next hand," Darryl said.

Percy decided to get into the trash talk. "Darryl, don't let your mouth write a check that your behind can't cash, now."

All eyes focused on him. Darryl looked at Carlos. "Did Percy just talk some trash? *Percy?!*"

"No, did Percy just talk, *period*?" Carlos added.

"Why it gotta be like that?" Percy asked. "Ya'll act like you never heard me talk before."

"Basically," Carlos told him. "I was beginning to think you couldn't."

"No, it's not that..." Percy was eyeing Andre's eight of spades that had cut Carlos's club. "I just wait until I have something significant to say, like take your hands off our book, Darryl." Percy slapped down a spaded ten to the delight of his partner and the dismay of Darryl, who was just reaching out to retrieve the hand he'd thought he'd won.

"So you saying you all out of puppy feet?" he asked Percy in disbelief. "Don't lie, 'cause I been counting the suits."

"I'm slap out, bru."

Carlos was keeping score in a notebook next to him. "Looks like ya'll about to be set, gentleman. Any last requests?"

Andre' and Darryl just glared at him. "It ain't over 'till the fat lady sings, bru—surely you've heard of that," Andre' reminded him.

Percy grinned and spread out his last three cards. The big dogs— the deuce of spades, the big and little joker. Andre' and Darryl ended up in the hole. Carlos jumped up and begin singing some bad opera in an even worse falsetto voice. Percy cracked up; Andre' and Darryl threw their remaining cards at him.

"Uh oh—they got my movie!" Rodney held up a videotape.

"What you got there?" Andre' asked, retrieving the cards from the floor and shuffling.

"*Cooley High*—I love this movie. Can I watch?" Rodney sounded like a child asking for a cookie.

"What you know about *Cooley High*? You were barely hatched when it came out." Carlos laughed and shook his head. He had about two and a half years on Rodney, and Andre' had just turned twenty-six.

"I was four—and very advanced for my age," Rodney defended, popping the tape into the VCR and sitting back against the couch. "Brian, you and Marcus can play the winners—I'm set."

"I can't believe you are watching that ancient movie," Brian said.

"You watch you mouth," Rodney warned him. "This is a ...a classic. Like Shakespeare."

"Yeah, if Shakespeare was black."

"You mean he wasn't?"

"Rodney's right about that," Andre' offered from the table. "*Cooley High* is a classic black movie of the seventies blackploitation era. Like *Mahogany, Shaft* and *Get Christie Love.*"

"Get *who*?" Brian asked.

"Man, you don't know nothing about that, do you?" Andre' laughed.

"Watch the board, Dre," Darryl warned.

But Andre' was on a roll. "See, back in the day, they made movies and music that had meaning. Not like this junk ya'll listen to today. All this hip-hop, rap, sexually explicit lyrics and violence. You didn't have all that when I was coming up."

Marcus migrated over to Percy's shoulder. "What you got against hip hop and rap?"

"Marcus, you think you can stop eating all over the living room? We do try to keep things reasonably clean around here." Darryl was a little miffed after he glanced over his present hand.

"What do I have against hip hop and rap? Well, first of all, it's hard to understand the words. Second, it's all about the same thing—sex, drugs and violence. What's the point?"

"Andre, rap is an expression of urban life," Marcus explained.

"What kind of message is it sending to the youth of America?"

Andre' was a high school counselor, and was constantly harping on the plight of the "youth of America."

"Here we go…" Darryl shook his head, knowing how his cousin was once he got started on an issue.

"But I'm serious, fellas." Andre put his cards down. "I know a lot of entertainers and sports personalities warn young people not to

234

make them a role model, but isn't that what they are by virtue of their profession?"

"Why do people who don't like rap always beat that dead horse?" Marcus took a seat back in the living room and sipped his drink. "Why not just say, 'I don't like rap' and leave it at that?"

"Marcus, it goes beyond that." Now Andre' got up from the table and went into the living room. Darryl threw down his hand with a sigh, and Carlos did the same.

"Put your hand down, Percy," Darryl told him. "When Dre gets going, he won't let up until he's finished."

"I think Andre' had a good point," Percy announced to no one in particular. Rap was big back in Jackson Park, and Percy used to be an avid listener. But when he saw his friends and neighbors trying to live out the lyrics, it turned him off from the music. "I think music like that glorifies an unrealistic lifestyle. It tears down family values and perpetuates the negative stereotype society already has about blacks."

For the second time, everyone turned to look at him. Even Rodney pressed the pause button on the remote and turned around.

"Well, let the church say, 'Amen!'" Marcus declared.

"Yo, Percy—the more you talk, the better you get at it," Darryl added.

"That was pretty deep," Brian joined in.

"My point exactly." Andre' strutted over to Percy and clapped him on the shoulder. "That's all I was trying to say, only Percy said it first."

"Can we please finish this game before I graduate?" Carlos pleaded.

"Must have a good hand," Darryl said, picking up his cards and slapping them down on the table again. "There sure ain't nothin' happenin' over here."

"So that means you gonna lose, right?" Carlos checked the score sheet. "Ya'll already down by one-hundred fifty something points."

Darryl was about to comment when Tamal suddenly burst through the front door, breathing like he'd run the whole way.

"Tamal, glad you could make it," Carlos greeted him cheerfully, which was out of the ordinary. Usually, Tamal seemed to work Carlos' nerves.

"'Sup, Carlos?"

"What happened to you?" Darryl asked, and Percy took a good look at Tamal. His pants leg was dirty and slightly torn on the right knee, and he was limping his way into the apartment.

Tamal looked down at his knee. "Ah…I tripped and landed on my knee, that's all."

"That looks kind of painful there," Andre' told him. "You sure you don't need to have it checked out?"

"Nah, man—I'm fine."

"You don't look fine, the way you're hobbling around," Carlos told him.

"It ain't no thang."

"All right…" Carlos went back to the game.

Tamal limped and pounded fists around the room. When he got to Percy, he hesitated, then slowly laid his balled up fist on his. It was more of a challenge than a greeting. But Percy had a news flash for ole' Tamal—he wasn't up for any of his nonsense anymore, and he was more than eager to alert him to that fact, injury or no injury.

"Tamal, have some pizza," Andre' offered, studying his hand. "Better hurry before Marcus starts nibbling on the boxes."

Marcus threw Andre' a look. "Tamal, we've been waiting for you to come so we can get up another game. Come on—I'm ready to whoop somebody."

"Better save your energy for Lambda Sig," Tamal told him. "You'll get your chance then." Carlos looked up sharply from his hand at that comment. "If the situation calls for it, Carlos. That's what we agreed on, right?"

"Why don't you just relax and have something to eat? Prop that knee up or something? We're not here to discuss business—we're here to have some fun."

Brian stretched out in his chair and hung his legs over the side. "Carlos is right. We're all wired up about it, but let's just unwind some. Guys night out."

"Yeah, we couldn't even invite any women over," Marcus complained around his umpteenth slice of pizza. It was a mystery to everyone how he was always feeding his face but didn't have a weight problem.

"I told you this was male bonding time," Darryl expressed, pounding his chest like Tarzan. "Women have their little 'girls night out' all the time. Why can't the fellas do the same?"

"No offense, Darryl…but I would rather be looking at a female than you right now," Marcus teased, causing an eruption of laughter in the room.

"Marcus, I think you need to concentrate on getting one first, brotha'. No offense." Darryl retaliated, causing more laughter.

Rodney turned up the volume on the television. "Can ya'll please keep it down? This is a very important part of the movie." The response was a barrage of couch pillows aimed at his head from Brian and Marcus.

"Rodney, why don't you take the movie back in my room and watch it?" Andre' suggested, watching Percy sweep up another book. Rodney immediately popped the movie out and headed down the hallway. "And ya'll pick up those pillows. Darryl, do you mind watching the board? In case you haven't noticed, we are losing."

"We're not losing," Darryl insisted. "We're just…not ahead."

"How long have you guys been playing?" Tamal asked. He had finally settled down with some pizza, and was flipping through a *GQ* magazine with his sore leg stretched out in front of him.

"They been playing forever," Marcus whined. "If you had been here earlier, Rodney wouldn't have been all into that movie and we could've had another game going."

"I had some Tri-AC business to take care of," Tamal told him.

Carlos put his hand down and stared down at the table. "What have you done, Tamal?"

"I went over to the Lambda Sig house with a few of the new members. That's where I tripped over a rock or something."

Even Andre' and Darryl dropped their hands then. Marcus stopped eating and Brian sat up from where he was lounging on the chair. The only noise was the movie coming from Andre's bedroom. Carlos didn't lift his head. You did *what?!*"

"I went to the Lambda Sig house," Tamal repeated confidently, standing. "I did some preliminary work. I went to map it out so we could plan…"

"Have you lost your mind?!" Carlos exploded, jarring the table as he pounded it. Percy, Andre' and Darryl all flinched, and Rodney came rushing out of the bedroom.

Tamal looked shocked. "No one saw me, Carlos."

237

"How do you know, Tamal?! You don't know who was watching you!" Carlos got up and paced around the kitchen. Percy hadn't seen him so worked up since the Lambda Sig trial early last month.

Everyone was taking turns looking at Carlos, then Tamal.

"I'm not hearing this," Andre said, getting up and heading down the hall. "If you guys are going to discuss what I think you're going to discuss, I'm outta here." Andre' had told Darryl that he refused to hear about any of their plans in case something went wrong. He wanted to be able to say he knew nothing about it.

Tamal limped over to Carlos. "Look, Carlos…"

"No, *you* look!" Carlos fired on him. "Who told you to go over there and check out anything?! And take the new members on top of that, who are supposed to know nothing about what we're doing?! Don't you know that a group of black men on that side of campus is sure to raise some suspicion—*especially at the Lambda Sig house?!* And then a week later, bam, some black men raid their house. Who are they going to point the finger at? Us, Tamal! The Tri-AC!"

"How are they going to point the finger at us if we're disguised? They won't know who did it! And I just told the members I took that I wanted to see what their house looked like—that's all."

Carlos dropped his head, either in a moment of reflection or in an effort not to choke the black man standing in front of him. "The bottom line is this—you were out of order. We are an organization—a team. We just don't jump out and do things on our own…"

"Oh, like you did when you put your boy over there on the board?" Tamal's tone was bitter. He pointed at Percy like Carlos didn't know who he was talking about.

Percy kept very quiet. He didn't even keep his eyes on Tamal because he felt his rage coming. *Let Carlos handle this.*

Carlos opened his arms wide and walked up very close to Tamal. "Is that what this is about?! You purposely try to sabotage our plans because you don't agree with Percy being on the board?!"

"I didn't try to sabotage anything. I just made a decision I felt would be best for the *team*—just like you did."

"But your decision wasn't best for us, Tamal…"

"I can say the same for yours, Carlos," Tamal interrupted. "So I guess we both made a mistake, right?"

You could've heard a pin drop in the apartment. Even Darryl was at a loss for words. Tamal was standing defiantly, looking down at

Carlos, who was a good three inches shorter than he was. Percy was fed up with him. He was tired of Tamal always talking about him in the third person, and looking at him like he'd just scraped him off the bottom of his shoe. Percy had been through too much in his life to take some mess off of a bully like Tamal, who constantly baited him for some mysterious reason. Bump the reason, now. This was getting too personal.

"Tamal, you a straight up fool, for real." Percy heard the words come out of his mouth before he could even think about them. "Yo, you need to grow up."

Tamal, who had his back to Percy, did a quick about face to look at him. "What did you say?"

Percy stood up. He learned a long time ago that you never challenged a person when you were lower than he was. "I said you foolish, bru—you acting like a child. I ain't stutter." He spoke in a low, controlled, even voice.

Darryl gaped up at Percy. Rodney sat all the way up in his chair. Marcus, who had resumed eating, dropped his slice of pizza. The look on Tamal's face said what everyone must have been thinking—they couldn't believe a new member, a freshman like Percy, was trying to break bad on somebody.

Tamal hobbled slowly towards him. "Niggah, who you think you talkin' to?!"

Percy stepped away from the table and right up to Tamal, who was about two inches taller and twenty pounds heavier. He didn't care. "You, niggah. Whassup? You got a problem wit me?"

"Yeah, I got a problem with you—you a punk freshman."

"You must want your *grill* smashed in..." Percy wanted to say more, but that's when Tamal grabbed him. In his neighborhood, when a brother put his hands on you, you didn't give him a second chance. Percy didn't have a clear recollection of the next few seconds—all he remembered was a jumble of arms pulling him back, and a lot of shouting. Tamal was holding his jaw and yelling, trying to reach for Percy, who was being restrained by Darryl and Marcus. Carlos, Brian and Rodney were pushing Tamal away, and Andre' came running down the hall.

"T—you out! Step!" Darryl yelled.

Tamal jerked away from the three holding him, glaring at everyone. "Oh it's like that, Darryl?! It's like that?!"

239

Darryl just looked at him.

Tamal rubbed his chin, where Percy realized he had hit him. "Ah-ight —bet! Bet!"

Percy looked down at his left hand, still balled up in a fist. His knuckles were throbbing. He didn't remember hitting Tamal, but it must have been hard, because Tamal's jaw was beginning to swell and there was blood coming out of the corner of his mouth.

"Look, everybody just calm down," Andre' interjected. "Darryl, get Tamal some ice and send him on his way. In fact, I think everybody needs to leave. Ya'll gonna get me evicted with all this nonsense."

"Andre, man—I apologize for the confusion," Carlos told him. He turned to Tamal, who was still glaring daggers at Percy, and Percy was staring them right back at him. "Tamal, meet me in my office in twenty minutes. Percy, I'll drop you back off by the school." Percy nodded, still dazed by everything. Tamal was limping angrily out of the apartment, not waiting for anyone and certainly not acknowledging Carlos' request.

"He won't show up," Darryl told Carlos.

"Then he'll be suspended indefinitely from the Tri-AC," Carlos responded, sounding like he meant every word. "We can't afford his attitude anymore. That's it."

"He won't like that, Carlos," Brian told him.

"So? Who's in charge here, Brian?"

"You are, Carlos—but I didn't mean…"

"I don't care what you meant, Brian. I care what you said. I don't run this organization based on Tamal's likes and dislikes. I run it based on what I feel is best…"

Whoa. Didn't Carlos just jump all over Tamal for running a one-man show with the Lambda Sig house?! Was that just an act to hide the fact that someone made a decision that he didn't authorize? Although Percy was one hundred percent in his corner about excommunicating Tamal from the Tri-AC, he still thought Carlos sounded a bit hypocritical.

Brian smiled nervously. "Come on Carlos. You know I ain't mean it like that…"

Carlos waved his hand in annoyance. "Squash that, Brian…you've said enough. Let me just say this for the record—if any of you don't like the way I'm running things here, you're welcome to leave at any time. I'm laying down some new law tonight. Tamal Bailey will be suspended indefinitely from the Tri-AC, no ifs, ands or buts about it. Anybody that cannot abide by the rules and regulations set up for the organization, or that has a problem following orders will be dealt with in the same manner. Do I make myself clear?"

Carlos didn't wait for an answer. He just looked at everyone like he meant business and went slamming out of the apartment. The other board members just stood around a minute, looking puzzled. "Well, let's clean up and get out of here." Marcus finally broke the silence and moved to pick up the pizza boxes.

"No, ya'll just leave," Andre' told them, sounding a little frustrated with the whole chain of events. "I'll clean up."

Darryl tapped Percy on the shoulder. "Come on Percy—I'll take back to campus."

Percy looked in Darryl's eyes for some signal, some reaction to what had just happened. Darryl's expression was tight, showing no emotion. His eyes flickered strangely, but Percy couldn't quite read what was there. If he had to venture a guess, he would guess confusion and disappointment. In fact, it was the same look he had minutes before the altercation at the Unity Meeting. Maybe his beloved leader wasn't the pillar of control he thought. Percy hated to admit it, but Carlos had sounded downright pompous and arrogant tonight. Maybe it was his anger at Tamal that made him forget that the Tri-AC was a team, but whatever it was, Percy was not too comfortable with Carlos at the moment—not comfortable at all.

"How's your hand feeling, man?"

"It's still sore. I had a real problem taking notes today."

The day following Tamal's announced suspension, Percy was walking with Marcus after their African-American Studies class let out. His knuckles were throbbing painfully by the time he woke up that morning, and he could barely bend his fingers.

"Tamal's face must be made outta steel."

Marcus laughed. "You hit him pretty hard. Hey, let's stop by the candy counter."

Percy couldn't understand it. Marcus had just eaten breakfast before their ten o'clock class, and here he wanted to eat again. And would probably have lunch in another hour.

"Yo, man...I think you need to have yourself checked for tapeworms," Percy told him. "You just don't have a normal appetite."

Marcus bent his right arm and patted it. "Muscle, man. It's all muscle."

They went to the candy counter in the Student Center, where Marcus brought a small bag of Brach's Maple Nut Goodies and immediately began chomping. Percy opted for the Sour Patch Kids.

"Yeah," Marcus continued as they left the center. "Tamal really surprised me last night. He's always been a tad temperamental, but *man!*"

"That's what Carlos and Darryl told me earlier." Percy's lips puckered as he chewed the sour, sticky pieces of candy. "To tell you the truth, I don't even remember hitting him. I just remember him grabbing me."

"Mmmh." Marcus worked his mouth furiously to break down the maple-flavored candy so he could talk. "Percy, you surprised everyone. As soon as Tamal grabbed you, your fist came out of nowhere—BAM!" He threw a jab out to illustrate his point. "You rocked that brotha's head—no lie. His eyes crossed up for about three seconds—seriously."

"Marcus, you know you lyin'. And I'm not exactly proud of hitting him." He wasn't, either. His mother and Mr. Dell would have a fit if they knew.

Because Marcus was already munching on a new piece of candy, his words came out slightly distorted. "He put his hands on you first."

"Yeah, no doubt. But I came from the streets, man. Fighting used to be a way of life—fight or catch a beat down or get killed. Nah, I'm supposed to be doing something positive with my life now."

"You right, you right. But I will say this about you, Percy—you got guts. That brotha's too big for me to be hittin'. I would've had to pick up a chair or something. But I would've went straight for that head, just like you—BAM!" Marcus punched out at his imaginary opponent again, which drew some concerned looks from passing students. "And what about his threat, Percy? What you gonna do about that?"

"Nothing." He looked at Marcus, who was studying him. "Oh, I ain't scared of him. I said I wasn't proud of fighting him. But if the brotha' wants to break bad, I ain't backing down."

"Hey, you got time to stop by the financial aid office with me?"

"Yeah."

Percy waited patiently for Marcus to finish his business with a financial aid counselor. He stood near a big window in the hallway of the department located in the Admissions Building, directly across from the Dean of Students building. Here, he had a clear view of the protestors bundled up in heavy coats in the still chilly March weather, chanting and marching every so often around the building. Every once and a while, a speaker would emerge with a megaphone—usually the ever vocal Terrell—and give an emotional speech on the injustice that was occurring and encourage the protestors not to give up the fight for racial justice. The campus officers were always present around the protestors now, looking grim and probably wishing someone would step out of line, just once, so they could break up the whole thing and go on with business as usual. In the nearly two weeks since the sit-in first began, no one had done anything out of line, and there were small signs of the protest happening all over the campus and at Hamel U sponsored events. But everything was very organized and legal. Tomorrow was the official last day of the two-month protest, anyway, since the Dean had agreed to attend the Forum. Everything the blacks were doing now was ceremonial—and the media had gotten wind of the turbulence now, so they had been on the scene for a couple of days.

Marcus emerged from the office, shaking his head. He and Percy made their way back onto campus. "They're trying to mess with my money for next year. I get tired of these people trying to tell me my parents make too much, they have to lower what they're giving me. You don't know how lucky you are, getting an all-expenses paid trip to college. Man, you and Tamal are walking brain cells, getting these scholarships."

Percy stopped walking. "Tamal?!" he echoed in disbelief.

"Oh yeah," Marcus nodded in confirmation. "I know he may not act like it, but that brotha' is always making the Chancellor's List. He's a whiz at math. He was on some scholarship that was paying everything like yours until last spring, when the school decided to make it a two year thing—freshman and sophomore year, only. It was called the T. Powell...Sam Powell...something like that."

"T. Samuel Powell?" Percy asked in a low voice.

Marcus nodded. "That's it—T. Samuel Powell. Tamal was pretty steamed about that. He had to get an emergency loan and do work study now. What was the name of your scholarship again?"

"Something—I don't need to remember the name, as long as they keep paying." Percy reached over and grabbed Marcus' candy to distract him.

"Man, don't play," Marcus warned, snatching his bag of candy back. "We'll be scrapping over some food, now."

Percy laughed, but now felt very weird. No wonder Tamal had acted so hostile toward him after he stormed out of the interview, and why he was automatically so cold towards him. He must feel like every time he wanted something, Percy was there to snatch right from under his nose—the scholarship, the recruiting position...he could almost feel sorry for Tamal now—at least, he could understand his attitude.

EUGENE

Even with the constant heaviness in his chest, he felt an immense sense of relief. Being able to talk to Irene about his feelings lifted a large burden off his shoulders. And he had a chance to apologize to her about last semester, about kicking her to the curb.

"I understand, Eugene. I didn't then, but when you told me about your father and about high school…it must have been a lot on you," she told him.

"Yeah, but you don't let color determine your friendships—or other people."

"It's o.k.," she reassured him, then fisted him playfully upside his head. "Just don't let it happen again."

"I won't—I promise."

Right now, they were sitting out in the deserted lobby area on Eugene's floor, trying to study but doing more talking, waiting for pizza to arrive and for Eugene's roommate, Monty, to finish his shower after his grueling basketball game. Afterwards, the threesome would walk over to the Student Center where the Forum was. Monty, whose full name was Montero Jaurez, was Hispanic, and had no problems with Eugene and Irene's friendship. "That's all you see in L.A.," he told Eugene in his relaxed, west coast accent.

"But we're just friends, Monty," Eugene insisted.

Monty had just shrugged. "That, too. People so crazy in L.A., you could be walking down the street with a martian and they wouldn't pay it any attention."

Eugene liked Monty. In fact, they talked about rooming together next year if Monty didn't bid for an on-campus apartment. He invited Eugene to bid with him, but Eugene didn't know if his dad would fork over the extra money. Not with their relationship in the state it was in.

"Have you seen Renee' lately?" Irene asked out of the clear blue. She had closed her psychology book, not even pretending to study anymore.

"I saw her today, but she really didn't say anything to me. I guess I owe her an apology, huh?"

"What do you think?"

"I hate it when people say that."

245

"Well, Eugene…if you feel like you were too hard on her, then maybe you should apologize. But if you don't, then don't worry about it." No wonder Irene was able to deal with challenges. She had developed a black or white view of life. There were no gray areas with her.

"I think she still likes you," Ms. Direct told him, giving him a playful clip on the chin.

"Not now, she doesn't."

"Sure she does," Irene insisted. "Women don't just turn their feelings on and off like a light switch. She's just mad at you."

Eugene flipped his notebook over to a clean page and readied his pen.

"What are you doing?" Irene asked.

"Taking notes on how women are. Now, does what you said apply to all women, or just college women?"

She narrowed her eyes at him. "Make jokes if you want, but I'm telling you the truth. Renee' likes you still. She seems likes a decent girl once you get past her attitude. She's very pretty."

"She's pretty decent, but she's not my type."

"What do you mean?"

"She comes on a little too strong. I feel like she would cut down everything I say."

"So your woman should be seen and not heard?"

Eugene balled up a sheet of paper and threw it at Irene. "No, I didn't say that. I just mean that I don't want to have to justify everything I say."

"You mean like proving how black you are?"

No use in beating around the bush. "Exactly. I don't want to constantly prove how black I am. I want someone that accepts me for me—not try to turn me in to who they think I should be."

"Like your dad is doing?"

All roads led back to his father.

"Don't you think it would be worth your while to sit down and talk to your dad, Eugene?"

He grunted. "We tried that already. All we did was yell at each other."

"Can you try again? Maybe if you two sat down and really talked, you would understand why he acts the way he does with you."

246

"I could," he admitted. "I just don't want to rock the boat while mom's sick."

Irene nodded. "I understand. And hey—your mom is going to be up on her feet in no time. She's gonna beat this thing."

"That's what we're all hoping for," Eugene said, hoping he believed the words. His mother had been on bed rest since her operation over two months ago, even though the doctor said she should only be down for about a month. She had good days and bad days, but she always tried to make it seem like she was on the road to recovery when Eugene called. Chip would tell him the real deal, however. Again, she insisted that Eugene not come home to see her until she was up and about—or if she happened to pass, which she kept insisting to Eugene was not going to happen.

Irene grabbed his hand. "I'm behind you, Eugene."

He smiled, looking into her pretty, green eyes. "I know. Thanks."

She kept squeezing his hand and looking back at him. Boy, she was a pretty girl. He found himself wondering why she wasn't dating anyone, and realized that they'd never even treaded that territory in their conversations. He couldn't take his eyes off of her emerald colored eyes—he'd never seen eyes so green—her rose-colored lips...Before he knew it, he'd reached out and stroked her hair, hanging loosely around her shoulders instead of in her habitual ponytail.

To his surprise, she laid her head into the hand stroking her hair and held it against her face.

"Irene..." He began as he leaned toward her. She closed her eyes and came closer, her hair tickling Eugene's nose. Just then, the door to his suite banged open. Eugene snatched his hand back and Irene flipped her hair and quickly opened her psychology book. Eugene's roommate came around the corner into the lobby, rubbing his wet head with a towel.

"Pizza here?" Irene asked in a way too cheerful voice. She dug into her pants pocket for her money. "How much is it?"

"No, the phone was for you, man," Monty said, nodding his head at Eugene.

"Was? What, they hung up?" Eugene asked, wondering why Monty looked so strange. "They didn't want to speak to me?"

Monty shook his head. "No—it was your brother, Chip. He just said you should come home right away."

247

Eugene ignored Monty and Irene calling his name behind him as he took off down the hall to his room and fumbled with the phone, trying to dial his number. Tears were already burning his eyes as his brother picked up, telling him that his mom had not passed but had taken a turn for the worse, and changed her mind about wanting to see her youngest.

"Chip...how bad is it? How bad is she?"

Chip sighed deeply. "Just hurry up, little bro," he told him in a quaky voice.

Eugene hung up and started throwing clothes in his suitcase that he snatched from underneath his bed, while Monty and Irene tried to coax him into talking. He managed to get out that he was going home and he mentioned his mother, but that's about all he could say.

"Is she...?" Irene started, her eyes already filling with tears. Monty muttered something in Spanish.

"She's getting worse—I need to get home." Eugene continued his frantic packing, pulling clothes out his drawers and closet without paying much attention to what he was packing.

"I'm going with you." Monty went to his closet for his own suitcase. "You ain't in no shape to drive."

"I'm going, too. Leave your car parked, Eugene—I'm driving. I'll meet you guys out front in about forty-five minutes." Irene headed out, while Monty continued to pack. Eugene wanted to express his gratitude, but he felt like if he said anything now, he would break down. He wanted to hold it together.

The three were silent for the most part, going down the highway. Eugene studied the view out of the passenger side, trying to hold back his tears. Every once in a while, Monty would reach out from the back seat and pat his shoulder, or Irene would squeeze his hand from the driver's side. He needed to say something to them, express how thankful he was for the company. He cleared his throat. "Uh...thanks for coming with me, guys," he told them in a husky voice.

"No problem, papi'. I just hope your family doesn't mind having us. I mean, we're basically gonna bust up in your house all unannounced—we're here," Monty said from the back seat.

"What are you worried about?" Irene asked him. "How's he gonna explain his white chauffeur?"

Eugene opened his mouth and laughed loudly. He hadn't thought about that when Irene said she was coming. He envisioned his father's face when they came strolling in, and laughed louder. Irene and Monty looked at him, glanced at each other, and then joined in.

When Irene pulled up to his house, several cars lined the street in front of it and filled his driveway. A few out of town license plates, lit up by the outside lights in the dark evening sky, told him that his aunts and uncles were already there. His paternal grandmother, Alice, was parked just outside of the garage, which let Eugene know she was the first one here. His dad's father died when Eugene was nine, and his mother's parents passed before he was born—he'd only seen them in pictures. Diedra's light blue Escort sat beside his grandmother's car.

Chip was waiting at the door when they came up the walkway. His eyes were red. "She's asking for you," he told Eugene after grabbing him in a big hug.

Eugene nodded briefly, and made his way into the foyer and the living room, trying to smile at the various relatives and friends who were greeting him. He heard Irene and Monty introduce themselves to Chip—he barely remembered hugging Diedra on his way up the stairs.

The door to his parent's bedroom was open. His was sitting on their king-sized bed, holding his mother's hand. Eugene had never saw his dad looking so weak and so sad in his life. His mother looked so frail laying up in the giant bed with her eyes closed, a respirator hooked up to her on one side, an I.V. on the other. A nurse wearing a multicolored smock and white pants was fidgeting with the respirator, and here came his pastor, meeting him at the door.

"God bless you, son—good to see you," he said in his gentle voice, giving him a warm hug. "You doing all right?"

Eugene shrugged. "Not really, Reverend Freeman."

Reverend Freeman nodded sympathetically, then led him over to the bed. "Come on and see your mother—she's been asking for you."

Eugene felt like a scared little boy as sat down opposite his father, staring down at his mother. Her eyes were sunk into her face and she had lost a tremendous amount of weight. He touched her arm lightly and her eyes fluttered open, happiness shining through the glassy look as she gazed at him. She tried to smile, then reached out slowly with her hand.

"Hi, baby," she whispered.

"Hi Mom," he managed, before he broke down, his shoulders shaking. She squeezed his hand and he brought her hand up to his face, holding on for dear life. He dad reached over and patted him on his back, then got up to let him have a moment with her.

"Mom..." He started again, but her eyes closed and he felt panic grip his heart.

"She sleeping, son," his dad assured him from behind. "Your grandmother's here. She wants to see you."

He turned toward the door. His father's mother stood in the doorway with her arms spread out. He hurried over to be enveloped in her warm embrace, dripping tears on her blouse.

"Sorry, Granny..." he began, but she shushed him.

"Don't you try to be strong for nobody," she instructed him sternly, still hugging him. "You grieve as much as you need to, you understand?"

He nodded. His grandmother pulled him into the hallway. "Granny, how bad is she?"

His grandmother looked into the room, then led him into the guest room across the hallway where her bags were already sitting. She shut the door and sat him down on the bed. She took a deep breath and grabbed his hand. "It could be anytime, Eugene. That's why we called the family to come."

Eugene dropped his head and squeezed his grandmother's hand. He couldn't believe this was happening. Last year at this time, his mother was vibrant and healthy, baking him warm, chocolate chip and walnut cookies and helping him get ready for graduation. "Granny, I don't understand," he choked out. "I don't understand."

"You don't have to, Eugene."

"She...she didn't even want me here. I didn't get to be with her..."

"I know, Eugene—she told me. I didn't agree, but it wasn't my place to say. But your mother wasn't trying to keep you away, honey. She said she wanted you to remember her the way she was when she wasn't sick because you were so close to her. She was trying to protect you, sweetie. That's what parents do. Your dad talked her out of it."

He looked up, shocked. "*Dad* did?!"

His grandmother nodded knowingly, looking at him with sympathy. "Eugene, I know Ray comes down on you pretty hard at times, but I guess it's because he had to grow up with so many challenges. You know, he was a lot like you growing up."

"No way, Granny. Chip—yes. Me—no way."

"Now, Eugene, I raised the boy—he's my son. He was just like you coming up. Always underneath me—never had time for his daddy. Of course, his daddy was always talking about how Raymond needed to do more manly things like playing sports, working out in the fields, instead of having his head in books all the time. Your father loved to read as a little boy, did you know that?"

Eugene shook his head.

"Yes indeed, he did. He wrote outstanding stories. The teacher was always sending home his work with gold stars or something. Said one time that Raymond could be a writer or teach if he wanted. Said he could get into any college he wanted if he wasn't black. That's how smart he was."

His dad liked to write? He couldn't believe it. And here he had come down on Eugene, telling him he was "wasting his time" with his writing.

His grandmother unzipped her purse that was sitting on the bed and pulled out her wallet. She opened it, and flipped to a slightly tattered, black and white photo of a young man that looked a lot like Chip in a football uniform. "Your father in high school," his grandmother told him.

"This is dad?!"

"Mmm hmm."

"Dad played football?!"

"One of the best players in high school. He was so good, Eugene, that he got a football scholarship to one of the best schools in Virginia."

"But I thought he had his head in the books all the time?"

"He did, honey. But he also listened to what your grandfather had to say about playing sports. And he still kept his head in the books. But anything your father put his mind to do, he did it well."

"So dad played college football?" Eugene was intrigued, almost forgetting that his mother was just across the hallway, breathing in her last breaths.

His grandmother shook her head sadly, and put her wallet back in her purse. "Never got the chance."

"Why?"

251

"Baby, the south in the early 1960's was not a rose garden for black folks. Things were segregated, and they just started trying to integrate the schools. Your dad had to be escorted by police to classes every day. Even then, he wasn't completely safe. They still spit at him, called him nigger, threatened to kill him—and when they found out he was going to play football on their team—well, your father had to have police protection at football practice. He was the only black on the team. Your grandfather tried to talk him out of going. Said he couldn't understand why Ray wanted to rush off to some lily-white school even on a scholarship, when there were some fine Negro schools around."

Eugene felt chills hearing his dad words to him echoed through his grandmother.

"Your father was so proud to be one of the first blacks at a white school. Your grandfather told him that he was just a token, and they wouldn't have him if he didn't play ball so well, but Ray didn't care—he was going to show them and the world what he could do."

"What happened?"

"He was finishing up practice one day and was cleaning up to come home. He couldn't stay on campus, you know that, right? He couldn't even use the locker room to change until all his white teammates finished and left. Then, he could go in and clean up. Well, one day when he was in there, three white boys came in and jumped on him. He said one of them had a baseball bat and kept slamming it into his knee. Then he said they just left him laying in there and walked out like they hadn't done anything wrong. Eugene, your father laid on the floor of that locker room for about an hour, yelling in pain. If the coach hadn't come back in the locker room that day to get the uniforms..." His grandmother trailed off, looking away like the memory was too painful for her to remember.

"They busted his knee, Eugene—and they did it on purpose. Your dad couldn't play football because the doctor said even when his knee healed and he could walk without a limp, he could never play sports because if he hurt it again, it could cripple him."

"So they kicked him out of school?" Eugene guessed.

His Granny nodded. "He tried to stay, but we didn't have the money to keep him there and they took the scholarship away since he couldn't play."

"What happened to the white boys that did it?" She looked at him like he should have known better. He snorted. "Nothing, I guess."

"That's right—nothing. The most we got was an apology from the coach, and the school paid his medical bills. That's it. They didn't even bring the police in."

He had no idea about his father. His grandmother had just dumped a cesspool of new information on him. Didn't Irene say something earlier about understanding why a person acted the way they did? And there was another issue—Irene was somewhere in the house with his relatives. He didn't care when they were coming down the highway—it was funny then. But now her being here could really cause some chaos with his father. He couldn't send her back and he wasn't going to, anyway. He just wasn't looking forward to her meeting his father.

"Eugene, I didn't share that with you to make you feel you had to change something about yourself. You are perfect just the way you are—we just didn't want you think your dad was picking on you all the time. It's not personal."

"We? Who's we?"

"Your mother asked me to talk to you."

"Can anyone talk directly to me?!" He was suddenly angry. Everyone wanted to make his decisions for him—everyone wanted to shield him from the truth. If his dad had been straight with him from jump street, they'd be getting along right now, no doubt. Chip probably knew the truth. Now, besides his mom dying, he had to worry about being a peacemaker between his father and Irene. He wanted to explode.

"This is not the time for that," his Granny was telling him. "Now, do yourself a favor and your mother a favor—try to be peaceful with your dad, o.k.?" She reached over to hug him again, then led him out the bedroom back across the hallway.

His mother's eyes were still closed. He could see the light rise and fall of her chest and felt relief. "She's resting," his dad said, back at his station beside her on the bed. "Why don't you go say hello to your aunts and uncles? I'll let you know when she wakes up."

He didn't want to leave—he was afraid it would be his last chance, but he nodded and slowly backed out of the room. He saw his father's head drop into the hand that wasn't entangled with his mother's, and Reverend Freeman came over to his side, bowing his head in prayer.

The living room was full of relatives—aunts, uncles and cousins—sitting around, talking in low voices. It was like an invasion, and Eugene wanted everyone out. He made his way into the dining room on the other side of the kitchen, where the table was decked out with food from one end to the other. Diedra was sitting at the table with Chip, whispering and wiping her eyes.

"Hey, little bro," Chip greeted him with a weak smile.

Eugene walked around Diedra and threw his arms around Chip again, who hung onto Eugene like he was being snatched away from him, too.

Deidra waited until he straightened up, then grabbed Eugene in a hug and planted a kiss on his cheek. "How are you, Eugene?"

"I'm trying to hang in there, Diedra," he told her. "Did you guys happen to see the two people that came in with me?"

"They're downstairs in the den," Diedra answered. "I fixed them a plate and sent them down there to eat. They looked a little tired and I figured they were hungry."

"Always the nurse," Chip commented lovingly.

Eugene took a seat beside Diedra at the table. "It was nice of them to bring you up here. I know you weren't in any condition to drive," Diedra said, rubbing Eugene's arm.

"I wasn't," he agreed. "I didn't even ask—they just told me they were coming with me."

"Monty—that's your roommate, right?" Chip asked.

"Yeah."

"I told Irene she was welcome to stay at my place," Diedra said. "It looks like you guys are going to have a full house."

"Thanks, Diedra. I sure didn't think about that on the way down."

Chip was frowning in confusion. "I thought you and Irene had a falling out or something?"

"We got things straight."

Now Diedra was frowning. "Now wait a minute—are you and Irene dating or something?"

Chip said "yes" at the same time Eugene said "no." They looked at each other and broke out laughing, but Eugene had to think again. What had almost happened between them earlier that evening?

"That's o.k.—don't tell me. I'll get the scoop later on at my place," Diedra promised. "We'll have some girl talk."

"Diedra, no..."

"Well somebody better start talking."

"Why, honey?" Chip asked, tugging playfully on a lock of her short hair. "Just let it go. That's Eugene's business."

"He's practically my little brother, and I want to know about the women he dates," Diedra declared.

"For the fiftieth time, we are not dating—big sister," Eugene told her, feeling very comfortable with his brother and soon to be sister— none of that "in-law" stuff for Diedra. She was already going around calling Eugene her little brother, and Eugene loved her like a sister. She certainly acted like part of the family—his parents adored her.

One of his mother's sisters appeared in the doorway. "Charles, Eugene—you guys better get upstairs right now. Your mom..." She broke off, turning back into the kitchen and sobbing out loud.

Eugene and Chip raced through the hallway and up the stairs, where all the relatives had gathered in the hallway, crying, whispering and praying. They parted when they saw the brothers coming, and lay consoling hands on them as they pushed them through. The nurse was just straightening up from bending over their mother, taking a stethoscope out of her ears. Eugene's dad was bent over the tall bureau beside the bed, with his arms covering his face, while Alice stood beside him, speaking soothing words to him. Chip and Eugene came in and sat on either side of the bed.

To Eugene's surprise, his mother looked better and more alert than when he first came in. Her face had more color, and her eyes had lost some of the glassy look. She grabbed both of their hands. Even her grip felt stronger.

"Look at my boys," she said, turning to smile at both of them. "I am so proud of my boys." She turned her head back to Eugene. "I changed my mind."

"I know, Mom," he said, trying to hold back the floodgate of tears threatening to break loose.

"Mom, you look better," Chip said hopefully.

"Chip, don't do this to yourself. We talked already, remember?"

Chip bottom lip trembled as he nodded. Behind them, the bedroom door shut. Somebody realized they needed their privacy.

She turned back to Eugene. "Baby, you know your dad loves you."

"I know, Mom."

"You understand now, don't you? Granny told you what happened?"

He bobbed his head, biting his bottom lip.

She gripped his hand harder and tried to lean forward. "I need to know that my boys will be at peace when I leave. I can't hold you together anymore."

"Mom, please don't go!" Eugene cried, not sure he could handle anymore. "I need you, Mom!"

"Eugene, I can't stay, but you'll be all right. I raised a fine young man—two of them. Her face was losing its color again, and her eyes were starting to get glassy. "I'm tired, baby—I'm so tired. Don't you worry—my spirit is at peace. It's my time, Eugene."

Chip suddenly got up from the bed, gagging like he was sick. Alice grabbed him and led him into the master bathroom, where Eugene heard him sobbing out loud. He could hear his father somewhere behind him, trying to cry quietly but getting louder. Reverend Freeman's gentle voice was somewhere to the right of him, praying with vigor, and he heard a female sniffling, and looked beside him to see the nurse wiping her nose with a tissue. He squeezed his mother's hand, determined not to let her slip away from him. Not his best friend—his support. His mother.

"Eugene, you remember the story about the baby robin and its mother—the one you wrote for me?" His mother's voice was fading. She slid down on her pillow.

"Yeah, Mom." He had wrote the story in first grade and was proud to bring it home to his mother. The teacher declared it to be the best story in the class. His mother had the pages laminated and bound in a leather cover. Eugene's huge, seven-year old scrawl about a baby robin and his mother had brought *his* mother to tears, just because he told her he wrote it for her.

"Tell me the story," she whispered. He looked down at her. There was no question she was slipping away. He would do this one last favor for her. It was his tribute to her.

"Do the voices," she added, gathering up enough strength to wink at him. She loved to hear him do the voices. Her breathing was getting shorter.

So he repeated her most beloved story of his childhood, squeaking out the voice of the baby robin who kept falling out of the nest because he wanted to fly like his mother, and lowering his voice to the soothing gentle tones of the mother bird, who would fly down just in time to keep her son from tumbling to the ground, where the mean ole' cat was waiting to gobble him up. Baby Robin finally learned how to fly after his mother taught him, and he had a grand time up in the air, flying around the nest. His mother was so proud of him.

"I love you, mom," Baby Robin chirped in Eugene's trembling voice. "Thanks for teaching me how to fly."

"I love you too, son," Eugene's mother recited before he could, like she always did when she had memorized the next line. "You can fly without me now. But remember, I'll always be here for you."

When he was small, his mother would touch his heart on that last line, then tickle his belly until he squealed. Now, her weak hand fluttered up and landed lightly on his heart. Her eyes turned up to his, and she smiled the most beautiful smile Eugene had ever seen.

"Thank you," she whispered, taking a sharp breath, and rolling her eyes upward.

She was gone.

He wouldn't let go of her hand—he couldn't. He didn't realize he was still holding it until he heard the Reverend's voice behind him, telling him to let go, she was gone—it would be all right. He stood up slowly, looking around the room in confusion. The room became a blur, and then it spun around several times. He couldn't breath. He heard someone yell, "Catch him—he's falling!" before everything went dark.

PERCY

In about forty-five minutes, the Forum would begin. In all, twenty-five black alumni and community leaders responded to the letters sent out by the Operation Blackout committee and were ready to come on campus to see just what the heck was going on with their land. They ran the gamut of lawyers, doctors, ministers and NAACP Board members. One of the keynote speakers was a Dr. Caldwell Williams, whom Carlos was making out to be some sort of demigod. Dr. Williams was one of the founding members and the first president of the Tri-AC at Hamel, back when it was just a group of brothers who were dissatisfied with the BSA and thought that black students needed a stronger voice. It wasn't even called the Tri-AC back when he was in school.

Carlos had everything mapped out. The Tri-AC would attend the Forum, of course, then head over to Darryl's apartment afterward. Darryl had their "uniforms" there—black jeans, black sweatshirts and black ski masks or black hats and scarves to cover their faces. Most of the board members had the items already. A member would be stationed a half mile up the road, in a car with no license plates. It would be close enough for everyone to make a quick getaway, but far enough away so as not to be spotted.

Percy sat on his bed, flipping through the channels with the remote. Television was something he didn't have a lot of time for anymore, but he wanted to do something to keep his mind off of what they were about to do. The phone rang loudly. Allen must have turned up the ringer again.

"Hello?"

"How's it going, 'Sugar Ray' Lyles?" It was Darryl. He gave him that nickname after the incident at his apartment.

"What's up, Darryl? You gotta squash that 'Sugar Ray' mess, man."

"He deserved it, Percy." Darryl had told him that at least fifty times since the incident. "Are you ready?"

"Ready as I'll ever be."

"All right, brotha'. Just remember that those boys deserve what they have coming just as much as Tamal deserved that punch. Keep that same attitude."

"I'm straight."

"Ah-ight."

"Hey—what about Tamal? Do you think he'll dime on us?"

Darryl snickered. "Not the way that brotha' feels about white people. Don't worry about Tamal, Percy. He won't be a problem. I'll see you at the Forum."

Percy hung up, telling himself that he could do this—Lambda Sig deserved it—just like Darryl said. Then, the phone rang again.

"Hello?"

"Percy? This is Dr. Adams. I hope I didn't catch you at a bad time."

"No...I'm fine. I'm just surprised to hear from you."

"I know, but I just couldn't wait to tell you the good news."

"Good news?"

Dr. Adams laughed. "Don't tell me you forgot already? The exchange program to England—you've been selected to go!"

"What?! Are you serious?!"

"Very serious, Percy. Congratulations! The board selected you—with my recommendation—out of one hundred thirteen students from Hamel. You should be very proud of yourself. You really deserve it."

"I'm going to England?! Wow...I mean...wow!" He couldn't think of any other words to fit the occasion. England! He hadn't been out of Jackson Park his entire life, except to come to Hamel. Now he was going overseas!

"All expenses paid," Dr. Adams continued. "And you get a monthly allowance. Percy, I can't tell you how fortunate you are to get this. Only ten students out of the seventy participating universities are selected."

Percy felt like his mother must have when he had gotten accepted to Hamel. England! All expenses paid! Opportunities like that just didn't come for brothers from Jackson Park every day!

"Thank you, Dr. Adams. This is great!"

"You're welcome. Oh! This is one thing I need to let you know." Her voice grew serious. "I know you've been involved in this boycott—Operation..."

"Blackout," Percy finished.

"Yes. I believe in what the African-American students are doing. I just want to caution you to avoid any violent activity."

"Dr. Adams, the boycott is non-violent."

"I know—please don't take what I'm saying the wrong way. I know it's non-violent. But I also know how tempers can flare and things can get out of hand. There are a lot of ill feelings out there right now. I just don't want you to get caught up in any…uncontrolled activity."

"What does that have to do with the exchange program?" But Percy knew the answer before he asked.

"You must be in good standing with the University—that is stressed. And 'good standing' means the period before you are selected, until you leave in August."

Dr. Adams filled him in on a few more details, told him he would get a complete packet of information during the summer, and then told him to call his family with the good news. Percy hung up, feeling heavy inside. The Lambda Sig raid certainly did qualify as "uncontrolled activity" and even though Darryl said that there was no way to be fingered, Percy still had his doubts. But he had given his word that he would be there. Now the question was, which was more important to him—his loyalty to his race and the fight against injustice, or what he considered a once in a lifetime opportunity?

The phone again. It was Grand Central Station in his room today. "Yeah?" he answered, figuring it was another Tri-AC call.

"*Yeah?!* Didn't I teach you to answer the phone better than that?"

"Oh—hi, Ma. I didn't know it was you."

"Well, you wouldn't until I speak. Don't lose your manners because you're away from home."

His mother would probably be fussing at him when he was an old man. But he loved the woman, and it was all good. "How are you, *Mother*?" he said with exaggerated formality.

"I just wanted to see how you were doing," she said, switching out of her scolding mode to a softer tone. "You came up during my prayer time, so I had to call."

His mom's uncanny sense of when to call unnerved him at times. "Guess what, Ma?" He brightened, remembering the previous call. "I'm going to London!"

"Where?!"

"London, Ma. London, England."

"I know where it is, Percy. What do you mean you're going…" She took a sharp breath. "You mean the exchange program?!"

"Yes! I was selected to go!"

He heard the phone clatter, and his mom let out a whoop that sounded like a fire alarm. He laughed, knowing that right now she was probably dancing around the room in a holy stupor. He heard thundering footsteps and a faint voice yelling, "What Ma? What?" His mom continued to yell.

"Hello?! Hello?!" Percy yelled into the phone.

"Who is this?!" Paul picked up the receiver.

"It's Percy, man."

"Percy, what cho' say to her?! Ma, calm down!"

"I told her I was going to England," he told Paul.

"Where? Oh, the exchange thing?"

"Yeah, man. I'm leaving in August."

"Hey, you going all the way over there? That's great! You something else, ain't you?"

"You know—just doin' what I gotta do, yo. You'll probably be taking a trip like that one day."

"Only if I join the military and they send me. Nah, bru—you got all the brains in the family. Well, I think Ma's calmed down some. Let me put her back on the phone."

His mother let out a "thank you, Jesus," a couple of "Hallelujahs" and got back on the phone, out of breath. "Percy," she breathed. "Baby, I am so proud of you! I tell you, God is so good!"

"Thanks, Ma. I'm pretty pleased myself."

"Percy, you are setting such a good example for Paul. He looks up to you so much."

"No he doesn't, Ma."

"Yes, he does, Percy. I hear him talking to his friends about his big brother in college. You just keep on doing what you're doing. It blesses my heart to see my children doing their best."

Percy felt a lump rise in his throat. Paul actually looked up to him. He didn't think he was anybody's role model.

"And you will make it out of Jackson Park," she said firmly. "Those buddies of yours are in a mess of trouble right now—I think one of them got arrested. What's his name, Checkers...?"

"Domino, Ma. Domino got arrested? For what?!"

"Attempted robbery and assault. He tried to rob the station next to Dell's—and he hit the cashier with a piece of pipe because the cashier tried to stop him."

261

Michele R. Leverett

Percy was surprised. Freddy, or Domino, as they called him in the street, seemed to be following in his footsteps. He did well in school, and also talked about going to school—community college. Obviously, the streets got to him before he could get out.

"I am so glad you pulled away from those boys when you did. You might have ended up just like Backgammon..."

"Domino, Ma."

"Whatever."

Percy glanced at his clock. "Ma, I have to go. I have to get to a meeting."

"Sure, son...I know I talked your ear off—I have another call coming in, anyway. Take care. I love you."

"I love you, too, Ma." He hung up the phone for the third time. So far, three people were counting on him to stay out of trouble—Dr. Adams, who had recommended him to study abroad, his mother, who said that he had blessed her, and his brother, who looked up to him.

Ring!

What now?! Percy just stared at the phone. It hadn't rung as much for him all year than it had today.

"Yeah...I mean, hello?"

"Percy, it's me again," his mother's excited voice was back on the phone. "Somebody wants to speak to you. I'm gonna leave the phone for a few minutes and let ya'll talk."

Percy smiled. It was probably his sister, Monica. His mother always announced her phone calls by telling Percy some anonymous person wanted to speak to him or by telling him, "some woman's on the phone for you."

"Percy?" The male voice that spoke startled him.

"Yeah...who is this?" Percy didn't recognize the voice immediately.

A pause. "This is your dad."

His dad?! What did he want? And why today, of all days?! Percy had no words, no feelings. He just breathed into the phone.

"Your mother just told me about you going to England. Congratulations."

"Thanks," Percy mumbled automatically. He hadn't talked to his father in almost six years by choice, and he still sounded the same. The voice on the other end was the same one that would promise he and Monica ice cream when he came home from work, or jump on

262

their tails when they would cut up. It was the voice Percy wanted to come back for about four of those ten years, and now didn't care about anymore.

"So how have you been, son?"

"Fine." Percy was curt.

"How's school going?"

"All right."

"Making good grades, and all that?"

"Yeah…"

"Well…good." There was an uncomfortable silence that followed. As soon as Percy could end this conversation and his mother got his father off of the three way, he was going to call her back and ask her what right she had to force him to talk to a man he never wanted to see again, let alone talk to. Once again, she had denied him the right to make his own decision.

"Percy, I know you're surprised to hear from me…" his dad started.

"You got that right."

"But you won't talk to me when I call the house, and I figured this was the only way I could talk to you."

"Ma conferenced you in," Percy reminded him, letting him know that he knew he didn't do it on his own.

"I *asked* her to after she told me the news. I wanted to tell you congratulations."

"She should have checked with me first to see if that was o.k."

"O.k. with *you*? Boy, that is your momma. She don't need your permission to do anything." His dad sounded a little testy. He had some nerve.

"I *know* who she is. She's the woman that raised us when you stepped out." All his anger was rising to the top and about to boil over. What made him an authority on parenting all of a sudden? He didn't hang around long enough to find out.

His dad sighed. "Your mother warned me you might be angry. All I can say to that is don't condemn a man until you've walked a mile in his shoes. But you go ahead and say what you got to say. Maybe it's time for that, anyway. Yell, holler…call me names if that makes you feel better. Then maybe we can sit down and talk about it, man to man."

In Percy's opinion, they were one man short. And didn't his father have some nerve, acting like Percy's anger wasn't justified? Maybe his mother could forgive and forget, but he wasn't there—no, not yet.

"We ain't got jack to talk about. I don't want to know why you skipped out anymore, 'cause I ain't got no father." Percy wanted to hurt him with his words, the way he had hurt for years with no father around—a father he thought didn't want them anymore. "What kind of man goes AWOL on his wife and three kids?! Ma cried her eyes out over you, man. You know how it feels to see your mother and sister cry and you can't do anything about it?! Paul was too young to understand—he was lucky."

"I know," his father agreed.

"You know?! Then why'd you leave? Why didn't you come back?! You left Ma to raise three kids by herself...you left us struggling for years..."

"Now you hold on—I sent your momma what I could..."

"That's supposed to make it right? That's supposed to make up for you not being there?!" Percy could feel himself losing control, which just made him angrier. "You reached into your wallet and sent us money when you felt like it, while Ma worked two jobs to keep us off welfare, put food on the table and send us to school with decent clothes?"

"Percy..."

"Where were you when Paul learned how to ride a bike without training wheels, huh? I was there—where were you? How about when Monica went to the prom. Ma was there, I was there, Paul was there—were you? Did you reach into your wallet when I got my license? How about when someone broke into the house and Ma chased him out with a steel baseball bat?! You didn't even come to my high school graduation, man. Or Monica's. You think sending some chump change and making a weekly phone call is gonna make up for you not being there?!" Percy felt terrible inside. He believed if his father was standing there in front of him, he'd tried to smash him. Right now, his words were his fists.

His father remained calm. Even that bothered him. "Percy, I understand how you feel. I felt the same way when my dad left my family."

If he expected sympathy for that one, then he was barking up the wrong tree. "Then you should have known better, if it happened to you."

"It's not that cut and dry. I was determined not to turn out like my father, but I didn't know any other way. All I knew is that I couldn't provide for my family like a man should. So I started drinking—I couldn't control it. I wasn't do any of ya'll any good. Your momma stayed busy trying to shield you kids from my foolishness, and try to hold me together, and work so we could pay the bills..."

"Ah, man..." Percy started, disgusted.

"Boy, do you understand what an addiction is? Do you? Do you understand that you don't think straight when you have an addiction? You're old enough to understand that, Percy. I was an alcoholic, I was out of control, and I was bringing my family down, so I left before I brought you down anymore..."

"What, you want a pat on the back for that?"

"Percy...boy...who do you think you talking to like that?! I know your momma taught you better! I'm still your daddy...!"

Percy jumped up, he was so angry. "Daddy?! You lost that right ten years ago when you..."

His mother picked up the extension again. "Whoa, whoa! What's going on? Percy, who are you yelling at?!"

"Evelyn, look...I'll call you later on this week—I'm not getting anywhere with this boy..."

"What is going on?!" His mother asked again. "Percy, what did you say?"

"I told him the truth!" Percy said, still bitter. "I ain't got nothing to say to him!"

"Percy!"

"Evelyn, I'll call you later. Give Paul and Monica my love..."

Percy slammed the phone down on his parents. He was angry at his father, but right now, he was angrier at his mother, who never seemed to consult him about the decisions she made for his life. He was eighteen years old now, not some nine-year old kid whose mother knew what was best for him. If he chose not to have a relationship with his father, that was his business—not hers.

The phone rang again, but Percy had no intention of picking it up. He knew it was his mother, calling to see what in the world was going on, why couldn't he make peace with his father, why he had to stay so

265

angry all the time. He couldn't understand why she couldn't see how he felt—how hard it had been for him to grow up, knowing that his father left the family, seeing her struggle to make ends meet, assuming the role as man of the family as a child when he could barely keep himself out of trouble.

The answering machine clicked, and Allen's voice came on, and then a beep. "Percy, pick up the phone…it's your mother…Percy…?" Percy stared down at the phone a minute, then grabbed his keys off his desk and headed out the door, on his way to the Forum. He closed the door on his mother's voice.

"Come on guys—let's roll." Darryl was running around his apartment, trying to get the remaining board members to move in a hurry. Clothes were strewn everywhere as everyone donned the "uniforms" left there earlier. There were eight members involved in the raid, and Carlos had taken his group on to the house. He wanted half to go ahead and the other half to wait at least fifteen minutes before leaving, so they would not draw any attention. The two drivers who were staying with the two cars were Marcus and a junior named Willis Reed, who'd been a member of the Tri-AC since he was a freshman, but never desired to be a board member. With the reception and all of the parties that were scheduled on and off campus, they really needed no alibi. Black folk were everywhere tonight.

Percy was back in Darryl's room, trying to tie his shoelaces with fingers that did not want to cooperate. His ski mask lay on the bed beside him—it was something his mother had brought him for school. *"It gets cold up there," she told him. "You don't want to catch a cold or pneumonia."*

This was a prime example of why he never let his mother shop for him. He had tried to argue that ski masks were played out, but she asked him which was more important—fashion, or protecting himself from sickness. He took the mask to stop her from nagging him, but he vowed never to wear it and shoved it in the back of one of his drawers. Allen had spotted it one day when Percy was switching his warm weather clothes out with his winter clothes, and asked if he planned to do any skiing.

"Yeah, man—that's exactly what I'm going to do," Percy answered, while Allen laughed. "Seriously, now. I belonged to a ski club in my neighborhood—that's all we did in the winter."

"*Really? That's awesome.*" *Allen, taking Percy seriously, stopped laughing and perched on the edge of his bed, ready to hear more.* "*Where did you guys ski?*"

"*Oh...a mountain close to the neighborhood,*" *Percy continued, not believing that Allen actually believed he could ski.* "*I could do all those high jumps and fancy moves, man. My ski coach wanted me to train for the Winter Olympics, but I had to give it up. Broke my heart.*"

Allen was staring with his mouth open, hanging on every word. "*Wow, Percy—I never knew. I mean—you were that good, huh?*"

"*Oh yeah.*" *Percy turned his head so Allen wouldn't see him about to laugh.* "*If it wasn't for that bad spill that I took a year ago, I would've been in the Olympics last year. Messed my knee up.*" *Percy glanced at Allen, who was now looking at him with some doubt.*

"*Percy, you're puttin' me on, aren't you?*"

"*Nah, Allen...what, a black man can't ski?*" *Percy asked, trying to keep a straight face.*

"*No, I didn't mean to imply that black people can't ski, Percy.*"

"*Allen, I'm just messing with you...don't get bent out of shape...*"

"*About what? Skiing or black people?*"

"*Both.*"

Allen frowned up a minute, then shook his head and started to laugh. "*You got me Percy, you got me. I thought you were serious there for a minute. Especially about the knee thing...*"

"*Oh yeah, man. I apologize—that was a bad joke.*" *Percy had forgotten that Allen had a real knee injury when he was younger and it was effecting his walk now.* "*You know I like to mess with you, man. Don't pay me no mind.*"

Allen leaned over and snatched up the ski mask laying on the bed, looking it over. "*From Ma, with love?*" *Allen laughed, reading the tag his mother had stitched on the inside.* "*Ahh, ain't that sweet?*"

"*Mind your business.*" *Percy snatched the mask back, embarrassed.* "*That's our little secret, Allen.*"

Allen crossed his heart. "*Your secret's safe with me.*"

Darryl's head popped around the corner of the room. "Time to go, Percy. We need to be over there in seven minutes."

"Yeah, I'm coming." Percy pulled the shoestring tight and stood up, grabbing his mask from the bed.

"You straight?" Darryl asked, stepping into the room. He was wearing a pair of black jeans that looked like they had been starched and ironed at the dry cleaner, and a plain, long-sleeved, black T-shirt that was just as crisp. Even his black Nikes looked new.

"Yeah, I'm straight," he told him.

Darryl looked out in the hallway, then slid the door shut. "You still have time to back out, Percy. We can say something came up, or something."

"Nah, man. I'm straight."

"I'm serious, Percy. You told me about your exchange program to England—that's important to you. So I'm just saying if you feel like tonight is too big of a risk, walk away, bru."

"No, I'm fine, Darryl. 'Preciate dat, though." Percy stood up and held out his hand. To his surprise, Darryl gave him the grip instead of a regular handshake.

"You all right, man," he told him. "Come on—let's get this over with."

Percy, Darryl, Brian and Marcus pulled up to the sidewalk just down the street from the Lambda Sig house. Carlos and the others were supposed to be parked further up around the corner. The road was dark and deserted. Darryl jumped out of the car and opened the trunk, while the others filed out quickly behind him. He grabbed two backpacks out of the trunk that held spray paint cans, three hammers, a couple of pairs of scissors. What they couldn't break or discolor, they would cut.

"Keep your voices down," he told the small entourage as they made their way up the street.

The house was almost out in the middle of nowhere. There was a fraternity row just outside of campus where several fraternities and sororities had houses, but Lambda Sig chose a secluded location just below the track field. Carlos told the Tri-AC that Lambda Sig chose the location so they could throw loud, drunken parties. Looking around as he walked, Percy couldn't understand his president's concern about Tamal being here a couple of weeks ago. Unless someone was on the track field late at night, Tamal was in no danger of being spotted. Maybe Carlos' real problem was Tamal stepping out on his own.

A light blinked somewhere beyond the woods. Once, then two quick flashes—the signal they had agreed on. Darryl stopped and blinked his flashlight back three times.

"They're in," he hissed to the rest of the group. "Let's roll."

They came to the end of a row of trees and rounded the corner to the Lambda Sig house. It was a large, two-story brick structure with the fraternity shield and letters painted down the side. There were no lights on in any of the windows. They quietly made their way up the steps to the porch.

"Ya'll hurry and get in here," a voice urged from the inside. A black, ski-masked face appeared in the doorway and gestured anxiously with his flashlight. Percy and his group hurried inside the house, where the mystery person shut the door behind them.

"Who is that?" Darryl asked.

The figure pulled his mask up and shined his flashlight. "It's Carlos. Now look, I need everyone to listen carefully. Is everyone here?" Carlos did a quick head count, including the bodies that had materialized behind him. "That looks like everybody. Now listen…our group ran through the house already, and everyone's gone. I'll give those boys one thing—they're smart. They probably didn't want to be within ten feet of this campus tonight, with all the things going on. So that changes our plans slightly. I want this house tore up from the floor up. Don't leave anything behind and be quick—we don't want any of those boys walking in and surprising us. Rodney, you didn't destroy that lock, did you?"

"No—their key should still work," Rodney told him. His dad was a locksmith who had, perhaps in a light moment, taught his son how to pick a lock. Rodney probably never realized that the skill would come in handy.

"Good. I want you and you…" Carlos pointed randomly at three bodies. "…in the living room. Two of you go in the kitchen. The rest of us will go upstairs."

Percy looked at Darryl, who gestured with his head to follow Carlos upstairs. He felt his heart thumping double time—this was it. He either bowed out now, or went through with it all the way. It was bad enough that he was trespassing in the first place, but once he started destroying things, he was a vandal—officially.

As he followed Carlos and Darryl down the dark hallway towards the stairs, thoughts flashed through his mind like a mental slide slow:

his mom telling him how proud he'd made her; Mr. Dell calling him son, telling him not to disappoint him; his boys back home, ragging him about college; his dad, trying to explain his absence; Tamal running up in his face; Allen grinning at him. Even pictures of England came to mind.

His mask was getting warm and smothering him—he couldn't breath. He stopped walking and snatched it off, using it to wipe perspiration off his face. Percy wanted to go through with it, but he didn't think he could—too many things were at stake. He heard a small voice telling him to get out of there—now.

"Darryl," Percy hissed ahead of him. He could hear glass shattering and small ripping sounds in the living room.

Darryl twisted his head around, his eyes looking sinister in the flashlight he was holding. "Yeah?"

"I..." Percy hesitated, sniffing the air. He turned completely around and sniffed again. "What's that smell?"

"What smell?" Darryl snatched his mask off and sniffed. His eyes grew round in concern.

"What are you two hanging around back here for?" Carlos asked irritably, doubling back to Percy and Darryl. "Why are your masks off...?"

That's as far as he got, because there was a whoosh of light behind Percy, and he cried out, "Fire!"

Smoke and flames seeped into the hallway as Percy stood there stupidly, looking behind him, watching the flames as they engulfed the open front doorway. Through the flames, Percy saw a figure in black running off the porch. There was something familiar about the way the figure was moving...

Darryl suddenly grabbed him. "Run!"

The others heard the commotion and came barreling out of the living room just in time to see Darryl and Percy whizzing by, followed by a trail of flame.

"Find the back door!" Someone yelled as they zoomed into the kitchen, crashing into the other members who were in there already, trying to escape.

Percy felt smoke and gasoline clogging his throat. Suddenly, he heard crickets chirping and he was being thrust through a doorway, where he tumbled onto damp grass.

"Get up! Run!"

Percy scrambled back to his feet, disoriented, coughing and trying to hold onto the backpack that was slipping off his shoulders and falling to the ground. He had enough wits about him to turn around and pick it up before taking off in a stumbling run. Pavement and trees whizzed by, and he found himself being pushed into the backseat of Marcus' car that immediately zoomed off, tires screeching. Percy fumbled for the window handle and rolled it down, breathing in big gulps of fresh, night air.

"You all right, Percy?!" Someone asked beside him. It was Darryl.

He nodded, and stuck his head back out the window, feeling like he wanted to vomit. He could almost taste the gasoline fumes.

"What happened?!" Marcus, the designated driver asked. "Ya'll weren't in there a good twenty minutes."

"Somebody set the house on fire!" Darryl panted at him.

"What?!" Marcus nearly ran a red light and came to a screeching halt. All heads in the car bounced back and forth from the motion.

"With gas..." Brian added in a trembling voice. He was pushed between Marcus and Carlos in the front seat. "We could've been killed."

Carlos, sitting in the passenger seat, was breathing hard but he was silent. He had his head leaned back against the seat, taking in short puffs of air. Sometime during the chaos, everyone had managed to pull their masks off. Percy looked down at the hand that should have been clutching his ski mask—nothing was there. It was probably on the floor in the backseat—he'd get it later. Right now, he was trying to accept what he saw running off the porch. Whoever it was had a gas container in his head that he threw to the side before he took off.

"Marcus, just get us back to Darryl's," Carlos finally spoke up, and Percy could've sworn he heard a little fear in his voice.

MARIE

"Why you tryin' to avoid a brotha'?"

Marie was just stepping out of the ladies' room and into the hallway when Cedric's voice stopped her. She had just excused herself from the intense Forum discussion in the auditorium. Cedric was leaning against the wall, hands in his pockets.

"Hi, Cedric," she said, with her body turned in the direction of the auditorium. She was in no mood for another phony conversation with him. Still, she was glad she was looking good this evening.

"So why you been avoiding me, Marie?" he asked again, walking toward her.

"I haven't been avoiding you, Cedric."

"Why haven't you returned my phone calls?"

"I've just been real busy. Sorry." She couldn't help but relish the conversation. man, it felt good to tell him in so many words that she didn't have time for him. It felt real good—and it was the truth. She hadn't talked to him in almost two and a half weeks when he called her trying to explain his association with Claudia.

He reached out and touched her arm gently. "So you been too busy for me, huh?"

What an ego. "I'm here right now. Was there something important you needed to tell me?" The look on his face made her want to turn a couple of cartwheels.

"No—I just wanted to kick it with you a little, see how you were doing." Some of the wind was definitely out of his little sails. Marie found herself enjoying it. She had to put herself in check.

"I'm fine, Cedric. I appreciate your concern." *Go, girl.*

"Yes you are *fine.*" He put his wolf face back on. "You looking good, Marie. You looking *real* good."

"Thanks. Nice talking to you." She wiggled her fingers at him and started walking away.

"Marie!"

She stopped again. "Yes, Cedric?"

"Why you acting so funny, like you can't hold a conversation with me for ten seconds?"

"I'm not acting funny. I just want to get back to the Forum so I don't miss anything."

"I think you're trying to get back to your little boyfriend," he said in a nasty tone.

Marie felt her head beginning to swivel. "Excuse me?"

He was smirking now. "The little guy I been seeing you with—he plays with the band. The one that acts so happy all the time."

"If you are referring to Tony, yes, he is waiting for me. Now if you will excuse me…"

"So you seeing him now, right? That's your new man?"

"What's it to you, Cedric?" She was trying hard to maintain her cool. He had some nerve questioning her like they had something going on, especially after his canine actions. She itched to tell him so, but she didn't want to come off bitter.

"That's the reason you ain't been calling me. Instead of telling me the truth, you try to play me—having me call you, and you seeing some other dude the whole time. You ain't nothin' but a phony."

Marie weighed her options. She could just walk away, or she could jump on him and try to beat him down right there in the hallway. It wouldn't be very ladylike, but it would sure make her flesh feel good for the moment. Never had she encountered such pathetic, brazen gall in all her life. She looked at him staring at her. He probably wanted her to go off and call him names, or have some type of strong reaction so he could proclaim the victory in getting to yet another female. She couldn't believe that she had found him so attractive. Right now, he was pitiful.

"Cedric," she began, surprised at how calm she felt. "I really don't have time for this nonsense. I really don't. You can just stand here and talk to yourself, or tell these walls what you think about me for all I care—I'm gone." She started to walk away again, congratulating herself on her mature approach to the situation. That's when Cedric lost his head.

She felt a hand around her arm, and a tug that swirled her completely around. "Don't you walk away from me!" he hissed with angry eyes.

Now Marie didn't have any brothers, but no one was tougher than her sisters, Davette and Rolanda. The three of them had gotten into some knock down, drag outs growing up, so Marie never felt like she was anyone's pushover. That's why she was able to stand up to Tallette—and mean it. She lifted her free arm and sent her hand flying through the air, where it connected with Cedric's face in a loud pop.

He released her so abruptly she had to steady herself against the wall to keep from falling backwards. She was shaking with anger and wanted to hit him again—all two hundred plus pounds of him.

"Are you crazy?!" He yelled, holding the side of his face and advancing toward her.

"Yeah, I'm crazy, Negro...are you?!" she shot back, not about to back down from some man that was trying to bully her. "I don't know who you think you messing with, but 'chu put 'cho hands on me again and we gonna find out who's crazier!" Her voice was shaking and she was probably breaking every rule of good grammar there was, but so help her, she wanted to hit him again. Grabbing her like he didn't have good sense! She glared daggers at him, wondering if he had tried that nonsense with any other girl, like Claudia...

Claudia! Shoot, Marie needed to check on her, especially with Cedric showing his true colors. No telling what he had done—or would do—to intimidate her. And although she had bucked up to Marie this semester, Marie didn't know if Claudia had the strength to stand up to Cedric. He might have even put his hands on her! That thought angered her even more as she glared into those eyes she used to melt over, and watched his face change from anger to remorse.

"Marie, I'm sorry," he said, backing up a little with his hands outstretched.

"Yeah, I just bet 'chu sorry," she snarled, not quite in a forgiving mood.

"I got carried away. He looked down and stuck his hands in his pockets. "Marie, when I thought about you with that brotha', and you weren't returning my phone calls..."

"Boy, don't even try that mess!"

"I'm serious, girl. I got a little jealous, o.k.? I know I messed up with Claudia, but..."

"So now you admit you had something with Claudia?"

He looked trapped. He *was* trapped. "No...I mean—Marie, I never thought I was good enough for you, so I jetted before I got hurt." He came closer and touched her face. "You know I've always been crazy about you, girl."

His voice sounded oily in her ears. Smooth, silky words that were meant to melt her heart made her want to throw up instead. She slapped his hand down. "I told you to keep your hands off me."

His face registered disbelief, then anger. Marie braced herself. How was it that no one had heard the commotion and come running?

"Forget you, then," he growled. "You can't do nothin' for me, no way. You ain't even all that."

Marie had heard enough. This boy either had a multiple personality disorder or he was stuck on stupid. She exhaled forcefully and started walking away—again.

Yeah, that's right," he called to her departing back. "You ain't all that. That's the reason I started chillin' with your roommate. She got more going for her than you."

Marie kept walking. The hallway didn't seem as long when she came down it earlier, but she was almost to the corner.

"I ain't never thought dark-skinned sisters were attractive, no way."

She stopped. She turned. Cedric was standing in the middle of the hallway where she'd left him, glaring at her. Never had he looked so physically unattractive. She could hardly stand to look at him. She had severely damaged his ego, that much was obvious. Now he was trying to hit her where it hurt—in the skin.

Marie suddenly felt sad—but she felt sad for him. She heard a Voice somewhere inside her speaking softly, telling her how to respond. "I'll be praying for you, Cedric," she told him, and had the satisfaction of seeing confusion come across his face before she turned the corner to head back to the auditorium.

"What happened to you?" Tony asked quietly as she slipped back into her seat.

"I…got caught up with something," she whispered back, not sure how to describe what just took place. She was still a little shook up. "What did I miss?"

"The whole thing, girl," Tony laughed. "It's just about over. I think the Dean's about to approve another trial. He doesn't want to be held responsible for the school losing some major funding."

"Good." She fumbled in her purse for her compact and just managed to drop it on the floor. She hissed when she heard the thing break.

"Hold on—I got it." Tony reached down and handed the pieces to her. "Are you all right? You look a little shook up."

No, she wasn't all right. She needed to check on Claudia and see if *she* was all right. "I've got to go, Tony."

"Wait a minute…Marie, what's wrong? What's going on? Can I help?"

Terrell stood up on stage, and started thanking each panel member and the alumni for their participation. "…and I also would like to thank the members of the Special Events Committee in the Black Student Association, who worked long and hard to make this event happen. Please come up when I call your name. "Edward Adams…""

Marie hunched down to start her exit out of the row. Tony's hand stopped her. "Marie, what's going on?"

"Tony, I can't talk about it right now…I have to go…"

"Tony Sadler and Marie Steeleton…the only underclassmen on the committee. You two come on up and take a bow."

The crowd turned toward them and applauded. Terrell smiled benevolently in their direction. Tony held out his hand to Marie. "That's us."

She reluctantly placed her hand in his and followed him up front, while the audience clapped, hollered and stomped their feet. She smiled and shook outstretched hands, hugged the necks of the panel members and gave a hug and a return thumbs up to Tony. The crowd was on their feet by that time. She would have relished this moment at any other time—especially with the media present—but she had Claudia on her mind. Marie hurried off stage when Terrell called the other black leaders up. Tony was behind her.

"I think we were supposed to stay on stage," he told her as she grabbed her purse from her seat and kept stepping.

"I can't, Tony." She nearly jogged up the aisle while students reached out to tap her and tell her, "Ya'll did an excellent job." She smiled, thanked them, and kept going. One thing was for sure— Cedric was tripping, and she needed to get to Claudia. She might not believe her, she might think she was just jealous, but she had to try and talk to her.

"Marie, hey…" Tony was bringing up the rear behind her, still trying to get an explanation. She continued on, pushing through the crowd in the lobby that was watching the Forum from the monitors because of the capacity audience inside the auditorium. She kept glancing around to see if Cedric was lurking somewhere, and nearly jumped to the ceiling when an arm swooped in front of her to push the glass exit door open.

"Yo, Marie—slow down." Tony was holding the door open so she could go out, and brought his concerned face around to hers. "You mind telling me what's wrong?"

She opened her mouth to speak, but didn't know where to begin. Did she start with Claudia, Cedric's actions a few minutes ago, or herself? Was it fair to slam Cedric and Claudia, when she had supposedly already forgiven them for what they did? She calmed herself. She wasn't going to be any help to Claudia if she couldn't keep her emotions in check.

"A friend of mine may be in some trouble," she explained hurriedly to Tony, as they made their way to the bottom of steps in the front of the Student Center. "I've got to get to her."

"You mean Claudia?"

"Yeah."

Tony nodded. "You need me to go with you?"

"No—it's not that kind of trouble. She might just need someone to lean on—you know. The guy she's seeing is tripping—hard. I need to get to her before he does something stupid."

"What, to her?"

Marie nodded.

"Whoa, that sounds deep. Maybe I need to come with you."

"I can handle myself, Tony," Marie snapped, suddenly tired of men thinking that she was some kind of weak pushover.

Tony didn't flinch. "I don't doubt that you can, Marie—you're a strong black woman. But if this guy is going to come on the scene causing trouble, you as a female do not need to handle him alone. Now that's just common sense."

Dang. The brother had put her in her place—nicely. Again. She was immediately sorry. "Tony, I'm sorry I bit your head off. I'm just a little upset right now. But that was no reason to catch an attitude with you. I'm sorry."

His face softened into a smile. "No problem, beautiful. I can be a little pushy at times. But I was completely serious about what I just said."

"I know—and you're right," Marie told him, visualizing the scene outside of the bathrooms just a few minutes ago. "I really don't think Cedric's going to show up at her room or anything. He'll probably just call her and try to get her over to his place."

277

"Wait a minute—Cedric who? Not Cedric Carter, the football player?"

Shoot. Marie hadn't meant to reveal his identity, not even to Tony. She reluctantly nodded while Tony whistled. "Tell your girl she needs to keep a few continents between her and that brotha'."

"You know him?" Tony was only a sophomore, so Cedric must have made quite a name for himself on campus. Still, it made sense— Tony, the best saxophone player on the school's band, followed the football team everywhere.

"He's from my hometown. We went to high school together, but I don't know him personally. I know *of* him."

Marie was looking at Tony expectantly, waiting for him to continue. But Tony just stared out at the street, looking troubled. "Tony, what do you know about him?" she asked impatiently.

Tony shook his head. "Let's just say he is not the guy your friend needs to be hanging around—if she's as nice as you are."

Marie was going to exercise patience, no matter how much she wanted information. Tony was not the kind of person that went around smearing anyone's name, but she needed the low down on Cedric, and she needed it now. "Tony, look—I know you don't like to talk bad about anyone, but my friend is mixed up with this guy so I need to know what he has done or what he may do so I'll know how to approach the situation, o.k.?"

Tony just shook his head again. "Just tell her to stay away from him."

"Look, Tony. That boy grabbed me tonight like he was gonna hit me before I belted him across his face." Oh—that got Tony's attention. He whipped his head around in alarm, and Marie could see anger creeping up in his eyes. "Yeah—the boy had the nerve to grab my arm and jerk me back because I walked away from him. Now I assume he has a violent streak, so you don't have to tell me that."

"Marie, when did this happen?!"

"Right before I came back in to the auditorium."

"Why didn't you tell me, girl? No wonder you were acting so shaky when you came back." Now it was Tony who was storming ahead of her across the street. Marie stepped fast to keep up with him.

"Tony, I handled it, o.k.? I'm not concerned about myself right now. I'm concerned about Claudia."

"I know you handled it, Marie, but that was serious. Why didn't you tell…" Tony stopped mid-sentence. "Never mind. It's none of my business." He continued to walk ahead of Marie, headed in the direction of his apartment. He seemed angry—a rarity for him—and at her.

Marie just stood there in shock. Behind her, she could hear the noise as people made their way out of the Benson Student Center. Some were hanging around for the reception, while others were probably headed to one of the various parties being held on campus that evening. Marie had declined the party invitations, thinking that maybe Tony would want to grab a bite to eat off-campus somewhere, or would just want to sit and talk. Now, she was watching his departing back because he was angry with her. She didn't know whether to be angry herself at his abrupt dismissal of her company, or get upset at something she didn't know she did. She waited a minute to see if he would return, but he just kept disappearing up the sidewalk.

Marie started to go after him, then remembered Claudia, then wanted to punch herself for still wanting to go after him. *I'll call him tonight*, she promised herself as she walked quickly to Belten Hall.

When she finally reached her floor, a little out of breath, she was momentarily stunned by the absence of noise. Of course—all of her African-American floor mates were at the Forum while the white residents, fearing a violent upheaval, had found pressing engagements off campus, or were seeking refuge in their rooms.

Someone was taking advantage of the evacuation. Marie heard soft music coming from the suite right next to the elevators—her old neighborhood. She pulled the heavy door open and saw a shaft of light from Claudia's room hitting the floor…and was that perfume she smelled? Yes, she caught the delightful whiff of Claudia's 5th Avenue—a scent that was definitely not in Marie's budget at the present time. And since Claudia was not an everyday perfume wearer, even after her transformation, she was more than curious. All the same, she was hesitant to approach her old roomie, not sure how Claudia would act after the dinner incident the other day.

"Oooh!" Claudia almost had a head-on collision with Marie, who was coming up to the door while Claudia was flying out, clutching her small makeup bag. She looked great, Marie noted; she was dressed in a gray, cotton ribbed turtleneck, black jeans and black short boots.

Michele R. Leverett

Her hairdresser's eye couldn't help but to rest on Claudia's wavy mane, which was pulled back from her face and wrapped in a bun at the nape of her neck. She looked good, but in all her splendor, Claudia's expression was still distasteful. She looked at Marie without speaking, waiting for an explanation on why her preparation for whatever was being interrupted.

"You look nice," Marie told her, trying to break the ice.

"Thank you," Claudia managed, still with the disapproving look. *O.k., what do I say now—'Claudia, if you're going out with Cedric, cancel it because he's violent?' That ain't hap*penin'. "Can I come in?"

"Sure," Claudia stepped back in the room, allowing Marie to enter. She was improving on her housekeeping skills—there weren't as many clothes on the floor and bed as there had been in the past. Marie stood by the desk, not sure if she should invite herself to sit down. Claudia, however, did have a seat on the bed, frown and all.

"How are you?"

"Fine."

"Missed you at the Forum."

"I had other plans."

"Oh, o.k." *Alright—I need to cut to the chase. But let's clear the air here first.* "Claudia, I'm sorry about the other day in the cafeteria. I didn't mean to offend you."

The transformation was immediate. Claudia's hard expression melted as she nodded. "Well, I'm sorry, too. I shouldn't have said all those things. I just thought you were trying to act like somebody's momma."

"Not hardly—just trying to be a friend."

That got a smile. "I know—I was acting grown, as usual."

"Nah—just every time you get your hair done."

They shared a laugh over that. Marie felt like pieces of the friendship might be falling back into place. "You're looking good, girl." She reiterated, and couldn't help but venture, "You got a date?"

Claudia shrugged, looking a little defensive. "Maybe."

"Is it Cedric*?" Ummph— should've been a little smoother with that. Ah well...*

Claudia blinked like she didn't understand the question. She started fingering her makeup bag. "What?"

"I asked if your date was with Cedric."

280

"Why do you automatically assume it's Cedric?"

"I don't know, Claudia. I just figured you were still keeping in contact with him."

"Not necessarily."

She should have known that Claudia would try and cover it up. Of course she was still messing around with him. She wasn't the type to get over a man that easily. Marie stood up. "Well, I'll let you finish…"

"Is that all you came for—to find out if I was still seeing Cedric?"

"No—I actually stopped by to tell you something."

"So why don't you tell me?"

"Well, there's no use in telling you now."

"Why?" Claudia sounded confused.

"Because you just said that you weren't keeping in contact with him—not necessarily."

"Oh." a look of understanding—and resentment—replaced the confusion on Claudia's face. "You were coming to dog out Cedric again, right? You don't quit, do you? Why even come over here to apologize if you're going to turn right around and do the same thing?"

This conversation was about to go to another level—Marie could feel it. "Claudia, I apologized for offending *you*—not for what I said about Cedric because it's the truth."

"You are a stone trip, Marie. Here lately you've been trying to act so holy and then you turn around and bad mouth somebody. That's hypocritical."

See, Marie was not even trying to go there with Claudia. She lifted herself off of the bed and headed for the door. "I did not come over here to argue with you. You said you weren't seeing him anymore, so there's no need for me to talk to you about him."

Claudia's voice stopped her just as she reached the door. "What if I was?"

What if you was—what?"

"What if I was still seeing Cedric?"

Marie sighed, already physically, mentally and emotionally drained from the Claudia/Cedric merry-go-round. "Claudia, I didn't come to play games…"

"I'm not playing games, Marie. Fine—I 'm seeing Cedric tonight. That's what you were digging for, right? You satisfied?" Claudia angrily unzipped her bag, opened her compact and started applying her makeup right there in her room. "So what now? What were you going to tell me?"

I just need to leave. Let Claudia do whatever the heck she wants—she's old enough to make her own decisions. But no—Marie just had to try and rescue her one more time. "I ran into Cedric at the Forum, tonight..."

"Uh huh..." Claudia looked like all her attention was focused on her makeup.

"He started trippin' again, Claudia, bottom line. He was asking me why I wasn't calling him and what was going on with me and Tony..."

Claudia stopped applying her makeup and had a seat on her bed again. Marie took that as a positive sign. Maybe she was getting through to her after all.

"I'm not trying to hurt you, girl. But I've been telling you that Cedric was a dog from jump street and he ain't changing. Even Tony said that he's not the one you want to be messing with."

Claudia's look was full of questions. "Tony?"

"He went to high school with Cedric, so now you know it's not just me—he's had a reputation for awhile," Marie explained. "Then he had the nerve to grab me when I tried to walk away from him. I had to put him in his place."

"And what did you do?" Claudia asked like she was addressing a child.

"I slapped the fool out of him," Marie realized she was rather proud of her reaction—she had to put herself in check. "I..." she noticed Claudia's intense listening face. She didn't believe a word Marie said. "You think I'm lying, don't you?"

"Oh, I *know* you're lying."

"What am I lying about, Claudia?"

"The entire thing—Cedric trying to talk to you, Tony—everything."

Marie could have slapped her—right there, right then—into the middle of next week, and felt very little remorse behind it. How in the world could she accuse her of lying when she was there trying to save her pompous tail from heartbreak?

"For your information," Claudia continued, "Cedric has been out of town, at home, the entire weekend. He just got back in town not too long ago."

4

"And you know this for a fact because you went with him?" Marie couldn't help her sarcasm.

"No I didn't."

She was dumbfounded. "And so you just believed that fish tale? Girl, I know you have more sense than that!"

Claudia said zilch. She just continued to stare at Marie like she was the one who needed the lie detector test.

Marie tried a new line of defense. "Have I ever lied to you?"

"No, not that I remember," Claudia admitted.

"Then what makes you think I would be lying to you right now, Claudia? We've been friends for over three years and I have yet to lie to you. Why would I start now?"

The most infuriating, nonsensical, totally irrational response came out of Claudia's mouth. "Because you're still upset over what Cedric did to you, Marie. Bad mouthing him is your way of getting back at him. And you're probably still jealous. Why can't you just be honest with yourself? And me?"

Now Marie *knew* it was time to go. "You know what, Claudia? You're on your own from this point on. I can't do anything else for you."

"I ain't ask you to."

"O.k. Have a nice evening." Marie exited quickly, shutting Claudia's door and heading out into the lobby towards the elevator. After punching the down button, she leaned against the wall. *Lord, I don't feel very friendly toward Claudia right now, but that child needs help. Right now, I don't think it's gonna be coming from me because my heart is not right toward her. So I want to ask you to please open her eyes about Cedric before she gets hurt again, or really does end up pregnant. Amen.*

Marie reached up when she felt a tickle on her cheek, and was surprised to find that it was a tear. In her three-year friendship with Claudia, that was the second time that she had ever actually cried over something she had said or done. *Well*, she thought as she wiped her cheek, *I'd better go call Tony and smooth things over with him, so the night won't be a total disaster.*

PERCY

The house seemed larger somehow. The hallway seemed to stretch for miles. The stairway loomed ahead.

"Come on, Percy. We'll take the upstairs," Darryl said from down the hallway, waving at him. But Percy felt like something wasn't right. He kept smelling something funny.

"Fire!" he yelled, turning to look back just as the blaze flashed behind him. He saw Darryl and the others scrambling down the hallway.

"Run, Percy!"

Percy turned toward the front door and saw a figure dousing the porch with gasoline in a red container.

"Percy, run!" Darryl was hollering at him from down the hallway.

Percy took off in the direction that Darryl was moving in, but he seemed to be moving in slow motion. His feet felt like lead as he tried in vain to run up the hallway. He could feel the heat of the fire behind him. He turned and the figure in black was on his heels, pouring gas on the floor and lighting a match. Fire licked under his feet. He tried running faster, but his cement block feet would not cooperate.

The figure was laughing—Percy could see the doorway to the kitchen ahead of him, but couldn't get there fast enough. He felt the gasoline container slam into his back and knock him to the floor, which didn't make sense because it was only made out of heavy duty plastic. The only sound he heard after that was the figure standing over him laughing, and his own screaming as the flames licked up his body...

Percy bolted upright in his bed, breathing hard. Sweat was pouring down his face. His sheets were tangled around his legs and his comforter was on the floor.

"Are you all right?"

Percy, still slightly disoriented, looked over to see Allen sitting at his desk, fully dressed in a denim button down and tan slacks.

"What?"

"You've been tossing and turning for about five minutes. Then you started yelling and woke up," Allen explained to him. "That must have been a doozey of a nightmare."

"Yeah. It was—it was..." Percy swiped at his face and let out a little embarrassed laugh. "I must have been dreaming about finals."

Allen continued to stare at him, then laughed a little himself. "Man, I thought someone was trying to kill you."

Percy grimaced at Allen's precise description of his nightmare. He swung his legs over the bed, feeling shaky, then stretched. His eyes caught the clock on the desk—he had missed his biology class again. It really wasn't that big of deal this time, since most black students were planning to skip classes today anyway after the Forum and the thousand and one parties that went on last night. He was about to fall back on his bed when someone knocked on the door.

"Come in!" Percy called. The door opened and Eugene stepped through the threshold. Percy felt like he was replaying a past moment here, with him still in bed and Allen up and alert and Eugene visiting.

"What's up Eugene?" Percy asked, sitting back up in bed.

"What's up, Percy?" Eugene responded, giving Allen the same wary look he had given him the last time he'd visited. He nodded cautiously in Allen's direction and Allen retaliated with his customary, "I love everybody" grin.

"You're not up yet?" Eugene asked, like it was the weirdest thing in the world to still be in bed at 11:15 in the morning.

"I actually just overslept. I forgot to set the alarm when I got in last night. What, you skipped class today?"

"No, they cancelled mine. No one was paying attention, anyway." Eugene gave Percy a strange look. "After what happened last night..."

"Somebody burned down the Lambda Sig house last night, Percy," Allen informed him in a calm voice. "It's been the buzz around campus all morning."

Percy's shock was real. "Burned down the house?!" He looked at Allen, who nodded gravely, then at Eugene, whose nod was tighter. Percy felt his heart slam dunk into his stomach. What had the Tri-AC done?! They were supposed to smash a few mirrors, rip up some furniture...what were they going to do now?!

"...surprised you didn't hear all the fire engines and police cars last night and early this morning," Allen was saying. "It took about four hours to get the fire out. It was fortunate it didn't spread further, with all that forest around."

"You mean you didn't hear about it?" Eugene asked him.

285

"I wasn't...I wasn't even on campus last night after the Forum," Percy explained, like he was on trial.

"Yeah—you got in pretty late. I don't see how you could have missed all the hoopla, though," Allen commented, with that same calm look on his face. It unnerved Percy for some reason.

The phone interrupted, ringing like it just had to be answered. Percy reached down on the floor and snatched it up without thinking. "Yeah...hello?"

"Percy, this is Darryl." Darryl sounded excited. "Get over to the office as soon as you can."

Percy cut his eyes over at Allen, then Eugene, who were both watching him. "Hi, Ma. I go the package you sent."

"What?"

"Ma, can I call you back this evening? I got company right now."

"I got you. Just get over here as soon as you can."

Percy put the phone down and got out of bed.

"Percy, you could've talked to your mother," Eugene told him. "I can come back later..."

"No—my mom calls me almost everyday, checking up on me. It's all good. But I do think I'm gonna grab a bite to eat—are the cafeterias closed, too?"

"I don't think so. Look, I'll catch you later, Percy," Eugene told him as he waved and left.

Percy waved back, a little puzzled by Eugene's sudden urge to rap with him. He did look like he had something on his mind when he came in, but why he picked Percy to talk to about it, he didn't know. But that was small potatoes compared to what was going on now.

Percy ran down the hallway for a quick shower and fumbled into some jeans and a shirt. He just knew this thing was going to get out of hand, he just knew it! And he alone saw the person who set the fire...

"Percy, you got a minute?" Allen asked him. He was still sitting at his desk with an open text book in front of him.

"If it's about that room assignment thing, I'll get back with you. I still don't know if I'm going to be on campus next semester." His living arrangements were the last thing Percy wanted to discuss. And he hadn't had the chance to tell Allen that he was scheduled to be in England next semester, anyway.

"No, it's...well, it'll wait. I'll talk to you later."

"Preciate dat." Percy got out of there and made his way over to the Student Center. As soon as he stepped outside, he could smell faint whiffs of smoke. Burned! He couldn't believe it!

"Ah, man!" he declared to himself as his fast walk turned into a jog. What were they going to do now? Percy was fuzzy when it came to who it was jumping off that porch. He wanted to say it was Tamal—that made the most sense—but somehow it didn't appear to be. Tamal couldn't be that stupid. Maybe it was one of the new members who'd gotten word and wanted to get involved. Perhaps he realized he'd gone a bit too far, got scared and ran.

Percy was completely confused by the time he reached the Student Center, and didn't feel any better when he saw the Board perched around the office, looking concerned.

"What's up, fellas?" Percy greeted half-heartedly. The men nodded and murmured in his direction. Carlos waved him into a seat near his desk as Percy quickly scanned the room. All of the board was present and accounted for except Tamal.

Carlos let out a few uncharacteristic sighs of frustration. Percy looked up at him and saw lines etched in his forehead. "No need in replaying what happened," Carlos began. "Who knows about it?"

The board members looked at each other, then at Carlos in silent confusion.

"Come on, come on....I know somebody knows *something*," Carlos insisted, his voice a little edgy. "Who set the fire?"

The board remained silent. Percy glanced over at Darryl, who had been staring at him, then looked down.

"Carlos, how would we know who started it?" Rodney asked him. "We were in the house just like you."

"How do I know that?" Carlos asked like a prosecutor questioning a witness.

"I know you don't think one of us did it?" This came from Brian.

Carlos, who had been sitting at his desk, got up and sat down beside Brian on the couch arm, as if to start a casual conversation. "I don't know, Brian. You tell me. All I know is that the Tri-AC was in the house last night, only board members knew about the raid, and nobody here seems to know anything about it."

"How do we know another black group didn't do it, like the BSA?" Marcus asked. There are over eight hundred students here who have a beef with Lambda Sig."

"How do I know it wasn't *you*, Marcus?" Carlos asked, standing and walking right in front of Marcus. "You were outside the whole time. Maybe you got a little gung-ho and started the fire."

"Man, you trippin'!" Marcus stood to face Carlos, who didn't flinch. "How was I supposed to start that fire, then run all the way back down the street to where the car was parked in that amount of time?!"

"Yo, Marcus, lower your voice," Carlos admonished calmly. "Unless you want folk to know we were in the house last night. If you didn't do it, then why are you all up in the air?"

"Because I can't believe you're accusing your brothers of doing that!" Marcus fired, but in a lower voice. "You've known all of us since we got here! How could you think one of us tried to hurt you?!"

"Maybe I don't know some of you as well as I thought," Carlos replied, still the picture of serenity. "And some of you, I don't know well at all." He went back to his desk and leaned against the front, studying his hands. "Percy, you awful quiet. What's on your mind, man?"

Percy could feel four sets of eyes on him. He shrugged. "Nothing. Just taking everything in."

Carlos looked up like he had just discovered Percy sitting there. "You were hanging around in the hallway for a while, Percy. What were you doing?"

"I was with Percy the whole time, Carlos," Darryl finally spoke up. "We spotted the fire at the same time."

Percy felt immediate relief, and forced himself to look at Darryl. Darryl was staring at Carlos with his mouth set in a tight line. Whether he was covering for him or he saw the fire the same time as Percy, he wasn't sure. Percy just knew that once again, Darryl didn't look too pleased with their esteemed leader.

"Well, it looks like I called this meeting for nothing. We have a room full of innocent black men—my bad," Carlos remarked sarcastically. "But all I know is this—the plan was sabotaged last night, badly. And we all could've been killed. Fortunately, that's a side issue now, because we're all here. But now we have some serious arson, and we have to make double sure that it doesn't come back on us. Anyway, I think I already know who did it."

The whole room started talking at once.

"You know… !?"

"Wait a minute—how did you find out... ?!"

"Who...?"

Carlos held up his hands for silence. Percy was staring wide-eyed at Darryl, then at Carlos. How did he find out?! And how could he be so calm?

Darryl leaned forward. "Yo, Carlos—how long have you known about this, man?! And why all the questions if you already knew?!"

"Because I was trying to give the brotha' the benefit of the doubt. I didn't want to believe that he would do something as fool as to try and take us out." Carlos' voice grew bitter as he looked around at everyone. "Come on, ya'll—think. *If* it wasn't anyone in this room, it doesn't take a rocket scientist to figure out that it was Tamal."

"You think Tamal did it?!" Darryl asked in disbelief.

"Oh, that fool did it, Darryl. Think about it—he knew about the raid, he got suspended and he's psycho. Sounds cut and dry to me."

The board starting murmuring in agreement. Even Percy had his suspicions that Tamal did it, but he still wouldn't swear to it.

"Whoa, whoa, fellas—let's not get so worked up," Darryl told everyone. "We don't know for a fact that Tamal did it. We're accusing him without knowing for sure."

"Who else could have done it, Darryl?" Carlos retorted. "I knew that brotha' was trouble from day one, intelligent or not."

"Why don't we just find out where Tamal was last night, first?" Darryl sounded like that should have been the obvious action.

"Tell you what, Darryl—why don't *you* ask him? See if he tells you the truth. As for me, I wash my hands of the brotha'." Carlos wrung his hands together and flung them out, dismissing the Tamal issue. "If somehow he gets caught, it serves him right."

Darryl's indignation lifted him to his feet. "What, you just gonna sell him out like that?! That's what we're about now? The heat gets cranked up, and we bail out on each other?!"

Everyone looked at Darryl in surprise, especially Carlos. The two were usually like a right and left foot—always working together, never having any flack with one another. Darryl had never questioned any of Carlos' decisions. In fact, he was known to back them up one-hundred percent—right or wrong.

Until now. Carlos walked over to Darryl, looking at him like he'd never seen him before. "Since when did you and Tamal become bosom buddies? The man tried to take your life, and you're defending him?"

"Nobody saw who did it," Darryl told him, and Percy flinched. He alone saw someone, and the only thing that stood out was the way the person moved—with a slight limp. That's what made him believe it was Tamal in the first place, who limped in the apartment the day he broke bad with Percy.

"...supposed to be about brotherhood," Darryl was telling Carlos. "We're not supposed to accuse one of our own with no concrete evidence. That's the same attitude racists took back in the day. Something went wrong, they lynched every black they could get their hands on, whether he did it or not."

If Percy had to judge by Carlos' look, he did not appreciate the comparison. He glared daggers at Darryl, who had somehow gained control of the room.

"Ahma put it to you like this—to all of you," Carlos began. "No matter what our *Vice* President says about brotherhood, unity, whatever, I'm not taking the fall for nobody. Now, as your *leader*, I would suggest that you get your alibis together, and make them good. If you choose to take the fall for Tamal, that's your business. This meeting is adjourned." Carlos grabbed his ever present briefcase from the desk and sauntered casually out of the door. The ones left in the room looked at each other, then down at the floor. They finally put their eyes on Darryl who, at least for now, was second-in-command.

Darryl, who was still standing, made a blanket statement. "I'm not going to tell any of you how to think. I just know I'm not going to sell the brotha'' out, no matter what his attitude is."

"But it does make sense, Darryl," Brian pointed out.

"A lot of things make sense, but it's still circumstantial evidence. We don't even know where Tamal was last night. He could've been long gone from campus."

"How about the way he acted at your crib?" Rodney added.

Darryl shook his head. "I'm not saying he ain't a hothead, and he did need to be reprimanded. He got what he deserved that night, no doubt. But I still don't think he's capable of what happened."

"If you want to know the truth, I think Carlos is the one we need to be watching out for. It looks like he's trying to cover himself, to me." Marcus still sounded a little heated over Carlos' inquisition. "Ya'll better watch that brotha'. Sounds like he's selling out."

"Well, even though I do not approve of the way things were handled, let's not make a rash decision with that, either." Darryl suggested.

"How much damage was done to the house?" Percy asked.

Darryl was silent for a moment. "From what I understand, it burned down to the ground. They got policemen crawling all over this campus."

The whole room went silent for a minute.

"Yo, I gotta run," Marcus stood up. "They cancelled my class over this, so I'm going home—I need to chill."

"Yeah, I'm gonna get up outta here, too." Rodney stood up. "I better get my dad's locksmith kit back before he misses it."

Marcus, Rodney and Brian filed out of the room slowly, nodding in parting at Darryl and Percy.

Darryl sat back down at his desk, sighing. "Well, man, I guess I owe you an apology," he told Percy.

"For what?"

"For my big black power spiel the other day. Don't get me wrong—I'm not sorry about what happened to their house, because they had something coming. But now we're involved—this thing got out of hand."

"You didn't hold a gun to my head, Darryl. I did what I wanted to do."

Darryl shook his head. "I don't understand Carlos, Percy. He used to be the one talking about unity and equality. Now he's ready to throw Tamal to the lions. Maybe I shouldn't even be saying this to you, because I know you have issues with the brotha', but I still don't think he would do something like that. I still don't."

Percy contemplated. He needed to tell someone about what he saw last night. All rational fingers pointed to Tamal, but if he could just hash it out with someone, Maybe he could put some pieces together. "Darryl, you got a minute?"

"Yeah…"

"We need to talk. I need to tell you what I saw last night…"

PERCY

It was a good thing he didn't live far from the bus station. The one mile hike from it to his neighborhood was no joke—especially when he was carrying luggage. Percy had been on that bus for over three hours trying to get home—escape, was more like it. When he finally reached Jackson Park, he was surprised to see that his neighborhood was quiet, even though the spring weather was warm and comfortable. Percy saw a few faces peeping out of their respective windows, but that was just about it. Even Ms. Cleo wasn't at her usual station on the porch, waiting patiently for a child that would never come back from the store. It almost gave him the chills, things were so silent.

As soon as he hit the porch to his house, loud, angry lyrics and a booming beat greeted him. His mother obviously wasn't home, because she wouldn't stand for Paul playing loud music, let alone rap.

"Paul!" Percy called as he opened the door. It was worse inside. The music felt like a hammer pounding away at his head. He couldn't believe that he used to listen to that nonsense.

"Yo, Paul!" Percy yelled again, dropping his suitcase and heading up the stairs to his brother's room. "Man, turn that mess down! Paul..." Percy opened his brother's bedroom door and stopped. His little brother that used to tag him like a shadow, the one that he had protected from bullies at school, had pillow fights with, and shot hoops with on the basketball court, was sitting on his bed, leaning over the small nightstand beside it, snorting in lines of fine white powder. He didn't even look up when Percy opened the door. He hadn't even heard him.

In one giant step, Percy reached the dresser in the middle of the wall and viciously yanked the cord to Paul's boom box out of the socket, ending some inane rapper's soliloquy about what was going down at some party he was rapping about. Paul jerked his head up at the interruption of his private party, and his eyes and mouth became round circles of surprise when he saw his brother standing over him. He jumped up and used his body to block what was on his nightstand.

"Percy...what you doin' home?" he asked, trying to sound casual even in his disoriented state.

"No, the question is what are you doing, period?! Man, have you lost your mind?!!"

"What?"

Percy could have punched him for trying to sound so innocent. Instead, he pushed Paul out of the way to reveal the crime scene behind him.

Paul let out a lazy laugh. "Oh…that ain't nothin'."

"Nothing?!" Percy stared in disbelief at Paul, who had fallen back on his bed. His eyes were wide and watery, which let Percy know he'd inhaled a significant portion of the stuff before he caught him in the act. Percy snatched a plastic bag full of the white stuff from the nightstand, dangling it like it was a dirty sock. "You call this nothing?!"

"Yo, watch out with that!" Paul was on his feet immediately, grabbing at Percy's hand. Percy held the bag just out of reach with one hand and fended his brother off with the other. "That's money you playin' around with."

He couldn't believe how nonchalant his brother was about the whole thing. Then again, he was probably stoned out of his mind. Who knew how long he'd been using drugs?! At fifteen, while his mother juggled two jobs to try and keep a roof over his head, food in his mouth. Percy wanted to pick him up and shake him like a rag doll. Where you get the money for the 'caine, man? You ain't got no job— where you get the money?"

"Don't worry about it," Paul answered rudely.

"Don't worry about it? You know how much this stuff cost?! Where you been gettin' the money?!"

"Don't worry about it."

"Come on, Paul—what, you been stealin'?"

"I ain't stole nothin'," Paul sulked like a child, then tried to grab the bag again.

"Then how…" A light bulb went off in Percy's head. He leaned right in Paul's face. "You sellin', ain't you?"

Paul kept quiet and just glared daggers at Percy, who lost all control then. He hurled the bag to the floor and snatched his brother up by his collar. "Are you stupid?! You snortin' that crap up your nose, making you stupider than what you already are?! What's your problem, fool?!"

Paul picked up his leg and stomped down hard on Percy's foot. He shoved Percy backwards and Percy landed on the bed. He sprang right back up to knock his little brother on the floor. Paul slammed hard into his dresser, but not before he punched out with his fist, catching Percy in the mouth and busting his lip open against his teeth. Percy ignored the pain and blood and grabbed Paul, turning him on his stomach and pinning his arms behind him. Paul, who was at least ten pounds lighter, was fighting back tooth and nail. Percy finally just sat on him to keep him still.

"Get off me, Percy!" Paul hollered, trying to free his arms but only making the pain worse. Percy shoved up on his arms and Paul cried out.

"Niggah, I should smash your grill in! Here mom is, trying to keep her family together, and you bringing death up in her house! You puttin' yo' life at stake and hers! What 'chu thinkin' 'bout?!"

"I ain't thinkin' 'bout nuttin'!" Paul cried from underneath his brother's crushing hold.

"You right you ain't thinkin' 'bout nothin'—you trippin'!" Percy gasped out his words, short of breath after the short tussle. He let up on his hold and got up from his brother's back. Paul rolled over slowly, wincing as he straightened out his arm muscles, and rolled his eyes at Percy.

"You get this stuff together, and you get it out of this house," Percy ordered him. "Flush it down the toilet. And don't you ever bring it back up in here again."

Paul's look was full of disbelief. "Who you think you are, Percy?! You ain't nobody's daddy. You don't tell me what to do!"

"Yo, I ain't even playin' with 'chu. You get rid of this 'caine. And you get your little butt out of whatever hustle you got going on out there in the street."

"Or what, Percy?! You gonna try and come at me again? What, you gonna tell Ma?!"

Percy just stared at him, feeling his jaw swelling and his heart pounding. He reached up to wipe some of the blood off his lip and flinched. Paul got up off the floor, but kept a safe distance away from his big brother's reach.

"Tell her then—what I care? She ain't here half the time, anyway. Wouldn't care even if she was."

Paul—how can you say that?! Ma is out there working two jobs to support this family! Tryin' to make sure you got a place to sleep, fool. How can you say that?!"

"All Ma cares about is going to church—and you. She's always throwing you up in my face—why can't I be more like Percy?—bragging to everyone about her intelligent son in college. She don't care nothin' about what I'm doin'.""

Remembering his last conversation with his mother, Percy wanted to believe that the drugs were doing more talking than Paul was. But there seemed to be some truth to what he saying. His mother was holding down two jobs, so she wasn't able to be home and spend a lot of quality time with her son. Percy sighed. The streets had almost snared him, too, but he had enough anger at his father and his situation to want to get out. Also, he still felt like the self-appointed man of the family, which kept him straight in a lot of situations. His brother had no where to channel his emotions—no wonder he sought the streets and drugs for release.

"Yo, man—you're playing with fire," Percy said, bringing his voice down to a lower volume and trying to understand his brother. "Drugs will kill you—know what I'm sayin'? You'll either fry all your brain cells or someone out there will bust a cap in you."

"I can handle things, Percy. Ain't nobody takin' me out. My boys got my back."

My boys—how many times had Percy said the same thing to describe his affiliation with *his* crowd? My boys—Percy remembered hanging with his boys. Everything was love-love, until he decided he wanted a better life than what Jackson Park was offering. All of a sudden, his boys excommunicated him from their little circle. Even came in Dell's to give him dirty looks. Percy had enough street in him not to be intimidated, but he watched his back all the same.

"No, Paul—I got 'cho back. Ma and Monica got 'cho back. Those fools you hanging 'round wit ain't got 'cho back—your *family* does, man." Percy just realized how true that was, especially in the wake of all that was happening on campus. Carlos had all but sold the entire organization out in his quest for political gain. Tamal put the Tri-AC in jeopardy because of a power trip—you couldn't trust anyone fully except family. Darryl seemed like the only stable one. So far.

"Ah, man…don't give me that bull," Paul sneered rudely. "Monica all the way over in Korea, Ma's working all the time, you off at college. Everybody's off doing their own thing, out for self." Paul's bottom lip trembled a little, then he immediately stiffened it, but not before Percy saw the pain behind all his toughness. "Dad won't even come to see us—he's off doing his thing. Everybody's out for self— why shouldn't I be? Oh, you thought I was too young to remember Dad leavin', huh? I remember when he left—won't tell me over the phone why he did. Ma won't tell me why he left—ah...bump this!" Paul jerked his arm in frustration and picked his bag of drugs off the floor. Percy watched stupidly as he carefully swept the remains from the nightstand into the bag and sealed it tight. Percy heard him sniffle and wipe his nose. He couldn't determine whether it was from the drugs or emotion.

"I'm out," Paul informed him, stashing the bag inside his pants and heading towards the door. Percy came out of his zombie state and blocked his way.

"What, we goin' another round?" Paul spread his arms out. "Look, who you think been helpin' with the bills around here? *Me*—that's who. Monica sends a little money, but she gotta live, too. I been buying grocery and paying the rent."

Percy couldn't believe what he was hearing. "Ma *knows* what 'cho doin'?!"

"Ma thinks I have a job after school."

"Where does she think you're working?! You ain't even old enough to have a real job, man!"

At least Paul had the decency to look embarrassed. "She thinks I'm working at the furniture factory. I told her the guy was paying me under the table since I ain't sixteen yet. Look—all she knows is that I'm helping to pay the bills. They done went up on the rent, she got bills that are behind...*you* ain't contributing nothing, Percy. Somebody got to be the man of the family."

Percy started to respond, but found that he had nothing to say. He knew what Paul was doing was wrong—dead wrong—but he couldn't counter with anything that would blast a hole in his argument. He didn't realize things were so tight at home. His mom never said anything when he talked to her, and probably wouldn't. She probably didn't want him to worry and think he had to drop out of school to help out at home, which is exactly what he was considering now. And she absolutely refused to go on welfare. "I'll depend on God to meet my needs—not the government," she would argue.

While he was deep in thought, Paul slid past him, ran down the stairs and banged out of the house. Percy ran behind him, but Paul's long legs took him halfway down the street by the time he reached the porch.

"Paul!" Percy yelled after him. Paul glanced behind him just as a blue car with gleaming silver rims and loud speakers came around the corner and stopped beside Paul.

"What's up, Paul? Yo, you wanna go chill?" The driver asked. Percy could see two other heads in the backseat.

Keeping his eye on Percy, Paul hurried to the passenger side and climbed in. The car revved unnecessarily and zoomed down the street past Percy.

Percy kicked the screen door in frustration. How did things get in such a mess? Before he left for school, Paul was as normal as a kid could be in Jackson Park. Now, he was using and selling drugs and lying to his mother. And here he was, in a mess of trouble over something he didn't even do at school.

This was the fault of one man—Edward Lyles, Percy decided. He moved them to this roach motel of a neighborhood then skipped out, leaving his mom working two jobs and his younger brother selling drugs to make ends meet. Percy's rage grew as he thought about his dad's last phone call, trying to act like a proud father, making excuses for why he left, calling once a week, like that would make up for not being there. Look at the mess this family was in.

He went back in the house and slammed the front door, looking around for something else to punch or dismantle so he could relieve his anger. What he really wanted to do was throw this mess up in his dad's face—show him where his cowardliness had led the family. He scrambled through the neat piles of paper, envelopes and books on the end table where the phone sat, where his mom usually kept her address and phone book. His dad's number was bound to be in there somewhere. He found the book buried underneath a stack of bills and flipped through it. H, I, J, K, L...Lyles. Edward Lyles—there it was, right before Monica's name and unusually long address and phone number in Korea. There was the name, but no telephone number. The only information listed was an address, and a strange one at that. Caller 232, a city, state and zip code.

Percy frowned and looked around the room in confusion, his eyes focusing in on a 10x14 picture hanging on the wall. It was a picture of his smiling parents, holding two small children on their laps—he and Monica. He had on a bow tie big enough to cover his ears and Monica was wearing Afro puff ponytails. He remembered asking his mother to take that picture down after he figured his dad wasn't coming back, but his mother refused. Percy climbed up on a chair and tried to take it down himself, but the picture slipped out of his hand and the glass in the frame shattered when it hit the floor. His mom wore his tail out, then made him clean up all the glass and use his allowance to buy another, more expensive frame. She put the picture back in the same place and dared him to touch it. Then she tried to explain, for the umpteenth time, that his anger at his father would only destroy...

The sudden ringing of the phone jolted him. He picked it up. "Yeah...?" Whoever it was took their sweet time to say anything. "Hello?"

An automated voice responded, telling Percy that there was a collect call from a...Low Valley Correctional Facility...*Correctional Facility?!*

The voice continued smoothly. "Caller, please state your name..."

"Edward Lyles."

Percy jumped straight up. Edward Lyles?!! Correctional Facility?!

"Will you accept the charges?" The computer-generated voice wanted to know. "Please press one to accept, or press two to refuse..."

Percy sank slowly back down to the sofa. His father was in prison?! That explained why he only called once a week...but why didn't he tell him that? Why didn't his mother tell him?! He put the receiver back in the hook and stared at it like it would ring back and his father would be on the other end. He just sat there on the couch, deep in thought. He looked out of the living room window at his neighborhood. *Prison!!* What was his old man doing in prison?! And how long had he been there?!

Percy felt numb—he just continued to stare out the window, unable to process any sensible thoughts. There was a little more activity out there now than when he first came home. He saw the Robinsons' daughter across the street coming home from work, dressed in her McDonald's uniform, he saw one of his ex-homies standing down by the corner, looking like he was waiting for somebody—*his father was in prison!*—he watched Ms. Fletcher bring her young daughter out on the porch, and place her on the steps between her legs so she could braid her hair, like she did once a week when it was warm out. And today was unusually warm for this time of year. Percy closed the curtain and grabbed the remote control instead. He flipped through channel after channel, until he finally settled in on a news show that didn't interest him in the least bit, but the anchor was a brother...

The next thing he knew, he was laying across the couch with his arm and legs hanging over the front and the remote on the floor. The living room was dark except for the flicker of the television screen. He heard keys jangle as the door opened and his mother came in, singing a gospel song like she always did. She stopped singing abruptly, and slowly wrapped her hands around the metal bat she kept by the door.

"Who's there?" she asked.

"It's me, Ma," he answered sleepily, not moving from his prone position.

She approached the entrance to the living room, and Percy could see a look of relief wash over her face in the light of the television. "Percy—boy, I was about to use this thing on you. What are you doing here? You get another break you didn't tell me about?"

"No, I just felt like coming home."

She settled down on the couch at his feet and patted his leg. "Percy, it's not that I don't like having you at home, but don't you think you should be saving your money? You have to come home for the summer, don't you? And you got to get ready for England. Riding the bus ain't cheap."

"I got it covered, Ma," he told her, staring at the television. The black anchor was now replaced by a cheerful white woman holding a gigantic bottle of vitamins, promising viewers they could lose twenty, forty, one hundred pounds in just weeks.

"What's wrong, Percy?"

"Nothing, really."

"You sure? You don't sound like nothing's wrong?"

"I'm fine, Ma."

"I haven't heard from you since your father talked to you. Why didn't you return my call?"

"Sorry about that Ma. I just wasn't in the mood to talk."

His mother sighed. "Percy, I understand how angry you must feel, but your father is trying to make up for what he did wrong. He just wants to have a relationship with his children. You shouldn't have talked to him like you did."

Percy just kept silent.

"Is that what's bothering you?"

"I'm straight, Ma—I mean, I'm all right." His mother hated when her children talked in slang.

She patted his leg again and stood up. "O.k.—you're home now. Let me go get some dinner ready. If I knew you were coming, I would've made a bigger meal. We'll just have to stretch what we have."

"I'm not hungry, Ma."

"You need to eat, Percy. And why are you sitting here in the dark?" She flipped the switch by the wall and Percy finally sat up, squinting from the light. "Percy!" His mother zoomed back to the couch and grabbed him under his chin. "What happened to your face?!"

Percy gently disengaged his sore face from his mother's hand. He'd forgotten about his lip for a minute—he could have at least wiped the blood off. "It's nothing…"

"Don't you tell me it's nothing! What happened?!"

"Paul and I were messing around and he nailed me, that's all."

"*That's all?!* You mouth is all busted open and bleeding and you say *that's all?*! What were ya'll doing? And where is Paul?!"

"I don't know. He left a couple of hours ago. It's no big deal, Ma. We both got a little upset and we scrapped."

"Is his lip busted, too?"

"No—Ma, it'll heal up. He didn't mean to."

His mother continued to frown. "I should go upside both your heads, because I told you not to be fighting each other like that. You're brothers and I'm not having it. I'm too tired to deal with it now. If I hear tale of it again, you both better duck, you understand?"

"Yes, ma'am."

She nodded, satisfied. "Paul's probably at work right now. I can never tell—he works such odd hours down at that factory."

Percy studied the T.V. screen again.

"Well, at least he's working," his mother continued, sounding like she was talking more to herself than to Percy. "He's not hanging out on the street somewhere. This is not a neighborhood to raise children, Percy. There so much out there, right in front of your face. I just praise God that all of my children were able to rise above it. And that extra money sure has been a big help around here. And Paul can buy all those fancy clothes he likes himself."

Percy swallowed. Guilt spread through his body like a cold chill. He had to tell his mother what was going on, but how? She was struggling with two jobs as it was. If she knew where the extra income was coming from, she'd probably take on two more. Just the thought of that clammed up his mouth, and then the other issue came to mind.

"Ma?"

"Hmm?" She had stood up again and was heading down the hall to the kitchen.

He took a deep breath. "Dad called."

Mrs. Lyles was back in the living room in a flash, her eyes wide. "You talked to your father today?"

"No—he just called. I didn't accept the charges."

His mother sunk down to the couch beside him for a third time. She sighed deeply. "I was supposed to talk to you before you found out where he was. I been snatching the phone up before you kids for years to keep you from finding out."

"How long has he been in prison?"

"About nine years now."

"Nine?!" Percy turned to look at his mother. "He's been in lockdown for nine years and I'm just finding out?!"

"Percy, you were too young to know what was going on when he first went in…"

"I was nine, Ma."

"Your dad asked me not to tell you until you were older. Then you never wanted to talk to him when he called, so he felt like you weren't ready to hear about it."

"Ma, can you blame me?! All I—all *we* knew was that dad called every Sunday at seven o'clock—that's it. I didn't know he was in prison. What he do, steal something?"

His mother was suddenly silent. She clasped her hands under her chin and studied the carpet.

"Ma, what'd he do? Why's he locked up?"

Mrs. Lyles shook her head. "Percy, it's not important what he did. The Word says to forgive and forget. He's paying for what he did."

"Don't I have a right to know?!"

"Lower your voice, boy."

A troubled thought came to mind. "He didn't beat you, did he?"

"No son—your father never raised a hand to me."

"Did he kill somebody?"

"No, Percy! Please…"

"Ma, what did he *do*? Don't I have the right to know something about my father?!"

His mother stood up. "Percy, I don't want to talk about this right now. Now you had your daddy on the phone a few days ago. You should have asked him why he left."

"I *did*! He wouldn't tell me, either!"

"Well then…just give it some time. Maybe it isn't time to tell you. You already know he's in prison, all right. So just leave the 'why' alone until he's ready to tell you."

Percy ventured a guess. "Monica knows, doesn't she?"

His mom eyed him warily. "Don't you dare call your sister and get some mess stirred up when I told you to leave it alone!"

"Did it have something to do with his drinking problem?" Percy pushed.

His mother advanced on him slowly. "Is there something wrong with your hearing, Percy?! Did I not just tell you to *drop it*?! That's your problem now, you think you're grown and you don't want to listen anymore! You ain't grown, so you just need to listen to somebody and stop flying off the handle all the time! Now I'm not going to say it again—leave it alone!"

"Don't matter anyway," Percy mumbled, more than a little miffed. "He still left before he did whatever he did. He still skipped out." He knew he was risking his mother's wrath by bad-mouthing his dad, but he desperately wanted some answers and he was tired of getting the runaround. He barely had time to get his hand over his injured lip and jaw before the back of his mother's hand came and caught him on the other side of his face.

"I told you to watch what you say about your daddy under this roof! You don't know what you're talking about, and you need to keep that big mouth shut!"

Percy had never seen his mother so upset, but he was just as angry. "Why do you keep protecting him, Ma?! Huh?! He left us! He ain't here!" he yelled, rubbing the side of his face and moving away, because his mother was advancing on him again.

302

"Shut up, Percy!" she screamed at him.

"What about us?! He left you working like a dog, Ma! You work two jobs—you don't even have time for yourself…and your youngest son's out on the street dealin' drugs for money because of that fool…!"

Whap! Percy felt his mother's ring scratch the side of his face again. He stumbled back and fell down on a large potted plant, knocking it over and sending soil flying. His mother stood over him, her eyes so angry they were almost bulging out of her head. She took a deep breath and pointed a finger down at him.

"You get out of this house," she said in a low, angry voice.

"What?!"

"You heard me Percy. I want you out of here! You want to keep bad mouthing your father, disrespecting me, find somewhere else to live. I ain't having no rebellious child up in my house!"

Percy jumped up, not believing his ears. His mother was throwing him out?! Over that sorry excuse for a man that left them high and dry?! "Ma…"

"Get out…" she repeated, grabbing Percy by the shirt and trying to drag him.

"Ma, wait a minute…!"

She turned and tried to strike him again, but he blocked it and held her wrists. "Ma, listen to me…!"

"Get out!" she screamed in his face, working a hand free and rearing back. Get out! Get out! Get out…!" His mother suddenly brought her hand down and crumbled to the floor, sobbing so hard that she was gasping. Percy was immediately beside her, wrapping his arms around her and stroking her hair that had come out of its neat bun.

"Ma," he started, feeling more frightened and helpless than when his dad left them. "Ma, what's wrong? Ma…I'm sorry. I'm sorry, Ma…"

His mother just kept crying, burying her face in her son's chest. Percy sat back on his heels and just let her cry, feeling like he would rather have his right pinkie finger slowly sawed off with a dull knife than to ever upset his mother like this again. The last time he saw her anywhere near this was when his father left, but even then she went into her room and closed the door until Percy couldn't take her faint sobs anymore and went charging in.

"Ma, I'm sorry," Percy repeated, feeling like he was going to cry himself. "I just wanted to find out why dad stopped caring about us...about you..."

Evelyn Lyles finally looked up, her beautiful face swollen and tear stained. "Stop caring?" she practically whispered. "How can you say such a thing, Percy? We were everything to your father...everything..."

"Then why did he leave Ma? And why is he locked up?"

Evelyn Lyles sighed, and it was the saddest sound Percy had ever heard. She sat up beside him. Percy got up and hurried into the kitchen, wetting some napkins and bringing them back to his mother.

She took them with a smile and patted his leg when he sat back down next to her. "You're always looking out after me, aren't you, Percy?" she asked, cleaning her face.

"I'll kill a man over you, Ma," he declared, dead serious.

His mother's face clouded back up, and tears started rolling back down her cheeks. "Please don't say that..."

"I'm sorry," Percy said immediately, not meaning a word. He had always been fiercely protective of his mother, especially after his father left. The only reason he didn't go to a local university or a community college that would allow him to come home every day was that Paul was still here to look out after his mother, but even that had changed. Paul couldn't even look after himself right now.

"You know, your father felt the same way, the very same way, Percy. That's why he's in prison."

Percy's eyes went wide. "So dad killed somebody?!"

His mother shook her head and gazed out into space. "No, but he tried to."

"Why?"

His mother continued to stare out at nothing, like Percy wasn't even there. "You remember when I worked down at that hardware store?"

Percy remembered. The store had been sold and was now a used car dealership out on Grover Street, in the ritzy part of town. His mother had worked there as a bookkeeper right until the time his father left ten years ago. He remembered riding with his dad to pick her up in the evening, when she and the owner would be the only ones left in the store. Percy never liked the owner, Mr. Brant, a late-fortyish white man with bushy eyebrows and slicked back hair. He always patted Percy on the head when he saw him and called him a "good boy" which, even at eight years old, Percy knew was a racial put-down. And he had an annoying habit of licking his lips and putting an arm around his mother like he owned her. His dad didn't like it too much, either.

"That man needs to keep his hands off of you," he told her one evening when he picked her up and thought that Percy was asleep in the back seat. "He pays you to keep his books, not put his arm around you and rub your shoulder."

"Edward, he doesn't mean anything by it—he's just touchy feely like that," his mother told him.

"Well, he can be touchy-feely with his own wife—not mine. I don't like him, Evelyn. I don't like the way that joker looks at you, licking his lips like that."

"That's just a habit."

"Well staring at you like a piece of meat ain't no habit!"

"Edward! Look at me—I'm a black woman with three children living in a low-income neighborhood and he's a rich white man," she laughed. "What does he want with me?"

"White men go after black women all the time," his dad argued.

"Baby..."

"I don't like you working there. You need to quit."

"Edward, I'm fine. We need the money."

"We don't need it that bad that I'm gonna let some man put his hands all over my wife!"

In the rear view mirror, Percy saw his mother lean over and place a soft kiss on his dad's cheek, and he saw the frown lines in his dad's forehead disappear. His mother had a knack for softening his dad right up. "It's o.k. Edward. I'll be fine. Look—if I feel like he's being fresh, I'll quit, how's that? Will you just trust me? This job is a giving me some good accounting experience so maybe I can find something better soon. Trust me."

"Dad tried to kill someone at the hardware store?"

"Yes, Percy. My boss—Mr. Brant."

"What?!" Percy knew his dad had his issues with him, but to try to kill the man because he touched his wife's shoulder was a bit extreme. "Why, Ma?!"

Evelyn finally came out of her trance and looked straight in her son's eyes. "Because he tried to rape me," she said softly.

Percy got up slowly, staring down at his mother like he didn't know who she was. He walked a few feet away and turned back to look at her, sitting down on the floor and looking like a scared little girl. "No, Ma…Ma, no…"

"Yes, Percy," she told him. "You wanted to know, so I'm telling you."

"Oh, Ma…" Percy zoomed back over to her and put an arm around her, tears forming in his eyes. She let herself be held for a few seconds, but then pushed away.

"He, uh…asked me to come to his office late one night after he'd locked up the door and I'd finished the books. He told me that he really liked the way I kept the books in order, and that he wanted to help me get started as an accountant—he had some connections. Do you know what that meant to me, Percy? Do you know how much I wanted to do something more than just work at a cash register or be a bookkeeper? I didn't have a chance to go to college and be something like you children do—that's why I push you so hard…"

Percy listened, feeling like he wanted to be sick, and his mother hadn't even gotten to the worse part yet.

"He…he asked me what would I be willing to do to get a better position, make more money. I just told him I guess I could go to community college part-time if my husband agreed. 'That's not what I mean, Evelyn,' he told me, then he got up and shut his office door. 'Did I ever tell you what a beautiful black woman you are?' And then I knew that your father had been right on the money all along. I got up to leave—that was the night that I was riding the bus home from work because your father had to work late. The bus station was about a block up the street. He…blocked the door, and then grabbed me, and threw me on the floor, tried to rip my clothes off…"

She stopped and dropped her head in her hands. Percy just sat there helplessly.

"I kneed him, Percy, and got away. He had locked the front door with a key so I had to go out the back door where they brought the supplies in. I never ran so hard in my life. I didn't even catch the bus—I just kept running and crying, running and crying…I don't know where your father came from. He told me later on that he called the store and no one answered and then he called home, and Monica told him I wasn't home yet, so he came out looking for me. Can you believe I was halfway home by that time? I didn't know I was out there so long..."

Now Percy was starting to remember things from that night. He was in bed but he heard the door slam shut downstairs and faint crying. He heard his parents coming up the stairs and jumped out of bed just in time to see his mother's back disappear into their bedroom and his dad behind her.

"Ma...?" he started.

"Get back in bed, Percy. Now!" He had never heard his dad sound so angry and pained at the same time. He knocked on Monica's bedroom door. "Come in here with your mother," he told her, flying back down the stairs and out of the house, but not before Percy saw the gun he was trying to shove inside his jacket. A couple of days later, his dad was sitting the children down and telling them he had to go out of town for a while, to take care of their mother while he was away. That was ten years ago.

"What did dad do to him?" Percy wanted to know.

"I wasn't there, but your dad told me that he was so angry he didn't even remember when he stopped hitting him. He just remembered that Mr. Brant stopped moving. Then he just left him out in front of the store—that's where he caught him when he came back, locking up the store as if nothing out of the ordinary had happened. He even had the nerve to smile at your father and tell him I had left over an hour ago. He said he was all set to shoot him, but when he saw him, he wanted to try and tear him apart with his bare hands. He did some damage to him, Percy—some serious damage. He had about five operations just to reconstruct his face."

"So...dad left so he wouldn't get caught?"

"He left to go live with some relatives so he could find some work and still send money to his family, Percy. That's why he left. The police came for him three days later after Mr. Brant woke up and told them who beat him up. They caught him. And the only reason he's not doing more time than he should be doing is because I didn't press charges against Mr. Brant. I'm not condoning your father's actions no more than I condone Mr. Brant's. He acted out of anger, and instead of us going to the police, he handled it himself."

Percy leaned his head back on the sofa and closed his eyes, calculating the number of times his dad had called but he refused to talk to him, and all the anger he had against him. His dad did exactly what he would have done in that situation. The police would have handled it just like the Administration at Hamel handled the Plot. His dad took justice into his own hands, but look where it got him. He missed out on ten years with his family.

"I can't blame him, Ma." Percy told her.

"Percy, I understand your father being angry. It was a horrible thing that happened. But anger can get you in trouble. Why do you think I tell you to watch your temper all the time? You can't just react without thinking first. What if he would have killed him?"

It would've served him right, Percy found himself thinking, then immediately changed his mind. What if someone would have been in the Lambda Sig house that night and they didn't know about it? What if the person burned up with the house? Did the punishment fit the crime in that scenario?

"So now you know your dad didn't just skip out on us…"

"What about what he said about being an alcoholic?"

His mother shook her beautiful head. "I hate to admit it, but that was a lie, Percy. We didn't want you to know what really happened just yet. You wouldn't even talk to your daddy over the phone."

"You were in on it, too?" Percy couldn't believe it. The way his mother pounded the Bible in their ears…

"Parents make mistakes too. I'm not proud of lying to you—it was wrong. We just wanted to protect you."

"From what, Ma? Dad already took care of the man."

"From hating white people. From being bitter and angry and doing something that would mess up your life. But lying was wrong—I'm sorry."

Their protection was too little, too late. Percy had let his anger and animosity get him caught up in trouble already. He knew one thing for certain—he was his father's son.

His mother started to rise from the floor. Percy immediately jumped up to help her. "Well, now that the fireworks are over with, let me get dinner started." She started toward the kitchen.

"You still want me to leave, Ma?"

Mrs. Lyles turned. She looked younger, stronger, like telling the truth was a catharsis that rejuvenated her. "No, Percy. I want you to go clean up your face and get ready for dinner."

"What about Paul?"

She closed her eyes and took a deep breath. "I can see there's a lying spirit in this house that needs to be cast out. But your daddy and me opened the door to it. I'll deal with Paul, Percy. You leave it to me."

Percy started toward the front door. "Let me go find him..."

"No, Percy. I'll handle it—I'm the parent. You children have been trying to take care of me for too long—I'll handle it."

Percy sat back down on the couch, his head reeling from all that had happened. He had never felt more confused in his life.

CLAUDIA

She got a lot of nerve, Claudia kept thinking as she bounced along in the Campus Police car. Ever since a student had gotten attacked a year ago while walking across campus, the University had provided an escort service for students traveling across campus at night.

Claudia was sitting in the passenger seat, listening to the squawk of the police radio and thinking about Marie's latest attempt to dog Cedric out. He had been out of town since yesterday afternoon, so how did Marie expect her to believe that story about him trying to get his rap on at the Forum? He called her about forty-five minutes ago, telling her that he had just gotten back in town and wanted to see her—all that jazz. Claudia wanted to tell him she was busy, maybe some other time...something to make her feel like she was in control. But what she ended up telling him was that she would see if she could come over later, knowing full well that she would be there. He told her he would wait up all night if he had to—he just wanted to see her.

Maybe he realized that no matter what, he still cares for me, Claudia told herself as she scurried around her room, trying to get ready. She just about had herself convinced of that when Marie decided to come by and dash a bucket of cold water over everything.

The officer rounded a corner and pulled into Cedric's apartment complex. His apartment was a short walk up the sidewalk from where they stopped, but illegally parked cars were blocking the street. The officer sighed in frustration. "I can't get any closer, honey," the female cop complained. "I don't know why the University didn't make this lot bigger—it would cut out on these cars parked along the sidewalk. I guess I can go in from the opposite direction..."

"I can walk," Claudia assured her, unstrapping her seat belt.

"Are you sure?"

"Yeah, it's no problem. I'm just going up the street there."

"All right, call if you need a way back. That's what we're here for."

"I will." Claudia climbed out of the car, and the officer stopped her.

"I'm going to stay here until you get to where you're going."

"Oh—thanks." Claudia started up the sidewalk and noticed Cedric's door standing open. He was standing outside the door, looking in the opposite direction. Her heart leaped in spite of herself—the boy was outside waiting for her!!! She promised herself that she was going to keep it in check no matter what. She decided then and there that she would not go back to Marie and gloat—she was going to be adult about the whole thing since Marie wasn't. Besides—she needed to keep her social life to herself.

Claudia turned back to the police car and pointed to Cedric, indicating that she was o.k. The officer nodded and pulled off. Claudia was just about to smile and call out Cedric's name when he suddenly stepped off his porch and strolled over to a car that pulled in from the direction opposite Claudia. She was about twenty yards from his apartment. She stopped in her tracks and watched his dimples appear as he broke into a wide grin, then opened the door of the car.

The driver climbed out— Claudia spotted the sleek, shoulder length hair even before Cedric ran his hand through it. The female turned just enough for Claudia to tell how beautiful she was, even from where she was standing. The mystery woman came around her open car door, grabbed Cedric in a big hug and planted a juicy kiss on his mouth. Cedric grinned again, then reached into the open car door and pulled out what looked like a small suitcase. He shut the door with his free hand, then leaned toward the girl for another kiss before he put an arm around her small waist and led her into his apartment. Not once did he glance down Claudia's way.

Claudia stood there in the chilly dark, feeling like her shoes had molded into the cement. She shook her head vigorously; she looked behind her to see if someone might have come upon the scene to witness the incident with her—someone who could corroborate her story, but the area was deserted. She didn't how long she stood there or what propelled her forward after that. All she knew was that one minute, she was standing rooted to the ground, watching Cedric kiss another woman and the next minute, she was knocking on his door. She heard a muffled voice and movement on the other side, then the door creaked open to reveal Cedric's surprised face.

"Hi! So you came, huh?" he said in a voice that was way too high-pitched and cheerful. Claudia tried to look behind him and thought she caught a glimpse of the bag she saw in his hand earlier, but Cedric's body was strategically blocking her view, preventing her from seeing clearly. She did notice that the lights were very dim inside, which meant he had on the tall, thin lamp in the living room

311

that he liked to call his "mood lamp." And was that the shower she heard running in the background?

"I tried to catch you before you left," he was telling her as he came out on the porch, easing the door shut behind him. "I was hoping you had just stepped out of your room for a minute."

Claudia just stared, wondering if he were going to tell the truth—wondering if she was going to explode in rage or crumble in a sobbing heap.

"I'm worn out after that long drive home and back. I just want to take it easy tonight." Cedric yawned, then managed to look remorseful. "I'm sorry, Claudia. I got you all the way over here for nothing. You want me to drive you back to your room?"

She was dumbfounded. How could he stand up there and lie to her like that? She felt ridiculous. Then, something on his face caught her eye. A raised, darkened mark was plastered right below his left eye. She found herself staring at it—it looked like he had been punched...

Or slapped.

"Claudia?"

"What?"

"I asked if you wanted a ride back to your room?"

Claudia found herself nodding. Where was she going to use a phone to call for an escort anyway?

"Uh, o.k. Can you wait here a minute? I'd let you in but the apartment is a mess—my roommates didn't clean up. O.k., let me go grab my keys." He slipped back inside and shut the door. Claudia heard a metallic click, which meant he had locked the door as well. Right now, he was probably making up some lame story about a friend, or some crazy, lovesick female needing a ride home.

Yeah, baby. It's this freshman girl. Stays up in my grill all the time. I keep telling the girl to step but she insists she's in love with me. I even told her about you, baby, but she don't care. She walked all the way over here and it would bother me to have her walk back this time of night by herself. No matter how much she irritates me, baby, I don't want her to get hurt out there this time of night. You know how mean people can be nowadays.

Claudia began to tremble, and not just from the cold. She bit her bottom lip and felt tears sting her eyes. She looked at the door, waited to hear approaching footsteps, then turned and almost ran away from the apartment. Let him worry about where she was. She walked faster, then she did break into a run, her boots making heavy, clunking sounds against the sidewalk. She turned corners and whizzed past trees, before deciding she was far enough away that Cedric couldn't see her.

It took her about fifteen minutes to reach Belten Hall. She swiped her I.D. card through the reader and flashed it at the desk attendant, then headed straight for the stairway. By the time she got back to her room, anger had replaced her sadness. She slammed her door shut and threw her purse against the wall, hearing a small shatter inside. Big deal. She grabbed the picture Cedric had given her—he was posed in one of his great football moments—and ripped it out of the frame. She studied it a minute, then proceeded to shred those dimples into small particles of chemically treated paper.

She dug through her jewelry box and found the chain he surprised her with the week after their "first date" at Cow Pattie's. That got slam-dunked into her trashcan. Then she went to her closet and pulled out the leather jacket he had let her wear one night when it turned freezing cold and her jacket wasn't heavy enough. Claudia fingered the jacket, brought it to her face. It still smelled like his cologne. She carried the jacket to her desk and pulled out a drawer, rifling through it to find her scissors. She was amazed at how calm she felt, like everything she was doing was part of a routine "to-do" list: tear up picture, check; throw away gold chain, check; shred leather jacket...

She found the scissors just as someone was knocking hard on her door. Maybe Cedric followed her, wanting to explain himself in person. She searched her heart—was she willing to forgive and forget, or was she going to slap his face and tell him to get lost? And who was that other woman anyway, with her long, pretty hair and her overnight bag?

The knock became more insistent. Claudia went over to the door and yanked it open. Marie was standing on the other side—the last thing Claudia needed right now was one of her lectures.

"Marie, if you are hear to preach to me, I am not in the mood," Claudia told her without hesitation. She actually felt like she would become physically violent if Marie so much as opened her mouth. Marie's tone was subdued. "I just came by to get my purse," she explained. "I think I left it in here earlier."

Claudia turned and scanned her room. The purse was lying at the foot of her bed. She left Marie in the hallway and scooped up the purse, noticing that Marie was looking at her peculiarly. She looked down and realized that she was still holding Cedric's jacket and the scissors in her other hand.

"Are you all right?" Marie ventured cautiously.

"Fine. Why?" Claudia asked, thrusting Marie's purse at her.

Marie just stared at the jacket and scissors.

"What, you like this jacket?"

Marie shrugged, looking uncertain, then nodded.

"You want it?"

"What?!"

Claudia held the jacket out to her. "Do you want the jacket?"

"Claudia, that's a leather jacket," Marie reminded her.

"I know."

"And you just want to give it away."

Claudia just shrugged.

"O.k.—why do you want to give it away?"

"I can't use it."

Marie let that statement sink in. "Claudia…"

"Take the jacket, Marie, before I cut it up." She went back to her bed and threw the jacket down, readying her scissors. She could feel a strong wave of emotion coming on.

Marie came in and shut the door. She didn't say a word as she picked up shredded pieces of picture off the floor and went to the trashcan. She paused, then reached into the can and pulled out the gold necklace.

"Oh, you can have that chain if you want—it's real. Do you want this jacket to go along with it? Last chance." Claudia's voice was at a higher pitch in an effort to control her emotions. Something was getting damaged tonight. It was either going to be the jacket, or it was going to be its owner. And Marie's silence was annoying her, by the way.

"I suppose you're waiting for an explanation," Claudia snipped as she finally sat on her bed, bringing the jacket close to her.

"Only if you want to tell…"

Claudia held up one hand like a crossing guard. "Do not do that, Marie. O.k.?"

Marie nodded, her eyes rooted to the scissors in Claudia's hand. "What did he do this time?"

No use in pretending she didn't know who it involved. "I guess I owe you a big apology, don't I? You had him all figured out. But I was too stupid to listen as always."

Marie, who had been standing by the door, zoomed over to sit beside Claudia, all caution gone. "Did he hit you?" she asked in a low, angry voice.

Claudia shook her head.

"What did he do?"

"He made like he wanted to see me so bad, then when I went over to his apartment, he was smooching with some other woman."

Marie drew in a deep breath, but she didn't look shocked. "You walked in on him and some other woman?"

"No, I was getting ready to walk up to his door and she was getting out of her car—with an overnight bag."

"Mmph."

"I felt like a straight up fool, standing there watching them kiss. He didn't even see me. So I went up to his door after they went in the house."

"You confronted him?"

"No—I just stood there and listened to him lie to me about the whole thing. You should've heard him, Marie. 'I tried to call you, Claudia. I'm just so tired after all that driving…' Just straight up lied about the whole thing." Claudia gripped the scissors tighter and looked down at the jacket. "He even offered to drive me back here. So when he went back to get his car keys—oh, did I tell you he left me outside in the cold while he did that?—I left. He hasn't even called to see if I'm here, if I'm o.k.—nothing."

She expected Marie to be shaking her head, saying, "I told you so." Instead, she was frowning in concentration. "What did the girl look like?"

"I don't know. About your height, I guess. Slim, lighter than me, shoulder-length black hair, nice figure, big dark eyes, full lips. It was too dark to see that well."

Marie held back a laugh. "That sounds like a decent description to me."

Claudia embellished, realizing she was just as upset with the mystery woman as she was with Cedric. "High heels, tight, little skirt that looked like it belonged to a four year old, a cheap, low cut blouse like some…"

315

"Oh, you didn't see her that well, huh?"

Claudia laughed, wanting desperately to find humor in the situation, or at least have a "Marie" reaction to it—let everything roll off of her back. Instead, she felt like crying for being so stupid. Cedric had played her and Marie in the same year—correction—he *tried* to play Marie, but she was too smart for him.

"Now tell me what she looked like one more time?" Marie asked. Claudia repeated her description. "Oh."

"Why? You know her?" Claudia was kidding, but Marie wasn't laughing back or denying the charge. "You *know* her?!!"

"Well..."

"Marie, do not do this—who are you trying to protect? Cedric?"

"I don't exactly know her. I know *of* her."

"And?"

"Claudia, come on..."

"Marie!"

"How's that gonna help you get over this, you knowing who she is? It's not going to change the situation. Just leave it alone. Leave Cedric alone and go on with your life."

"O.k., so let's pretend some guy—let's just say it was Tony—played you with some other woman in front of you—you wouldn't want to know who she is? Is that what you expect me to believe?"

Marie sighed, rolling her eyes. "All right. I don't remember her name, but she sounds like his old girlfriend from back home." Marie paused, and looked down at her hands. "Sounds like his...baby's mother."

Claudia jumped straight up. "His wha-who-what?!!! Did you say his *baby's mother*?!"

Marie nodded reluctantly, looking up at Claudia with pity.

"You're telling me that Cedric is somebody's daddy?!!"

"From what I know."

Claudia had to take a seat at her desk on that one. Cedric was a daddy. He had a child somewhere back home. And she was just fortunate enough that he didn't have another one on the way. So maybe this "old girlfriend" wasn't so old. Maybe she was always in the picture, and Cedric was seeing both of them at the same time.

"Now I only told you that because it should make you feel better," Marie was saying, squeezing Claudia's arm. You don't want to get wrapped up with all that baggage, girl. You are a young, beautiful, intelligent woman, and you have your whole life ahead of you..."

Claudia was only half listening. Yeah, yeah, she knew the drill. She had her whole life ahead of her, there would be many Cedrics in and out of her life before she settled down—blah, blah, blah...that whole spiel that was designed to make jilted women feel like they could conquer the world again. Well it didn't take away the pain and humiliation she felt at giving her virginity away to a man that didn't deserve it.

"He played me like a cheap fiddle," she said out loud, not even necessarily addressing Marie. "He probably saw me coming a mile away. Here comes one of those stupid, desperate females who'll do anything to keep a man. I can't blame him—he's a dog. Dogs are supposed to go after, stupid, desperate..."

Marie got up and put her arms around Claudia, who had dropped her head in her arms and starting crying. "Let it out, girl," she whispered, smoothing Claudia's hair. "Go on and cry if you need to."

She needed to. She cried until her voice felt hoarse and her nose stopped up. Marie sat her on the bed and handed her some tissue from her desk. "Blow," she commanded, like a mother.

Claudia blew. Her eyes felt like golf balls pushed in her sockets, and she just knew her face was beet red. "How do I look?" she joked, after clearing her sinuses.

"Beautiful."

"Don't lie."

"Have you eaten yet?" Marie asked.

"No. I thought Wonderdog would feed me once I got over there."

"Let's order a pizza."

Food was the last thing on Claudia's mind, but she wanted some company for a while. "That sounds good. Your treat?"

"No—yours. I don't have any money for pizza."

"Then why did you suggest it, Marie?"

"Because I'm hungry." Marie smiled mischievously and fished around in her pocket book, producing a dollar. "Ohh! I can treat us to some sodas! What kind do you want?"

Claudia looked at her in disbelief. "You are seriously going to run this game on me?"

"But I'm getting the drinks!" Marie insisted, trying to look serious but failing. A big, contagious grin spread across her face. Claudia had to laugh.

"All right, Marie. The pizza's on me. But I'm getting it all the way."

"You know I don't eat all that trash on my pizza!" That was their word for things they didn't like—trash.

"Oh, excuse me...but this is *my* pizza, Miss 'I ain't got no money but I can get the sodas.'"

"That's cold, Claudia. Just for that—I'm getting you a Mountain Dew." Marie moved toward the door with her dollar.

"Don't you bring that trash in here!" Claudia hated Mountain Dew with a passion.

By that time, both girls were laughing their heads off and for a moment, Claudia forgot that she was supposed to be upset.

EUGENE

Eugene was sitting out on the back patio just off the kitchen, still wearing his suit from the funeral. His mother had been buried not more than three hours ago, right next to her parents' plot. Mercifully, the funeral had been brief, the way his mom had requested. She had been laid to rest in a rose-colored casket trimmed with gold and surrounded by white roses, her favorite.

He had no tears left. He had cried until all he could do was moan, and the pain still didn't go away. He was all alone now. Chip had Diedra to lean on, but he had no one.

"Eugene?" Irene and Monty came out on the patio. They had changed clothes and were carrying their bags. Monty told him he had to be back in time to meet a study group for his test tomorrow. Chip and Deidra would drive Eugene back to school in a couple of days or whenever he felt ready.

Irene sat down beside him on the long cushioned lawn bench and grabbed his hand. Monty sat on the other side. He didn't look at either one of them. He looked out into the backyard at the garden his mother had planted years ago. She showed him how to take care of it when he was ten.

"Eugene, Monty and I have to leave shortly. I just wanted to let you know."

He nodded, still staring at the garden.

"I'm sorry, papi'," Monty said with remorse. "This dumb calculus test—I'd skip it, if I could."

"Monty, it's all right," Eugene half whispered. "I appreciate you guys being here as long as you were. You don't have to apologize for anything."

That seemed to relieve Monty. He squeezed Eugene's shoulder—a male version of a hug. Eugene patted his hand and studied the yard.

Irene stood up. "Well, I guess we'd better hit the road. Call me anytime, o.k.? I mean that."

Eugene stood beside her, nodding. Irene reached up to touch his face, then grabbed him in a big hug. "I'm here for you—remember that," she muffled into his shoulder.

Eugene tried to respond, but he felt his tears coming and his will to stop them leaving. He heard the glass door slide open, and then his

319

father was standing there, watching them hug. Eugene pulled away from Irene and eyed his dad, almost daring him to say anything. He had just seen his beautiful mother laid to rest, and he wasn't about to put up with any of his father's racial nonsense. But his father didn't look upset. He just looked like he was waiting for Irene to finish consoling him.

Irene followed Eugene's gaze behind her, and released him, too. She turned and walked over to his dad, holding out her hand. "Mr. Wright, thank you for having us," she said, shaking his hand. "If there's anything that I can do…"

"Just being there for my son means a lot," Mr. Wright responded, and Eugene almost fell over. "You two have a safe trip. Come back anytime."

Eugene had to have a seat then, especially when Irene reached up and hugged his father's neck and he hugged her back.

Monty gave his dad a brief handshake and hug and disappeared back in the house with Irene. Mr. Wright stood at the door a minute, then took a seat beside Eugene. Both of them just stared out into the yard for a while. It was the longest moment Eugene had ever spent in his father's company and felt comfortable. Even with his dad's silence, Eugene felt like something had changed between them.

"How are you feeling?" Raymond finally asked.

"I'm all right," Eugene told him. "You?"

"I guess I'll make it, I guess I'll make it. It's tough, though."

"Yeah, I know."

Silence again. Eugene shifted—his dad shifted. One of them coughed.

"Is Chip o.k.?" Eugene asked. Chip had done one of his numbers at the funeral, passing out in front of the casket. He was carried out by two cousins who were pallbearers.

"He's upstairs laying down, but he's fine. Momma's up there with him."

"Where's Diedra?"

"She went home to get some clothes so she can stay over a few days. She'll be back later on."

Eugene nodded, grateful that his brother had someone to comfort him, and even his dad had his mother to console him, but who did he have? He thought he had mentally prepared himself for the whole thing, but at that moment, he felt just as confused and lost as he did when he first found out his mother was sick.

"You ah...going back to Hamel?" his dad asked. His question didn't hold the disapproval it had in the past. He just sounded like he wanted to know his plans—period.

"I don't know, Dad. I haven't really thought about it. I know that's what...mom wanted."

"What do you want?"

What his dad really asking what *he* wanted?! "I don't know, Dad. I don't know what I want to do now. I don't even want to think about it right now."

His dad nodded in understanding. "Sure, son. I didn't mean to push."

Eugene looked down at his hands and searched for the right words. "Uh, thanks for making my friends feel welcome."

"They're nice kids. It was good of them to be there for you."

And Eugene had to push further—had to. "I thought you might have a problem with Irene. I wasn't sure what kind of reception she would get from you."

He thought his dad might get defensive; instead, he laughed softly. "I can tell you this—she's only the second white person to be in this house since we bought it twenty years ago."

"Who was the first?"

His dad looked at him sideways. "The real estate agent."

Eugene cracked up. His dad joined in, laughing heartily. Eugene couldn't remember a time when he and his dad had shared a laugh. Even with the tragedy they were facing, he couldn't help himself from laughing. The laugh was a release of pent-up emotions—of wanting for years to be close to his dad, and not being able to. It was an expression of his anger at not being athletic, not being black enough for the people in high school, and feeling like he always had to prove himself. And finally, it was the sadness he felt at losing his mother, the only person he ever thought loved him unconditionally.

He didn't know when his laughter turned into tears—all he knew was that he was sitting up one minute and laying on his father's lap the next, crying loud while his father held his shoulders and told him to let it out. The patio door slid open and he felt Chip's arms go around his neck as he added his tears to Eugene's. Finally, his father broke down, holding his sobbing sons tight.

321

Suddenly, Eugene felt a peace fall over him like a warm blanket in the winter. He heard the musical trilling of a bird, and slowly lifted his swollen, tear-stained face just in time to see the red robin that had been sitting on the ledge of the balcony. It stood there a minute, seeming to make eye contact with him. *I'm so proud of my boys*, he heard a soft voice whisper from somewhere inside of him. The robin hopped around to face the yard before it soared up into the sky.

Diedra gave him a big hug and a kiss on the cheek when she and Chip let him off in front of his residence hall.

"You take care of yourself, little brother," she said. "Call if you need anything."

Good Lord—she sounded like somebody's mother. The thought sent a pinprick of pain to his heart. His mom always told him that when she called. Diedra and Chip and had driven him back to school four days after the funeral. They had tried to persuade him to stay home and take some incompletes in his classes, but he refused. His mom had wanted him to finish no matter what, and he would do just that.

Chip was still nestled in the passenger side of his burgundy 360, ready to go to sleep. He drove to Hamel and Diedra would drive back home. His dad decided to stay home and "get things situated," as he put it, and Chip told Eugene that he and Granny were probably going to go through his mother's things. Mr. Wright had been talking about selling the house a couple of days after the burial, until his mother mentioned that she might want to move to Harrisburg from Virginia. Mr. Wright suggested—almost begged—that she move in with them. No sense in a four bedroom house going to waste.

After Eugene got his bags out of the trunk, he went around to the passenger side. "What—no goodbye kiss?" he teased Chip, who grimaced in disgust.

"Please—I just ate."

"Your woman gave me one."

"Well then—let that be from both of us."

"Charles Michael, what is wrong with you? Get out and say goodbye to your brother." Diedra chastised, shaking her head. She loved to see the two of them cutting the fool, but she would never admit it.

"Yeah, man—where's the love?" Eugene added.

Chip leaned his head back against his seat and closed his eyes. "Right now, it's tired from driving."

"Chip!" Diedra growled.

"O.k., woman—o.k." Chip grinned and got out of the car. His joking expression turned serious as he grabbed Eugene in a bear hug. Eugene could feel the pain through his hug. He almost cried again.

"You call us, all right?" Chip said, letting him go.

Eugene nodded, not sure if he wanted them to hurry up and leave or hang around a while. He shifted his suitcase to the other hand.

"Eugene, are you sure you're ready to be back here?" Chip asked. "You can come on back home with us. We can put your stuff right back in the trunk and take you back."

The idea was tempting. He had gotten in a little routine during the past four days, and being at home made him feel closer to his mother's memory. He would go in her room several times a day and sit on her bed, talking to her. His dad hadn't slept in there since the medical crew took her body out the day she died—he was crashing in the extra guest room downstairs near the den. And even he and Eugene had gotten closer. He had taken him fishing a couple of days after the funeral while Chip was out with Diedra. They didn't catch anything, but it didn't matter. It was the first real quality time they had spent together.

Eugene clapped Chip on the shoulder. "Thanks, big bro. I think I need to go ahead and finish what I started."

Chip nodded. "Well, if you change your mind, call us on the car phone. We'll turn right around and come back for you."

"We sure will, Eugene," Diedra added.

"Thanks guys, but I'll manage. You guys just go ahead and set a wedding date before Diedra discovers what a loser you are and changes her mind, Chip."

"Boy, let me tell you something—this woman could travel to the ends of the earth and never find another man that she loves more than me," Chip declared, throwing his arms around his fiancée. "Ain't that right, baby?"

Diedra looked like she was about to get him told, but he leaned over and kissed her. She giggled in response.

"Uh—look guys...I'm getting kind of queasy so why don't I just go up to my room?" Eugene put his hands on his stomach and pretended to retch.

323

"Oh, you'll understand one day, Eugene," Diedra trilled, winking at him. "Tell *Irene* I said hello."

"No way, baby. My money's on Renee'," Chip said. Eugene shared his experience with Renee' with his big brother and Chip was all for it—especially when Eugene described her. Of course, he also said that Irene was pretty cute after he met her.

"Bet," Diedra challenged, shaking Chip's hand in agreement. "Ten dollars."

"You're on."

Eugene couldn't believe his ears. They were actually placing money on who he would date. "You two need some professional help," he told them, laughing.

Before he got back in the passenger seat, Chip reached out and squeezed his brother's hand. Eugene squeezed back, getting the message loud and clear—they would be there for each other for the rest of their lives.

"Have a safe trip." Eugene waved until he could no longer see Chip's car. He turned around to face his residence hall. Now, the real test would begin.

CLAUDIA

"Girl, you know I care about you. I think I'm falling in love with you."

"Claudia, we're going to be together for a long time."

"Why would I be running a game on you? I'm a man—I ain't got time for games, baby."

Everything made sense when Marie was here. Dump the loser, leave him be, don't even talk to him. But Claudia's chest was burning with rage and pain. How dare Cedric take her heart that she gave so willingly and grind it under his shoe? Then go off with another woman like it was nothing?

Claudia had actually felt very confident about their relationship after that night in his apartment when Cedric first tried to make his move on her. They had eaten the pizza, watched the movie, laughed and talked until it was late. Cedric drove her back to her apartment, walked her up to the Belten and leaned down. She immediately jumped.

"I just wanted to give you a hug," he told her.

She let him hug her, then he grabbed her face and kissed her on her cheek, letting his lips linger there awhile. She felt her spine tingle. "Sorry, Claudia. But you have to leave a brotha' with some type of pleasant memory," he told her before winking and telling her he would see her later.

He called her everyday for two weeks after that, telling her how much he enjoyed their conversation, he was glad they had cleared the air, how much closer he felt to her—more than any other woman, how free he felt knowing that he could talk to someone who wouldn't judge him. Even if he'd seen her two or three times in a day, he was still calling her that evening. Claudia was floating—she was on top of the world. They were an official "item" on campus. He held her hand when he walked with her, and she could see the envious stares of other girls. Yeah, this was her man. Look, but don't touch.

The only thing that really bothered her was when they saw Marie, who tried to act like she didn't see them together. Cedric would sometimes immediately drop her hand or start to walk a little faster when that happened. Claudia still felt happy regardless because she had not compromised herself and Cedric was respecting her. What more could she ask?

One Thursday night two weeks later, Cedric called her at about ten o'clock.

"I'm downstairs," he told her, sounding strange. *"Can you come sign me in?"*

"Are you o.k.?" It was very rare for Cedric to come to her side of campus. most of the time, he would come and pick her up, take her back to his apartment.

"No, not really," he told her sadly.

Claudia hurried downstairs. Cedric was leaning against the wall in the lobby with his head hanging, looking like he had lost his best friend. She quickly signed him in and took him back upstairs. He was silent on the way up.

"You want something to drink?" she asked him when they got to her room.

"Nah, I'm straight—can I sit down?"

"Sure." Claudia threw her sheet and comforter back over her bed where she had jumped out of it when he called. She had never seen him look so sad—or so attractive. "Is it someone in your family?" She asked him.

"No—it's nothing that, Claudia. It's..." He sighed and shook his head, standing. *"I better go."*

"No," she told him with a little force, pushing him back down to a seated position.

" Claudia, I almost scared you off before with my crazy emotions. I don't want to risk losing you again."

"I want you to talk to me, Cedric. You know you can talk to me about anything. That's what I'm here for."

Cedric smiled at her. He told her that he went to bed right after he talked to her that evening, and he just couldn't sleep. He got up and tried to watch a little television, and finally just got in his car and drove around. That's how he ended up at her place.

"Why can't you sleep?" she asked, not realizing she had grabbed his hand and was rubbing it.

He told her he couldn't figure it out until he got in his car and drove—had some time to reflect. He said there was something different on the inside of him, and it took him a while to figure it out.

"What's going on, Cedric?"

326

He looked her in her eyes. "Claudia," he began. "I think I'm falling in love with you."

Claudia stopped. Had she heard correctly? Had he told her that he was falling in love with her? Did he just echo what she thought had been going on with her almost since day one?

Cedric stood up again. "I should go."

Claudia pulled him back down. "No, Cedric. Stay."

"I scared you off again, didn't I?"

"No, Cedric."

He smiled, leaning toward her to cup her face in his hands, and bring his lips to hers. This time, Claudia didn't shy away.

She didn't have a clear recollection of what happened after the kiss. All she knew was that she woke up the next morning and Cedric was already gone and she had missed her eight o'clock class. She called his apartment and one of his roommates told her that he was asleep, but he would give him the message. A few hours went by, and no return phone call. She called again after she had gotten dressed and eaten lunch, figuring she would catch him before her two o'clock class but all she got was their answering machine.

So she went to class and came back to her room, positive that he would want to hook up like they did every Friday night. Her message light was blinking, but there was no message from Cedric. So she waited another three hours and called his apartment again—he was there but said he was just about to jump in the shower, could he call her back a little later? So she waited another two hours but Cedric did not call. When she called him back, his roommate said that he had left—he didn't know what time he would be back or even if he would be back because he didn't say. That's when Claudia started to feel funny.

"Just leave it alone, Claudia," Marie told her when Claudia called her, in tears again. "I know it hurts, but Cedric ain't worth it."

"I just want to know why he felt the need to use me?" she sobbed loudly. "Why did he tell me all those things if he didn't mean them? Why would anybody do that?"

"Trust me...you're not the first person he's played, and you won't be the last. But whatever you do, girl, do *not* let him know that what he did hurt you this much. Don't confront him about this, Claudia. Chill out."

"I'm trying to."

"Do you need me to come over and stay with you?"

"No, I'll be fine. I'm going to bed after I take my shower. I'll be fine tomorrow," she sniffed, hoping she meant what she said.

"You call me if you need me tonight, o.k.? Corrie's at some conference, so you won't be disturbing anybody."

"I appreciate it."

"I mean it, Claudia. I don't care what time it is. I'd rather have you call me than him."

"I know you do, girl. I do appreciate it, but I'll be fine. I'll call you if I feel like slicing something up again."

Marie laughed. "Take care, sweetie. Get you some rest."

Claudia did feel like she would be fine after she hung up the phone. She ironed her outfit for the next day—something she rarely did—took her shower, snuggled in bed and grabbed her remote. She glanced at her clock—10:00. There wasn't bound to be much on. She didn't do too much television viewing at this time anyway, because Cedric would usually make his evening call and... No, she had to keep her mind off of what they used to do. There was no longer a "them." After a couple of rounds, she found a movie that looked a little interesting and settled in.

Claudia's eyes were beginning to droop. She really wanted to finish the movie, which was about a young couple torn apart by adultery according to the emotional announcer of the woman's channel the movie was on. Claudia rooted for the woman, who threw her cheating husband out on his ear after finding evidence of his infidelity. After many trials and tribulations, the man came crawling back to his family, vowing never to be unfaithful again. His wife and baby meant too much to him. He was a fool, he confessed to his teary-eyed wife.

Claudia's eyes flew open. "Don't do it," she advised the actress on television, wanting some company in her personal misery. The actress continued to cry; her play husband took her in his arms.

"I love you, Nadine," the traitor blubbered. "You mean more to me than anything."

Claudia found herself crying. O.k...maybe he was really sorry. He was certainly crying hard enough to convince her. She continued to cry as the man met his former mistress in the park the next day, telling her that it was over. She couldn't accept that, she told him. She was his, and she knew that deep in his heart, he loved her too, and she would wait for him.

"You'll be waiting forever. I love my wife," he told her firmly. "Forget about me—I'm a married man. Go on with your life."

"Don't do this to us, Frank," she begged, grabbing his wrist. "You told me you were falling in love with me!"

Frank gently disengaged his wrist from her hand, told her one more time to forget him and go on with her life, and left. The woman screamed after him before she finally collapsed in a depressed heap in the park, sobbing her heart out.

That's when the burning rage started in Claudia's chest. Frank decides that he has had enough of his little rendezvous, and just tosses the woman to the side like a piece of trash. After, of course, lying to her about his feelings for her just so he could have his way. Granted, she was wrong for fooling around with a married man, but she was just a lonely woman looking for love and found it in the arms of a married man. And she naively believed that he would leave his wife for her. But she should have known that she was Cedric's first love, and he'd never gotten over her and she was beautiful, probably funny and smart...

The next thing Claudia knew, she was pulling a T-shirt and a pair of running pants out of her drawer. She found one sneaker under her bed but couldn't find its mate to save her life. She rifled on the floor of her closet, found a right foot sneaker from a different pair and rammed her foot into it, pulling it around her heel with a finger. She grabbed Cedric's leather jacket from her bed and found her keys on her desk. She didn't know what she was doing or what she planned on doing, but she was going over to Cedric's to do it. She heard a baby's happy gurgling, and turned as the credits rolled over the happy, reunited family on television. Frank tossed the baby in the air, making her squeal with excitement, then turned and kissed his wife passionately.

Call Marie. Call Marie. Claudia started across the lobby to Marie's room, then hit the elevator button instead. That was taking entirely too long, so she headed down the eight flights of steps leading to the lobby.

The desk guard looked up from his magazine and gazed at her strangely—wild hair, too big T-shirt, wrinkled running pants, mismatched shoes and a leather jacket. Yep, she looked like she had some deep issue but, unfortunately, he didn't get paid to counsel residents. He went back to his reading and let her go.

The night air was a little crisp. Claudia clutched Cedric's jacket tighter around her and headed up the sidewalk, walking at a firefighter's pace. She glanced down at her watch, surprised to find that she even remembered to put it on. 12:13. No wonder that desk guard was giving her that peculiar look. What a sight she must be, marching across campus at this time of night with the way she looked. Judging from the lights in the windows of the residence halls she passed, the majority of the student population was asleep. Those that were up were probably studying, talking, or trudging across a dark, empty campus in the middle of the night.

It took her about twelve minutes to reach the apartment. The burning in her chest wasn't as bad now that she was almost there. She felt mature—they could handle this issue like adults. They could reach a conclusion and go on with life from there. All she wanted was an explanation—something Marie had talked her out of. But she wasn't Marie—she was Claudia, and she needed some answers.

Maybe it was a close friend, or one of his roommate's girls. Maybe that wasn't even Cedric I saw outside. It could have been Vince. They're about the same size, about the same complexion. It was dark and I was upset. He said he cared about me and he might. We can make this work, but I have to stop crowding him, start trusting him. Men don't like insecure women. And so what if he is a daddy? I like children, I think. It was probably just a bad situation he got into in high school or something—or maybe some female trapped him. A lot of them do that. Maybe we can talk about that, too. Maybe I can stay over and we can just talk—I won't let anything else happen. I can handle it this time.

Claudia found herself at his apartment door and reached up to knock, then instinctively ran her hands through her wild hair. She must be a mess. She tugged at her too big shirt and looked helplessly down at her mismatched shoes. She could see the flicker of the television through the window, so somebody was at least within hearing distance. Maybe Cedric was restless again, mulling over how he felt about her. She knocked, listened, then knocked again. She finally heard shuffling feet and a groggy voice mumble, "Hold up," on the other side. The knob turned and Travis squinted out at Claudia over the chain lock.

"Hi, Travis," Claudia greeted him, trying to sound cheerful. As if that would make up for being at his apartment in the middle of the night. "Is Cedric here?"

"Uh, Claudia? Mmm, hold up—let me wake up." Travis yawned and rubbed his eyes. He closed the door, unlocked the chain and let her in. "You all right? What's wrong?" he whispered.

"Nothing. I just came to see if Cedric was here."

"He's asleep," Travis said like she should have known better. "I mean, it is…late."

"I know. I'm sorry I woke you up. I have his jacket. I thought he might need it," she explained, holding up her arms to show him the jacket.

"You can leave it with me and I'll make sure he gets it when he wakes up. Did you walk all the way over here?"

She nodded, feeling even more stupid. "It didn't take long."

Travis looked down at her like she'd lost her mind. She wasn't there to explain anything to him, though. She wanted to see Cedric. Travis didn't understand, either.

"What does Vince's girlfriend look like?" she asked out of the clear blue.

"Huh?!"

"Is he seeing a girl with long black hair?"

"I…I don't know…why are you asking me this?" Travis asked, running a hand through his disheveled hair.

"I need to know, Travis."

"Claudia, honey…I ain't trying to be rude, but I got to hit the road early in the morning and everybody else is asleep. Why are we standing here talking about who Vince dates? Are you all right?" he asked her again, a cross between concern and frustration.

"Are you trying to hide something from me, Travis?" She could feel the burning coming back. "Is there a girl staying here?"

"Claudia let me take you back home." He started back towards his room.

"No, that's all right, Travis. I came to see Cedric." Claudia's voice got louder and started down the hall after Travis to Cedric's bedroom.

"I told you he's asleep," Travis reminded her in a louder, firmer voice.

But she was determined. She had to talk to him. He wouldn't mind if she woke him up. How many nights had they talked until the wee hours of the morning? Didn't he come to her room late that night when...

"Travis, turn that television down, man!" an angry voice called from behind Cedric's door where Claudia had stationed herself.

"I got it, Cedric, sorry," Travis called, then added in a whisper, "Claudia, you need to go home. Do you want me to call an escort for you?" He moved around behind her, like he wanted to lead her back to the living room.

"Travis, I told you I came to see Cedric. Now he's up, so I'll just go see him and you can go back to bed." Claudia turned the knob on Cedric's door. It was locked. She yanked at it.

"Cedric, it's Claudia. Can I come in?"

Sheets ruffled. "Claudia?!"

"I need to talk to you."

"Claudia, what...what are you doing here?"

"I have your jacket and I need to see you. Open the door, please." Claudia pounded on the door and listened. She heard Cedric's low voice and a sleepy female response. The burning became a flame inside her chest. She pounded harder. "Open the door, Cedric."

She heard the click of a door opening beside her, and Vince stepped out of his room, frowning and looking very tired. "What's going on out here? Claudia, what are you doing here?" He looked over her head and frowned at Travis for an explanation, and she turned just in time to see Travis point at Cedric's door before quickly reaching to scratch the back of his head.

"I know somebody's in there," she informed the roommates.

Vince started to open his mouth, then looked away; Travis suddenly decided his messy hair wasn't presentable and ran both hands through it.

"Cedric, open the door! Who's in there?"

"Girl...go home! What are you doing at my house making all that noise?!"

Claudia pounded harder. She was getting some answers tonight if she had to wake up the whole complex to do it. "Open the door, boy! I know she's in there!!" She yanked on the doorknob again, trying to force it to turn. She heard the female voice again, this time asking something like, "Who is that?" and her rage increased. She could hear somebody getting out of bed and coming closer. She banged on the door again.

"Claudia, I don't know why you're here, but you need to leave. Now." Cedric said from right behind the door, trying to sound calm and rational.

"Cedric, why are you doing this?! Why did you have me believing we had something and you got some other woman in there with you?!" Her voice caught and tears were beginning to spill from her eyes. "Why did you lie to me like that?!"

"Go home, Claudia!"

"Claudia look, maybe you should just calm down a minute." Vince was beside her and gently grabbed her arm. "Just come sit in the living room a minute and get yourself together."

She snatched her arm away from Vince. "Let go of me! Cedric!" Claudia turned her attention back to the door. Vince stepped away and went back to his room and Travis at some point had done the same. He was no where in sight. "What's her name Cedric?" Claudia asked the door. "Is that your baby's momma?! Open the door!" Claudia pounded and cried, going for broke now. She had already made a fool of herself—might as well see her little special project through to the bitter end. And she wanted to see the girl close up—she wanted to see who she was being kicked to the curb for.

She saw a shaft of light from underneath his door and heard frantic movement. The door cracked open and Cedric tried to slide through it, but not before Claudia caught a glimpse of shiny black hair and long manicured nails running through it. She tried to see more, but Cedric slammed the door shut behind him. He was wearing the same pair of khakis from earlier this evening—now wrinkled—and an open button down.

He grabbed her wrist and pulled her into the living room. She punched at his hand with her free fist, then dug in with her nails when that didn't work. He yelped in pain and turned on her angrily. "Girl, have you lost your mind?!" he barked, sucking at the broken skin. Claudia, now several levels past out of control, hauled off and hit him again in his arm, which felt like a brick.

"Who you think you are, Cedric?!!! Who do you think you are, lying to somebody?!" Claudia punctuated her words with blows that she tried to land on his face, but ended up connecting with the arm that was blocking her.

"Claudia. Claudia!! Calm down!!"

"Don't you tell me what to do! Don't you tell me to calm down and you got some other woman in there!" Claudia had broken free when she dug her in nails in Cedric's hand and rushed back to his bedroom door. "Did he tell you about me?!" she asked the girl in the room. "Did he tell you how he tried to play me and told me that he was falling in love with me just so he could sleep with me...?!"

Cedric snatched her arm and yanked her away from the door, pushing her in the living room. Claudia grabbed the first thing she saw—the remote control laying on the table—and threw it at his face. It hit his shoulder instead.

"Girl, you better chill. Go on, now!" Cedric warned, grabbing both her wrists in his hand. "You need to leave, Claudia. You need to go on and leave." He started pulling her toward the door again.

Claudia struggled but couldn't get free this time. She folded up her leg and kneed him in his hamstring as hard as she could. He lost his balance and let her go, and she pushed at him while he was trying to straighten up.

"Claudia, don't make me hurt you! You better leave!"

"Do it, Cedric! Do something then! You a man—you want to beat me up?! Do it!!"

"Yo, Claudia, chill!" She heard Vince behind her, and felt him grabbing her free arm that was raised to do some more damage to the dog standing in front of her, who—no he was *not* trying to hold back a laugh—oh no he wasn't. Claudia yanked away from Vince again and her eyes landed on a long, brass candle holder sitting on top of the stereo system. She grabbed it and started swinging at Cedric, the leather jacket she still had on made swishing sounds as she swung. Cedric's eyes rounded in surprise and he ducked. The candle stick connected with the wall behind him where his head had been milliseconds before, making a loud thud. The pictures that had been hanging above shattered to the ground.

Claudia, put that down!!" Vince yelled, trying to grab her swinging arm and avoid getting injured in the process.

Claudia didn't know what was driving her anymore. Everything became a blur of arms, legs and shouts through her tears. She continued to swing and chase Cedric around the living room. Swinging and chasing, swinging and chasing, with Vince shouting behind her. She knocked over the table and sent magazines and a couple of knick knacks flying, trying to get to Cedric.

"Claudia," Cedric started, crouched to run on the other side of the dining room table. "You need to calm down! Let's talk."

"Talk?! About what?!" Claudia picked up the candle holder and banged it down hard on the table. "You wanna talk about how you dogged me out, huh? How you told me you were falling in love with me but you got some other tramp in your bed?" Claudia attacked the table again, the thought of his baby's mama in his room, in his bed, making her so angry she felt nauseous.

"Girl, you done lost your mind! Yo, you 'bout to pay for a new table!" Cedric yelled at her.

Claudia let out a yell that sounded animal-like, and charged around the table after him. She heard a female voice call her name and swung in the direction of it, thinking it was that tramp from the bedroom, coming to rescue her baby's daddy. She was surprised to see Marie rushing through the front door. Marie's presence distracted Claudia enough for Vince to grab the candle holder from her. She turned around in surprise and tried to grab it back.

"Claudia, what's going on?!" Marie grabbed her arm and yanked her away from Vince, who was trying to restrain her with one arm and hold the candle holder away with the other.

"You a no good lying dog, Cedric!" she screamed, ignoring Marie and trying to advance on Cedric, who had rolled over onto the couch in an effort to get away. "How many other girls you slept with, huh?! Does she know about your other girls?!"

"Claudia, come on and let's get out of here," Marie told her gently, trying to pull her out of the front door.

"You know what? I hope you sleep with the wrong person one day and catch something you can't get rid of, you nasty..." She called him some heavy names, and went on in detail about what she hoped his future disease did to him. Again, Cedric looked like he was trying to hold back a laugh.

"Marie, you better get that fool out of here before I call the police! That girl is straight trippin' up in here!" Cedric said, sounding amused and angry at the same time.

"Marie, let me take ya'll back to the room." This came from Travis, who came back into the living room now that the fireworks were over. He glanced around at the chaotic mess and almost shuddered.

"No, we'll walk. She needs some air, anyway. Thanks for calling me, Travis. Come on Claudia." Claudia let Marie lead her to the door and looked around at the different expressions in the room. Marie's face had a concerned, determined look; Vince and Travis were looking at her with a mixture of pity and confusion and Cedric was sucking on his nail marks again, still looking amused.

"Ya'll sparring partners, or somethin'?" he asked Marie, chuckling.

"Cedric, you need to shut your mouth! You so stupid!" Marie told him, wrapping her arms around Claudia.

"Marie, come on. You ladies don't need to be walking by yourself this time of night," Travis told her.

"Yeah, why don't ya'll at least let me trail ya'll over in the car?" Vince added. "Travis man, go to bed. You got to hit it early in the morning." Vince started back to his room, holding tightly to the candle holder.

"No, we'll be fine. Come on Claudia."

"Can I get my jacket?" Cedric, out of any immediate danger now, asked in a mock cheerful voice.

"Yo, Cedric, chill. Let these women get home," Travis told him.

"What about my jacket?" Cedric insisted. "Yo, that's straight leather."

Claudia jerked his jacket off her shoulders and walked towards him, now wishing she had destroyed it when she had the chance. She threw it at his face and walked out the front door; Marie followed. Cedric was yelling something about his lip being busted. Marie slammed the door shut on him.

Claudia was still in a daze. She was shaking, but she wasn't sure if it was from the night air or because of what just happened. She knew she had acted up, but could not remember at what point she decided to lose her natural mind and start tearing up stuff. *I handled that wrong. I was supposed to chill out about the whole thing. I should have left it alone like Marie told me. I should have left it alone.* Other girls acted like that back in high school. Females went ballistic on television like that—not her. Now, on top of being used, violated and dissed, she shamed herself in front of three locker room athletes, who were probably yucking it up over what happened right now.

That girl is off the hook, man. You needed to dump that load. Did you see that when you hooked up with her?

Nah, I thought she was straight. I didn't know she had a mental streak like that. She 'bout tore up this apartment. I ain't trying to pay for no damages.

Cedric, you've had some wild ones in here before, but I ain't never seen nothing like that. That was straight off of television.

That girl is crazy.

Pyscho.

Looney tunes.

Shell.

Crazeecrazeecrazycrazee

"Claudia!"

Claudia just made it to the bushes beside the apartment before she brought up her dinner from earlier. Marie was right beside her as she coughed and gagged her system dry. Marie sat her down on the curb and fished in her pocket for some tissue. Claudia cleaned her face up and sniffed out, "I'm sorry."

Marie didn't say a word. She just wrapped her arm around Claudia's shoulders as Claudia dropped her throbbing head into her hands.

The door opened up behind them. "Is she all right? I thought I heard somebody throwing up out here." Vince had thrown on some more clothes and his shoes, ready to drive them back.

"She'll be fine," Marie whispered, pulling Claudia closer in a hug. Claudia allowed herself to be cuddled. She needed it, she didn't feel good and she was too ashamed to say anything else, anyway.

"Come on...let me take ya'll back to the residence hall."

Marie lifted Claudia up and walked with Vince to his car, parked in the lot across from the complex. Claudia crawled in the back seat and buried her face in her arms. She wanted to make this thing right— she needed to say something to justify her stupid actions, explain to Vince that she wasn't crazy. She was just a rejected female pushed too far to the edge. She couldn't tell him what made her confront Cedric at midnight, because she didn't know herself. She needed some release, she needed some answers, she needed to get rid of the burning in her chest and the ache in the pit of her stomach. She opened her mouth to explain all that, but all that came out was a moan.

Marie immediately twisted around in the passenger seat. "You, o.k., honey? You feel like you need to be sick again?"

"I'm fine," Claudia croaked, trying keep whatever was pounding on her head still. She heard the distant sound of sirens getting closer and stupidly wondered if Cedric had made good on his threat to call the police. She could hear Vince and Marie whispering something up front, but she couldn't make out what they were saying.

She woke up with a jolt as the car lurched to a stop. Were they there, already? She felt content just to lay there in the back seat and sleep. She was exhausted.

"Claudia, we're here."

Her head felt like a sack of wet concrete, but she lifted it up. Marie thanked Vince, led Claudia out of the car and into the residence hall. Claudia didn't even want to look at the desk guard when she came in, figuring she probably looked worse than when she left. She kept her head down until they got to the elevator.

Marie led Claudia to her door. "Where's your key?"

Shoot. Her key. "In Cedric's jacket pocket."

Marie turned the knob anyway. In her haste, Claudia forgot to lock the door, something Marie was always on her case about. She told her she was too trusting; she wasn't cautious enough. "Girl, how many times do I have to tell you to quit leaving your door unlocked?" Marie chastised as Claudia entered her room and immediately fell on the bed. Her mouth tasted terrible. She dragged herself up and grabbed her toothbrush. "I'll be back," she mumbled to Marie as she headed toward the door.

"I will, too—just sit tight," Marie told Claudia, heading out the suite door.

Claudia swished water around in her mouth to clear out the last of the toothpaste. That was better. She felt like she could open her mouth again. She had been trying to avoid her reflection but now looked up in the mirror. Yup, straight out of a horror movie. Her face was tear-streaked, fire red and swollen, like her eyes. Her fly away hair was all over the place and her head ached terribly. She ran some water and doused it on her face—still, it didn't not wash away the sadness and defeat that she saw. What a mess she'd made of things—what a mess *she* was.

Marie wasn't there when she got back to the room and in a way, Claudia was not surprised. What did you say to a person that did what she did, anyway? What kind of comfort did you give to a girl who had made a straight up fool of herself over a man and in front of his roommates—and his other woman? *Well, I'm sure you did what you thought was best at the time*—uh...no. All you could do was stay away, like Marie was doing—it was almost more than Claudia could bear and she felt the tears coming again. There was no sense in her crying anymore—what was done, was done, and she managed to alienate everybody she'd grown close to here...

She had dozed off when she heard a knock. Marie open the unlocked door quietly and tiptoed in. She had two mugs and two packets of cocoa in one hand and a big Bible in the other. She had been wearing a pair of jeans and a light jacket when she came to Cedric's apartment, but now she looked ready for bed in an oversized t-shirt and cotton shorts—and her big, pink, fuzzy bunny slippers. Claudia had to smile. Marie told her she had always wanted a pair of big, pink, fuzzy bunny slippers, and Claudia got them for her as a graduation present last year.

"Sorry—I didn't mean to wake you up," Marie apologized, easing the door closed.

Claudia sat up from her reclined position on the bed. "No—it's o.k. I was waiting for you to come back." Hoping, was closer to the truth.

"Yeah, I'm sorry I'm so late getting back. I was trying to see about your keys—Travis got them from Cedric. You want some hot cocoa?"

"Sure—that sounds good. How'd he manage to get them from Cedric?"

Marie busied herself at the counter where the microwave and refrigerator sat. She poured bottled water into the mugs—both girls had the same kooky rule about water—they didn't really like to drink it but if they must, it had to be bottled, so they always kept it on hand—and tore open the packs of pre-mixed chocolate. "I called and talked to Travis. He said he'd get them. Then Vince called me back and told me they got them. That was it."

"I know Vince and Travis think I'm some kind of psycho."

Marie put the mugs in the microwave and set the timer. "No, they don't, Claudia. Don't you worry about that now, o.k.? You hungry? We have leftover pizza, don't we?" Marie open Claudia's refrigerator again.

"There's some popcorn over there—I know you don't want to eat pizza this late."

"It doesn't matter—pizza's good, popcorn's better. I ain't going to sleep no time soon—unless you're tired, girl. I can go and let you sleep..."

The last thing Claudia wanted was to be left alone. "No, Marie, please—stay. I have all this room in here." When Marie left, Claudia had pushed the two twin beds together to make one big bed. She had a humungous comforter that her mother brought for her, apparently forgetting that college students were just one step away from sleeping on cots. The comforter had drowned her little twin by itself, but it was just the right size to cover both beds.

Marie smiled. "All right, honey. Whatever you need."

Claudia was beyond shame now. "I need you to stay. Barricade the door, if you need to, so I don't escape and start trippin' again."

"You'll be alright." *Ding!* The microwave announced the completion of the cocoa, and Marie carefully handed a mug to Claudia, then stuck her popcorn in. "And look, if you still want to go to sleep, go ahead. Don't feel like you have to keep me company or anything."

"No, I'm fine..."

"Claudia," Marie said gently. "I'm not going anywhere."

She couldn't measure the relief she felt—or the guilt. If she ever had any doubt about Marie's friendship, all that was history now. She had turned on her best friend—broken all the rules of friendship and sisterhood—and here Marie was, still trying to be there for her. Then Claudia realized something that made her want to dig a hole in the ground and crawl in it until she graduated. She had never sincerely apologized to her—her shame and guilt kept her from it. "Marie?"

"Hmm?" Marie had settled on the edge of the extra bed, waiting for popcorn. The room was filled with the wonderful, buttery scent.

"I need to tell you something."

She twisted around to look at Claudia. "What is it, Bambi?"

The use of her nickname started the floodgate of tears. Marie immediately came around to sit closer to her. "Claudia, don't do this to yourself—everybody goes overboard sometime..."

"No, no. That's not what I wanted to say." Claudia took a few seconds to gather herself. "I just wanted to tell you how sorry I was for what I did to you, Marie."

Marie interrupted immediately. "No—it's o.k. You don't have to say..."

"Yes, I do. I need to say this."

"All right."

She started again. "You have been there for me since day one. Ever since the day Tallette squirted mustard on my shirt. I realize that sometimes I relied on you too much to fix things for me in high school. I felt safe with you, Marie, you know what I mean? I mean, you are always so sure of yourself—you always know what you want to do and how you want to do it, and everyone liked you, they still do. And you're so beautiful..."

Marie looked like she wanted to blush, if that were biologically possible. "Girl, don't go there..."

"You are Marie, you are! You may not admit it to yourself, but you are beautiful. Junte' was right—you look like an African queen. And your hair always looks so good—you don't have that black issue like I do. Do you know how tired I was of having people pick on me because of my color? And I hurt you, Marie. I got so fed up with always feeling like I had to rely on you for everything—my friends, my self-esteem, my decisions—that when Cedric came along, I got stupid and thought that this was someone I could have on my own. No Marie, this time. Just Claudia. Something Claudia got on her own.

"And I messed up—I dissed the best friend I ever had. Marie, I love you—you're like a sister to me and I just..." Claudia got to a point where she felt she couldn't talk anymore, her tears were so heavy. "I'm so sorry, Marie. I am so ashamed of myself for the way I treated you," she sobbed. "I—wouldn't blame y-you...if you never wanted to have anything to do with me again." There, she'd gotten all out. To her surprise, Marie was crying just as hard as she was. Tough, confident, and who Claudia thought was sometimes unemotional, Marie. Rarely had she seen her cry, and definitely not as hard as she was crying now.

She threw her arms around Claudia. "Thank you," she heard her whisper over and over. So they sat there holding each other and had a good cry. Then, they dried their eyes, drank their cocoa, ate popcorn, watched T.V. and talked until they couldn't keep their eyes open anymore.

They didn't wake up until noon the next day, and Claudia, disoriented from her sporadic sleeping pattern, got anxious thinking she'd missed class again before Marie reminded her that it was Saturday. They ate lunch in the dining hall, the only place open on the weekends. The early March weather was still a bit chilly, but they bundled up and decided to walk off campus to the shopping center down the street and rent some videos. When they got back to campus, they ran into a girl that Marie knew who told them about the spades tournament in Conrad Hall later on that evening. Marie, who was an excellent spades player, taught Claudia the game in high school. It seemed to be all the black students played at Hamel. Claudia told Marie she was game, so they watched a couple of movies (both had been careful to steer clear of any romances and select action/adventure instead) and headed across the walkway to Conrad for the tournament.

On Sunday, Claudia agreed to go with Marie and Tony to church. She was a little amazed at how lively the church was—nothing like her church at home where people just nodded their heads in agreement or said a small "Amen." This church had a live band, a group of singers who got everyone riled up and singing right before service, and people who would take off in a spontaneous lap around the church, lay on the floor like they were unconscious, or lapse into what sounded like Spanish to Claudia.

"It's called speaking in tongues," Marie informed Claudia when she asked her about it later on.

"How do they do that?" She wanted to know.

"You have to be baptized with the Holy Spirit..."

"What?!"

"I'm still learning about it myself, Claudia."

"You mean you can talk like that?"

"Not yet," Marie sounded disappointed. "But I hope to one day."

Claudia didn't ask her anymore about it—but she could see that the church and spirituality had become very important to Marie. She couldn't shake the image of Marie at church, her arms straight up in the air like she was under arrest, and her face wrapped in a glow of peace as she closed her eyes and sang along with the rest of the congregation. She'd never seen her look more beautiful or more peaceful. She would have loved to ask her about it, especially when she and Tony got into an excited conversation about the service later on at his apartment and she felt a little left out. Claudia finally agreed to have dinner with him—and Marie was right...the boy could throw down in the kitchen. She had fun with the two of them, and it was obvious Marie and Tony had a very special friendship. They boy was hilarious—Claudia couldn't stop herself from laughing.

Yes, Marie had made sure that her weekend was filled with activity, but Claudia knew she still had to face this thing alone eventually. She got her chance Monday morning after her eight o'clock class.

She was just coming out of the English Building, headed toward the Student Center to kill time before her eleven o'clock class when she ran into Vince, who was coming out of the Center.

"Hi, Claudia," he greeted, and although Claudia didn't detect anything in his voice, she was still uncomfortable.

"Hi, Vince," she mumbled back, trying to smile.

Vince was returning her smile. "You feeling better?"

"Yeah, I'm fine."

"I was a little worried about you after I dropped you two off, but Marie told me that she was going to hang out with you."

Man, did she feel weird. She suddenly felt like a big kid that had to be babysat. "Yeah, I'm fine," she repeated, not knowing what else to say but really wishing she could end the conversation.

"Claudia, I just want you to know that I don't think anything bad about you or anything. I know you feel bad about what happened, but Travis and I don't think you're some kind of tripped out female or anything like that. You were upset, and sometimes people go overboard when they're upset, yo. But you all right. I told Marie the same thing the other night."

Claudia felt herself relaxing. How sweet of him to tell her that after she'd trashed their apartment. "Vince I am so sorry for getting you and Travis involved in all that. Just let me know if there's any damage to the apartment…"

Vince was shaking his head. "The apartment is fine. There's just a little dent in the wall, but there were dents when we got there—it's all good."

"What about the table?"

Vince waved his hand. "We'll put a tablecloth on it. They'll just take it out of our deposit…"

"No! You guys shouldn't have to pay for what I did…"

"Claudia, it's all good. It can't be that much. Don't worry about it. I'm sure we ain't gonna get no deposit back anyway with the damage we've done," he concluded with a chuckle.

"But the noise. I know I disturbed your neighbors…"

Vince was still shaking his head. "Nobody said anything about any noise. We haven't heard a thing from anyone around us. They were probably out of town, anyway. Most of our neighbors get ghost on the weekends. I told you not to worry."

Claudia was feeling better, but she still had to know something. "I know Cedric probably trashed me after I left, right?"

"No…he was complaining about his lip, but he didn't really talk about you since he had his girl…" Vince widened his eyes and laughed nervously. "Yeah, you probably know about all that, though."

Yeah, she knew about his baby's mother. "Still, he'll probably get in the locker room and tell all his teammates…"

Vince reached out and grabbed Claudia's hand. "Claudia, I know you and Cedric and Marie all had some drama going on, and Cedric is the type to brag about his women and what he does and whatnot. But he hasn't said a word about you or Marie like he does with his other women. For some reason, he hasn't done that with you."

Claudia felt an ocean wave of relief and gratitude wash over her. She had to force back tears. She looked up into Vince's eyes, but couldn't read any deception there. "Well, I guess I learned a hard lesson, huh?"

"It's all good," he told her again. "You may have taught me and Travis something about how to treat women. I don't know about Cedric, though. Next time, a girl might actually have to do some physical damage to get it through his head. I'm not going to lie—I used to admire the brotha' for it. But that kind of lifestyle can get you in trouble. I don't have time for all that nonsense—it's too much wear and tear on your body. I have to start thinking about my future and getting out of this place. See, Cedric has this false sense of security about his game—he's good, don't get me wrong, but anything can happen and ain't no guarantees about going pro. And the way he's living his life, he'll tear his body down with all that. I have to stay focused, yo."

"Yeah?"

"Definitely. In fact, I have a little friend I just met. She stays over in Belten where you are."

"Do I know her?"

"You might. Her name is…"

"What's up, Delaney?"

Both Claudia and Vince turned in the direction of the deep voice and a very big, husky, bald brother headed their way. He gave Vince a grip and stared at Claudia with what looked like interest. Or recognition. Despite what Vince just told her, she still felt her stomach do flip flops.

He nodded in her direction. "Hello."

"Hi," she said shyly.

Vince made the introductions. "Claudia this is one of my teammates and homies, Keith. We call him Big Rig. I guess I don't need to tell you why."

No, he didn't. And she already recognized the name from her football conversations with Cedric and from around campus. This brother was hard to miss. Big Rig was aptly named, because he looked like an eighteen wheeler barreling down the highway. He was tall and huge with a bald head, a bearded chin and a fierce look on his face. Right now, he was looking at Claudia again.

"Nice to meet you, Claudia." Big Rig pumped her hand with what was probably gentleness to him, but felt like a vise grip to Claudia. He smiled at her and winked.

Vince addressed that. "Rig, man—I know you got at least a hundred pounds on me, but I'll take you out if you look at my little sister like that again," he warned, trying to frown up at the giant like he meant business.

Big Rig laughed, no doubt assured in his ability to not only take Vince out, but half the football team—with one arm. "Delaney, you never had a sister that looked this good. Not unless ya'll had a different set of parents. But I feel ya, man. I feel ya. Claudia, I'm sorry but I'm all man, baby. I can't help but notice a beautiful young lady."

Claudia smiled up at him warmly. For all of Big Rig's intimidating looks, he was a great big teddy bear. "No problem, Keith. Do you prefer Keith or Big Rig?"

"You can call me whatever you want, sweetheart," Rig told her, and Vince plugged him in his massive arm. "Nah, honey, I'm serious. I'll answer to either one. And check this—any little sister of Vince's is a little sister of mine, 'cause this here's my boy. Anyone give you any trouble, you let me know. Even if it's my homey here." He plugged Vince back in his arm, and Claudia saw Vince flinch a little.

She felt another wave of emotion. "All right, big bro," she told him.

"And that's exactly what he is—big," Vince added. Big Rig eyed him.

"Did ya'll hear about the Lambda Sig house?" the giant asked, then filled Claudia and Vince in on the events of Friday night/Saturday morning. Claudia was surprised to learn that while she was having her schizophrenic attack, the Lambda Sig house was burning to the ground. That was probably the siren she heard on her way back from Cedric's and the smoky smell that was lingering in the air even now. No wonder the students were congregated into mini-huddles —it was probably the buzz on campus.

"Bet it won't take a protest to get the University moving on this one," Vince predicted bitterly.

"And every black face is guilty until proven innocent," Big Rig added. "Well, let me go on. Delaney, you ready to run laps?"

"I'll be on time, Rig."

"Remember what I said, Claudia. You have any trouble, I'm your man, baby."

Claudia laughed. "I won't forget."

Rig winked at her, pounded Vince on the arm again, and sauntered off as only a tractor trailer could. Various students, black and white, male and female, greeted him with a guttural, "Big Riiiig" as he pounded fists, slapped hands and returned their greeting:

"What's up, baby? How ya feel, how ya feel?"

"I almost forgot to give you these." Vince dug in his pocket and pulled out Claudia's keys.

"Thanks, Vince. I hope you didn't go through any trouble getting them."

"Nah. He went to go fix his lip and Travis grabbed them when Marie called. He still thinks the zipper or something caught him in the mouth and cut him. We didn't tell him any different. Claudia, you know Big Rig means what he says about having your back. You can't find a better friend than a six foot seven, three hundred seventeen pound defensive tackle."

"I can use a friend like that."

"You got one. And listen—I got your back too, all right? Don't worry about a thing. Any guys get flaky with you, call your big brother. Well, I'd better run. Take care of yourself. Remember who you are, young lady. Some guys aren't worth your time."

"I will. Thanks Vince." Claudia reached up and hugged the neck of the man who was the complete opposite of his canine roommate. After he walked off, she stood there for a minute, thinking that she could start feeling good about herself again, and this time for the right reason.

MARIE

Two more weeks, and her freshman year would be history. Marie couldn't help but feel a twinge of sadness as she stepped out of the residence hall and headed over to campus. The usual parade of students rushing to class was reduced to a trickle here and there with finals going on—it felt like a ghost town. She wasn't so much worried about her finals as she was about her plans for the summer.

What was she going to do? Claudia and her family were going to the Bahamas for a month, Tony was going home to Florida—where was she going? She didn't particularly want to go home—there was really nothing to do except find a part-time job, fuss with her sister, twiddle her thumbs and wait for the fall semester to begin. When she was in high school, she threw herself into her extracurricular activities to stay busy—to fill the emptiness she felt when she stepped into her house in the afternoons. Claudia always thought Marie was so active, so smart. She never suspected that Marie was just trying to stay occupied so she wouldn't think about what she didn't have.

She stopped at the Block and sat on the wall, took a mental inventory of things. She and Claudia had gotten a lot resolved this year. They had found out some things about each other, things that took three years and a different set of circumstances to rise to the surface. It still amazed Marie that Claudia had envied her. Shoot, Claudia was the one with the tight family. She and Harland were practically best friends, and the whole foursome acted more like buddies than parents and children. Claudia lovingly referred to her family as her "peeps." That's why it was so hard for Marie to understand why her best friend came to high school with such low self-esteem. It sure didn't come from a dysfunctional family situation.

And it wasn't that Marie's family life was so terrible. Granted, they weren't as close as Claudia's and she and her sisters did fuss quite a bit—well she and Rolanda mostly—but they had their fun times, too—plenty of them. Marie did wish she was closer to her mother like Claudia was—Claudia was always bragging that she could tell her parents almost anything. Almost. But Mrs. Steeleton was old school—she believed in letting things roll off the back, go on with business as usual, don't waste time with tears or emotions. Her dad didn't live at home with them. Her sisters had their own life, their own friends—she often felt isolated at home.

"Hey! Marie!"

She looked up to Tony grinning and waving frantically at her from his car. Her heavy mood fell off of her like unlocked shackles, and she smiled widely as he parked and made his way to her.

"What's going on, beautiful?" he greeted, giving her a quick kiss on the cheek as he sat down beside her. He held a long white envelope in his hand.

"Nothing much," she told him, trying to sound cheerful.

"What wrong?"

She was surprised that he'd picked up on that. "Wrong?"

"Marie, don't play—this is me you're talking to."

I'm going to miss this boy over the summer.

"What's wrong?" he asked again, taking her hand.

"Nothing much," she shrugged. "Just trying to figure out what I'm going to do this summer."

"Aren't you going home?"

She snorted without meaning to. "Yeah, but that's about it. Claudia's going to the Bahamas and my roommate is doing an internship in Canada. I'm going home. Whoopee."

"Is it *that* bad?"

"It's not that it's bad, it's just boring. Believe me when I say there is absolutely nothing to do in my hometown."

"You weren't planning on clubbing, were you?" he joked, giving her hand a squeeze before he released it.

Usually Marie would be cheered by his off-the-wall sense of humor, but she was so completely distressed by spending a dull summer at home she barely managed a smile.

"You're serious about this thing, aren't you? I'm sorry, beautiful. I didn't mean to make light of it." He wrapped his arm around her and pulled her in for a hug.

"It's o.k." It *was* o.k., now. His cologne was providing some serious aromatherapy for her.

"Marie?"

"Hmm?" she answered absentmindedly, lost in the comfort of a man she could consider for a life partner.

"I want you to think about something for me, o.k.?"

"Kay."

"You're family's not born-again, right?"

"I don't think so—I'm not sure."

"I know, you told me that before—you have some doubt."

"Right." Where was this going, she wondered?

"But you want to remove the doubt, right?"

"Right…"

"Maybe the Lord wants to use you at home this summer to bring them on in."

Marie unraveled herself out of Tony's embrace and looked at him, hard. "Use *me*?!"

"Yeah."

"Why me?!"

Why *not* you?"

"Tony, my family is not like that."

"Like what?"

How could she explain? "They're not going to listen to me tell them about the Lord. They'd probably laugh at me. Unn uhh."

"How do you know what they'll do? You've never witnessed to them before."

"Because I know my family, that's why." She felt herself getting agitated and was sure it was starting to reflect in her voice.

"Marie, you won't be the one doing the work—it'll be the Lord working through you."

Now she was confused and even more upset. But she didn't know if she was upset with Tony, or what she felt was an unfair assignment from the Lord. How in the world was He going to use her to get them saved? "Oh, so now I have to go home and get my family saved?"

"Marie, don't get upset about what I said—Maybe I shouldn't have said anything about that—it's kinda deep for you right now. Sometimes I run my mouth too much." He shook his head, looking like he wanted to kick himself.

Marie's heart automatically went out to him. "It's all good, Tony. Don't worry about it. Look, let's not talk about me anymore—what's going on with you this summer?"

"A lot." Tony grinned, then immediately looked like he wanted to take the grin back.

"Tony, stop that! Go on and tell me, please!"

He grinned on cue. "Girl, God is working it OUT!"

"Tell me, tell me!" her enthusiasm didn't reach her heart, but she could fake it.

"Here," Tony handed her the envelope. "I'll let you *read* about it."

"Let me guess...you won a million dollars?"

"You been reading my mail, right?" Tony gave her such an adorable look that Marie wanted to grab his face. *I think today might be the day for some realness. Yup, it might be just about time to lay some cards on the table.* Whoa—this was the first time she ever wanted to let a guy know how she felt about him. Now that was deep. But she would read his good news first. Maybe after that, she would have worked up enough courage to tell him. Yeah, it was about time.

"Dear Mr. Sadler...*Mr.?* What's up with *that?*"

"That's called respect, girl." Tony winked at her which he should have never done, because she found herself leaning in to grab like she wanted to do earlier.

"Whatever. Let's see...Dear Mr. Sadler. We are pleased to offer you admission to Florida A&M..."

Tony grinned wider.

"You're going to FAMU?! FAMU in *Florida?!*"

Tony nodded, his grin looking like it would split his head in two pieces.

Marie felt her heart plummet to her stomach. Florida! That meant Tony wouldn't be around next semester...or any other semester after that. He was leaving...her.

"So you're leaving Hamel?" she found herself asking, like she didn't fully comprehend what *We are pleased to offer you admission to Florida A&M University* meant.

"With pleasure."

She stared at him. "What do you mean, *with pleasure?*" she asked with an edge to her voice.

If Tony noticed her tone, it didn't reflect. "I mean *with pleasure,*" he repeated. "Marie, I'm going to FAMU on a band scholarship. You know how good FAMU's band is? Do you know how much I've always wanted to play in FAMU's band?"

No, as a matter of fact, she didn't. Nor did she care. She just wanted to know what gave him the right to just up and leave her, after practically *forcing* her to fall for him.

Tony wasn't finished celebrating. "I auditioned while we were on break and I'm just hearing back from them. I got a SCHOLARSHIP,

Marie! A full ride scholarship—everything is covered as long as I play and keep my grades up!"

"Well, congratulations," she said with a tight grin, handing back his stupid acceptance letter. She rose from the wall, preparing to leave, but Tony grabbed her hand.

"Marie, what's wrong?"

She refused to look at him. "Nothing."

"Aren't you happy for me?"

"Should I be?"

"I would think so—do we need to talk about something?"

Right now, that caring attitude of his sounded condescending. It wasn't cute anymore. "I don't need to talk about anything. I told you, I was going home for the summer."

"Yeah…?"

"And that's it. I'm going home, you're going back home to Florida—what else do I need to say?" She finally turned her head to look down at Tony who seemed confused, but then nodded in understanding.

"Marie, I know you're upset about going home, but…"

"It's not about me going home! Why can't you just leave that alone, Tony? I don't need you to fix that problem!" she blurted with a sudden burst of emotion. *It's about you, me, us…why can't you see that?!!!*

But Tony couldn't read her thoughts and she definitely did not want to share them. Her eyes were angry as she stared at him—his look of hurt confusion angered her further. Where was her fairytale confession of his undying love? Why wasn't he tearing up his acceptance letter from FAMU right now, claiming that if she couldn't go with him to Florida, wild horses couldn't drag him there? No, the only thing he could do was act like he was from Backwoods, USA, where the men had no clue when a woman has fallen in love.

"Then what is it?"

She couldn't do this—if she kept on, he was going to drag her feelings out without her knowing how he felt. He was giving her a pretty good indication now, because he didn't seem to be the least bit upset about leaving her behind at Hamel. "It's nothing, Tony. Nothing. You got your acceptance to Florida A&M, you're happy, you don't need to be concerned about why I'm not."

"Marie, what are you talking about? If you want to talk about something, I'm here."

"Don't do that, Tony."

"Do what?"

"Act like a good Samaritan. I don't need your sympathy, and I don't need to rain on your parade anymore either, do I?" She turned and headed toward her residence hall, her eyes burning with tears. Tony was calling her name behind her, but she wasn't about to turn around and let him see her emotions.

She could hear the phone ringing just as she put her key in the lock, and managed to pick it up before it completed the second ring. If it was Tony, wanting to find out what in the world was going on with her, she wasn't quite ready to talk to him yet. "Yes?" she answered cautiously, assuming a concerned Tony was on the other end.

"Marie, it's Claudia."

Her disappointment was obvious. "Oh. Hey, girl."

"You all right?"

"Yeah, why?"

"You sound kind of...depressed. Is it Tony? You're gonna miss him over the summer, aren't you?"

Marie sighed. She suddenly realized that she wanted a pity party right now, and Claudia was going to get the first invitation. "Don't say that name," she moaned.

She could almost see Claudia's wide-eyed look over the phone. "Come again?"

"Tony's leaving."

"To go home over the summer," Claudia concluded, sounding like a parent patiently explaining something to a clueless child. "You are too, Marie. Most of us are."

"No, Claudia. Tony's leaving Hamel."

"What?!"

"He got accepted at FAMU."

"Really?!! That's great!"

Marie didn't respond. She just flinched and breathed hard into the phone.

Claudia caught the hint. "I mean—that's terrible. Oh, that is just horrible for you, girl. What in the world was he thinking?"

"Don't be funny."

"Oh, you're really upset about this, aren't you? I'm sorry. You really like him, don't you?"

"Girl, I thought he was it, you know?"

"Yeah."

"He was sweet, funny, respectful, nice-looking, saved…he had it going on."

"Marie, the boy ain't dead."

"Yeah, but he's leaving. Just picking up and going to Florida," she pouted.

"Well…"

"Can you believe that?" she asked Claudia.

"Well…"

He's leaving *me*! He leaving *us*!"

"Yeah, well…"

"Can you say something besides that, please?"

If Claudia took any offense, she didn't show it. "Do you want an honest answer, or do you want me to make you feel good?" she asked in an irritating, logical voice.

"What is that supposed to mean?"

"Just what I said, Marie."

"Of course I want you to be honest," she lied.

"You know you're being selfish, right?"

"*Selfish?!* He's the one that acted like he liked me, then decided to hightail it off to FAMU! How am I being selfish?!"

"Because you are."

"Because I am?" Marie repeated.

"Yes."

"Mmm hmm."

"Marie I know you like the boy, but you can't be upset with him because he's going to school somewhere else. It's not like you guys are married or engaged or anything. Get a grip."

Claudia was a lousy counselor. Even when she was painfully shy and lacked self-confidence, her "comfort" always had a hard edge to it. Marie knew she meant no harm and probably thought she was being helpful, but her words stung sometimes, shoot. But she was right. She was acting extremely selfish, extremely ghetto. Here the boy was, trying to do something with his life beside sow some wild oats and she was straight trippin'.

Marie sighed heavily again. She actually felt like crying. "I just about laid him out over this."

"Na uhh."

"Yes I did. Had the nerve to get an attitude."

"Girl!"

"I made a straight up fool of myself—over a man," Marie realized with shame.

"Join the club," Claudia responded dryly.

"All right—I know what I need to do."

"You need to go apologize for acting so uncouth, that's what you need to do."

"Who asked you?"

"You like my word?"

"What, uncouth? Yeah, that was good, Claudia. Proud of you."

"Thought you'd appreciate that—I been sitting on that one all day long."

"Don't hurt yourself, now." Marie found herself laughing with Claudia, back in high spirits. That's what good friends did for you. "Listen, nut. Why did you call me in the first place?"

Silence.

"Claudia? Did you hear me?"

"Yeah, I heard you. I just can't remember why I called you."

"Must not have been important."

"Yes it was!"

"Look—when you remember, call me back or just stop by."

"All right. Hey, you want to do dinner around six?"

"That sounds good. I'll stop by your room about quarter till."

"Gotcha, love ya."

"Bye, girl. Love you too." Marie put the receiver down then picked it up again, all set to dial Tony's number.

No—I started this mess in person, and I need to fix it the same way. With that resolve in mind, she grabbed her keys from the dresser, glanced at herself in the mirror—might as well look good—and headed out the door for Tony's apartment.

PERCY

""Percy, I apologize for being late. Old Diane here just conked out on me earlier."

"Don't worry about it—I'm straight." Actually, Percy had been waiting close to two hours at the bus station. Allen had agreed to pick him up when his bus came in, and the air conditioner in the station would have to be malfunctioning on what had to be a record high temperature for a spring day—ninety-one degrees. He kept going to the bathroom and splashing water on his face to cool off.

Allen got out of the car to open the trunk and did a double take. "What happened to you?" he asked, staring at Percy's swollen lip.

"I got into a little tussle with my baby brother that got out of hand."

"Is he o.k.?" Allen chuckled.

"Yeah, he's cool. Came away without a scratch."

Allen slammed the lid of his trunk down after Percy put his bags in, then climbed back behind the wheel. "Old Diane" sputtered a few times, coughed out some fumes, then roared loudly to life. "That's my girl," Allen said, patting the dashboard like the car was an obedient pet.

"It's hot." Percy wiped sweat from his forehead. "Yo, man—you got some AC up in here?"

"Sure do," Allen grinned. "But this old girl can't take too much power at one time. I turn it on, we'll be walking back to campus in the heat."

"Ah man...you mean we gotta ride with no air?" He couldn't believe it! He now understood why the crime rate was so high when the weather turned hot. He rolled down his window and stuck his head out, trying to find some relief in the warm breeze.

"Sorry, Percy. The Cadillac's in the shop."

Percy pulled his head back in. "Nah, it's all good, Allen. I don't mean to sound all ungrateful 'cause I appreciate you picking me up. This heat just gets up under your skin, you know?"

"It's all right. It's about time to put this girl out to pasture, anyway. She's on her last legs as it is, and it's costing me a fortune to keep her running." Allen frowned up for a minute, then his trademark grin spread back over his face.

"Allen, you need a horse or a dog, or somethin'."

Allen laughed like he'd never anything so funny, and Percy caught a glimpse of something white near his hand. Allen's left forearm was bandaged up with gauze and tape. There was some redness and swelling where the bandage didn't cover his arm.

"What happened to your arm?"

Allen looked down at his arm in surprise, like he didn't know it was wrapped up, and chuckled. "Oh, I had a little accident."

"You all right? That looks kinda painful."

"Yeah, sure," he assured Percy quickly.

"What happened?"

"What happened? Oh, it's really...stupid. I was looking under the hood of the car and burned my arm on the engine."

"You had the engine running?"

Allen frowned. "Well, I—she cut off on me. Remember I told you she cut off on me today? I tried to fix her myself and burned my arm. The engine was still hot."

"Is that why you were late? What'd you do—go to the emergency room?"

"What? No—I keep a first aid kit in the trunk. I was a boy scout—always prepared." Allen changed the subject. "How was home?"

"You mean besides me getting my lip busted? It was fine, man." Nothing was further from the truth.

"Family doin' good?"

"Family's doin' fine."

"You tell them about all the hoopla on campus?"

"No—we didn't get into all that."

"Seriously?! It's just about the biggest event that's happened at Hamel!"

"I just didn't. I try to leave school at school." Percy was starting to feel a little funny about the conversation.

"How do you think this is going to affect the black students, Percy?"

He forced himself to chill out and think about his answer carefully. "Well, it's obvious, Allen," he began. "Who do you think they're going to blame the fire on? Us, of course. We'll be the first ones they'll look at."

"They're already asking a lot of questions," Allen told him. "The police have been all over the place since Friday afternoon. The press is sticking microphones in everyone's face. It been quite a carnival. Good thing you decided to go home, huh?"

"I guess so." For some odd reason, Allen's questions were beginning to sound loaded with other meaning. It didn't appear to be a casual conversation anymore—not that arson was a casual issue. He decided on a counter-attack. "Hey Allen...why are you asking so many questions? You working undercover or somethin'?"

"No, Percy. I just thought...well...I just wanted you to know that you could confide in me if you needed to, that's all."

Now Percy was sweating for real. He had to play dumb. "Confide in you?! Confide in you about *what*?!"

"Oh, any old thing, Percy."

"I think the heat got to you, man. You ain't makin' sense."

Allen sighed, glanced at Percy, then pulled out a plastic grocery bag from underneath the driver's seat. He handed it to Percy, who took it with no small measure of confusion. When he looked inside, he felt all the blood drain out of his body.

His ski mask.

"I thought you might need that back," Allen said gravely.

Percy swallowed and thought quickly. He had completely forgotten about losing his ski mask. He know remembered that he'd thought it was in the back of Marcus' car, but then he forgot about it. *Where in the world did Allen did my ski mask?!! Where did I leave it?!!*

He decided to play dumb. "Allen, why would you bring my ski mask? You been snooping around in my stuff?" he asked angrily.

"Percy, I think we both know I didn't find that mask in your drawer. I told you—you can confide in me. I won't say anything."

"Say anything about *what*, Allen?! I'm not gettin' you, man. First, you make some off-the-wall comment about confiding in you, then you bring me a ski mask when it's ninety something degrees outside. What's your problem?!"

Allen looked disappointed. "I understand, Percy. You don't trust me—I understand that. Look, you don't have to say anything until you're ready. I just wanted you to know that I got your back." He took a deep breath, then glanced at Percy again. "I found the mask near the Lambda Sig house Friday morning after the fire—well, what's *left* of the Lambda Sig house."

"*What*?! What do you mean, you found it by the Lambda Sig house?! That's impossible!"

"I went over there that morning before class," Allen continued, like he hadn't even heard Percy. "It was a mess. It's a miracle that fire didn't spread to all those trees around it. There was a crowd of students, police—it looked like the whole campus was over there. It was funny—I just happened to be walking around the back on my way back to class, and I stepped right on this ski mask." Allen held his thumb and pointer finger an inch apart. "I was this close to taking it to the police, then I saw a white tag in it. 'From Ma, with love.' I realized it was yours, so I brought it back to the room...tried to clean it up for you. I still didn't get all that smoky smell out of it, though."

So that's why Allen was acting so funny the morning after the fire. He had the ski mask the whole time, and was waiting for Percy to say something about it.

They were pulling into the parking lot near the residence hall, now. Allen swung into a space and cut off the engine. "Old Diane" jerked and fluttered a few times, then settled into a dead silence.

Allen sighed heavily. "Percy, don't worry. I'm not gonna squeal on you. I guess you guys felt what you did was right. I mean, Lambda Sig did mess with your property first, so you guys retaliated by burning down their house."

"Yo, I didn't burn anyone's house! Like I said before, I don't know what you're talking about. You come up with this off-the-wall scenario about what happened, and you blame it me because you say you found my mask somewhere I didn't leave it. You trippin', Allen—you trippin' hard!"

Allen nodded the whole time Percy was talking, like a psychiatrist listening to a delusional patient. Percy reached for the door handle and climbed out of the car. He rammed his hand down his pocket and laid some bills on the passenger seat.

"I don't want your money," Allen told him mournfully.

"Take it—take it."

"Percy, you don't have to buy my friendship or my silence. Friends don't charge each other for gas. I'm your friend, man. Why can't you understand that?!"

"I'm outta here, Allen. Something is seriously wrong with you, on the real. I'm out." Percy took off towards the residence hall. Shoot! What was he going to do *now*?! He walked in the direction of the residence hall until Allen's car was no longer in sight, then he took the shortcut through the woods and headed towards the campus entrance, running as swiftly as he could in the almost unbearable heat. He crossed the street and headed to the shopping center, huffing and wiping sweat out of his eyes. The phone booth he needed was right there on the corner, and when he reached it, he leaned against the glass interior, trying to catch his breath. He fumbled some coins into the slot.

"Come on, come on!" he urged on his end.

"Hello?"

"Darryl! This is Percy. Look, I need you to come get me!"

"Where are you?" Darryl asked with concern.

I'm in front of the shopping center near the school."

"Percy—I kinda have company right now. Are you o.k.?!"

Percy almost yelled in frustration. "Man, you need to send her on her way, 'cause things may be blowin' up—in a *big* way!"

"All right, all right…give me a few—I'll be there."

"O.k., Percy—let's try that one more time, and slowly," Darryl instructed to Percy, who had rambled off everything that happened as soon as he climbed in the car. Darryl took him back to his place, told him to sit down and fixed him a glass of iced tea—told him to cool off for a minute.

Percy sucked down the last of his tea, and leaned forward on the couch where he was sitting. "All right, Darryl—here it goes again. My roommate knows I was in the Lambda Sig house."

"How?" Darryl was still too calm for Percy's comfort.

"He found my ski mask on the ground the next morning. I must have dropped it when we were running out of the house. He gave to me today when he picked me up at the bus station."

"And how did he know the mask was yours?"

"My mom sewed a tag in it with my name, and he made a comment about it when he saw it a couple of months ago." Percy was impatient. He'd already explained all of this in the car. He didn't want to wade in details—he needed solutions, quick. "The bottom line is that he *knows*, Darryl! He started telling me how I could trust him and how he wouldn't say anything. I played it off."

"Good, good. Where's the mask now?"

Percy handed the plastic bag that he had a death grip on over to Darryl, who reached inside and took out the mask. He studied it, turned it inside out, and sniffed it. "Still smells like smoke."

"Allen said he tried to clean it up, but couldn't get the smell out."

Darryl had been sitting in the chair opposite Percy, but now got up to pace a small circle in the middle of the room. He said nothing for what seemed like forever, then, "Do you think he'll say anything?"

"Man, I don't know. He's seems all right, but he still ain't one of us. What, you think I should tell him?"

"No...I didn't say that."

Percy was at the end of his rope. "Look, man...I got a lot riding on this situation. A lot. You and I both know that nobody in that house set that fire, but if Allen's not on the up and up, who's gonna believe it?"

"Just calm down. We have figure this thing out." Darryl had a seat again. "O.k., for right now, you keep playing stupid about the mask. Right now, it's your word against his, and you have the evidence..."

"Word, word..."

"That's not the final solution, trust me. We've seen where Hamel's loyalty lies when it comes to race relations, so he could still make some trouble for us. I'll take care of this mask."

Percy felt a little better. "Ah-ight."

"And whatever you do, Percy, don't tell anyone else in the Tri-AC about this. You saw how shaky Carlos was acting the other day. He gets wind of this, he'll go shell like he did about Tamal." Darryl turned looked at Percy sharply. "You really think it was Tamal you saw on the porch with that gas can?"

Percy had told Darryl the same thing several times since he first revealed his suspicions. "To tell you the truth, I don't know. Sometimes I think it was, and other times I am not sure."

"You say whoever it was walked with a limp?"

"Yeah, and you know Tamal busted his knee up that night he came over here. But the person I saw—he wasn't as big as Tamal, or maybe I looked so quick I thought he looked smaller. Has anyone heard from Tamal lately?"

Darryl shook his head. "I don't know if that's good or bad. Look bru, Andre's out of town this week at a counselor's conference, so why don't you crash over here for a few days—get your head straight? That way, you won't have to worry about puttin' up a front for your roommate."

That's the best news Percy had heard since he'd been back in town. He didn't think he could deal with Allen's "you can trust me" speeches anymore. "'Preciate that, man. I left my clothes in my man's car, though. I need to go get 'em."

"No problem—let's go do that now. I got your back, Percy, all right? You'll be sending me a postcard from England next semester."

"Thanks, bru."

When Percy got back to campus, he left Darryl parked in front of the residence hall and headed up to his room. Allen was sitting at his desk, reading.

"Where'd you disappear to, Percy?" he asked with his customary grin, like nothing unusual had happened. "I thought you came back up to the room."

"I need to get my bags out of your trunk," Percy told him coldly. He grabbed his bookbag out of the closet and started loading his books and extra clothes into it.

"Sure, sure. I guess you forgot them when you got out." Allen dug in his pants pocket for his keys, then stopped. "Percy..."

"Look Allen, if you're gonna start that nonsense about me burning down the Lambda Sig house, then forget it. I ain't figured out why you'd try to pull a stunt like that, but to keep me from smashing your grill in, you'd better leave me alone and let me get out of here."

Allen nodded, almost sadly. Percy finished packing, grabbed the keys from Allen's outstretched hand and started out of the door.

"Percy, I still don't blame you guys for what you did..."

Percy turned around to face him. "Man..."

"O.k., so maybe you didn't start the fire, but someone did. Think about this just for a moment. Don't you think it was poetic justice?"

"What?!"

"It's simple, Percy. That had it coming—don't you think? For what they did to you guys."

Percy's shock was real. "Allen, their house burned down—it wasn't just a broken window or graffiti—people get killed in fires!"

Allen just shrugged, looking eerily calm.

"Doesn't that register with you, man?! If someone was in the house that night, they could've been seriously hurt, or worst yet, dead!"

Allen frowned. "Percy, for years your people have been ridiculed, injured, crippled and killed and for what?! For just fighting for basic human rights! Now the racists who started it are getting their payback, and if a few people have to die…well—that's just the way it is."

Percy felt like he was in the room with a madman at that moment. "Are you for real?" he asked in a low voice.

"Heck, yes! Percy…we owe your people for years of suffering…"

"So you think this fire—that could have taken someone out—was payback?"

"It was a small down payment, Percy. And whoever did set that fire…well—they're a…a hero, kinda like Joan of Arc or Martin Luther King."

Percy just stared at him, not believing his ears.

Allen looked down at his hands a moment. "You ever seen a fire, Percy? There's something so…powerful about it—almost majestic. All those strong colors. Think about it—one small match has the destructive power of…ten armies." He made a whooshing sound and opened his hands, smiling at Percy.

Oh…that was it. This was some spooky stuff he'd seen on those psychotic horror movies. He was getting outta there. "Yo, you are one crazy…" He reached for the door handle, never taking his eyes off of his roommate, opened the door and slammed it shut. He heard Allen call his name as walked down the hall, but he just kept stepping out into the lobby, even taking the stairs just in case Allen wanted to finish the conversation and a slow elevator made it possible.

When he got downstairs, Darryl was in the lobby, looking very unhappy. "Brother, where have you been?!" he asked, falling in step beside Percy. "I ain't tryin' to melt out there."

"Let me grab my clothes out of his trunk, and I'll be ready."

"You mean you have to take his key back up to the room?" Darryl sounded none to pleased.

"Nah…I'll leave 'em under the mat in the front, and I'll call and tell him where they are."

"Is that safe?"

"Darryl, nobody in their right mind would steal Allen's car."

"O.k." When they reached the car, Darryl laughed, understanding. Percy half-heartedly joined in, still reeling from Allen's little psycho theory on retribution in the room. He had just under a month left in the semester, and he didn't see how in the world he was going to spend it with a crazy roommate.

He lifted up the trunk lid and grabbed his big suitcase. "Hold this for me?" he asked Darryl, handing it to him. He reached back in to get his overnight bag and froze. Right underneath his suitcase was a black ski mask and a red gasoline container.

Great day in the morning.

Now it was coming together—Allen asking about his ski mask, being upset about the Plot, that speech in the room, the limp. *"Whoever set that fire...is a hero..."*

Allen was the arsonist. He set that fire that nearly took them out.

EUGENE

He couldn't figure out how he made it from one day to the next. Classes seemed to last forever, and the walk back to his room was like a trek across the desert without water. Once he finally reached his room, he felt claustrophobic. Irene called him everyday and came by at least twice a week, checking to make sure he was o.k.

Chip and Diedra alternated calling him every day for a while, making sure he hadn't changed his mind about coming home. According to Chip, his dad had some rough days but having Granny around seemed to help him cope better. He was more mellow, Chip informed him, and was easing off his "Black Pride" kick. Mr. Wright called his son once a week but he never talked long. He did tell Eugene that he wanted to plan a family vacation this summer and he was welcome to invite anyone he wanted, even the "young lady."

And Eugene thought about his mother everyday. When he came back to school, he had taken down all the pictures in his room that she was in because they were too painful to look at. He sometimes cried at night, burying his face in his pillow so Monty wouldn't hear him. One night Monty heard and climbed down from his top bunk to sit on Eugene's bed, patting his shoulder awkwardly. Eugene tried to dry up but couldn't, so Monty patted until he finally drifted off to sleep. The next morning, Eugene found a note on his desk: *Hope I didn't wear your shoulder out. Don't be afraid to cry. Monty.*

One night, Eugene was making an Olympic effort to control his tears despite his roommate's note. He bit his pillow and sniffled, hearing Monty fumbling for the phone that he'd taken up to his bunk. There was a muffled conversation; he heard Monty say, "We'll be ready," before hanging up.

"Eugene—you awake?"

Eugene rolled over. "Yeah—what's up?"

Monty jumped down and turned on the light. "Come on—Irene's on her way over. We're going to get some breakfast."

Eugene blinked. "Monty, what time is it?"

Monty looked at Eugene's clock on the desk. "One forty-seven," he answered casually, sliding into the jeans and T-shirt he wore the day before. "Come on—she'll be here in about fifteen minutes."

365

Eugene sat up and watched his roommate run his fingers through his curly black hair, then grab one of his many baseball caps stacked neatly on his dresser.

"Monty, don't tell me you woke Irene up this time of morning because you were hungry?"

"Ah-ight—I won't tell you that."

Eugene sighed, embarrassed. "I'll be all right, man. You guys don't have to baby me. I won't crack."

Monty studied him a minute, then picked up the jeans Eugene had slung over his chair earlier and tossed them at him. "I don't know why you're over there trying to be a hero. If my mother died and my friends didn't try to help me through it, I'd look for some new friends. Now get dressed and quit trippin'."

Eugene got dressed in silence. He really wasn't sure what to say, anyway. He and Monty met Irene downstairs and they headed to the nearest pancake house. Before Eugene knew it, he was eating a hearty breakfast and nearly choking as he laughed at Monty's wild stories about his family and his neighborhood. Fortunately, Eugene's first and only class was two o'clock that afternoon, so he had plenty of time to sleep. Irene had a lab and Monty's class started at 9:30—he kept insisting that he had it under control.

Later on that morning, Eugene rolled over at 10:30 and saw Monty's hand dangling down from the top bunk.

"Man, it's chill," he told Eugene later on that day. "I was going to skip that class, anyway."

By April, one month before the end of his freshman year, Eugene had found a tolerable pace to operate in. He kept mostly to himself, but still spent a good part of his time with Irene and Monty. He had even decided to bid with Monty on an apartment for next semester. He found that throwing himself into his schoolwork helped, too—a little. The warm spring air reminded him of working in the garden with his mother, even though she would be doing most of the work while he played.

Monty and Irene had something planned for him every weekend. A picnic here, a movie there—Eugene wondered how they kept up with their school work. He appreciated everything they were doing, but sooner or later he was going to have to face this thing alone.

One week before finals, Eugene was sitting out in the study room on his floor, trying to get an English paper together. His African-

American Literature professor didn't require as many papers as Grapevine had, but she was known to assign five books in one week to read. And her paper length requirement was longer. He looked up when he heard the ding of the elevator, and saw none other than Renee' step off, holding what looked like a cake container and looking around in confusion. She finally spotted Eugene in the study room and smiled briefly, taking hesitant steps toward him.

"Hi, Eugene," she said, standing in the doorway.

"Hi," he greeted cautiously. What was this all about, he wondered? He hadn't talked to her since right before the Forum, which was close to two months ago. He saw her on campus a few times but she usually just swished by without even looking at him. At times, he wanted to stop her and apologize for coming off so harsh, but he felt too ridiculous to actually do it.

Renee' appeared nervous. She looked down at the floor. "I—uh, just came by to tell you how sorry I was to hear about your mother." She lifted those cat eyes to stare sympathetically at him. "I just found out this week. I'm sorry, Eugene."

"Thanks, Renee'. I appreciate that." He gathered his books that were sitting beside him on the couch, and put them on the floor. "Why don't you have a seat?"

She looked surprised, then pleased as she walked over and sat beside him, fingering the container she was holding. "I made you a cake," she blurted out, looking embarrassed.

"Really?! Wow—thanks!"

"I hope you like Seven-Up cake."

"Seven-Up?"

"Yeah."

"You mean like the pop, Seven-Up?"

Renee' smiled. "Exactly. It's made with real Seven-Up."

Eugene scratched his head. "Well—that's a new one on me, but I'm sure it's good."

Renee' still looked uncomfortable. Eugene was beginning to feel sorry for *her*.

"Can I try a piece?"

"If you want. I sliced it up for you." Renee' lifted the lid and a delicious aroma traveled up Eugene's nostrils.

Cake made with pop, huh? He pulled out a slice and bit into it. "Mmmph," he mumbled, chewing quickly so he could take another bite. "Renee'—this is good!"

Renee' looked doubtful. "You really like it, or are you being nice?"

Eugene was already munching on his second bite. He reached over and grabbed the container off Renee's lap, causing her to laugh. After two more bites, that slice was finished and he was looking longingly at another. He reached down, then looked sheepishly at Renee'. "You, ah, want a slice? I didn't mean to act like a pig in front of you, but this is good."

Renee' smiled and shook her head. Eugene never noticed how pretty her smile was. He had been too busy concentrating on her eyes. In fact, Renee' looked nice today—period. And she smelled wonderful, like fresh strawberries.

"No, I'm fine. I've had my share, believe me," she assured him. "I'm glad you like it. My mother taught me how to make it."

At the word "mother," Eugene blinked but tried to cover it up with a smile. Suddenly, he lost his appetite.

"Eugene, I am so sorry! I didn't mean…"

"No—you're fine. I've got to deal with it, don't I?"

She nodded and to his surprise, laid a gentle hand on his arm. "If it's any consolation, I kind of know how you feel. I lost my sister a couple of years ago."

Eugene had been leaning on the arm of the couch, but now he sat straight up. "Man, Renee'—I never knew. I'm sorry to hear that."

"Yeah. I don't talk about it much because it still hurts, but—yeah…"

"How do you—how do you deal with it?" Eugene asked, thinking that losing his mother was hard enough but to lose his brother, the one he had grown up with, man…

She shrugged. "I just try to take it one day at a time, I guess. It's getting easier—there was a time I couldn't even think about her, let alone talk about her like this." Renee' looked toward the wall. "I still have days when I think about her and just—have a good cry."

Eugene stayed silent. He found himself laying a hand on her shoulder when he saw her swipe at her eyes. She turned those feline orbs, full of tears, to look at him, then smiled. "I'm sorry—I'm over here talking about myself and I came to see how you were doing…"

"No, no—this helps, trust me. I'd been thinking that I had to hurry up and pull myself together, but I'm glad to hear that I don't have to."

Renee' shook her head. "No, you don't. You have to deal with it the way you need to deal with it. See, I let other people make my decisions for me, Eugene. I wanted to stay closer to home to be around my mother and my family kept telling me, 'no—you should go away to school—keep your mind off of it.' So I ended up here at Hamel."

He could relate because his mother did the same thing to him, trying to protect him. But he was kind of glad that she forced the issue. If he was home, he might not be dealing with it the same, being so close to her memory. He could let go a little more here. He smiled at Renee'. "I'm glad they did make that decision for you—I would have never met you if you stayed at home."

Man, what a beautiful smile. It lit up her whole face. He'd drown her in compliments all day long just to see that smile.

"Thanks for sharing that with me, Renee'. I know it took a lot for you to do that." Before he knew it, he was reaching over to give her an uncustomary hug. The fresh strawberries surrounded him. He inhaled deeply before he released her. He liked strawberries. "I apologize for blowing up that day at the boycott. I was dealing with a lot of stuff, and I guess I took some of it out on you."

Renee' was shaking her head. "No—I'm the one that needs to apologize. I shouldn't have tried to guilt trip you because you weren't marching. I was wrong, Eugene. Every black person didn't participate and you or them don't have a thing to prove, so you were right."

"O.k."

"And my little speech at lunch last semester…"

"Don't worry about that…"

"No—that's why you stopped talking to me, right?"

Eugene nodded reluctantly. "It did kind of catch me off guard, like I had committed a crime or something because I talked to a white person."

"I know. I was just—I was a little mad at you and Irene's friendship, Eugene. I'm sure you know by now that I am a very straight forward person. I know I need to tone it down a little, but that's who I am. So when I approached you that day in the Student Center and Irene showed up—I just went off the next time I saw her. I guess I was a little jealous."

"Irene and I are friends—that's it." He hoped he was telling the truth. The day that they were sitting in the same study room on the same couch flashed in his mind. He didn't know what he was feeling at that moment—he knew that he found her very attractive and that she made him feel comfortable and good about himself. It was just so confusing, and they never talked about it afterwards—not like they had the opportunity to talk about it.

But he was intrigued by Renee', especially now since they had cleared the air about some things. No doubt he thought she was more than pretty, and even her self-proclaimed boldness had an appeal— she had a mind of her own.

Renee' was nodding. "I know that now. That's the same thing she told me."

Eugene blinked. "*Irene* told you?! When did you talk to her?!"

She giggled at his reaction. "I ran into her yesterday on campus. She stopped me and told me about your mother. We discussed the other stuff at lunch."

Eugene blinked again. "*Lunch*?! You guys had *lunch*?! *At the same time?!*"

She laughed loudly. "At the same time, at the same table. We got some things straight—I told her I was sorry for being rude to her that day on the patio. My mother didn't raise me like that, Eugene, trust me—that was all *me*. Irene's a really nice person."

Eugene couldn't agree more. "Yes, she is—she's special."

Renee's face brightened, like a light bulb popped on in her head. "Hey, why don't we all get together and do something before finals?"

"That sounds like a great idea, Renee', but…"

Renee' frowned immediately. "It would be too awkward for you?"

"No, no—I just wondered if maybe we could go out first. Just the two of us."

Renee's grin was slow and wide. "Eugene, are you asking me out on a date?"

Now *he* was the bold one. "That's exactly what I'm doing."

"What took you so long?" she teased giving him a playful nudge in the arm. "And *when*?"

That sounded like an affirmation to him. "How about Friday night?"

"How about that sounds good?"

"Great—Friday night, then. Did you want to do anything special?"

Eugene suddenly realized he didn't know *how* to date, let alone where to go on one.

"I'll leave that up to you. Why don't you surprise me?"

"All right—I will." It would be a surprise to him, too.

"But let me know in advance, so I'll know how to dress," she warned.

"I'm sure you'll look pretty regardless," Eugene found himself telling her. There went that diamond smile again. Chip would be so proud of him, especially since it was beginning to look like he would inherit ten dollars from Diedra.

Michele R. Leverett

Epilogue

"Eugene! What a surprise!"

"How's it going, Irene?" Eugene asked as Irene opened her door and let him in. He had just finished an afternoon final, and decided to head over to Irene's side of campus instead of back to his residence hall. Irene lived where most of the female volleyball players did—in the suite buildings on the other side of the academic campus. Eugene walked in, admiring the size of the living room area that she shared with three other roommates. She still had to share a room, but you couldn't beat all that living room space.

"Have a seat?" she offered as Eugene took a good look at her. He had never seen her with glasses before, but it gave her a cute, studious look. She was wearing a huge volleyball T-shirt and jogging shorts. She looked like she was studying, because there were books spread all over the coffee table, and she had an open one in her arms.

"I don't want to disturb you—you look like you're studying..."

"No, you're fine. I'm taking a break." She down beside him on the couch, folding her leg under her. "What?" she asked, catching Eugene staring at her. He pointed to her glasses. "Oh...yeah—I go total nerd at home."

"No—they look cute on you."

"Ya think?!"

"Yes, you look...intelligent."

"I *am* intelligent!"

"No arguments here!"

She laughed and plugged him in the arm. "Oh my God, I can't believe you finally came over to see me! What gives?"

"Well—I just finished a final and decided to see what you were up to."

"Taking advantage of my roommates not being here. This is only like the second time this year I've been here by myself. Otherwise, I'd be at the library. You want a soda or something?"

"No, I'm fine."

She reached over and rubbed his hand. "How's it goin', kiddo?"

He knew what she meant. "It's hard, but I'm dealing—thanks to friend like you and Monty. And Renee'."

Her eyes got wide. "You talked to her?"

"She stopped by last week. Hey, thanks for telling her what happened."

"No problem."

Yeah, we went out Friday."

She gasped. "No way! Get out! How was it?!"

"It went well. We had a good time, we ate, saw a movie…."

"And…?"

"And…that was it. I dropped her off by her dorm and said goodnight." Irene smirked and raised her eyebrow. "What?!"

"Nothing else happened? No goodnight kiss?"

He laughed. "Come on, Irene! It was our first date! I'm a gentleman!"

"O.k….you don't have to tell me…"

"Seriously! No goodnight kiss!"

"All right! I believe you," she laughed. "You like her?"

"I do, but we'll see how it goes. We talked about everything. She's a really sweet person once you get to know her."

"And pretty."

"Definitely pretty. Like you."

Irene blushed. "Yeah, for a four-eyed nerd."

"Even as a four-eyed nerd."

She smiled at him. "Eugene, you're a special guy, you know that?"

"So I'm told."

She smiled. "So…you guys gonna go out again, keep in contact, what?"

"Well, my last final is in two days—I'm going home after that. Hopefully I'll see her before then, but if not, we'll keep in contact over the summer. Maybe somebody can make a trip north or south, who knows?"

"I'm happy for you, Eugene. For both of you."

"We're not getting married, Irene," he chuckled.

"No, but you found someone that you like, you can talk to, that's always nice."

He reached over and tugged on her ponytail. "I found *two* someones."

She threw her head back. "You are too much! Please leave before you spoil it for other men!"

He laughed and got up. "I'm going…"

"I was only teasing…"

"No, I need to get back to the room, do some more packing and studying."

Irene walked him over to the door. He opened it and turned back to her, ready to say goodbye again, and she grabbed him a big hug. Whoa…

"You take care of yourself," she told him. "Keep in contact, o.k.?"

His emotions were doing overtime. "You know it."

Irene pulled away and looked him in the eye. "Eugene, should we talk about that night in the study room?"

He looked down at her, remembering when he first met her in Grapevine's class with her cat green eyes, their falling out, her driving him home to see his mother, making sure his weekends were filled afterward…before he knew it, he reached down and planted a quick kiss on her surprised mouth. "No—we don't," he told her, walking into the hallway and out of the building.

MARIE

It took about fifteen minutes to walk to Tony's apartment complex, clear across campus. On the way over, she did some serious reflecting. *What's wrong with me? Acting like an insecure high school girl whose boyfriend is going off to college. I am NOT in high school anymore and Tony is a young man—not some little thuggish teenybopper trying to act like one. I need to show him I can handle a long distance relationship. Yeah. He's trying to do something positive—I can't hold him back. In fact, that's how I'll approach him. He'll really appreciate that. Who knows? I may even get my first kiss.* That thought alone sent a delicious shiver through her and hurried her along.

Tony's door was open when she got there and a delightful smell met her nose. *He's cooking again.* She smiled. The boy was amazing. He sang, cooked, and here she was about to make a mess of things with her selfish attitude.

"Tony?" She knocked lightly on the halfway open door. ""Hello? Is anyone home?"

There was movement in the kitchen, and a female came around the corner, wiping her hands on a dishtowel. "Hello," she greeted Marie with a smile. She was very pretty, Marie observed. She had a warm, honey brown complexion, and her sleek, short hair was combed back from her face. She was a little on the heavy side, but still had one of those figures where everything fell in the right place—solid. Marie guessed that she was a friend of one of Tony's roommates, but she appeared too pleasant to be associated with Tamal and Tony's other roommates were white—but anything was possible.

"Hi," Marie responded. "I'm looking for Tony. Is he here?"

Suddenly, the girl's pleasant disposition was replaced by an intense look of curiosity. "You must be Marie."

"Yes," Marie told her. O.k., what was this about? Girlfriend knew who she was, but Marie was clueless.

"I'm Vonjie," she told her, like she should have known better.

The name meant nothing to Marie. "Vonjie?" she repeated, frantically searching her brainhousing group for an answer. Nothing. The one thing she did know is that she wasn't entirely at ease with the way Vonjie was looking at her, like she was trying to see right through her.

"Marie, I didn't know you were coming by. Hey, I see you two have met." Tony came in the open door, holding a plastic grocery bag. He looked a tad bit nervous to Marie.

"Well, not exactly," Marie told him, not sure if she was comfortable with the scene emerging before her. A female coming out of the kitchen like she lived there or at least had been there several times before, able to identify Marie automatically and staring at her, Tony appearing uneasy with Marie's presence, when he had made it clear several times before that she didn't need an invitation to stop by.

"Well, I'm glad you came. I was going to call you later…" Tony faltered, then stopped. Why was he acting so jumpy? He absently handed the plastic bag to Vonjie, who immediately looked inside and frowned.

"No, Tony. I said lemon *flavor*, not lemon *juice*," she told him. "Vonjie, you told me lemon *juice*."

"Why would I say lemon juice when I'm trying to make a sweet potato pie?" She playfully clouted Tony upside his head. "You of all people should know better. Where'd you put my pocketbook?"

"It's back in my room, why?" Tony asked as Vonjie headed down the hallway, returning seconds later with her pocketbook. "I'll go get it, Vonjie, it was my mistake."

"No, you stay here with your friend." *Friend?!!!!* "I'll be right back. Marie, won't you join us for dinner?"

To Marie, Vonjie sounded like she was just being polite by asking her. She didn't sound like she meant it. "Oh, no—thank you."

Vonjie just nodded and disappeared out the door. What, she didn't need directions to the store? She knew where she was going. *Something ain't right…*

Suddenly, she and Tony were left alone in the apartment. O.k.— where did she start? Who was supposed to talk first? Apparently, Tony thought he should get things going. "So, Marie," he said in his normal friendly voice. "To what do I owe the honor?"

Was he serious? Was he just going to bypass the Vonjie thing? "I came by to apologize for earlier," she told him.

Tony waved his hand and sat down, motioning for her sit, too. "Don't worry about that. I understand."

"You do?"

"Yeah, I realized afterwards that I would have been hurt if you wouldn't have shown some emotion about me leaving. Marie, I consider you one of my best friends. I don't know how you feel about me, but you there." He patted his chest near his heart.

"As are you." She told him, staying on safe ground. At least now she knew where she stood with him. He considered her friend—a best friend, but still just a friend, and Vonjie had called her the same thing earlier. Now things were starting to make sense. If Vonjie were more than a friend to Tony, she may not have felt comfortable leaving them alone like she did; however, if Tony had her categorized as a friend, and Vonjie didn't want to come off as the jealous type, then the noble thing to do was to show Tony just how much she could trust him. But it still didn't mean that she was entirely comfortable, which would explain the intensity when Marie arrived. Still, why hadn't Tony mentioned her?

"Vonjie seems like a nice girl," she said with small pangs of jealousy.

"You think so?" Tony sounded nonchalant.

"Don't you?"

"Yeah, I guess I do. She needs to quit mothering me so much though."

"Have you talked to her about that?"

Tony had been lounging casually against the couch but now sat straight up, frowning. "It doesn't do any good, Marie. She won't stop, and I don't really mind it too much."

Oh, o.k. She couldn't believe she was sitting here talking to the man she adored about his girlfriend or friend or whatever the heck she was. It was painful, but she had to be mature about it. Tony didn't need to know that she had a tremendous crush on him.

"So, how long have you two known each other?"

Tony actually laughed. "All of our lives, Marie. Girl, you something else."

"Well, have long have you two been dating?"

Tony's eyebrows went straight up. *"Huh?!"*

"Aren't ya'll dating?"

Tony's eyebrows went up another notch, then he fell back against the sofa, hollering with laughter.

"What's so funny?! What?!"

Tony tried to speak but when he did, he laughed harder. In fact, he fell face forward on the sofa, holding his stomach.

Marie was feeling strange. She didn't know if it was a good strange or a bad strange, but it was strange all the same. "Tony what did I say that was so funny?"

"You—you think Vonjie's my girlfriend," he managed to squeeze out.

"Well, who is she then?!"

"Marie, Vonjie's my big sister," Tony told her patiently, wiping tears from his eyes, before going off in another round of laughter.

"Your..."

"Sister," he repeated. "Don't you remember me telling you about my three sisters?"

He probably did. But let's see...what did Marie have on her mind this year? Oh yeah—there was Cedric, then there was Claudia with Cedric, then Claudia without Cedric, the boycott, then Cedric trying to push up on her again, then Claudia with Cedric again when she should have been without, then Claudia without Cedric—again. Then, in between all that drama were the classes, the books, the studying, adjusting to being away from home, living with someone from a totally different background...no wonder she didn't remember old girl's name.

Marie sat there a minute, hearing a low sound deep in her belly. When she opened her mouth, she was laughing as hard as Tony had been earlier. In fact, Tony joined in again and both of them were soon laughing like they'd taken leave of their senses.

"That was funny," Tony said breathlessly, after he'd calmed down again. "Vonjie—mmm." He looked like he wanted to lose control again.

"Tony, I am so sorry. You must think I'm an idiot."

Tony waved his hand, still in a light mood. "Don't even worry about it, beautiful." He gave her a strange look. "Should I be flattered?"

She smiled, suddenly feeling very giddy—and bold. "Maybe."

He grinned widely in response. *Oh yeah—today could be a hallmark moment. I'm not sure, but I think I'm about to let a guy know how I feel about him.*

"I'm glad you stopped by," Tony was saying.

"Oh yeah...I almost forgot why I stopped by in the first place."

"Well, I hope it was to see me."

"It was." Marie didn't know what had happened in the last couple of minutes, but something significant was going on in her and Tony's relationship. If she had to give it a label, she almost wanted to say that they were—flirting with each other. "I wanted to apologize for earlier on the Block. I got an attitude with you instead of rejoicing with you over your good news. It was selfish of me and I'm sorry."

Tony nodded warmly. "No problem. I understand, Marie. But you might actually have a fun summer. Don't give up hope on that."

Marie smiled nervously. "That's not what I meant by me being selfish, Tony."

"What do you mean, then?"

Should she say it? Did she dare? *O.k., girl. You know once you say this, you can't take it back. It's out there. What's done is done. Now, up until this point, you've managed to keep yourself pretty well protected from being hurt by a guy—and letting him know it. Are you sure you want to move into unfamiliar territory? Tony ain't Cedric,* but he's still a man. "I...I'm going to miss you, Tony. And—I really...I really like you a lot and I just didn't want you to leave me, that's all." There—she'd said it. It was out, finally. And instead of feeling scared, she felt relieved.

And instead of a look of disgust, pity or confusion crossing Tony's face, he looked pleasantly surprised. He came toward her and held out his hands, lifting her to her feet. Before she could even think, his face came towards hers and he planted the sweetest, softest kiss she had ever known on her lips.

No, this boy didn't just do what I think he did. This boy didn't just kiss me. He didn't just give me my first, real kiss. He didn't just...

"Marie, you better go." Marie opened her eyes and Tony was standing a good three feet away from her. The magic moment was broken.

"Tony, what's..."

"I'm...gonna have to talk to you later." Tony looked extremely bothered and agitated. He turned and swiftly headed toward the door and opened it. He looked down at the floor instead of at her.

Marie stood there a minute, frowning in confusion. What in the world was going on with him?! What had just happened?! One minute, he was planting a kiss on her, and the next, he was practically pushing her out the door. What had she done?! "Tony, please tell me what's wrong? What did I do?"

Tony just shook his head and continued to stare at the ground. "I just think it would be best if you left, Marie. I'm sorry," he said in a soft voice.

She could not believe what was happening—and who it was happening with. Tony was stone dissing her after she bared her feelings to him…she wanted to cry. Then she got mad at herself for wanting to cry. Then, she got mad at Tony for making her want to cry and get mad at herself as a result.

Well, she didn't tell Cedric what she thought about his doggish ways because she was trying to be nice—a good Christian. But Tony was going to get an earful. She walked up to the door, stood right in his face.

"You know what?" she began in a low voice. "You are about the sorriest excuse for a man that I have seen. You came off all nice, grinning in my face, cooking for me and sweatin' me like you had an interest, and then you pull some okey doke mess like this. I thought you were different Tony. You made me believe you were, too. And you even had the nerve to slam Cedric, when you ain't no better than he is…"

"Marie…"

"No, don't say jack diddly squat to me, Tony! You have to be about the biggest hypocrite…how dare you treat me like this! I didn't ask you to kiss me—you did that on your own!"

Tony looked wounded. He reached out to grab her hand. "Marie, listen…"

She snatched her hand away. "Don't touch me! Don't touch me and don't talk to me! You ain't no different than any other doggish…canine male out here." Her tears were flowing now. It was time to leave. Tony didn't stop her and it probably would not have been a good idea for him to try, either. She stomped down the steps and away from the apartment complex.

"Where were you?" Claudia was knocking at her door some two hours after Marie came back to her room. Corrie wasn't there, as usual. She was probably on the tenth floor somewhere studying for finals with Amanda and Chrissy. That was a good thing—she had pumped Tony up so much to her roommate that she probably thought he walked on water. Marie had been walking around campus, crying and trying to make sense out of what had just happened at Tony's apartment. "I've been calling your room for about two hours!"

"I forgot about meeting you for dinner, Claudia. Sorry," she told her in a husky voice, turning away immediately once she opened the door.

"Sorry don't cut it for me, Marie. You know my appetite," Claudia joked. "Where have you been?"

"Nowhere really," Marie shrugged, sitting on her bed with her head down.

"Nowhere..." Claudia lifted Marie's face up. "Marie! You're crying! What's wrong?"

"Nothing," Marie said, before bursting into tears. Claudia immediately sat beside her and pulled her into an embrace, smoothing her ponytail. *She'd better not rub too hard,* Marie found herself thinking through her grief. *It might come off.*

"Marie, talk to me. What happened with Tony? What's going on?"

Marie tried to compose herself so she could explain to Claudia what she didn't understand herself. "Tony kissed me."

Claudia pulled away from Marie. "He kissed you?!"

Marie nodded.

"Was it that bad?"

Marie just looked at her, in no mood to joke.

"Marie, I'm a little confused. You like Tony—he kissed you. Why are you upset?"

"Because after he kissed me he threw me out of his apartment, that's why!"

"What?!"

So Marie took Claudia to the beginning—meeting Vonjie, thinking she was his girl but she was actually his sister, making up her mind to be honest about her feelings and then the magical moment— the kiss. Then Tony acting like he'd kissed the devil himself afterwards.

Claudia was shaking her head, looking troubled. "Oh, Marie. I am so sorry...did you ask him why he was acting so funny?"

"I tried, but he just kept telling me I needed to leave. And trust me—I left something behind for him, too."

"You went off on him, didn't you?" Claudia asked, very familiar with Marie's character.

"I tried my best…but I still didn't say everything I wanted to say."
Marie paused to blow her nose. Her tears had stopped because she
was angry again, thinking about Tony's actions.

The phone startled both of them. Marie went for it, but then
stopped midway to her dresser.

"You're not going to answer it, are you?" Claudia asked.

"I don't have anything to say to him, Claudia. As far as I'm
concerned, Tony is no different than any other dog out here. He ain't
no different than Cedric…" She stopped, forgetting for a minute about
Claudia's drama with him.

But Claudia just smiled. "It's all good, girl."

"Well, I told him the same thing…" The phone stopped after three
rings. One more and Corrie's answering machine would have picked
up. "And I told him he was the biggest hypocrite I'd ever met."

"Marie, there's got to be a logical explanation for the way he
acted."

"Because he's a dog, that's why! I knew I should have kept my
mouth shut!"

"No—Tony is not a dog. *Cedric* is a dog. Tony is not like Cedric.
I don't even know him as well as you, but I can already pick up on
that."

"Then why treat me like that, Claudia?" Marie wanted to know,
standing and gesturing with her arms. Why act like you all interested
then diss me…" Tears were threatening again. "And why are you
defending him?!"

"Marie, I am not defending him. All I'm telling you is that I
honestly don't think that Tony was out to hurt you. From the few
times I been around you two, I can tell that he likes you."

"Yeah, right."

"You're upset right now. Look, what time is Corrie coming
back?"

"I don't know."

"Why don't you come spend the night with me? We'll order
another pizza and I can babysit you—make sure you don't go over
there and attack ole' boy with a brass candleholder."

Marie tried not to laugh because she wanted to grieve about this
thing, but the sound came out her mouth before she could stop it.
"Shut up! Stop making me laugh, Claudia! Get on my nerves!" she
pouted.

"You need to laugh, Marie. We are not going to let these men get us down or cause us to make fools of ourselves anymore. We are strong black women and we don't need men to make us happy, o.k.? Forget him. Let's eat."

See, that's exactly what Marie was talking about—Claudia was a lousy counselor. She didn't say one thing that Marie wanted her to. She did not accept the invitation to Marie's pity party and agree with her that Tony was a dog, or tell her she understood how hurt she was and how in the world could he do this to her. No—she gonna come with some powerful, "Sistagirl" speech that made perfect sense, make her laugh when she wanted to cry, and eat when she wasn't even thinking about food. What a rotten counselor.

And what a wonderful friend.

"I love you, girl." Marie threw her arms around Claudia and squeezed the life out of her.

"I love you, too," Claudia choked out. "But I can't breathe."

"Sorry. Come on, let's order a pizza. Your treat?"

"No, see…you are not going to do that trash to me again!"

They went across the lobby, arguing about who was going to pay for the pizza this time.

PERCY

"Percy!"

Percy was just leaving his Intro to Business final when he heard someone calling his name. He turned to his left, and Eugene was sitting against the wall on a cushioned bench. He stood and weaved through the crowd to him.

"What's goin' on, Eugene? I didn't know you had a business class."

"I don't. I was looking for you," he told him, falling in step beside him.

"How'd you know where my final was?"

"I ran into one of your brothers this morning and he told me where it was. I came by your room yesterday evening and Allen said you weren't staying there that much."

"I come and go," Percy told him. Actually, he managed to spend about two nights a week in his room, crashing on the couch at Darryl and Andre's the rest of the week. He didn't feel too confident about closing his eyes around Allen, and Darryl offered him the couch after he'd shared his discovery with him. He didn't want to take advantage of his hospitality, but since they had a similar class schedule three days out of the week, he felt no qualms about chilling out off campus away from his psychotic roommate. The nights he did sleep in his room were restless at first, but lately Allen had been coming in the room extremely late or not at all.

"What did you need to see me about?"

Eugene looked around the crowded hallway. "Can we talk outside?"

They headed down a flight of stairs to the first floor and out of the building. Eugene led him over to Yardley Tower, already filling up with students taking a break between finals, and sat on the edge of the brick structure. Percy sat beside him.

"So what's up?" Percy asked again.

"I need to show you something." Eugene reached in his pocket.

Don't tell me I dropped something else at the house! Percy watched Eugene bring a closed fist out of his pocket, then open his hand to reveal a gold plated, rectangular key chain with two Greek letters on it. He frowned, confused.

"What's that?"

"You don't recognize it?"

"Should I?"

"I don't know. You've never seen it before?"

"No, I haven't." And he was tired of playing games with everyone, just for the record. Allen, Carlos, now Eugene. "I ain't even got time for no game, man…"

"Percy," Eugene looked him directly in the eye and asked calmly, "Don't you recognize the letters?"

"No…" Percy took the key chain and looked closely at the letters. One of them he'd seen from the black Greeks on campus—a sigma. The first one did look familiar right away…"Lambda Sigma?"

Eugene nodded.

"Why do I care about a Lambda Sigma key chain, Eugene?"

"Turn it over."

Percy flipped the small rectangle over and looked at something inscribed on the back. His right eyebrow inadvertently raised itself in alarm.

Downing—Hamel University.

"Where'd you get this?" Percy practically whispered.

"I found it in my pants pockets—the ones I let Allen borrow when he locked himself out of his room last semester. I didn't even bother to look in the pocket until I wore them when…when I went home," Eugene hesitated, and blinked.

Percy's radar went up. His RA informed the whole suite what had happened in his family. "Yeah…I heard about your mom passing. Sorry to hear that. I should've said something the day you stopped by. It slipped my mind."

"Thanks, man." Eugene gave him a quick, grateful smile. "Oh—congratulations on England! I read about you in the school paper."

"'Preciate that." But now was not the time to remind Percy about England, once a signed, sealed and delivered deal. It now depended on how this whole thing with the house and Allen panned out. And he realized he was protecting that trip with his silence and his lying. Wouldn't his mother be proud of him.

"So you're telling me my roommate is a Lambda Sigma?" he asked Eugene, getting back to the subject at hand.

"Isn't that his last name?"

"Yeah…"

"All I know is that I found it in the pants that he borrowed. It certainly isn't *my* key chain."

Percy's mind was reeling. He had rooming with a member of that hateful, racist destructive fraternity almost all year, and didn't know it?! And what about his little speech on restitution and payback?! Was that just a bait and switch to see if Percy would reveal anything to incriminate himself?! He didn't know how much more he could take.

Eugene continued. "I wanted to show this to you when I first found it. That's why I came by your room that morning after the house burned down. That's really why I stopped by. Percy, I'm not trying to be funny, but Allen seems a little off to me."

"You noticed it too?"

"Yeah…o.k., when he returned my pants, he made some weird speech about how grateful he was to see the day when 'my people' could afford a quality brand of clothes like my pants were or something. He said that we should be furious with his people for keeping up in coarse potato sacks and substandard shoes for years…it was really kinda crazy sounding, like he was just…disconnected or something."

"Tell me about it. He gave me a song and dance a couple of weeks ago. That's why I don't stay there much."

"There's something else…"

"Yeah…?"

"I could've sworn I saw Allen over at the Plot the morning I stopped by and told you about it. He was just standing there, then he walked away. That's why I was acting so funny when he acted like he didn't know what happened to it."

"You say Allen was there *before* you told us about it?!"

Eugene nodded. "It *looked* like him. If it wasn't, then whoever it was had on the same clothes Allen had on that morning. That's why I couldn't understand him asking about it. And doesn't he drive an old green car? A Grand Prix, I think?"

Things were getting stranger by the minute. Percy's mind was doing overtime. His roommate was psycho, that much he was sure of, and he had set the fire—he was 99.9% sure of that. The only thing he couldn't figure out was what to do with the information he had, or how it would keep him and the rest of the Tri-AC from being fingered in the fire. He knew he would have to face Allen one more time to see if he could make heads or tails of what had transpired, which meant possibly listening to some strange spiel on race relations.

"Can I keep this?" he asked Eugene, holding out the keychain.

"Sure. I certainly don't want it, but what are you going to do with it?"

That remained to be seen.

CLAUDIA

"That's foul. That's foul. You know I would do it for you."

"Trust me …this is something I'm doing for *you*, Harland. You don't want that girl's number."

"Claudia, let me decide that. Look, just give her the home number then, ah-ight? Give her the home number, tell her to call me."

"Harland…"

"Come *on*, Claudia. Hook me *up*, yo!"

Claudia sighed, wanting very much to end this telephone conversation with her brother. He had been calling her everyday this week, bugging her for Vanessa's number. A few more weeks had passed since that incident with Cedric; she'd barely seen him around since then.

Not that she wanted to. After talking with Vince that day, she'd felt almost human again. It still hit her hard from time to time and the few times she did see Cedric, it hurt the worst. She and Marie caught the bus to the mall a couple of weeks after she tried to use his head and a brass candle holder for batting practice, and she saw Cedric there—with his woman. And the bad thing was that they were in a jewelry store.

"Let it go, Claudia," Marie told her when Claudia practically stopped to stare at the couple.

"I'm straight."

"No, you're not. You're wondering why that's not you all snuggled up to Cedric looking at rings instead of her, aren't you?"

She was. Cedric's baby's mother looked so beautiful standing there in her little short dress, long legs and her glossy, pinned up hair with just a few strands falling softly on her long neck and around her oval face. Cedric whispered something in her ear and she held up her hand to admire a ring as she laughed charmingly, throwing back her lovely head. Then she reached up to rub his face with her long, artistically manicured fingers and they kissed, smiling into each other's eyes.

Claudia wanted to know what she was still doing in town. Shouldn't she be at home taking care of her baby? What kind of mother was she to leave her baby miles away just so she could take off on a rendezvous with her man?

"The kind you don't need to concern yourself with," Marie told her when she mentioned to her later on that day. "Let it go, Claudia."

"I want to, Marie. But it comes back and I don't know how to stop it sometimes."

"Just take it one day at a time."

One day at a time. That's exactly what she had been doing—one day at a time...one long day after another. Finally, after about three weeks, she settled back into a routine of normal college life—if there actually was such a thing—and thought of biology labs and sociology tests instead of Cedric.

Right now, she was thinking of a way to get her brother off the phone so he would not call her back again over the same issue. Telling him about Vanessa's character didn't work. "Harland, I think Vanessa is seeing someone, anyway," she told him, not exactly lying because she had her suspicions. She had been seeing less and less of Vanessa around the residence hall and when she did pass her, there was always a whiff of perfume trailing behind. She never stopped to talk because she didn't have that kind of time or patience, but part of her was curious about who could actually stand to be dating Vanessa.

"And...?" Her brother answered.

"And...I think she's seeing someone. Isn't that enough?"

"Is she married?"

"I'm not even answering that dumb question..."

"Is she engaged?"

"Boy, no. At least, not that I know of."

"And you're not even sure that she's seeing someone."

"No. I think she may be, though."

"Girl, hook me up with them digits!"

The boy was on a paid mission to work her last good nerve. She almost wanted to agree with what he wanted just to get him off her back. No, that would open up another can of worms. Then he would be bugging her even more, wondering why Vanessa hadn't called, having Claudia keep tabs on her for him...nah.

"Harland, you know mom and dad are going to kick your tail when they see the phone bill. I know you ran it up because you've been calling me everyday for a week and a half."

That hit home. Harland got quiet. He was probably remembering when he was punished a couple of years ago for calling some girl in Florida he had met when they were on vacation there. He accepted

389

collect calls from her and they would talk for hours. When his parents got a three hundred dollar bill in the mail, all the non-physical approaches to discipline they were trying to put into practice were abandoned. Her father gave his fifteen year old son the whooping of his life. Claudia joked that her father whooped Harland like a black dad.

"O.k., then just get her number for me or give her mine or somethin' and write me. Or call home like you want to speak to mom and dad, then ask for me and tell me what's up."

In other words, lie to help him out. "Bye, Harland..."

"Claudia! You gonna do dat for me?!"

Claudia smiled, then hung up the phone. She didn't expect to hear from her brother for a very long time. And she had no intention of talking to Vanessa about the weather, let alone asking her about an overly-testosteroned, seventeen-year old high school kid who wanted to impress his homies. What a conversation that would be.

One warm spring day at the beginning of May, Claudia was on her way to the Appetizer for breakfast before her biology exam. She had studied hard the night before, taken her shower, ironed her clothes, and woke up early in the morning to go to breakfast so she could concentrate during the exam. She felt rather proud of her responsible planning. But at 7:30 in the morning, the Mouth of Belten Hall was lurking about, looking for a victim to devour with her endless, gossipy prattle. As soon as Claudia stepped out of the front door, Vanessa, coming down the walkway, made a beeline for her.

"Claudia!"

Claudia looked around for an escape route. She could run back inside the building, or she could just run right across Vanessa's path and head into the woods. There was no one there she could fake having a conversation with. She would just act like she was in a tremendous hurry to get to her exam. Surely Vanessa could understand that. Claudia didn't know why she didn't just come out and tell Vanessa what a busybody she was and that she didn't feel like hearing all her gossip, so just go somewhere, sit in a corner and shut up.

"I been trying to catch up to you all week," Vanessa smiled at her, already in first gear.

"Really?"

"Yeah. I hadn't seen you around lately. How are you?"

"I'm fine, Vanessa. Thank you for asking." This was an interesting approach. Usually, Vanessa just came right out with her information. Now, she seemed to be easing her way into it. Or maybe Claudia was being too hard on her. Why couldn't she just be making friendly conversation this morning? Maybe if she was in a relationship, it was mellowing her out—the tiger was changing her stripes. Maybe...

"So how are you and Cedric doing?"

And maybe Claudia would get a visit from those clearinghouse representatives, telling her that she'd just won ten million dollars.

"Vanessa, I have an exam this morning, so I really don't have time to talk." Claudia started walking away, thinking Vanessa got off easy on that one, because she wanted to go slam off on her. Instead, she decided to take the mature approach and just walk away. She had already reached her quota for foolish confrontations this semester, anyway.

"It's o.k., Claudia. I already know that you're not seeing each other anymore."

Claudia turned, anger on the way. She had just about had enough of these trifling folk in her life. "If you knew, then why did you ask how we were? And excuse me, but I don't think it's any of your business what..."

"Oh, I didn't mean any offense. I just thought you might not know that he was sick."

Claudia found herself back in Vanessa's face. "What do you mean, he's sick?"

Vanessa looked a little vindicated from Claudia's outburst. "I figured you didn't know since you weren't together anymore."

"No, I didn't know. Is he o.k.? Is he in the hospital or something?"

"No—at least, not yet." Vanessa paused, then delivered a bombshell. "He has AIDS."

"*What*?!! He has *what*?!!! *AIDS*?!!"

Vanessa was nodding.

"How do you know?!"

"Through Vince."

"Vince?!" She didn't even realize Vince and Vanessa knew each other. And even if they did, why would Vince tell her something as personal as that?! And if he told her that, what else did she know?

Vanessa mistook her confusion. "You know Vince? He's one of Cedric's roommates." She tried to smile shyly before adding, "We're talking."

Claudia didn't know which was more earth shattering—Cedric's condition or the fact that Vince was dating Vanessa. A memory came tumbling back to her mind. Vince had mentioned that he was seeing a girl in her residence hall, but no way did she ever imagine it was Vanessa, the Mouth, the Eternal Tongue Wagger, the Gossip Hound, the Busybody. Did he know what he'd stepped into?! Claudia had a quick visual image of Vanessa chattering away to Vince and him with his hands clamped over his ears, screaming at her to shut up.

"You're seeing Vince?" Claudia asked absentmindedly.

"Uh huh. I met him at a Sigma Phi Mu party. He's such a sweetie, don't you think?"

Claudia desperately wanted to get back to the conversation at hand. "Vanessa, you said Vince *told* you Cedric had AIDS?" Claudia grabbed Vanessa's arm and led her away from a couple of passing students. She tried to keep her voice low. The last thing she wanted to do was spread some vicious rumor, even if it was about Cedric.

"No, he didn't exactly tell me. I went over there to surprise Vince and I heard Cedric telling him about it. Their front door was open a little and I just walked in—Vince didn't know I was there. I said I found out *through* him, not from him. Vince doesn't like to talk about other people's business."

That's a relief. That means he probably didn't tell Vanessa about what happened with me and Cedric. That means that…wait a minute!! She just told me that Cedric had AIDS!! I was with him!! Does that mean that…?

"Oh, no." Claudia slipped down to the steps in front of the residence hall, feeling very weak and scared. Her heart felt ready to explode inside her chest—her mouth was dry. She could feel tears coming—she was going to lose it right there in front of Vanessa, whose hand she had in a death grip.

"It shocked me, too." Vanessa must have thought Claudia's reaction was out of concern for Cedric.

God, is this Your way of punishing me? For what I did to Marie? For giving myself away before marriage? Oh, no…not this!! Anything but this!! I'm sorry for what I did, Lord, but please don't punish me this way! I'll do better, I will!! But don't let me die!!

"...really kind of awful how she did it," Vanessa was saying.

"What?" Claudia was still in a daze and she was still trying to hold it together in front of Vanessa. She just wanted to get back to her room. She'd skip the biology exam.

"I was saying that the way Shamelle did it was awful, just leading Cedric on and then giving him that blow."

Nothing was making sense to Claudia anymore. "Who is Shamelle?"

"His girlfriend from back home," Vanessa explained. "Well, I should say his ex-girlfriend now. She's the one that gave it to him. And didn't even tell him about it."

Claudia sat statue-like—all the feeling had left her body. "Why?"

Vanessa rolled her eyes. "Well, Cedric told Vince that Shamelle was upset because he cheated on her and wasn't sending any child support. Just kind of left her high and dry. So the last time she came down he said she got even with him. Told him it would teach him a lesson for messing with her or something like that."

Claudia sat up straight. "The last time she came down?!"

"Well, that's when she supposedly gave it to him. The last time she was down. Last month. Did you know that he proposed to her? Brought her a ring and everything. Cedric was saying that she had tested positive for the HIV virus some time last semester and then passed it on to him. She told him never to come near her or her child again. I think he said she's going to marry some other guy. And she won't give Cedric the ring back."

The blood rushed back to Claudia's ears and head with tremendous force. Her fingers and toes started tingling again.

"Cedric's not looking too good these days. I think he was crying when he was telling Vince. But who's to say that Shamelle is telling the truth? She sure has him convinced, though. I mean, I guess he went and got a test, but I hear it can take ten years for the virus to even show up. Either way, I wouldn't want to live under all that."

Vanessa was going on about her other opinions on the matter, but Claudia was too busy having a mind celebration to hear her. Balloons and streamers were flying about in her head, and those crazy sounding, paper party horns were going off everywhere. Her mind party banner read: *CONGRATULATIONS, CLAUDIA!! YOU JUST DODGED A BULLET!!!*

"Claudia, where are you going?"

In her dazed, happy state, she had gotten up and started walking away from Vanessa without realizing it. "I have to get to my exam."

Vanessa looked a little offended. "But what about Cedric?"

"I feel sorry for him. I'm sorry he has to go through that. And Vanessa…" Claudia walked back up to her. "Please don't tell anybody else about this. I'm sure Cedric didn't want many people to know, and he did tell Vince in confidence what was going on."

Now she really looked offended. "I only told you because I thought you might want to know. You *were* seeing each other. I didn't think you would tell anybody, Claudia."

And you also wanted to find out if I had been with Cedric in that "special" way. You ain't slick. "I won't tell anybody. It's nobody business and you have a tendency to talk, Vanessa." Might as well be honest this close to the end of the semester. And she knew she was being slightly hypocritical, because she had sat and listened to Vanessa tell her what she knew. But doggone it, she really did need to know, no matter how the information came.

"Claudia, how can you say that to me?"

"Because it's the truth, Vanessa. And I think you know it." She didn't know where her courage was coming from, because the Claudia at the beginning of the year would not have told anyone about a character flaw. Then again, she had plenty of practice going off this semester. Heck, she was an old pro by now.

Vanessa opened her mouth to say something and from the expression on her face, it didn't look like it was going to be very nice. Then suddenly, she just shut it and poked her lip out much like a child.

"I'm not saying this to be mean," Claudia told her. "But I know Vince very well. You're right, he is a very sweet guy. And you're probably a very sweet girl, but you run your mouth. Seriously. Now you just told me that Vince doesn't like sharing other people's business—what makes you think he wants to date a girl who does?"

Vanessa's eyes got big over that. Claudia saw something click. She must really like Vince.

"Well, I feel awkward. I guess I need to say thank you for looking out for me," Vanessa said in a strange, low voice.

"No need to thank me, Vanessa."

"I'll just…keep what you said in mind, Claudia."

"Good. Hey, I'll see you around. I have to go."

"Good luck on your exam."

"Thanks." Claudia waved goodbye and walked away, feeling like she had made a difference. Vanessa wasn't a bad person. Who knew? Maybe they could even be friendly now that she knew where Claudia stood.

"Portia!!! Girl, I've been looking all over for you!!"

And maybe instead of winning that ten million dollars, she would inherit it from a rich relative. Claudia turned and saw Vanessa already deep in conversation with another unfortunate victim. She shook her head and walked a little faster. There was a plate of hot grits, bacon, eggs and a buttery biscuit with her name on it at the Appetizer.

Epilogue

Claudia had just finished her last final in Biology I late one afternoon when she ran into Cedric. It was like some weird déjà vu. Their paths had crossed earlier last semester after her biology class, only this time, he wasn't yelling out her name and he wasn't running up to her. When Claudia stepped out of the building, she saw him headed down the path in the direction of his apartment. He stopped when he saw her.

I'll just speak and get it over with, Claudia thought, surprised to find that a small tinge of resentment was stilling hanging around. She felt awkward, running into the guy whose apartment she'd nearly trashed, but what else could she do, not speak and come off as a bitter, jilted female?!

"Hi, Cedric," she greeted when she got to where he was standing still, like he was waiting for her. She continued right past him, not waiting to see if he would speak back.

"Hey, Claudia?"

She turned around.

"You got a minute?"

A minute for what?! She turned and came back up to him. This had to be about his apartment—had to. But didn't Vince tell her not to worry about it?

Claudia found herself staring at him. Wow—he didn't look so good. His eyes had a sad, tired look to them, and his glowing skin had a sickly, ashen tinge to it. And while they were together, Cedric always looked clean and crisp, right down to his shoes—now, his jeans and T-shirt were slightly wrinkled, and his sneakers had splotches of dirt all over them. This was not the black Adonis she had fallen head over heels for last semester—this looked like an average Joe who had some serious issues.

"Are you all right?" She found herself asking before she could stop it.

"Yeah, I'm cool. Been under the weather lately, but nothing serious."

"Sorry to hear that."

"I uh…" he looked off, chuckling and shaking his head. "I need to say something to you…"

She braced herself.

"I need to...apologize for playin' you like that. I messed up. Sorry." He shrugged.

She couldn't believe what she was hearing. Did Cedric just apologize to her?! Did he just admit he played her, he messed up. No...she was in some ghetto version of the *Twilight Zone*, because even with her limited experience with men, she knew that guys like Cedric did not say what he just said.

But maybe this HIV thing had grounded the brother. People died with AIDS; maybe that reality hit him like a ton of bricks. Strangely enough, she found herself feeling sorry for him.

"I...thank you, Cedric. Thank you for saying that," she told him. "I guess I need to say I'm sorry, too, for making a fool of myself and tearing up your apartment..."

"You were hurt—it's all good."

She nodded, feeling very relieved. And bold. "Can I ask you a question?"

He just looked down at her, waiting.

"Did you ever like Marie?"

Cedric looked off and chuckled again. "You pullin' from a brotha', aren't you?"

"You don't have to answer..."

"Nah...if I can say 'sorry', I might as well be real, right?" He looked down for a minute, then back up. "Marie was a sweet girl. Intelligent, ambitious, all that. And very attractive. Yeah, I was diggin' her..."

"Then why..."

"Why did I diss her and hook up with you? Ahma be straight up with you, Claudia. You're a fine sister. Fine. The kind that makes a brotha' thinks he has something when he's with her..." He stopped. "You don't get it, do you?"

Oh, yes...she did. By now, Claudia was no novice to this complexion thing. See, she had been through the Tallete McNeil complexion training camp, dealt with the rolled eyes and necks in high school, and lost her best friend and her virginity because of her hang-ups with her looks. And here Cedric was confirming what she had been trying to ignore for years. Complexion made a difference, but it wasn't her fault, nor was it her selling car. No, not anymore.

"You mean because of my light skin and wavy hair right?" She asked directly.

Cedric looked a little shocked. "Yeah...yeah—that's what I mean."

"And that's why you dissed Marie over me, right?"

Now Cedric looked a tad embarrassed. "Basically. I'm not sayin' you ain't a sweet girl..."

"No, it's o.k. Trust me, I've dealt with the complexion thing before. And I knew deep down that's the main reason you were with me. I'm glad you were honest enough to admit it, as sad as it is."

He still looked uncertain. "That don't bother you?"

"It did at one time, but I know that I'm more than a pretty face, trust me. A whole lot more."

He frowned up a minute, then grinned just a little. "Yeah, you're right. You and Marie—ya'll got a lot going for you."

"Thank you."

He looked at her again, smiling this time. "You got big plans this summer?"

"Well, I'll be out of town most of the summer. My family's going to the Bahamas."

"Word?! That's ah-ight!"

"How about you? I guess you'll be busy with football practice all summer, huh? Getting ready for next year?"

Cedric exhaled. "Nah...I won't be back here next year, Claudia. For football or anything else."

"What?!" Was this about the AIDS thing?!

"Yeah. I kinda messed up with my grades one too many times—I got kicked off. No scholarship, no school."

"I'm sorry to hear that, Cedric. So...what will you do now? I mean, you're still a junior, right?"

"Go back home, chill out with school for a little bit, spend some time with my son—get things in perspective, you know?"

She nodded. "How old's your son?"

"Almost four. I been away from him a lot, being in school, playing football and whatnot. Yup." Cedric exhaled again, looking off. "Well, I ain't gonna hold you up. You take care of yourself." He held out his hand to her.

Claudia took his hand, shaking it and looking directly into his eyes. "You too," she told him, meaning it. He nodded and walked away. She started back to the residence hall, feeling a mixture of sympathy, confusion and triumph. Wow...Cedric had a lot on his plate, a lot to deal with to be so young. Now, her experience with him didn't seem so traumatic, so useless. Sure, she'd lost something valuable, but now that seemed small compared to what she could have lost—her peace of mind, her education, her freedom—everything that Cedric had lost.

O.k., she needed to talk to Marie some about this thing with God, whom she felt kept protecting her for some reason. Maybe her best friend could shed some light on it. Claudia smiled, walking a little faster. Marie was going to get a kick out of this conversation!

MARIE

Saturday, May 9, 1991—Last day for all residents to be in the residence halls. Please turn your key into your Resident Advisor and leave your room door open for inspection.
Thank you,
Residence Life Office

"You ought to be ashamed of yourself, with this much stuff!" Marie was complaining to Claudia as she helped her pack. As usual, Claudia had waited until the last minute to get her stuff together. They had already packed two, huge suitcases and a trunk full of clothes, two medium-sized boxes filled with other stuff and now they were working on a third box. They had been at it for two good hours now. Marie had starting packing her things last week and now was ready to move. She was just waiting on her mother and sisters to come help her. Corrie had left early yesterday morning on her way home to Florida. She, Amanda, Chrissy and another girl were going to the apartments in the fall. She made Marie promise she would keep in contact with her over the summer.

"I am so glad I had a chance to room with you," she told Marie with tears in her eyes. "I'm going to miss you!"

"I'm going to miss you too, Corrie," Marie told her, giving her a hug.

They exchanged numbers and addresses. "You come visit me if you come to Florida this summer...after I get back from Canada." Corrie said.

"If I make it down that way, I will certainly look up my white sister."

Corrie screamed with laughter. "And if I come up your way, I'll drop in on my black sister!"

Marie had not seen or talked to Tony since that day in his apartment two weeks ago. That wasn't unusual—finals had been going on last week and nobody was keeping a decent schedule. He hadn't called her, either. And she actually found herself rushing back to the room when she was out to see if he had called. She finally broke down and called him earlier today, all set to demand an explanation from him, only to be told by one of his roommates that he

400

had already left for home—that's when she decided to go and help Claudia pack—she felt her newfound emotional volcano threatening to erupt again. Claudia had told her the other night, in all seriousness, that she was glad Marie was crying so much—she was beginning to think she wasn't capable of producing tears.

In a way, she felt bad for how she had went off on Tony—he looked so hurt when she told him what he was and was not. And now that she was about to begin what she thought would be a long, boring summer, the impact of Tony's actions hit her even harder. She would probably have too much time on her hands to sit around and think about the whole thing.

"Claudia, I'll be right back," Marie told her. "I need to go see if my family is here."

"Uh huh."

Marie headed across the lobby to her room, not really in a rush to go anywhere. But she knew if her family was there and didn't see her immediately, her mom would have a fit. No—no one was in the hallway—but what was that white envelope taped to her door?

Marie, the front of the envelope read. She didn't recognize the handwriting. It was probably just a goodbye letter or something that the RA's were sending around to their residents. As she walked in her room, she was all set to toss it in her book bag to read later, but something told her to open it.

Marie, the letter began. She sank to her bed—it was from Tony.

I know I'm the last person you want to hear from after the other day, but I did want to explain to you why I acted the way I did. You don't know how many times I called you, but I always hung up without leaving a message. I guess I just didn't have the courage to face you yet, but it made me feel like I was doing something to make the effort. First of all, beautiful, I want you to know that YOU DID NOT DO ANYTHING WRONG...it was me. I wasn't acting that way because of something you did—I was acting that way because of the guilt I felt. Marie, I liked you the day I first set eyes on you. You are so beautiful, inside and out. I don't even think you realize how special you are. You have a regal attitude about you, like a queen. Please don't think I'm just feeding you a line—I mean every word that I'm writing to you. And because I liked you so much, I really wanted to be able to get to know you—legally. What does this boy mean? I know you must be asking yourself that, so let me explain. The Bible says not to be unequally yoked together. What that means to me is that I can't consider a young lady even as a "special friend" unless she is saved. And it's not that I wanted you to come to Christ just so I could get to know you, but that was part of it. You know the best part of it—having a relationship with Him far outweighs any human relationship you can have, believe me. It's more important than any friendship, any family relationship, any boyfriend/girlfriend relationship...it is THE relationship. Marie, nothing is more important to me than my relationship with Him. Ever since I gave it over to Him right after I graduated high school, I have never experienced the high I get when I'm in His presence. I try so hard to live according to His Word, and I never want to do anything to displease Him—not intentionally, anyway. Now, of course, I make mistakes just like any other child of God 'cause we far from perfect, but I know He is faithful and just to forgive.

When you came over that day to apologize, I know you thought I was acting weird around my sister. See, I told her all about you and she was more than ready to meet this young lady I kept bragging about. But you have to know my sister—I love the girl dearly, and she is one of my best friends in this world, but she loves to embarrass me. When I came in and you were there, I was sure Vonjie had just told you everything I had said about you and I wasn't sure I wanted you to know just yet. I never mentioned it to you, but I used to see you with Cedric Carter. For a while, I thought that was your type—the handsome, popular athlete. I would think, "well, she won't even give a brother like me the time of day," but I thought it wouldn't hurt to be your friend. Then when I didn't see you two hanging anymore, I was happy. I always knew that you were too good for him and it looked to me like you realized it, too. And when you told me about Claudia dating Cedric, I knew something had went down between you two, but I didn't want to ask, so I just starting praying for your friendship. She's a sweet girl. You two care so much for each other—it wasn't nothing but the devil that tried to split you two apart. When you talked about giving her a shoulder to lean on that night, and she was dating a guy you used to be friends with or whatever, I thought, "this woman is amazing...and she just got saved!" I don't know how I would have handled that situation. But you...

Why do you think I got so angry that night after the Forum when you told me he grabbed you? Girl, I was hot—and that ain't God.

Now I know that brother outweighs me by a good one hundred pounds, but I must confess that I wanted to beat him down. When you called me that night, I didn't tell you the complete truth. I just told you I got mad because he put his hands on you, but I was also upset because I wasn't there to protect you. I know that sounds strange, but that's how I felt—I should have been there to protect you. And feeling that way just confirmed that I felt more for you than friendship, so I tried to walk away—from the feeling. Of course it didn't work. I want you to know that I WANTED to kiss you that day. I wanted to kiss you long before then, but I managed to keep myself in check. But when you told me you liked me…girl, I was turning cartwheels on the inside! I was thinking, "this beautiful, absolutely gorgeous, sweet, strong, intelligent young lady likes me… AND NOW SHE'S SAVED!! SHE'S SAFE!" I couldn't believe it. But Marie, kissing opens up a fleshly door that we can't go through. At least it does for me. I know I'm saved, but I'm also a man. I hope you understand what I'm saying. See, I had to get you out of that apartment before I lost my salvation. I know the way I did it was messed up, but I just reacted. I am so sorry I wasn't a gentleman about it. I don't blame you for going off on me like that, or thinking that I was a dog. I would have had some pretty bad thoughts too, if the shoe was on the other foot.

And you weren't the only one that was upset…when my sister came back and asked why you weren't there for dinner, I told her what happened. Marie, that girl went ballistic on me! I thought she was going to take a swing at me. She told me I'd better call you and get it right or she was going to do it herself. That's why I'm writing you this letter. The kiss I gave you was also very selfish. Marie, you are new to this walk—you are just starting your relationship with Him. You should have the benefit of getting to know Him without the extra burden of an outside relationship. I haven't been in it as long as others, but I have still been in it longer than you, which means I have experienced some things that you still need to experience. I've had the privilege of developing a relationship with Him and you deserve that same opportunity. I was a little selfish in wanting you to get to know Him, and I guess I just want to make it right by pulling back now so that you can know Him. I would love to call you my lady, Marie, even from Florida. But I would much rather call you my sister in the Lord FIRST.

Well, I have to close so I can study for my finals. I pray that you forgive my stupid actions and that we can still keep in contact over the summer. I left my phone number and address below. You can call me collect if you want, or just write me.

You will always be my lady, Marie.

Your friend and brother in the Lord ALWAYS, even if you never speak to me again,

Tony

Oh, here I go again, Marie thought as tears streamed from her eyes. So now she had her answer. And she felt like the world's biggest heel for the way she acted. *Lord, can you ever forgive me? I am so sorry. I dogged Tony out.* She carefully folded the letter again, stuck it back in its envelope and zipped it up in her purse. That was staying close to her and as soon as she got home, she was going to give the boy a call.

"Knock, knock," a male voice called from the other side of her door. Marie quickly wiped her eyes, opened the door, and nearly knocked the man down standing on the other side when she jumped and grabbed him in a strangle hug around his neck.

"Daddy!" she cried, giving him a juicy kiss on his bearded face.

"Hey, baby girl," he greeted her, squeezing her back.

"What are you doing here?"

"He came to help get you home, girl." her sister Rolanda answered with her usual sarcasm, pushing her way into the room. "You been at college for a whole year now and can't figure that out?"

Marie started to retaliate, but that wasn't who she was anymore. Instead, she walked over and gave Rolanda, who almost jumped straight up in the air, a hug. "It's good to see you, Rolanda."

Rolanda frowned. "What's wrong with you?"

"Nothing. Just happy to see my big sister."

"Oh, Lord. The girl done flipped down here, Daddy."

"Whew-girl, don't you move on the eighth floor next year. You know how I hate riding elevators." Marie's mother appeared in her room, fanning herself. She always claimed to be a tad claustrophobic, and would much rather take a flight of stairs than to be stuck in an elevator any day. But eight flights of stairs was a little too much, apparently.

"Hi, Mom…" Marie stopped on her way to hug and shock her mother, too. She did a double take. Her mother looked wonderful. She had always been a little on the heavy side, but she looked like she had dropped some weight, she had her thick hair cut in a nice style— and…gasp…she was wearing makeup!

"Momma, you look terrific!" Marie exclaimed, giving her mother a hug. To her surprise, her mother hugged her back and even gave her a quick kiss on the cheek.

Her mom couldn't hide her smile. "Thank you, honey. I had to do something. I got tired of looking in the mirror at myself."

Out of the corner of her eye, Marie saw her sister pointing and mouthing something to her. She stopped when Ms. Steeleton caught her.

"All right, Rolanda. Don't start that mess. Let's get some of this stuff downstairs. Marie, I'm happy to see you have everything packed up and ready to go—you got one of those pulley things to put this stuff on?"

"Claudia has one in her room. I'll go borrow it." Marie started out in the hallway. "Where's Davette?"

"Davette's working her second job. You know she's getting her own place, and now she's talking about getting another car because hers is giving her so much trouble. She said she would be home by the time we got there. She wants to see you." Ms. Steeleton realized that Marie treated Davette like a second mother. She didn't seem to mind, because she was just not as emotionally in-tune with folks as her older daughter. It wasn't her way.

"Marie." She had just reached the lobby when Rolanda stopped her. "I was trying to tell you about Momma and Dad in the room."

"What about them?"

"They trying to work things out…"

"Really?!" Marie wanted to shout—Rolanda quickly shushed her.

"Sshh, girl! Don't let Momma know I told you. Let her tell you herself."

"But what's going on, Rolanda?"

"Well, they been out on a couple of dinner dates—ain't that the grossest thing you ever heard? Our parents are dating. Anyway, you know Momma. She said ain't nothing etched in stone but that daddy sure is giving it his all. He been taking her to nice restaurants, bringing her flowers, coming over…why do you think she looks so different? Girl, Momma's wearin' perfume and everything."

Marie could not believe what she was hearing. She wanted to take a few laps around the lobby, shouting at the top of her lungs. She had been praying for her family to come back together—now it looked like it was happening. "Thank you, Lord," she said, noticing that her sister was looking at her strangely.

"Girl, what is wrong with you? Hugging on somebody, thanking God…you getting religious on us? Let me get back in this room before Momma comes out here looking for me. I know she knows I'm out here telling you something." Rolanda disappeared and Marie was beginning to think her summer wouldn't be so bad, after all.

"Claudia, guess what?" Marie flew into her room and grabbed her best friend by the shoulders. Claudia was in the middle of taping another box and dropped her role of heavy-duty tape. "My parents are dating!"

"What?! Are you for real? That's great!!" Claudia hugged Marie and both of them jumped straight up and down. "What happened? Tell me, tell me!"

"I don't know all the details myself, girl. But I'll find out from my sister. We'll see each other this summer. We'll talk. I need to borrow that cart so I can take my stuff down. I'll bring it back." She headed to the corner to retrieve the steel pulley that belonged to the maintenance man.

"Oh, o.k. Yeah, you can tell me all about it on the boat…"

Marie was just trying to maneuver the cart out into the hallway. "Boat? What boat?"

Claudia looked like a cat that had swallowed a canary. "Oh, didn't I tell you—you're going with me and my family to the Bahamas this summer."

Marie hadn't heard her correctly. "What did you say?"

"I said, you're going with us to the Bahamas this summer, Marie."

Marie's heart was pounding. "Claudia don't play with me…"

She laughed. "I am not kidding you. My dad told me and Harland that we could bring somebody along on the cruise—and his company is still paying for it! And check this out—we'll be there for *three weeks*, girl! In a double condo! We won't even have to see my parents unless we want to!"

Marie was standing as still as a statue. "Claudia, you're serious, aren't you?!"

Claudia was nodding and grinning at the same time. "Yes! We leave in two weeks. Oh, and check this out—after we get back, we'll be home for another two weeks and then we're all going to Florida for three weeks—we're going to Disney World! You're going, too! And it's not going to cost you a thing!! What do you think about that?!!"

But Marie was too busy screaming and jumping around Claudia's room to answer her question. Claudia grabbed her hands and joined her in her little praise ceremony. Then, a thought came to Marie's mind. "My mother...I have to ask her..."

Claudia was still jumping. "Girl, that's the best part—your mother already said you could go! My mother has already talked to her! You remember the day you went over to Tony's and I said I had something important to tell you? Well, I lied and said I forgot because I hadn't heard back from my mother yet. She called me while you were over Tony's and told me that your mother was o.k. with you going!"

Marie started screaming again and Claudia joined in. It was a good thing that Claudia was the only one left on her hallway, because they were doing some serious violating of the noise policy. They stopped screaming and Marie had a seat on Claudia's bed that she still hadn't stripped down yet. Claudia sat beside her. They looked at each other and screamed again.

"I'm going to the Bahamas...and Florida! I can't believe it! Thank you, Jesus!" Marie threw her arms up in the air. This had to be a gift from God. Here she was, wondering what in the world she was going to do this summer, and God had this present prepared for her all along. The majority of her summer was going to be spent on a cruise ship, on an exotic island, or chillin' out with Mickey and Minnie. And she might be able to visit Corrie and Tony while she was there. By the time she got back, it would almost be time for fall semester to start. Tony was right—God was GOOD.

"Girl, let me get ready...I mean, get back to my house, I mean my room...I mean...I don't know what I mean!" Marie was so excited she couldn't get her words straight. Claudia just laughed at her. "Wait a minute—why didn't you tell me I was going the night you found out?"

Claudia just shrugged. "I wanted it to be a surprise. And I just felt like keeping you in suspense until the last minute, all right?"

"You are rotten, Claudia! You *know* that trash is wrong!" Marie was flying high. She couldn't wait to get back to her room and thank her mother. She was sure her new relationship with her dad had a lot to do with her being so willing to release her youngest for almost the entire summer. She started back to her room.

"Marie..."

"Yes?"

"You forgot this." Claudia handed her a flat white piece of cardboard. Marie turned it over—*A Friend Like You is a Priceless Treasure*. It was her card that she had so angrily returned to Claudia.

O.k., if she cried one more time..."Thank you," she told Claudia, who also had tears in her eyes.

"I don't ever want this card returned to me again. You understand?"

"Yes, ma'am," Marie told her, grabbing her around the shoulder. "Come on and say hello to my family, girl."

The two made their way back to Marie's room. She told Claudia about the letter on the way there, and Claudia told her about Cedric apologizing—they had to stop in the lobby for another screaming session.

Epilogue

It turns out Davette wasn't working a second job, after all. When Marie walked through her front door, she was greeted with a banner strung across the entrance to the dining room that read, *Welcome Home, Marie! We Are So Proud of You!,* a table filled with some delicious looking home cooking, a white sheet cake that said *Welcome Back!* and Davette jumping straight up and down yelling, "Surprise!"

Marie ran to hug her oldest sister and looked back at her other family members, who were grinning like Cheshire cats. Davette had stayed home to finish the preparations, her mom explained, and this was just the family's way of showing how proud they were of this daughter and sister who was the first in the family to go to college.

Marie just let the tears flow then. They had never, ever done anything like this for her before, not even when she graduated from high school. She thought she would burst from all that she had been blessed with in one day.

Later on after the family had eaten, listened to Marie's stories about college (the experience with Cedric and Tony's kiss excluded, of course) and laughed together like they had never done in the past, Davette and Rolanda starting cleaning up and Marie's parents took cups of coffee out on the porch to "talk." Her mother looked like a giddy teenager. Marie hadn't seen her that happy in a long time.

"Momma, I need to call a friend long distance, is that o.k.? I can take it out of my allowance." Marie stuck her head out of the front door.

"Go ahead, Marie. Just don't be on the phone all night. And don't worry about your allowance. You save your money for when you go out of town."

"Oh yeah, Marie. I'll be by next week to take you shopping for your trip," her dad told her.

Marie couldn't resist. "That's if you aren't back home before then."

"Girl, get back in that house with that!" Her mother aimed a balled up napkin at her but Marie giggled and shut the screen before it could connect.

She went upstairs to her mother's room and flopped on her bed with the letter. She dialed the phone, waiting for it to ring on the other end.

"Hello? May I speak to Tony, please? Tony, this is Marie. I'm wonderful, how are you? Good. Yes, I got your letter…"

PERCY

He could not believe what he was doing. All he knew was that he wanted to get it over with as soon as possible. Percy knocked on Eugene's door one evening during finals' week.

"Can I borrow your ride, man? I'll fill it up with gas."

Eugene, who was studying, walked back to his desk and turned over the keys without even looking up from his book. Percy couldn't believe how easy it was.

"Are you sure, Eugene? I'll be careful with it."

Eugene looked up at him with a small smile on his face. "It's o.k., Percy. It's just a car."

Percy nodded and smiled back. "Preciate that, man. Hey, let's hook up for lunch or something before school lets out."

"Sounds like a winner to me."

Sounds like a winner…he definitely talked a little different, a little nerdy. But he was a nice guy; he definitely wasn't the Uncle Tom Percy had first labeled him to be.

Eugene's car was an older model Nissan Sentra, but compared to Allen's tin can on wheels, it was a Rolls Royce. The AC and the radio worked in Eugene's and at the same time. Percy adjusted the radio station as he drove off campus and onto the highway, glancing down at a piece of paper that told him how to get to where he was going. He didn't tell anyone what he was doing—not even Darryl, who had given him the directions in the first place.

"Who do you know on that side of town, Percy?" Darryl asked when Percy called him.

"A dude I need to get some information from," Percy told him.

"Be careful," Darryl warned. "That ain't the side of town you need to be caught in—especially in the evening."

Once Percy neared his destination, he could see what Darryl meant. A street sign pointing to the right guided Percy right where he needed to go, and he turned into a wooded area with two big stone walls forming an entrance. "Doe Run Lake Estates" the wording on the wall read. This was it—this was a neighborhood where a black man could be arrested just for driving through. Percy drove slowly and gawked at the huge houses that were bigger than three houses in Jackson Park put together. A lot of the houses had three or four car garages that probably held Benzes, Beamers, Lexuses and big, overpriced SUV's. He couldn't take his eyes off of the perfectly manicured lawns with grass so green it looked fake. Most of the houses had the curtains thrown open with the lights on inside, unashamedly showcasing crystal chandeliers, long, swooping staircases and heavy, cherry furniture.

People actually lived in paradises like this?! He had seen pictures of this stuff in magazines and on television, where, once a week, a man with a funny accent showed lower income kids like Percy what they couldn't have because they weren't rich or famous, but he never thought that it was this close to home.

There were a few people out in the twilight. Some were wrapping up a jogging session, some were walking dogs and others were chitchatting with neighbors as they warned their active children to stay out of the road. No matter what they were doing, nearly all paused to stare at the unfamiliar black man in his older model economy car, cruising by. They knew that neither he or his vehicle belonged in their pristine neighborhood.

The long road he was on finally ended in a cul-de-sac of sorts and according to the address he had, the house in question had to be somewhere in the bend. The cul-de-sac was actually a steep hill, and at the bottom of the hill behind a large, three story mansion was a huge lake that was most likely responsible for the neighborhood's impressive name. The numbers on the mailbox at the top of the steep driveway told Percy that he had found what he was looking for. Slowly, he coasted Eugene's Sentra down the driveway, feeling certain he was going to slip and end up in that lake behind the house.

As he neared the house, lights came on from nowhere, illuminating the driveway and the front porch. It really didn't look like anyone was home, but someone had to have turned on all those lights. Percy was surprised to find that he was nervous—nervous about being in this neighborhood and nervous about what he was doing. *What am I doing here?!!* He took a deep breath and opened the car door. His slow, deliberate steps led him to the front of the house with its tall, white columns. Three marble steps took him to the big, heavy-looking oak door that boasted a brass, lion's head door knocker, and on the side was a small, marble doorbell surrounded by that same brass. He pressed it and sent a melody of bongs vibrating through the house. Somewhere behind the door, Percy heard the "rup,

rup, rup" of a dog's bark. There was the sound of dog nails clicking on the floor and the bark came closer.

"Anastasia! Come away! Come, girl!" a woman's voice ordered.

Anastasia—Percy pictured a small to medium-sized dog with long ears and a golden coat. The door slid open; the wide, green eyes of a woman somewhere in her late forties or early fifties stared out at Percy behind the glass screen door, taking in his face and appearance. For this little field trip, he had chosen his outfit with care. He was wearing a lightweight, dark blue sports coat with tan slacks, a tie and his Sunday shoes. He felt like a sell-out, dressing up just to go to a certain part of town, but he could pick up his racial principles after he did what he had to do.

The woman tried to smile at him, but her eyes held confusion. "Hello—May I help you?"

"Uh, good evening, ma'am. My name is Percy Lyles. I'm here to see Randall. Is he available?" Ebonics wasn't the only language he could parley.

Anastasia "rup rupped" at him from around the woman's legs. Just as Percy had guessed, the dog was a long-eared, golden-furred cocker spaniel.

"Heel, girl," the woman told her, but Anastasia was too excited to obey. She hit the screen with her front paws, barking and making such a ruckus until her owner finally opened the door and let her out. Anastasia moved towards Percy, sniffing at his shiny shoes. Those checked out, so she moved her wet nose up his leg to his hand. *If you smell wrong, I have no problem biting you.*

"I attend Hamel University with Randall," Percy explained further.

"Oh—all right. I'll tell him that you're here..." She was still eyeing Percy with uncertainty. "Is he expecting you?"

"No, ma'am, and I do apologize for the intrusion. I wanted to speak with him briefly about some issues of interest concerning the school and his fraternity."

By that time, Anastasia had grown bold enough to lick his fingers. Percy reached down and rubbed her head, receiving a longer, wetter licking for the attention.

The woman's wide-eyed look grew wider. "She usually doesn't do too well with strangers," she said, sounding bewildered.

413

Michele R. Leverett

"I like animals," Percy told her, stooping to rub the excited dog under her chin.

"Well—Percy, is it?"

"Yes, ma'am…"

"Won't you come in?" The woman opened the screen again and allowed him to enter.

So the dog decides who gets in and who doesn't. I guess if Anastasia would have bit my hand off, I would have been waiting for the ambulance outside on the porch, bleeding.

"Why don't you wait right here in the living room and I'll get Randall for you. By the way, I'm Alyse, Randall's mother." Alyse offered her hand. Percy shook it quickly and gently.

"I'm very pleased to meet you, ma'am." Good thing his mother had raised her children to have impeccable manners. Even though Randall's mother had introduced herself by her first name, Percy would stick with "ma'am" just in case she was a single mother or still used her maiden name, which he assumed was Bennett, since that's the last name the school paper listed as Randall's, and was what he looked under to find his address in the Student Directory.

Alyse left to find her son and Anastasia lingered behind for a moment, looking like she was torn between following her master or playing with her new friend. Family ties finally won out. *I'd love to stay and chat, but it's this loyalty thing—you understand.* She clicked down the hallway after her owner. Percy studied the room he had been ushered into, which was big enough to sit his living room and kitchen in with room left over—plenty of room left over. Heavily framed pieces of artwork with somber looking people in them covered the walls. Crushed velvet, Victorian furniture with deep mahogany arms and legs were flanked by dark mahogany end tables. There was a tall, matching bookcase that fit into the perfect V shape of a wall corner. Percy looked down, wondering why he felt like he was walking on a cloud. Below his feet was the plushest, deep red carpet he had ever stepped on. He felt like taking his shoes off and wiggling his toes in it.

He wanted to sit, but the hostess hadn't directed him to do so. She just said, "wait in the living room." He could only imagine how she was announcing her son's company: *Randall, there's a young Nee-gra boy here to see you. He says he's a student at Hamel. I didn't realize you knew any Nee-gras. You don't? I'll call the police.*

414

Percy's eyes caught some pictures on the massive, marble and stone fireplace mantel There was an older picture of Randy's family—a man that he assumed was his father—the man strongly reminded Percy of someone...someone he felt like he knew. There was also a much younger and very pretty Alyse, two young boys, an older girl and a baby girl grinning from Alyse's lap. In fact, everyone in the portrait was grinning except for the youngest boy, who was standing beside his mother, looking sad, confused, angry or something unpleasant. He looked stiff and uncomfortable in his little blue sailor suit with a white sailor cap. Percy chuckled, thinking he would have screamed bloody murder if his mother would have tried to put him in a get-up like that when he was younger. No wonder ole' boy looked so unhappy.

The next picture showed only the children, a little older now. The young sailor suit victim was now wearing an outfit that was identical to the one his older brother was wearing, with a wide, striped tie. Though he looked like he was now trying to smile with his mouth, his eyes still held that same troubled look from the previous portrait. After these, there were various, individual pictures of each family member. The children's pictures had matured into graduation photos, prom portraits, wedding pictures of the oldest girl, and one of her with whom Percy assumed was her husband and a baby boy. There was a large group photo of Randy sitting with other smiling, rich looking young men around a large golden plague: Lambda Sigma Fraternity, Hamel University, 1989. Funny, there didn't seem to be any pictures of the youngest boy after the first two...

"Hello."

Percy turned at the sound of a voice behind him. There stood Randy What's-His-Name—Bennett, actually, looking at him in curiosity and confusion. Alyse stood behind him, and Anastasia could not resist coming back with them to give her new friend another lick to his hand. *O.k., so I like you. I'm not sure how my masters feel, but you smell all right to me.*

Like his mother, Randy was surprised at the dog's friendliness. "It looks like Anastasia made a new friend," he commented.

"She's a good dog," Percy said.

"Randy, I'll just leave you and Percy alone," Alyse commented, a cross between a statement and a question.

"Sure, Mom. Thanks."

"Anastasia, let's allow these young men to talk. Come, girl."

Anastasia looked reluctant, for she was having such a joyous time with Percy. She threw Percy a remorseful look, then tipped out of the living room and down the hall after Alyse. Percy's feelings were a little mixed too, being in the same room with a racist. Here was the man that spearheaded the whole Plot incident and he, like Allen, was a little rich kid. But he fought against his anger because he needed some information. And Randy just might need him, too.

"I'm afraid I don't recognize you…"

"Percy."

"Percy. My mom said you needed to see me." Randy was smiling and gestured with his hand toward the crushed velvet, antique looking couch. Percy perched on the edge of it and Randy sat on a matching chair diagonally from him.

"You don't know me," Percy told him. I'm a member of the African-American Awareness Coalition at Hamel."

Randy nodded, but looked confused.

"We had some property destroyed by members of your fraternity."

Randy dropped his smile. He looked like he was about to stand but changed his mind. "We've already sent out apologies on that," he explained. "And like we said in court, we're willing to make restitution…"

"I know all that, Randy. That's not why I'm here."

"Then why are you here?"

Percy reached inside his sports coat and produced the key chain. He laid it on the mahogany and glass coffee table in front of him.

Randy stared at Percy, then reached over for the key chain. He frowned down at it, then up at Percy. "I'm afraid I don't get it."

"That key chain belongs to my roommate, Allen. Allen Downing." Percy watched as immediate recognition washed over Randy's face. Something else was there, too—it looked like disgust.

"I don't know any Allen," Randy told him, giving back the key chain. Good—Percy thought he might try to keep it.

"Sure you do, Randy. He is or was a member of Lambda Sigma, right? Otherwise, why would he have this key chain?"

"I can't answer that for you, but I don't know him."

At least Allen had been telling the truth about one thing—there was no love lost between him and the fraternity. That much was

416

evident. Randy was trying to keep a poker face, but from the minute Percy had mentioned Allen's name he had turned as red as a lobster.

Now he was standing, apparently ready to end Percy's visit. "I'm sorry you wasted your time, Perry…"

"Percy…"

"Sorry—Percy. I don't know where your roommate got a Lambda Sigma key chain from, but I'm not familiar with him. You know you can get just about anything you want put on a key chain."

Yeah, Randall—good one. Percy stood up too and moved toward the entrance. "Well, I guess it was a waste of time, then. I just thought if you could help me, I might be able to piece together some things about your fraternity house but you guys probably have that under control…"

"Hold on." Randy actually grabbed Percy's arm to prevent his exit. Percy looked down at his hand and back up at Randy. He got the message and let go quickly. "What do you mean by that?"

"Your house was burned…"

"Uh, yeah. Everybody kinda knows that…"

"Uh, yeah…but everybody doesn't kinda know who did it," Percy said, mocking Randy's sarcastic tone.

"Are you saying you do?"

"I'm not saying anything until you tell me about Allen." Percy's voice rose slightly in his frustration. He chilled just in case Alyse was around the corner.

"Look, if you have information on the house, it is your moral duty to report what you know, Percy," Randy told him firmly, like a parent.

Was he for real?! Percy cocked his head to the side like Anastasia probably did when she was confused. Did he mention something about a moral duty?! *You're doggone skippy, Randy. I forgot about my moral duty—thank you so much for bringing me into the light. I'll mosey on down to the police station right now and fulfill my "moral obligation" as a citizen of these fine United States, who has treated our people wonderfully for years.*

"What?! Like you did when you and your moral, upright race loving vandals destroyed our property? Man, be for real! You and your boys opened up the can of worms. Don't talk to me about being moral. Ya'll set the rules to this game—we didn't!" Percy was really ready to leave then. Whatever happened from there on out just

417

happened, because if he had to spend one more minute in the same room with this hypocrite he was going to be in trouble for much more than just trespassing. Besides—he had probably ruined any chances he had of Randy's cooperation. He headed for the entrance again and Randy's voice stopped him.

"O.k.—maybe I do know Allen. Now what?"

Percy almost let out an audible sigh of relief. Randy sat back down in his chair, looking at Percy expectantly and anxiously. Percy stuck his hands in his pockets and stood near the massive fireplace.

"You're right—Allen was a member of Lambda Sigma about a year and a half ago."

"What happened?" Percy wanted to know.

Randy snickered, sounding very bitter. "What did *he* tell you?"

"He said the fraternity booted him out because of his views on race relations."

Randy snorted in that same bitter fashion. "Good one, Allen!"

"I didn't believe it, either. Race relations just doesn't seem to be on the agenda for Lambda Sig."

Randy looked uncomfortable, but didn't address that dig.

"So what's the real reason Allen got kicked out?"

"Allen just was not suited for the fraternity, Perry…"

"Percy…"

"He just wasn't a good fit, that's all."

"Nah, man…that ain't all."

"Look, that's privileged information!"

Percy didn't say a word. Didn't they just go through this song and dance? He just stared at him.

Randy gave up. "Allen just came unplugged. He just went postal—out of control. We couldn't even reason with him anymore. Not like that's the first time he ever…" Randy stopped suddenly, like he had said too much.

"You sound like he isn't your favorite person," Percy noted, helping himself to a seat again.

"He isn't. If I had my way about it, he wouldn't have gotten in the fraternity in the first place."

"Then why'd you let him in?"

"Let's just say I didn't have a choice."

"What—did he have something on you? Was he blackmailing you?"

Randy stood again. "Look—our agreement was to tell you what I knew about Allen. I did. He's a mental case from Nebraska. Now you tell me—what do you know about the fire at our house?"

"Nothing, except I think Allen had something to do with it."

"What?!"

"I think Allen's your arsonist."

"Allen?!"

"Yeah—why are you shocked? You just said he was a mental case and had a good reason, right?"

Randy shook his head. "No way…"

"He all but confessed, Randy. I talked to him yesterday."

"No."

"I found some evidence in his trunk!"

"What?!"

The evidence wasn't going to make sense to him—not with out telling Randy that he and the other board members were there. Percy took a deep breath and stood up. "I saw him do it—with my own eyes!"

Both of them just stood there, quietly staring at each other. Percy had just implicated himself—Randy had just discovered the full extent of Percy involvement. They stared at each other in disbelief until a noise at the front door broke the tension. Anastasia came from somewhere in the house to investigate, rup rupping all the way. Randall's mother was at her heels, as if the dog needed a chaperone at all times.

"Hello, dear," Alyse greeted someone at the door. Percy looked out in the hallway and almost fell over. In walked a tall man that, with the exception of the gray in his hair and the small wrinkles around his eyes, looked like the spitting image of…

"This is one of Randy's friends from school. Percy, isn't it?" Alyse asked.

"Yes ma'am," Percy replied, staring at the tall stranger.

Alyse continued with the introductions. "This is Randall's father, Percy."

The man smiled and extended his hand. "Nice to meet you, Percy. *Doug Downing.*"

Downing?!!! Percy froze in disbelief. The slightly confused looked in Doug's eyes jolted him and he remembered to put his hand out and shake.

No wonder he had looked so familiar in that picture. This man looked like Allen about twenty or thirty years from now.

"Hi, Dad," Randy greeted, sounding reluctant.

His dad nodded and smiled briefly at him. "Listen, I won't keep you young men from your visit. Nice to meet you, Percy."

"You also, sir."

Alyse, Doug and Anastasia disappeared down the hall. Percy turned to Randy, who looked very much like a child with his hand caught in the cookie jar.

"Allen's your brother?" Percy almost whispered.

"Afraid so."

"But he told me he was from Nebraska..."

"We are. We moved here about twelve years ago."

"Twelve years?!"

"Yup."

"But your last name's not..."

"I know—I use my mother's maiden name at school."

Percy couldn't believe his ears! *Brothers*?! "Why...why didn't you tell me that when I first mentioned him?!"

Randy just shrugged, looking uncomfortable. "You feel like grabbing a cup of coffee?"

They ended up at a doughnut shop not far from campus. Percy opted to trail Randy, not really knowing if he could or even wanted to try and hold a conversation on the way to wherever they were going—it would also allow him the freedom to leave at his discretion. He was still reeling from the news that Randy and Allen were actually brothers! What in the Sam Hill was going on?! And why did Randy keep it such a big secret, because Allen surely never mentioned his relations with his brother, either?! *He must have been the sad looking kid in the picture*, Percy rationalized as he followed behind Randy's 1990 Jeep.

While they were in line, Percy realized that he had only a couple of bucks on him but it didn't matter, because after Randy ordered something called a "Swiss Vanilla Mocha Delight" and a couple of glazed doughnuts, he told the cashier to add Percy's order in with his.

"No, that's all right..."

Randy sidled over to whisper to him. "It's not charity, Percy. I'm just trying to be hospitable. Can you drop your pride for a minute?"

Percy looked at him, then shrugged. He ordered coffee and a sour cream doughnut. Maybe he was being a bit prideful.

They found a seat in the almost empty shop and Randy leaned over his drink.

"That smells pretty good," Percy commented.

Randy sipped his drink and wiped whipped cream off his nose. "It's the best. It's all I order when I come in here. You should try one."

"Nah...I'll stick with plain old coffee." Percy sipped his coffee and felt an immediate rush of adrenaline hit his head. Whoa...

"So you're my little brother's roommate, huh?" Randy asked around a mouthful of doughnut.

"Yeah. Hey, why the big secret about him being your brother?"

Randy shrugged, tearing another small piece from his doughnut. "Allen and I don't exactly get along, Percy. My brother has a bitterness towards me that I can't explain."

"So that might explain the house..."

"I never said I believed you on that!" Randy immediately corrected.

"But it's possible." *O.k., don't push him too far.* "Sorry...go ahead."

"I'm sure you see a side of Allen that makes you think he's the happiest guy in the world, or that he's all about righting the wrongs of this world. But Allen's got another side to him. If things don't go his way, he can be very...mean." To Percy's surprise, Randy leaned over and used his hands to part a section in his hair. Behind the hair was an ugly, long, red scar. He straightened back up. "Allen did that when he was seven years old. I was nine. We were outside playing and Allen wanted a toy that I had. I didn't give it to him and when I turned my back, he floored me with a heavy tree branch. Knocked me unconscious. It took thirty stitches to sew my head back up."

"What did your parents do?" Percy asked, thinking that if Paul did that to him, his mother would be locked up.

"What, to Allen?" Randy snorted. "They sat him down and told him why it was wrong to hit his brother. Oh, and they made him apologize. *Made* him."

"They didn't...they didn't discipline him?"

"Who—*my* parents?! No, my parents use the *Brady Brunch* approach to discipline. They talk. They even got upset with me and

421

said I provoked him by not sharing—can you believe that?! *I* provoked *him*. It's my fault, and I'm the one with thirty stitches in my head."

Percy could almost touch his hostility. Randy was bearing a lot to a person who was a stranger until about an hour ago and a person who he might be prejudiced against. But he sounded like he needed to get this thing with his brother off his chest, and his audience was not his primary concern at the moment. Anastasia could have been perched on the other side of the table, tongue hanging out and ears perked up for all he cared.

"That wasn't the only time he lost control," Randy continued. "My parents took him to psychiatrists, psychologists and they even tried a psychic once to see if there was some 'hidden' meaning to his behavior." His shook his head and sipped his coffee again. "And I can't tell you the number of times my parents either blamed me or expected me to cover up for his behavior. I think the only time they sided with me over Allen is when I threw him out of Lambda Sig after my father practically threatened me to bring him in so he could follow in the proud tradition of the Downing men."

"Your father was a Lambda Sig?"

"*And* my grandfather. That's what the men did in my family—you go to college, you join Lambda Sigma. I guess Allen had no choice."

Or you, Percy thought, surprised to find that he was beginning to understand Randy, and perhaps even sympathize with him. "But why did you kick him out?" he asked, hoping he had caught Randy in a weak moment.

He had. "Allen was embezzling money out of the treasury. I made him the fraternity treasurer. I thought it was a low-key position, but it sounded 'important' enough to my dad. Important enough to impress people." Randy looked Percy in the eye. "I guess you're wondering why a little rich kid like Allen would be stealing money from the fraternity?"

Percy shrugged. That's precisely what he was thinking. "Why did he?"

"For the attention, Percy. He thought it was a great big joke. He really didn't think he'd done anything that terrible—but he never does. Not even when he was nine and we had to move because he..." Randy clammed up, shoving more doughnut in his mouth.

Percy let him finish chewing. He was already getting a pretty good picture of the Downing family. "What does your dad do?"

"He owns four nursing homes," Randy told him. "What about yours?"

"My ole' man's in prison," he said, expecting shock to register on Randy's face. He braced himself, ready to jump on the defense again. Instead, Randy just shrugged.

"Sounds like we both got skeletons in the closet, huh?"

"I guess so," Percy replied, feeling strangely grateful for his reaction, and little more comfortable talking to him.

"What'd he do?"

"He beat up a man that tried to hurt my mother. He almost killed him."

"Can't say that I blame him," Randy told him. "If someone tried to hurt my mother, I'd be arrested, too."

"Yeah?" Percy found himself smiling.

"Sure. My mother or my sisters. They'd have to throw me under the jail cell."

Percy found himself laughing. He never thought that white people felt the same way he did about family—about mothers, especially. "I hear you."

"You have any sisters?"

"One. She's over in Korea with the Army. I got a little brother, too—Paul."

"Hope he's not like Allen."

No, but he was well on his way, Percy thought, remembering the altercation at home. There was one blessing in his situation—at least his mother wasn't trying to cover up for what Paul was doing. By now, Paul should be wearing a long brown coat with a hood and a rope belt, taking a vow of silence.

Randy finished off his coffee with one big swig. "So tell me, Percy. You say you saw Allen set fire to our house?"

Percy was back on his guard, thinking the pleasant conversation was a set-up to this. "Maybe."

"Maybe? You told me back at the house that you saw him for sure."

"Did I say that?"

Randy laughed. "Percy—I'm not going to turn you over to the cops or anything. Why should they believe me? It would be my word

423

against yours. Who's going to believe that the two of us sat down and had a conversation, anyway?"

Now that made sense. To the black students at Hamel, Lambda Sig were a bunch of racist. In fact, Percy couldn't even believe he was sitting in a doughnut shop with their leader, sipping coffee and sharing family secrets. "I *might* have seen him. I *might* have been in the house that night."

"What *might* you have seen?"

"I *might* have seen a dude in a black ski mask throwing gas on the outside, then limping away. I found a gas can and a mask in the back of Allen's trunk. And Allen had a burn mark on his arm. I'm sure you've seen it. Then he gave me some speech on how blacks have suffered for years and that whoever set the fire was a hero for the black people or something. It sounded kinda psycho to me."

Randy's eyes slid shut as he pounded his fist on the small table, making it jar. He let out a few explicatives then banged the table again.

"Are you all right?" Percy asked.

"No—Percy, can you keep a secret?"

With all that had been revealed, why not? "Sure..."

Percy shoved the last bag in his mother's trunk and closed it. "Can I drive?" he asked.

She didn't hesitate. "Sure, but be careful, Percy."

Percy got behind the wheel of the loaded down car and eased their way off of Hamel's campus, glad to be going home. This had been one of the most interesting and challenging years of his young life, and he was glad it was over—almost.

"Hey, how come he gets to drive and I can't, Ma?" Paul protested from the back seat. Percy was delighted to see his little brother coming through the doorway of his room, looking like he'd lost some weight and some sleep, but smiling none the less. He gave Percy a cautious grip before Percy gave him a brief bear hug and pounded him on his back. His mother smiled, looking like she was fighting back tears at the reunion. After that, they just quietly started carrying boxes and clothes downstairs.

"Because you just got your license and you need more practice," his mother told him.

"Ma, I got plenty of practice."

"You might not want me to know that, boy," she warned him, and Paul shut up, getting the message. Paul had driven a few stolen cars, hanging around his druggie crowd.

"So, are you excited about England?" His mother asked, as he pulled onto the highway.

England. He had so much to do before he got ready. He almost felt guilty because he was still going, but not guilty enough to call it off. Technically, all he did was trespass, because he didn't have time to break anything in the house, which is exactly what he had told Randy the night they had coffee.

The house—that was another bombshell. After Randy told Percy how his family had to move from Nebraska because Allen had set fire to his neighbor's horse stable, nearly killing the horses whose owners risked their lives pulling the animals to safety. Randy told Percy that when the fire started and the family couldn't find Allen, he went out and find him standing in their backyard, watching the fire like a zombie.

"It was like he was…worshipping it, Percy," Randy told him.

The Downing family paid for a new horse stable, packed up and moved east, away from the small town where the stigma of an unstable son was sure to linger forever.

He finally told Percy that he believed Allen started the house fire, because he had threatened Randy after he got booted out of the fraternity. He wasn't trying to kill anybody that much Randy was sure of, because he knew the guys were going to Miami that weekend for a convention.

And Allen—his father came through for him, again. Randy saw Percy on campus during finals and told him that he had shared his suspicions with his father, who immediately promised to pay and have the house rebuilt, and make restitution to each of the brothers that lived there. The last word Percy heard was that the house fire was ruled an "accident" by some unknown faulty wiring or something, and that new house was scheduled to be finished by next spring. Allen had gotten away with almost murder—again.

Percy had also made up his mind to drop his affiliation with the Tri-AC, who seemed to be growing further and further apart after the house burning. Carlos was still determined to win his election for Student Body President, Tamal still had a beef with Percy, but knew better now than to run up in his face, and Darryl had been asked to campaign for President of the BSU, replacing Terrell, who was graduating in two weeks. Terrell had "put in a good word for him," as Darryl put it, recognizing his commitment to improve the status of black students, despite the rivalry between the two groups. Darryl was also dropping his affiliation with the Tri-AC and agreed to run for BSA president.

But the thing that impacted Percy the most was his conversation with Randy, who was also graduating that month. That was the first time he had sat across from a white person who wasn't his teacher or an authority figure, and shared experiences. White people had issues just like he did. They had estranged relationships with parents, fought with brothers and sisters, covered up embarrassing situations and felt bitterness, anger, resentment, hostility, sadness—hopelessness.

"Good luck to you, Percy." Randy had told him in parting that night, shaking his hand. "I'm glad I got a chance to talk to you."

"Yeah, you too, Randy." Percy replied, meaning it.

Pieces of his life were starting to come together, but there was one more situation he had to handle, one more bit of housecleaning he had to do before he flew overseas. And he needed Mr. Dell's help to do it.

Epilogue

Percy sat down on the hard, plastic cushion, thankful he didn't plop down like he started. The non-resistant sofa would have done him some serious harm. *What did you expect? Plush furniture?! You're in a prison,* he thought to himself. He still couldn't believe that this is where his father was—behind bars, at least for six more months. Then he was coming home, but Percy didn't want to wait until then.

He looked up just in time to see the heavy gray door of the visitation room wheeze open, and a handful of inmates dressed in denim work shirts and jeans enter. They looked around the room almost in sync, then made their way to their respective visitors, who greeted them with hugs, squeals of delight and loud hellos. No one came Percy's way, so he figured his father wasn't among this crowd.

"Shoot it! Shoot it!" Percy looked over at the loud commotion, and Mr. Dell was practically jumping straight up and down in a small corner that had a couch and a big floor model television set. He saw Percy staring and smiled sheepishly.

"My boys are smoking over here, Percy," he told him, referring to the NBA playoff game he was watching. "I got to keep them encouraged."

Percy laughed. "Don't let 'em lose, Mr. Dell."

Mr. Dell shook a fist at him and turned his attention back to the game. Percy realized how fortunate he'd been to have a Mr. Dell in his life, who did not hesitate for one second when Percy came to him the day after he got home for the summer, asking if he would take him on the two hour drive to see his father. He refused the gas money Percy offered him for the trip, and even packed a lunch for them from his hot bar in the store—barbecued ribs, cornbread, turnips and fresh iced tea. Since Mr. Dell was driving he didn't get to eat much, but Percy smacked his lips and licked his fingers up the highway, which would have driven his mother bonkers.

"Use a napkin, and stop sucking your teeth like an old man with loose dentures," she would constantly tell him. Mr. Dell wasn't that persnickety. He just kept reminding Percy that there was enough food there for two people, so please leave him some.

Percy was about to ask Mr. Dell about the score when he felt a shadow over him. He looked up and a tall, slightly gray haired man with sad eyes and a thick mustache was staring down at him. Percy immediately jumped up and looked closer. The complexion, the eyes, the shape of the nose—he was looking at himself twenty-five years from now. A glance down at the nametag clipped to the man's shirt confirmed his suspicions—Lyles, Edward. He was face to face with his father, after ten years.

He couldn't move; he couldn't speak. He could only stare in disbelief. Ten years had passed between them. Ten years of growing up with bitterness, anger, heartache, good times, bad times—and now Percy was staring at the man he used to look up to. He wanted to laugh, cry, holler, ask questions—but all he could do was stare stupidly at him.

His father looked like he had the same emotions running through him. He reached up to rub his face like he had to remove the feeling from it. He sniffed, then blinked at Percy like he had just appeared before him.

"Percy?" he asked in a soft deep voice that was oh so familiar to Percy. Percy managed to nod his head. He nodded again, just in case his dad didn't catch the first one.

A slow grin spread over Edward Lyles face. He chuckled in disbelief. "Son...is that you, all grown up?!"

This time Percy opened his mouth. "Uh, yeah, yeah. It's me." He kept looking at his dad, trying to picture him ten years ago, when he stormed out of the house and almost beat his mother's boss to death for trying to devalue her. He tried to envision him living with relatives and working on the sly, just so he could send money back home to take care of his family. He saw him smiling, loading him, Monica and his pregnant mother in the car for ice cream after dinner, always saving the last part of his cone for his son who loved ice cream so much. And then he saw himself at that moment, throwing his arms around his dad, crying like he had never cried before, and his dad squeezing him back and crying just as hard. "I'm sorry dad..."

His dad sat him back down on the couch. "It's all rig..."

"No, no...those things I said over the phone...Ma told me what happened. She told me why you were here."

Edward nodded. "I'm glad you know. I tried to keep it from you kids..."

"Why, Dad?" Percy asked. "You were trying to protect Ma—I would've understood that."

"I didn't want you kids to think that violence was the way to solve your problems."

"But Mr. Brant tried to …hurt my mother." He couldn't even say the other word, not in connection with his mother. It was still too painful.

Mr. Lyles shook his head. "What I did was wrong. Yeah, at the time I was angry—I wanted to kill him, I did because like you said, he put his hands on my family. I did what I did for the right reason, but look what it cost me—it cost me ten years with my family. I didn't get to see my children…" He stopped, looking off in the other direction. "Violence is not the answer Percy—it never is. The cost is too high. I understand your anger at me. You were standing up for your mother, for your family, just like I thought I was. I can never fault you for that."

"I can't fault you either, Dad." Percy told him.

His dad turned back to look at him, tears in his eyes. "That means a lot to me—son." He grabbed his hand and squeezed it. "I'm proud of you. Your mother did a good job with you."

Percy looked over at Mr. Dell and saw him watching them, smiling and trying to act like he wasn't watching. "She had some help," He told his father, nodding in Mr. Dell's direction.

His dad stood up. "Is that Oscar Dell?" He asked loudly.

Mr. Dell came over to the twosome and patted Percy's father on the back. "Lyles—you look good! Whatcha know good?"

"Oscar, it sure is good to see you! Man, it's been a while!"

"I hear you're coming back to us soon."

"Six more months—I'm out."

"I hear you, I hear you."

Mr. Lyles looked at Percy. "Oscar, I can't thank you enough for looking out after my boy…you don't know how much I prayed in here that my kids would be o.k."

"My pleasure. He's a good boy. I had to snatch 'im up a few times, but he turned out all right."

The two men shared a hearty laugh, and Percy found himself joining in.

"Yeah, you keep on doing that, Mr. Dell. I'll need some help, even after I get out."

Michele R. Leverett

Mr. Dell looked at Percy, pointing a finger at him. "You heard your dad, Percy. Get out of line…" he shook his fist at him.

Percy held up his hands. I hear you." Percy sat back contently as Mr. Dell and his father lapsed into a conversation about old times. His dad was coming home, he was going to England…yeah, it turned out all right after all.

About the Author

Michele Leverett is a college English instructor, playwright, wife and mother. *Tears Turn into Laughter* is just the beginning of her "real life" stories. The native Pennsylvanian resides in Tobaccoville, North Carolina.

Printed in the United States
1132400002B/220-222